merciless mermaids

TAILS FROM THE DEEP

EXECUTIVE EDITORS
KEVIN J. ANDERSON & ALLYSON LONGUEIRA

WFP
WORDFIRE PRESS

MERCILESS MERMAIDS: Tails from the Deep

Kevin J. Anderson and Allyson Longueira, Executive Editors

Editorial Team: Scott T. Barnes, Lois Bartholomew, Jennifer Daniels, Tracy Eire, Jessica Guernsey, Briannon Holifer, Lila Holley, Rob Johnson, Kelsey Kusnetzky, Katharine Meeks, Heidi Moone, Mckenzie Moore, Aubrey Parry, Victoria Rose, and Logan Uber

EBook ISBN:
Trade Paperback ISBN:
Hardcover ISBN:
Cover art image from Shutterstock, designed by Allyson Longueira
Published by WordFire Press, LLC
PO Box 1840 Monument CO 80132
Kevin J. Anderson & Rebecca Moesta, Publishers
WordFire Press Edition 2023
Library of Congress Control Number:
Printed in the USA

Join our WordFire Press Readers Group for sneak previews, updates, new projects, and giveaways. Sign up at wordfirepress.com

contents

introduction

Think deep—the deep of the sea, the deep of space, the deep of our souls, our fears, ourselves. Here, it's not the monsters under your bed. It's the mermaids under your boat.

Old sailors tried to warn us. You can find their accounts in water-stained journals and letters throughout histories and cultures. People of the land laughed at the stories as mere legends or fairy tales.

Can you see the shapes in the waters that watch you? Can you hear the mermaid's call?

We are the instructors for the master's degree program in Publishing for Western Colorado University's Graduate Program in Creative Writing. Each year's group of grad students brainstorms a concept for a new anthology, funded by Draft2Digital—a book that they will produce from start to finish. The first three Publishing cohorts produced the excellent anthologies *Monsters, Movies & Mayhem, Unmasked,* and *Gilded Glass.*

This year, after vigorous discussions, the fifteen students developed *Merciless Mermaids: Tails from the Deep*, then sent out the call for submissions—and received more than 600 stories in the slush-pile. After reading and rating, and debating, they chose these 24 short stories and six poems reflecting the darker side of mermaid lore.

They wrote rejections, they wrote acceptance letters. They issued contracts, they worked with the individual authors to copy edit the manuscripts. They chose the cover art, and they prepared to market and release the book. For their graduation, they will celebrate with a gala book launch on the university campus in Gunnison, Colorado.

They are new publishers ready to produce books for avid readers everywhere, and they have this anthology as their calling card.

We hope you enjoy these tales of malevolent and merciless merfolk of all kinds. Some are murderous, some are humorous. The tales are set across numerous cultures and time periods, some modern, some ancient, some mythical.

Deep down you know that the darkness has a tail.

—*Kevin J. Anderson and Allyson Longueira*
Executive Editors

bones to lay to rest

L.N. WELDON

DR. MCCORMACK HAD ONLY BEEN at the inn two days when he found the bones.

The sun had set and the moon was breaking over the horizon when he called us down to the beach with the eagerness of my little sister Elsie on Christmas morning.

He was young, for a doctor, and I had admired—blushing—the way his hair waved with the same gold as the sand below our inn. He'd been secretive about why he was here, in our little coastal hamlet, but I knew he was a naturalist of sorts—he had shown me his book of sketches: butterflies and shorebirds and the odd things one found in tide pools just after the sea had slipped away.

Alice had known what he was looking for.

He led us down the trail to the shore, talking the whole way and carefully showing us where to step as if we didn't climb those cliffs every Sunday after church to gather salt figs from the dunes.

We followed him anyway, silent and pale against his ruddy-faced enthusiasm. I matched his strides, the shape of his wide boots in the sand nearly swallowing my smaller steps. Alice came behind me with her hands clenched in her skirts, and the aunts followed her, word-silent as ever.

The bones were half covered with drifted sand. They never

should have washed up, and my gut twisted, heart beating faster until it drowned out even the surf. I could see as I neared—picking my skirts up to tread carefully and keep from tangling in the dried surf-weed—that the rope tied to both wrists had worn through. Rubbed against rocks, maybe, or chewed by something nibbling away at the body.

Flotsam.

"I *have* to show you," Dr. McCormack was saying, kneeling beside the bones with a ginger respect that forcibly slowed his excitement. He took a soft brush from his coat pocket and started sweeping the sand away, exposing the shell-white bones. "I need witnesses. This is—this is *incredible*. It'll be revolutionary!"

He kept pattering away, brushing the sand back, revealing rib after rib. His touch was reverential, but my skin crawled with the profanity of his eagerness. I stood there, my toes shifting into the cool sand, and looked up at my sister, Alice, over the waves of hair on his bent head. Her face was as white as the bones, but her teeth were set in determination. She shook her head at me and hummed softly.

Say nothing.

"Look at this!" McCormack sat back on his heels, one sun-browned finger tapping along each bone as he counted. "Nine, ten...fourteen, *fifteen* sets of ribs! And it goes on!"

"Doctor," I ventured, earning a warning glare from Alice. "Surely we ought to call the authorities? This is a body—perhaps some sailor whose family thinks him lost at sea." I made a face at Alice over the doctor's head and hummed in the back of my throat. *If we can get him out of here, we can put her back.*

She nodded.

"My dear girl, this is no sailor!" Dr. McCormack pushed himself to his feet and brushed the sand from his trousers with vigor. Some of the sand dusted back down onto the bones, filtering into the empty eye sockets. "Don't you see these ribs? And look! This is what caught my attention to begin with!"

He moved to his right and gestured at a bit of debris

protruding from the dried seaweed and driftwood. Dutifully, I stepped in to see better, though I already knew what he'd found.

It was dried and ragged, the delicate frilled edges now sharp and knifelike in the sand. It had lost the pearlescent blue sheen it once had, but was unmistakable in its shape: a fin—large enough for a shark. Dr. McCormack leaned down to excitedly show me where the fin met the bones, the extra ribs pausing briefly at the pelvis before resuming smaller and smaller down the length of the serpentine spine.

I fought the urge to be ill. This was desecration, and it was at least in part our fault. Who had last checked the knots when we surrendered the body to the deep? Who had made certain the ropes were strong enough to withstand the clumsy bites of the dumb scavengers who would help to return the body to the sea? Was it Alice? Me? One of my aunts, perhaps?

Keep calm, Alice hummed, her deep alto thrumming beneath the crashing waves.

Aunt Sofia and Aunt Beatrice, standing just behind me with their hair beginning to drift in the wind, agreed in counterpoint soprano. *We can't let him escape.*

They were right. The doctor had seen too much and there would be no convincing him that this was a hoax or an illusion.

Alice reached for my hand, her arm stretching across the splayed bones like a benediction. Dr. McCormack looked at us, his eyes wide with delight that turned to puzzlement at Alice's dark look. My heart panged with regret; he didn't deserve this.

"Ladies, I know this may be a lot for your sensibilities, but I assure you—this is not the body of a person in need of burial." The doctor gave a paternal smile, his tone reassuring. "This is nothing more than an animal, but in terms of a scientific discovery—"

He never got the chance to finish. At the words "nothing more than an animal" my regret flashed into storm-swift anger, and I grabbed my sister's hand, reaching behind me for my one of my aunt's.

We sang.

Our voices—a braid of kindred notes twining together as one song—rose above the sound of the tide crashing against the cliffs and wove enchantment into the briny air. The song was the sound of gulls, of breaking shells, of angels and drowning and eternity. It was sand-rough and salt-dried and it scratched against my throat... But it slid into the doctor's ears with the silk of wet seaweed and the force of a riptide.

McCormack's eyes went empty, stagnant tide pools floating with dead things. His mouth slowly fell open. Somewhere in the back of his mind, I believe he knew what was happening; he understood who—what—we were. They always know, I think.

It didn't matter.

Maybe he at least realized we weren't animals, before he walked into the waves and sank deep beneath the moon-dark surf. Maybe he understood, before he tried to sing with us, that the women whose roof he had slept under, the women whose kitchen he had visited for tea, the women he had shamelessly flirted with, the women he had pulled down to the sandy shoreline were not truly women at all.

Maybe, as the salt filled his willing mouth and the water filled his willing lungs, as we followed him down, and his dimming eyes saw our skirts and shoes dissolve into foam, revealing long sinuous forms that undulated with the tide...

Maybe he knew. As the salt filled his willing mouth and the water filled his eager lungs, as we followed him down and our skirts and shoes dissolved into foam, as his dimming eyes saw our long sinuous forms undulating with the tide... Maybe he understood that we had no choice. His life was not worth the freedom of the sea.

He would wash up down the coast. His wallet was still at the inn, and he was a stranger. Those who found him would have a hard time finding where he belonged, if they ever found it at all.

But that was no longer our concern.

And we had bones to lay to rest.

LoriAnn Weldon is an artist, writer, librarian, and all-around nerd who lives in the midwest with her mad-scientist roommate and a black cat named Jedi. In between working in a potentially haunted library, writing stories, and creating digital art, she enjoys gaming, exploring the Ozark countryside with her sister, and trying to figure out how there are always more books in her house than there are bookshelves for them to live in.

pretty maids all in a row

MERCEDES LACKEY

IT'S THE PERVO'S HOUR," sighed Lori, looking into the mirror as she carefully applied her waterproof makeup, her tail neatly curled around the base of her stool. The other girls in the back-of-house dressing room murmured in assent or echoed her sighs with sighs of their own.

"Pervo's Hour," otherwise known as the "Six PM Show at Silver Bubbles, Spring of Live Mermaids," had been subdued, mostly half-empty, before it got taken over by the sickos. Good reasons for that, of course. After a day of sightseeing, people were hungry, not looking for more entertainment. Families with little kids were in the car, stuffing their tiny faces with non-caffeinated beverages and burgers, in hopes that they'd nap going back to the motel. Families with older kids were on their way to places that stayed open later—the six p.m. show was the last one on the weekends, partly because after that, attendance dropped off like someone had peppered the arena with dead fish, and partly because the rest of the park emptied around dinner time too. The only on-site dining was a burger stand, and after having the limited menu for lunch, no one wanted to repeat it for supper, so it closed around five. Some diehards—the kinds of people that packed their own food and water—roamed around the garden and wildlife paths, or swam until the actual closing an hour before sunset—but most people bailed. No point in any (expensive) underwater lighting around the mermaid viewing area. Not these days, anyway.

The last show hadn't always been "the Pervo's Hour"—before the COVID pandemic it had had the usual mix of people who actually came here to see the show, and people who were just looking for a place to sit down in air conditioning before venturing back out into the park for more swimming, hiking and wildlife viewing before the park itself closed for the night. COVID had changed things. And since the show had re-opened, that last show of the day had taken a turn for the worse. The half-filled seats were generally filled with a mix of men—well, "boys," really, even if their chronological ages stretched from late teens well into their fifties. No children, God forbid. No wives, no daughters, no girlfriends.

Pervos.

When this first started, the management had been forced to turn the music playing over the loudspeakers up to drown out the catcalling and sexual come-ons. That hadn't made a difference to the girls, not really; if you happened to look at the viewing windows, you could see them in there, in the light that came from the spring-side. Mouths moving, hands making obscene gestures, forbidden booze-flasks coming out from under shirts, as if they all thought they were at a strip club. And worse shenanigans as well, real pervs, though the ones that masturbated or just hung their dicks out usually kept away from the main mob, off to the side. Park employees had told Lori that the Pervos would linger until the park closed too, as if they were hoping to catch one of the girls alone after the show. Little did they know the girls all lived on-site, unlike the other park employees, and the closest they were going to get to any of them was standing or sitting on the other side of that series of a dozen thick glass windows, and millions of gallons of water that stood between them and the girls.

"I am likink the little *devushkas* best," mourned Anya. "Why can it not be them at this show?"

"Why can't they just cancel the damn show, I'd like to know," snarled Betty, carefully applying her exaggerated eye-makeup, inspired by the Blue Tang fish.

"Because the Pervos' money spends just as well as any other kind of money," Lori reminded her. "And after the hit we took from the Plague we should all be grateful we still have this place. It could have closed, just like Alligator Alley, Florida Down Under, and Magnolia Gardens did. And then where would we be?"

"Counting our blessings, girls. Counting our blessings. They let us stay and kept us fed, even when they weren't making money." That was Sophia, the oldest and one of the most supple of the Mermaids, whose red hair always made the little girls ask if she was Ariel. And she was right. Every time Lori thought about how precarious her life had been before she joined the show, she knew that even dealing with the Pervos was worth it. She had a nice room in a four-girl suite, and didn't have to worry about rent, utilities, food…not anything, really.

"Balderdash," snorted Siobhan, whose clipped British accent made her stand out as much as Anya's Russian did. "They got pandemic money from the government, didn't they?"

It was a tale as old as—well, not time, but certainly as old as when Florida officially "opened" back up again, and the discussion wound its way through all the girls as it always did, following well-worn paths just like the springwater did, finally coming to a rest when Betty put down her mascara and said, grudgingly, "Well, they do treat us right. Nice digs. Full healthcare. Decent pay. And you can't beat the food."

Nods all around. It was always the food that brought peace again. The food really was top notch.

Then again, management knew better than to short the girls on their food and quarters. Being a "live mermaid" was hard work. Making it look effortless was even harder. The girls burned through a lot of calories, and management always came through.

Then again, management also knew what was going to happen if they didn't come through. The girls might put up with being ogled by incels and open masturbators and—well, who knew what else was on the other side of that glass?—but short them on their meals and quarters and...

...well, the result wasn't going to be pretty.

Lori liked the dressing room, even though it was showing its age. It would have looked strange to a showgirl; completely tiled in ceramic, in a shade of "harvest gold" that dated back to the 70s, and the usual makeup tables and lamps were painted a matching color. Although the room was air-conditioned, there were also a pair of industrial-grade dehumidifiers working full time. There were no windows, of course, and the lighting used bulbs with a bluish-green tint that replicated the color of the light under the water.

A dozen and a half girls crowded in here, most wearing tails, some not; a lot of the adagio moves looked better when you had legs to make pleasing poses with. Each one had her own dressing table, and in that, it looked like every other dressing room back-stage of any theater; intense lighting, dressing tables and mirrors crowded around the walls.

Except for three things. One, all the stools had wheels. Two, the "costumes" that would normally compete for space with the dressing tables were limited to a single rack of fancy "clamshell" or scaled tops. You might snatch a spare top off the rack if yours had had a wardrobe malfunction, but the tails were custom-fitted to each girl, so there were no spares on the racks. Three, there were four open holes in the floor, with water just below the floor level. Those holes were the openings to underwater tunnels that took the girls out into a deep hole where the source of the spring was, tunnels that emerged below the viewing area, so they could appear and disappear without breaking the mood or setting. When their makeup was ready, the girls without tails just walked over and jumped in, and the ones with tails could easily wheel themselves right up to their entrance and slip off the stool into the tunnel to appear right on cue.

The management had recently decided to try to combat the Pervos by changing the last show from the standard one to a more "artistic" performance. No rock and roll, no hip or shoulder shaking, just gentle, melancholy classical and show-tune music, no voice-over from the control room except to announce the beginning and ending of the show. Lori didn't think it was going to work, but she loved the program so much she'd been one of the volunteers to agree to swim the extra show, besides being the one to record the vocal numbers. Even so, there hadn't been a lot of volunteers; nine, to be precise, and two of them were two of the three shark-girls, who were just as tough as they looked.

Altogether there were just shy of two dozen mermaids and most of them swam two shows a day; the management felt that the more girls there were in the water at the same time, the better people responded. Lori supposed they were right; to keep this place going you had to compete with the huge stage shows the theme parks put on, plus peoples' expectations from what they saw in fantasy and superhero movies. That was why, for the girls that wore artificial tails, the management had gone all out. They wore the finest silicon tails available, with exaggerated dorsal, anal, caudal, pectoral and ventral fins and real scales, not just scales printed or molded on. Lori had one of those; even though it was a complete pain to get into and out of, and required a partner to zip up the back and close the panel that hid the zipper, she loved it dearly and always looked forward to being in the water with it. Hers was metallic greens with hints of gold that somehow matched her blond hair exactly.

Hers was one of the prettiest of the silicon tails because she was a featured performer. Although the fins on her tail were not as extensive as they would have been in a scorpion fish, that was what they had been modeled on. If the management went all-out on the tails, they went over the top for one of the soloists. And Lori was always in the non-existent spotlight. Even when she wasn't performing a routine, she was in a high-visibility spot, and lip-synced to the songs she herself had recorded, flanked by two of the three shark-girls.

"Showtime, ladies," said Jett, one of the shark-girls. All three of the shark-girls were in startling contrast to the others; needless to say, they had tiger-shark tails. They alone were allowed to look as sinister as they cared to, and they sported Mohawks and dreads, black tops, multiple piercings, and lots of chains, and generally carried black tridents underwater.

Jett rolled herself up to one of the holes and tilted herself head-first down it. Lori made sure her seashell crown was firmly affixed to her head before diving down her own entrance-tunnel, sending her stool back into place at her table with a practiced flick of her tail as she dove.

This was not a job for anyone who suffered from claustrophobia. Even though the tunnel was well-lit, and the open water at the end easy to see, Lori didn't much care for how close the walls were and was always glad to get out into the spring. There had been a "show" of sorts—mostly synchronous swimming—in the 50s, but the entire place as it was now had been built in the 1970s, when just about any environmental atrocity you wanted to commit was just fine in Florida. Some of those chickens were coming home to roost now in other places in Florida, but fortunately, although the mere fact of the theater's existence made some environmentalists weep, the breathing system, the auditorium and the tunnels *had* been built with great care for the pristine spring, and any damage had long since healed over.

Lori emerged from her tunnel into the watery light beyond and took her place at the front of the twelve windows of the auditorium, at what would have been stage-front if this had been a theater. The blue ruched curtains that hid the area until showtime were still down, but the underwater speakers fed by the same sound-system in the auditorium were playing an orchestral version of the "Skye Boat Song," so curtain-up wasn't far off.

She took her place in the middle of what Sophia called "The DaVinci Ring" at center "stage." It, and the four spinning "stripper poles" were newish, installed during the pandemic, and they made a world of difference for what the mermaids could do underwater. The problem with underwater acrobatics always had been that there were very limited options because unlike a ballet dancer or a gymnast, you didn't have gravity to work against, or a floor to push off of. Now, though, the girls could build up momentum swinging around a pole, they could push off from the pole and catch another, and all of them had started watching pole-dancer videos to see what they could adapt.

They had all been pretty skeptical of the poles until Sophia and Lori tried them out. That was when they discovered the clever engineering underlay what looked like a metal stick. It was actually a solid pole inside a hollow one, spinning on ball bearings. With the slightest wave of a hand or a tail, you could spin around the pole in a static pose in about any orientation you chose that looked amazing, and that was just the shallow end of the trick-pool. Skepticism very quickly turned into enthusiasm.

And if it wasn't that they had to put on those two wretched evening shows on the weekend, performing would have been sheer joy.

Cal, the other shark-girl, emerged from her tunnel to take her place beside Lori and Jett, the rest of the girls came to stage-front to pick up their air-hoses and take their places, and then there was the moment of silence from the speakers before the curtain came up.

Ugh. There they were. She recognized several of the Pervs from other shows. They were all crowded up to the glass, not sitting in their seats like they were supposed to. Before the first number began, one of them, a man in a gimme-cap, jeans, t-shirt and beer belly, pounded on the glass with his fist. *"Show us your tits!"* he bellowed, the words muffled, but distinct, even through the two-inch-thick glass and the water.

The management had decided to open the show with Lori singing a children's nursery rhyme put to harp music, naively hoping, she supposed, that invoking "Mary, Mary, quite contrary, how does your garden grow?" would settle the monkeys down. "Silver bells and cockle shells" fit the setting, and the languorous moves they made, as if they were all lazing about on a summer day, were supposed to quiet the audience down.

It didn't. They kept right on hooting.

Did these idiots *really* think the girls were going to break the rules, pull off their bras and do an underwater strip-tease routine? She sighed mentally, made a sweeping circle of bubbles with her air-hose, to emphasize "Pretty maids all in a row," and went on with the show.

Instead of bringing the curtain down between numbers, a curtain of bubbles came up at the frame of the glass, enabling girls not in a scene to get down out of sight deeper in the spring, while the others changed places. Lori, however, was "on" for the entire show, either in the foreground or the background—the management was going to get every last dime they could out of that expensive tail!—so she had plenty of chances to see what the Pervs were up to. Mostly just carrying on like they were at a strip club, without the ability to try for a fast feel-up while tucking a dollar into a g-string, and she wondered, as she always did, just what brought them *here* when there were plenty of actual strip-joints all up and down the Orange Blossom Trail. That was the real-life seedy side of Florida tourism; for every theme park, there were probably a hundred strip clubs, peep shows, and sex toy shops.

Maybe they'd been thrown out of every club nearby and this was the closest they could come to their preferred entertainment. Or maybe they were just cheap; you didn't get much for twelve bucks at a strip club, but twelve bucks got you access to the whole park for the whole day.

Lori's voice floated out of the speakers into the water, and she mouthed the words of "Ebb Tide" as the other girls performed and Jett and Cal traded their tridents for long, trailing strips of blue-green fabric as they made helical patterns around her. It was a lovely number, slow and dreamy, and a reasonable person would have expected that the Pervs would finally sit down, calm down, and enjoy it.

Lori had no such expectations, and she was unsurprised when

the music ended and there was another chorus of *"Show us your tits!"* before the bubble-curtain came up and the noise of the bubbles drowned out the muffled shouting. "Dirait On," "The Flower Duet" from *Lakme,* the Bacarolle from the *Tales of Hoffman* —it didn't matter. The monkeys kept hooting like it was all "Love in an Elevator."

Finally came the Grande Finale, performed to Lori's version of "Bali Hai," with Caitlin and Anya gently herding a pair of the big turtles that shared the spring with them past the window. The turtles didn't really need to be herded at this point; they knew the show as well as the girls did, and also knew there would be an offstage treat of fresh lettuce if they did their job. Sometimes there were even manatees in this part of the spring complex, but wildlife laws prevented interference with them, so no one counted on them to do more than glide around and excite the children; the turtles, however, were almost as old as the show itself, and the management had gotten an exemption for their single choreo-graphed passage across the window.

Lori's weariness, as the bubble curtain came up and the phys-ical curtain came down, had nothing to do with her exertions in the water. As they all neatly coiled their air hoses in the proper places and swam up the tunnels to the dressing-room, she sensed that same weariness in the rest of them. Or maybe it was depres-sion. Here they had been spending the last hour making something beautiful, and instead of getting energy from an appreciative audi-ence, all their energy had been sucked away by a bunch of shaved apes pawing their own genitals and hooting.

"Eto piz'dets," Anya swore, "Filthy pigs! Lori, your solo was beau-tiful, as always, and your voice is perfection. Don't let those animals ruin it for you."

Lori smiled wanly. "No more Pervo Hours for the next five days, anyway," she pointed out. "But I don't envy the cleaners tonight."

Annika, one of the two adagio swimmers who hadn't worn tails tonight, shuddered. "Ew," she said. "Just...ew. Jett—why are you smiling?"

"Because I am imagining a shower of Portuguese jellies cascading from the ceiling into their laps when they get their peckers out," Jett said sweetly.

Well, that made everyone laugh. "If only!" said Sophia.

That seemed to turn everyone's mood around. As the girls faced their mirrors and the challenge of getting off waterproof makeup intended to last the length of an hour-long show, they traded salacious quips and jokes about the Pervos. Although this was what usually happened after the shows, the banter was particularly good this evening.

Lori's sensitive skin meant that she needed to be very thorough about getting the gunk off, particularly around the eyes, or she risked not only finding herself with raccoon eyes in the morning, but an eye infection. So, as usual, she was alone in the dressing room after all the others had gone, still in her tail, when she heard the door to the hallway open. Thinking that it was either someone coming to see if she was done yet, or maybe management, she swiveled on her stool to face the door, lips parted to utter a greeting that didn't even get as far as her throat.

And she froze with absolute terror.

It was a stranger, a man, a young blond man, but that wasn't what had her complete and undivided attention. It was the military-style rifle he held.

Now, she didn't know anything about guns. All she knew was that it was big, painted in a camouflage pattern, and had a curving thing coming out of the bottom of it. The young man was dressed in camouflage to match, with a heavy-looking vest—was that body armor?—and stood there looking at her with a sneer plastered across his face.

Terror affects different people in different ways. It made Lori cold all over, her stomach knot, and her hands shake—but it made her mind as clear as the crystal waters of the spring, and seemed to slow down time.

Instantly three things flashed through her mind. That this was clearly someone who had come here intending to murder plenty of people; she knew just enough about guns to know that the curved thing held ammunition, and she saw several more of those things in pouches attached to his belt. That she was the only thing standing between him and not just her friends, but everyone else still in the park. She kept up with the news. She knew how these things always went. Mass killers didn't stop with single victims. And all too often mass killers intentionally targeted women they imagined had somehow wronged them.

And she knew that she had to get control of this situation *now,* or it wouldn't just be her who died tonight.

It's been so long since I used my full powers. Will they still be strong enough?

She didn't bother to hide her shivering. She wanted him to see fear. She tucked her chin in so she was looking up at him as a child would, submissive and harmless, and sang, quietly, "What is it, dear sir, that I can do to help you? *Is there something you'd like to say?*" She half-sang the last, ending on an imploring note.

Something you'd like to say—that was what she concentrated on, putting her power into those words, because if he was talking, he wasn't shooting, and the longer he spoke, the more chance she had for the full force of her will to work on him. The air conditioner hummed away, the only sound in the silence but the lapping of water in the tunnels.

He stared at her, still angry, but he didn't point that weapon at her, not yet anyway. It was going to take more than a few notes for her power to work, so as he opened his mouth to answer, she continued to sing, deep in her throat, thankful that the sound system was still on and still playing innocuous showtunes. It didn't matter *what* it was playing, just that she could use it to hide, and yet carry, her voice.

He began to speak. She didn't pay any attention to his words; they weren't very memorable, to anyone who had been reading the news the last several years. A recitation of his manifesto, apparently. Just a long, vicious diatribe against women in general and the mermaids in particular, though he wasn't at all clear about *why* he was so angry at her and her fellows. To be honest, he wasn't really coherent about anything, and the magic behind her song had unleashed not only his tongue, but every pent-up grievance against every female creature he had ever encountered in his entire life. If he hadn't been holding that gun, if he hadn't come here with the express intention of murdering as many people as he could, she might even have felt some sympathy for him.

But he was, and he had, and she was going to show him just how *not* helpless a "mere female" was.

As she sang, some of the notes right outside of the range he could consciously hear, the torrent of bile began to falter. His eyes lost some of that hard glitter.

But he was fighting her power. He didn't know *what* he was fighting—how could he?—if he had known, he would have come equipped with earplugs. But he sensed that something wasn't going the way he'd planned.

He took an angry step forward. "Hey, bitch! What the hell are you doing to me?"

She shrank into herself. "I have not moved, what could I do to you?"

"How should I know? Gas? Mind control? *Do you work for the government?*"

She shook her head carefully, and tried not to panic. It had been too long since she actually used her voice for anything but singing! "Please, mister!" she sang. She almost sang "master," but she was afraid that would set him off. "I just swim and sing! I don't know what you're talking about!"

Oh great Father Rhine, my powers aren't working! I can't enchant him! Both her hands flew to her throat. She didn't know what to do! All her long, long life as a Lorelei and Rhine Maiden she'd simply *sung* and men fell swooning at her feet, or dashed themselves against the rocks trying to reach her. But that wasn't working—now what?

All she could think of was to try and *bludgeon* him with sound.

Time slowed to a near-standstill. The muzzle of the gun slowly swung in her direction. She filled her lungs to their greatest capacity, and poured out a single, pure, ultrasonic note that was louder than anything she had *ever* produced in her life.

He stiffened all over immediately. The gun clattered to the tile.

With blood oozing from his nose and ears, he toppled to the floor backwards, landing first on his head with a satisfying *crack*.

I...don't think he's going to walk away from this.

Reflexively, she massaged her throat, which felt abused, and waited for her heart to stop pounding so she could think. By the time the others—not just the girls, but Udo the bear-sark who acted as Security—came pouring in by the dressing room door and the tunnel entrances, she already knew what to do, informed by a lot of binge-watching police shows.

"Strip him. Find his phone," she ordered, as she got Betty to unzip her tail so she could wiggle out of it. That wasn't possible for more than half of the girls, because their tails were natural to them, but that didn't matter right now. What mattered was finding out if he had told anyone he was coming here. Then erasing him from the world. "Strip him naked," she continued, "Get his phone, his car keys if he has any and separate everything he's wearing into clothing and weapon piles."

Betty held up his phone in triumph. "Give it to Udo, he's good with tech," she continued. "Udo, find his social media and find out what he's been telling people about this place and if he planned to come here."

Udo swiftly had the phone unlocked using the stranger's face. "Looks like he posted a manifesto to a couple sites, but he didn't say where he was going, just that he was going to 'give a bunch of bitches what they had coming to them.'" Udo flushed. *"Entschuldige mir*, Lori."

"No offense taken, Udo. Betty, can you get that pelican you like so much to take the phone and drop it in the ocean?" Udo was already wiping all prints from it with the face wipes they all used to clean off their makeup. He wrapped it in a wipe and handed it to Betty, who dove down one of the tunnels without a word.

"I've got a seagull that can take his wallet down to one of the strip clubs on Orange Blossom," Sophia offered. One of the girls that hadn't swum tonight, Yulia, volunteered another that would take his car keys and leave them somewhere in town. Both girls wrapped their objects in wipes and took them down the tunnel.

"We can burn his clothing in the incinerator, but what about the—" she said hesitantly, and was interrupted by Udo, who had a huge, feral grin on his face.

"No worries, *meine schatzi,* I have a forge that will make short work of them. As for the body armor?" He examined it. "Nothing personal on it, and it fits me." He glanced around, spotted the wheeled trash barrel, and pulled out the liner, dumping the clothing, boots, and body armor in it, and replacing the liner. "I'll go tidy up," he quipped, wheeling the barrel out the door.

That left most of the girls with her and the rapidly cooling body. They were eyeing it avidly, and she didn't blame them. He was in good condition, but the American fast food diet would leave his muscles all nicely marbled with fat.

"All right, my loves," she said, feeling a sudden surge of pure joy that she had survived this—and evidently had a new weapon in her arsenal. "Go sink him in the deepest part of the spring, and when the park is closed, we'll invite him to dinner." The rest laughed, as she had known they would. "I'll 'tidy up' here, as Udo would say, and tell Management what happened."

Two hours later, they were all in the aqua communal dining room, which, like the dressing room, was accessible by tunnel into the Springs. They all lived in a complex of hurricane-proof pink-painted cinderblock houses linked together by the communal rooms that dated back to the 50s, supplied with ramps so the girls with tails could wheel themselves around in light wheelchairs. Poseidon had been so effusive in his praise at her quick thinking that she was still a little pink. Once the parking lot emptied out, he was going to call a towing company to impound whatever it was the fellow had been driving. "I'll have that cow put on ice for tomorrow," he'd concluded. *"Kalí óreksi!"*

The others had done a good job of dismembering and butchering. And now they were all gathered around a horseshoe shaped aqua table set low to the ground, so everyone could dine in comfort, tails or no tails. The shark girls were already feasting on the entrails, Betty had cracked into the skull after first offering it to Lori as a sign of her conquest. Lori had taken a very nice piece of thigh, which was, as she had hoped, well-marbled with tasty fat. They didn't often get man these days, and often the carcass was underfed. But this time there was enough to go around and leave everyone feeling sated. Poseidon's magic, feeble though it was these days, was equal to making the pile of bones they would leave disappear once they were done and he came to say goodnight.

Lori nibbled the succulent flesh and looked around at her sisters—because, really, although they were dissimilar in origin, they *were* all water-sisters. *Rusalka* from Russia and Nereids from Greece, mermaids from the Med and shark-guardians from the Pacific Islands, the handful of other mythics that worked the park, and she, the one lone Rhine Maiden, were bound up in a way she could never have foreseen when encroaching humanity forced her to flee her home. And thanks to Poseidon, who these days looked like a jolly old Greek fisherman and rejoiced in strolling around his park dressed like shrimp boat captain, *this* was now a home for all of them in ways the poor human Management would never understand—and if they knew, would probably choose to *un*know.

And, she thought to herself with content as she took another tasty, red bite, *You can't beat the food.*

Mercedes Lackey was born in Chicago Illinois on June 24, 1950. In 1985 her first book was published. In 2022 she received the SFWA Grand Master Award, and also in 2022 she won the Dragon Award for Best Alternate History (*The Silver Bullets of Annie*

Oakley). She has to date traditionally published 146 books, in many series, including the Secret World Chronicles, Hunter, Valdemar, Elemental Masters, SERRAted Edge, Elvenbane, and Obsidian Mountain series, as well as many standalone books, written solo or in collaboration.

the lonely rusalka

AMANDA CESSOR

I FIRST MET VIOLETTA, my precious flower, on a sunny day in the spring. The water of the pond had become frigid with the melt off from the snowcapped mountains hemming in the little village of Pyagda, the town of my life and my untimely death at the hands of my own husband.

I'd lost track of how many *Maslenitsa* had come and gone in the time since my lover betrayed me on the holiday, yet it was a day that always made me ache in my stilled heart. The week of *Maslenitsa* always filled me with that vengeful anger that was the burden of all *rusalka*.

At least, until I met her. My Violetta.

She came to my pond on the first day of *Maslenitsa* and cried quietly, salty tears into the cool water as I watched her from beneath the pond's surface. I wondered what made her cry so; I yearned to reach my icy fingers towards her, to smear the tears off her face and tut soft words of comfort. So long it had been since I'd felt anything but anger, yet I could think of nothing but bringing a smile to her face.

I coaxed a water lily from beneath the surface to grow, urging it to wake from its slumber and brighten the day while winter still tried so hard to keep its firm grasp on Pyagda.

I sent one, then another, and then more and more, until I stemmed the flow of her tears. She gazed with her beautiful blue eyes at the gift I'd given her. The wonder I saw on her sweet face made me curious. So fierce was my curiosity that I couldn't bear to stay hidden from her. I needed her to know that I was haunting this pond as the ghost of who I once was.

I surfaced some distance away from her, allowing one of the largest lily pads to rest on top of my head.

She lay there on the short dock, dressed in her *Maslenitsa* finery. Her headband marked her as an unmarried woman, a bright shade of yellow that stood out starkly from her raven hair, her fine white blouse and her woolen skirt were covered in sunflowers and daisies. I watched her carefully, my nose and mouth still submerged beneath the water. What need did a *rusalka* have to breathe?

Then she lifted her gaze and she saw me.

I froze, body going entirely still in the water. Would she scream? Would she think I sought to lure her to her death?

The moment stretched between us like a great valley; I feared she would run away and never return.

But she only folded her arms beneath her chin and smiled.

"Did you do this?" she asked me. "Did you create these flowers for me?"

I blinked before allowing my pale lips to surface, lily pad still on my head as if it was a hat.

"You were crying," I said as an answer.

"I thought I was doing so in private," she said with a small gust of a laugh. "I suppose even little ponds in the middle of the wilds aren't uninhabited."

Her smile left her face, and I floated nearer. I clung with my cold, wet fingers to the edge of the dock and pulled myself up onto it, folding my arms in the same way that she did and resting my chin on them.

"Why are you crying?" I asked. "Did someone hurt you?"

My closeness gave her pause and she rose a bit from her reclined posture.

"Are you going to try to eat me?" she asked.

I shook my head.

"We don't have need for food like we did when we lived. The hunger we have is more for the peace of rest."

She looked at me for a long time, blue eyes searching mine. I felt self-conscious—I was certain they had turned to black or even an unnerving milky color since my death. I couldn't even remember what my eyes had looked like when I was alive.

I was just about to slink back into the water and vanish when she suddenly reached out and adjusted a strand of my hair.

"You're quite beautiful, Rusalka," she said. "You look like a porcelain doll."

Had I still possessed a heartbeat, it would have been hammering in my chest.

"You're the beautiful one. You look like a sunflower given form," I said with a sheepish smile.

She gusted a little laugh and swiped the remnants of wetness from her face.

"My mother wants me to marry a boy in the village. She's making me do a sleigh ride with him today," she said. "To answer your question about why I was crying."

I rolled my head a bit to the side, looking up at her. "You don't like this boy?"

"No," she answered. "I'm not interested in any of the boys in the village."

I reached out for her hand, and surprisingly, she allowed me to take it. Her fingers were warm on my clammy skin, and I basked in the vitality coursing through her. It was like standing in a pool of sunlight.

"Don't let anyone tell you how to live your life," I said.

"Easy to say when you're already dead," she said.

I flinched, taking my hand back from hers.

"W-Wait, I'm sorry." She said quickly, reaching for my hand

again and holding onto it. "I'm just feeling sorry for myself. That was a cruel thing for me to say."

It was cruel, but I found myself incapable of staying upset with her.

"You could just stay around here, you know," I offered. "You can say you got lost. There are many spirits that call these wilds home who would love to confuse a pretty girl like you, even just to be close to your warmth."

"Spirits like you?" she teased.

I shrank a little. Had I been so obvious?

She laughed warm and bright, but her hand only squeezed mine more insistently. "I'm Violetta," she told me.

I inhaled to introduce myself, but so long had it been since someone had uttered my name that I didn't remember it. She must have read as much on my face, because a moment later she reached with her free hand and pushed more of my hair out of my face.

"Liliana," she said. "Because of the water lilies you made for me."

I fell in love with her right then.

Violetta spent that day with me, avoiding the sleigh ride altogether. I eventually joined her on the dock, the pale white of my ghostly shift like the tail of a fish or an eel, keeping the connection between me and my watery prison.

We talked for hours until the lilac sky of dusk descended over us.

"It's getting late, Violetta," I said. "You should go back home before the ground gets icy."

"I don't want to go. I wish I could just stay here with you; this is the most fun I've had in ages."

"Nothing like a dead woman to give you riveting company," I joked.

"I mean it, Liliana," she insisted. "Mother and Father, the people in the village, they don't seem to understand me like you do."

I looked at her pretty eyes, a comfortable silence falling

between us. In that quiet, I could hear the steady beat of her heart, feel the warmth of the day rolling off her in waves. I took her hand one last time and gave it a firm squeeze.

"You're always welcome at my pond, Violetta. Whenever you'd like," I said before picking up her hand and pressing a kiss to the back of it.

A beautiful shade of pink dusted her freckled cheeks, and I could hear her heartbeat stumble and falter before it quickened. She lifted her free hand and smoothed it over my cheek, brushing her fingers into my now-dry hair.

And then a sound came from behind us, causing us both to start and yelp.

Then we both laughed, the contact between us breaking.

"Goodnight, Liliana," she said as she stood up.

I slinked down into my pond, looking up at her. "Safe travels, Violetta."

After that day, Violetta's visits became a regular occurrence. The time we spent together gave my afterlife a sense of passing time. Violetta could only come in the middle of the week, in the middle of the day, when her mother was visiting a friend and her father was working. Instead of my existence being marked by the passing of seasons, it was marked by the visits I received from my beautiful flower.

We never ventured into the intimacy we had the first day, but I didn't mind. I had her smile and gossip from the village to warm me.

Some days were harder than others, though. Some days, she came with a fresh bruise on her face. Some days she barely spoke, no matter what I did to try and coax her warm demeanor from within her.

Spring matured, melting the rest of the snow, summer falling in line just behind it.

Our friendship deepened, and so did my love for her.

Of course, I wasn't enough of a fool to ever talk to her about those feelings, her life was becoming complicated enough from what I could glean. She didn't like to talk about her family or their expectations when we were together, but I could piece together some of what I myself experienced so long before when I'd been alive.

It all culminated in one particular day we spent together, though.

She came to the pond especially early, her freckled cheeks flushed as if she had run the entire way. Her eyes were puffy, and I could tell that she'd been crying. Yet, when I asked her what was wrong, she only shook her head.

"Nothing," she said. "Everything's fine. I just wanted to come spend the day with you."

Only moments later did she start undressing.

I stammered, somewhat flustered, "V-Violetta, what are you doing?"

She undressed down to her linen *rubakha* before starting to peel off her fur-lined shoes. "It's a beautiful day," she said as she hopped on a single foot, fighting with her stubborn footwear. "I'm going to come in and swim with you."

"Wh-What? You are? Wait, Violetta, look out for—"

Before she could even manage to take off her shoes, she hopped too close to the edge of the dock, her sole catching the edge and sending her crashing into the water of my pond. I swam quickly to bring her back up from the murky depths, scooping her into my arms and going back to the surface. When we broke through to the air, she sputtered the water out of her mouth and broke into a bright and happy laugh.

"Violetta, your shoes!" I cried.

"Guess I'll just have to stay here till they can dry in the sun!" she said, completely unbothered.

And she did stay, from the early part of the morning, all through the warm afternoon, until we once again sat perched on the dock, overlooking the lily pads and the now calm waters of my home.

We watched the sun make its descent behind the trees, and it was then in the slanted angle of the sunlight that I finally saw it.

On her hand was an ornate golden band set with a dazzling topaz.

"Violetta..." was all I could manage to say.

She looked at me and then followed my gaze to her engagement ring. She hastily covered it with her other hand as her face flushed crimson.

"I'd finally managed to forget that it was there," she said, biting her lip.

Tears collected in her eyes, threatening to overflow—clinging to her long, dark lashes.

I lifted my cold hand to swipe them away, her skin warm with the sunlight she'd soaked in all day. She looked at me, eyes wandering down to my pale lips before meeting my gaze.

"If you could leave this place, would you have run away with me?" she asked. "Would you have come with me and built a little hut deep in the forest? Where we could have always been happy together."

My frozen heart broke. Had I been able, I would have burst into tears.

"Yes, Violetta," I said. "If I could leave these waters, which I've been cursed to wander, I would have...so happily made you my wife."

Her face crumpled and she let out a low, mournful sob as she curled into me for comfort.

"I hate him, Liliana," she wept. "He's cruel and sadistic. He only wants me to give him sons and be a trophy on his arm. And—and he said that I won't be allowed to come to the forest anymore. So I..."

She forced herself to unfurl from where I consoled her. She held my face in her perfect, warm hands. They smelled like soil and sunshine—they smelled like life. I closed my eyes and let out a tearless sob of my own.

"You won't be able to return here," I finished for her.

I would be alone again. Again, time would soldier on without end, the sound of the frogs and crickets the only companionship in this eternal prison. Yet, even in my own distress, I remembered feeling hers. I remembered the day I was promised to a man I thought would protect me, and I remembered the day of his betrayal.

I would have an eternity to nurse this wound, but only this moment to console Violetta. I would only be able to soothe her heartache and give her what fleeting love I could.

So, I pulled her into a tight embrace, petting a hand through her silken hair, committing every precious moment to my failing memory.

"You will find joy again, Violetta," I whispered, pressing a kiss to the top of her head. "Even if you hate your husband, even if he makes your skin crawl and your stomach twist, the children you have with him will be your whole life. And you will read books about adventure, and it will feel like you're the one taking them."

"I don't want an adventure without you," she sobbed.

"Shhh, shhh, my little flower," I cooed through a tight throat. "No matter what happens, Violetta, I'll still be here. And every day I'll think of you, and every day I will love you, and one day when I'm able to get free of this place I will spend my eternity with you."

"I love you Liliana," she whispered, her breath warm against my neck.

"I love you. I have since the first day I met you."

I held her until the evening came, and then we watched the first light of the stars and the moon blink into life. I treasured every second of that time with her until she had to go. When she finally got fully dressed, and once again donned her fur-lined shoes, neither of us could bear to say goodbye. Not when we both knew it would be the last time. It was too painful.

I only dropped into the frigid water of my pond and watched

as my flower, my very reason for existence, disappeared into the dense vegetation that she had bloomed from like a serendipitous sunflower after the waning of winter.

She did not return.

It was a black night in winter when I awoke.

The moon and stars were obscured by the dense cloud cover of a looming snowstorm. I'd long stopped trying to entertain myself in the dull days of my afterlife. Nothing was interesting after Violetta, and after watching the trees for years after she walked out of my life, I'd come to accept that she would not be returning.

So, I allowed my spirit to disperse in the waters. I became the unthinking tadpole, the stagnant beds of algae, the buzz of the mosquito in the banks.

Perhaps if I could just hold still long enough, I could forget that I was *rusalka*. Maybe I could just cease to exist.

At least until that dark night. There was the sound of an argument, a man's voice, a woman's, and a child's scream. Then there was the crack of something hard against the ice. Once, twice.

And then I heard her, my sweet Violetta.

"Run, Liliana."

The command was wet, as if sputtered through a mouthful of honey, but it roused me.

I came back to myself as the third crack sounded, and with it, the sound of a body breaking the icy surface of my pond. I collected the wisps of my soul from where I'd stored it, beneath the stones, within the ice, in the roots of the eelgrass.

And when I could open my eyes again, I saw her.

My flower, my Violetta.

But it was all wrong.

She screamed from beneath the surface of the water, a plume of blood and air leaving her mouth. She grasped the arm of a man, and even in the dark the band of her gold and topaz ring shone.

She was trying to keep him from pulling her up, from taking her away from me again.

No, that didn't make sense, she wasn't trying to get to me at all. She was turning red, her heart was hammering erratically.

She was drowning.

Every detail came into sharp relief then. The hand on her chest was her husband's, the sound of the cracking had been her skull against the thickening ice over my pond. I could see, now, the ribbons of red blooming from her head where her *kokoshnik* was pinned to her braided hair.

I could only watch as the circumstances of my own death flashed before my eyes. I marveled at how close the details were; how I'd also fought and wept fruitlessly, how my heart had felt as if it might burst, how I could do nothing but gasp in lungs full of icy water. The first horrific moments of my eternal prison. Waking as a spirit bound to these waters, with the mission of seeking vengeance for the life stolen from me. But my husband had never returned, he'd died peacefully in his bed, and I lived on.

But if Violetta died like this, then we could haunt this pond together. We could spend eternity laughing and playing. If I could watch her perish in this terrible lonely way, then I could finally end the torment of my loneliness.

Violetta looked at me, her beautiful eyes pleading. She removed her hand from her murderer, and I thought she might reach out to me.

But she didn't. Instead, her hand drifted up to the ice, pressing against it. I followed the movement, followed Violetta's gaze. And I saw a girl who could be no older than twelve, with raven hair and pale blue eyes. I watched as she pulled on her father's coat with all the strength her small body could muster, and I watched as he struck her down to the rotting wood of the dock and she fell unconscious.

She had not been urging me to flee, I realized.

Those words were for Violetta's daughter, her stunning daughter who she had named after me.

Centuries of rage bubbled from deep within me, and for the first time in my non-existence I felt the unfamiliar curling of bloodlust rise from some angry, dark crevice in my soul.

I became the monster I was promised, I found the strength I had purchased with my cold and lonely death.

I scooped Violetta into my arms before I smashed through the cover of the ice, one black claw sinking into the thickest part of the ice where I dragged us out of my watery grave. I opened my mouth—no—my maw, to accommodate the rows of rotting teeth that formed there.

The murderer, the abuser, stared at me. The color drained out of his face as he wailed, he skittered back like vermin, the stink of urine left in his wake. Too slow, though.

After carefully lying Violetta on the ice, I spirited myself behind him and seized him by his shirt, lifting him off his feet as he kicked and screamed like a frightened little boy.

"Mercy! I beg for mercy, spirit!" He begged.

My voice was a guttural, otherworldly sound as I promised him, "There is no mercy for those who prey on the weak."

I was grateful that little Liliana was unconscious as I dragged him into the depths with me, tearing him to wisps of crimson viscera.

I devoured every cruel, cowardly morsel of him. I did it with pleasure.

Some hours later, after I'd cleaned her husband's blood off my body and calmed the fury that had run through, I sat alongside Violetta's sleeping body. Liliana had awakened shortly after I'd devoured her father, but she didn't ask many questions after I'd explained that he'd run away. She had seen to building a fire while I coaxed the water out of her mother's lungs, then she helped keep her mother warm as the sun rose and broke through the dense cloud cover over us.

Liliana kept her distance, and I was okay with that. I could rest easy knowing that Violetta's heart was thumping strong in her chest and knowing that she wouldn't be harmed by her husband ever again.

Violetta finally woke when the sun was high in the sky, and she came to join me where I sat looking over my pond.

"You saved me," she said, her voice rough and raspy.

I looked at her and smiled as my heart warmed. She still had her sun-kissed skin, her beautiful freckles, her hair was still black as a crow's feathers and her eyes were still the same icy blue. But she had new lines on her face, framing her mouth, crinkling her eyes.

I lifted my hand to gently brush over the lines at the outer corner of her eye.

"You've smiled so much," I murmured.

As if I'd conjured it, she gifted me a vibrant beam.

"You were right," she said. "I hated my husband, but I love my daughter, more than anything in the world."

Then she shrunk a bit from me. "Th-That is, it's a different love than—"

I shook my head. "Don't—Liliana is a vision, Violetta. Just like you."

"I have missed you so terribly," my flower sighed as she cupped my face.

I leaned into the warmth of her hand and heaved a mournful sigh. I was so close to having her forever. Could I really claim I loved her if I subjected her to the prison I'd been trapped in for so long, though? Perhaps it was a momentary temptation, but it was never a real solution to my isolation.

"I can come see you whenever I want, now. Now that you've— that he's—"

I shook my head and kissed her palm.

"You must keep running. They will blame you for it."

"That doesn't scare me," she said. "I don't feel sorry for him being gone. Do you know what he wanted to do to my Lili? He wanted to marry her off to an old man—sell her like chattel for land."

"That old man will come looking for her hand regardless of whether or not your husband lives," I told her. "Go, take an adventure."

"But—" Violetta looked out over the pond that was already starting to ice over again. "But you'll be all alone."

"I can take it," I promised, forcing a smile for her sake. "I'll be able to rest easy knowing that you've gotten out from under his thumb and rescued your daughter from a similar fate."

"*You* rescued her, Liliana," she insisted. "If you hadn't saved me..."

She trailed off, and silence fell between us. We looked at each other for a long time, her warm thumb brushing against my skin.

"You haven't changed at all," she said. "You're just as beautiful as the day I left you."

"So are you," I huffed.

"I don't regret my Lili, I don't even regret that I had to marry that monster to get her," she said. "But there is one thing I've regretted for the last fifteen years."

"What is that?" I asked.

Violetta closed the distance between us and pressed her warm, raspberry-colored lips to mine. I drew in a breath through my nose, and smoothed my hand on her face into her tangled, obsidian hair. I put my other on her ample waist, wanting to feel her warmth.

Her warmth spread through me from the point of contact on our lips. It bloomed in my chest like a drink of strong liquor, flowing through my veins like life renewed. For the first time in centuries, I felt the cold of the winter around us. My teeth clattered against hers and she parted to look at me.

"Liliana," she gasped. "Y-you're *glowing*."

I laughed, feeling happier than I ever had. "Of course I am. I just got to kiss you."

"No, Liliana, look." She pulled my hand from her waist and showed it to me.

She was right, I was literally glowing as bright and warm as the sun itself.

"What's happening?" she asked.

"I—I don't know," I said.

I looked down at where my ghostly shift floated in the water and watched as it started to vanish like dispersing mists on a sunny day.

"I think that I'm finally being put to rest," I whispered.

"Wait—to rest? As in a true death?"

Violetta's hands seized my shoulders and I beamed at her from ear to ear. "I've been trapped in this pond for so long, Violetta," I told her. "I'm finally going to be free."

"No, you can't," she begged. "I've only just gotten to hold you again."

"You'll be able to again," I promised. "I've waited hundreds of years for you to come into my life, my flower. I can wait another forty or fifty."

"You swear it?" she wept, clinging onto me and cupping my face. "You promise you'll wait for me?"

I pressed my forehead against hers as my shift continued to unravel, revealing my feet, my legs. "Of course, I do, Violetta. I would wait a hundred more lifetimes for you."

She kissed me again, desperate and hungry, clinging to me as if she could stop the inevitable. I curled my arms around her and basked in her as long as I could. My heart hammered in my chest, and it soared up and up, until I was as warm as I was when I was still alive.

I parted from her and blinked my eyes open to look upon the heaven I'd been granted finally.

And I found myself seated on the dock, naked as the day I was born, with Violetta gawking at me.

"I-Is this—the spirit world?"

"Not so far as I know," Violetta said.

I looked down at my hands and found them soft and pink with life, but no longer glowing.

Violetta brushed her thumb across the sensitive skin of my lower lip, before pressing that same thumb to the side of my neck.

"Your heart is beating, Liliana," she whispered in awe. "You—you've been brought back to life."

I pressed my hands between my breasts, waiting in the quiet that fell between us.

And there, as I sat across from the woman that I loved, near the pond where I'd been trapped for far too many lifetimes, I felt the steady drumming of my own heart against my fingertips.

Amanda Cessor is a historical fantasy author and fiction ghostwriter. They publish the serial novel *The Hallowed Wilds* on substack and have their debut novel *With Love, Juniper* slated for release in Fall 2024 with Inked in Gray Publishing. Amanda lives with their husband and their fur children in sunny southern California. Find them on Twitter @AmandaCanWrite.

five times more

AKUA LEZLI HOPE

Helped from treacherous land back to shining sea
    lifted by her human shoulders,
    scale-dappled waist,
    fin-engulfed ankle

Grateful mermaid grants
    each man a wish.

One asks for twice his wisdom
    and poof!   spouts Shakespeare's sonnets
    and sculpts

The second asks for three times his wisdom
    and voila!   knows
    quantum physics, architecture, chaos theory

The third man asks for more: five times his base allotment.
    Mermaid warns: "So much, so much are you certain?"
    He insists, "Are you granting wishes or what?"

"But this will change everything,"
    She troubles sweet water,
    "This will change everything"

"Five times more wisdom," he demands.

and Boom!   He is made a woman.

AKUA LEZLI HOPE, a 2022 Grand Master of Fantastic Poetry (SFPA), is a paraplegic creator and wisdom seeker who uses sound, words, fiber, glass, metal, and wire to create poems, patterns, stories, music, sculpture, adornments, and peace. Her collections include *Embouchure: Poems on Jazz and Other Musics* (*Writer's Digest* book award winner), *Them Gone, & Otherwheres: Speculative Poetry* (2021 Elgin Award winner). A Cave Canem fellow, her honors include the NEA, two NYF fellowships, Science Fiction and Fantasy Poetry Association award, and multiple Best of the Net, Rhysling, and Pushcart Prize nominations. She won a 2022 New York State Council on the Arts grant to create Afrofuturist, speculative, pastoral poetry. She created the Speculative Sundays Poetry Reading series. She edited the record-breaking sea-themed issue of *Eye to the Telescope #42* and *NOMBONO: An Anthology of Speculative Poetry by BIPOC Creators*, the history-making first of its kind (Sundress Publications, 2021).

mer-made

URI KURLIANCHIK

YOU GOTTA GIVE the mermaid mafia their due, or the only place you'll be sailing is the bottom of the ocean. That's a law as old as gravity, and I'd rather take my chances jumping off a plane than sailing without the mermaids' say-so.

Now, not all mermaids are in the risk-management business. Others run underwater smuggling, seaside gambling, good old piracy, and even prostitution, believe it or not.

And don't even think about diving for pearls or sunken treasure. If they find you with anything shiny you didn't buy, you're gonna be jealous of the last fish you had for dinner.

Way they figure it, they were there first, so they own the sea. Anyone making use of their property gotta pay rent. Or something like that. Who the hell can say what's going through a fish's head? I guess it's the same as the harpies and their blasted mountains, except you can shoot a harpy as easily as any other critter. Mermaids are a whole lot tougher.

These gals are covered in hard scales tits to tail and are shielded by half a million cubic miles of water. Sure, there ain't much they can do on dry land, so you can sit on the pier and snipe at them all day long. Hell, you can even get a few; their brains fly from their heads as easily as yours or mine, but then you have yourself a war.

All they lose is their Sunday tan, while we lose the sea. Not a great bargain for a community that lives off fishing and beach tourism. Besides, you start shooting these fishy ladies, and public opinion will be on you like the tax authority on a wealthy orc.

There's a rumor some eggheads in the city are working on some kind of chemical you can put in the water to keep the gals away from ships and ports. A mermaid repellent if you will. But hell, I ain't holding my breath.

And speaking of holding my breath, you're probably wondering what a two-hundred-pound diving dress with a fancy bronze helmet is doing in the office of a hydrophobic private dick like me. Well, it ain't here for decoration like knight armor in some lord's mansion. It's not for leisure either. I don't even like going to the beach. Not after my last job.

The job, the one I'm reminded of every time the weather shifts and the old scars make themselves known. I'd never have gone toe-to-toe with the mermaid mafia just for a salary. That's what crazy people do.

Besides, I've got everything I need right here, on the good green earth God intended humans to walk on. Praise be to Him, there's never a shortage of folks suspecting their spouses are fooling around or wealthy, old ladies looking for their missing Chihuahuas.

But this job was different. It was the right thing to do. I was promised very little compensation and didn't get even that. Well, that's not true; I got this useless, old diving dress and enough scars for people to mistake me for a flesh golem.

It all started when my wartime CO walked into my office looking like a boy who just broke Mom's favorite plate. Now, Tim and I were veritable gods of war and closer than brothers back in the old days when the Demon Emperor Shin came riding the dragon Khol'Znavoth and threatened to enslave mankind, but after the war, our lives took different courses.

Tim, full of dreams like a six-year-old in a V-day parade, went into the academy to make a difference wearing blue instead of green. During the war, we'd taken plenty of shortcuts. Some of those would land us in jail if they became public knowledge. Back here, though, Tim believed things should be done differently—the right way, by the book.

I decided I'd ruined enough uniforms with my blood and opened this office, where the toughest battles I had to fight were with soon-to-be-ex-husbands caught *in flagrante delicto* and bums conning insurance companies with fake broken limbs.

I spent the years staring at the walls, while Tim spent the years punching them. Tim was a good cop and had a few good men, but the rest of the force stank like a kraken carcass washed up on the shore. Half of them took pearls from the mermaids, and the other half took nuggets from the harpies.

Tim was convinced some cops were directly involved in smuggling Eldritch Slime into the country, except he had no proof and no one would talk to him. Yeah, that was the story of our life—doing things by the book and never getting past page one.

One evening, a once-in-a-lifetime opportunity fell into his lap. One of Queen Daga's girls got tired of being passed over for promotion and indicated she'd give a full list of every cop who was on the take in return for being transferred to a safe body of water. Problem was, the mermaids kept a tight watch on the coast. Just swimming would be suicide, and not the painless type.

So Tim devised a plan. That's what Tim did: he made plans. He beat his enemies with brains.

Tim told me he had a few good kids under his command, honest cops who wanted to do the right thing but didn't yet know how. They never fought demons with swords when guns proved useless or ran toward the AA guns while everyone else ran for the lifeboats. These kids needed a real tough guy to lead them. There wasn't anyone else he could trust, so he turned to me, his last surviving comrade-at-arms with enough limbs to work a boat.

His plan was simple: me and the young'uns would switch our

cheap suits for cheaper sweaters and pretend to be fishermen. Piloting an old trawler, we'd go to the designated spot, grab the informant code-named Silver, and hide her in the fish tank. Not a comfy ride, but at least she'd have something to snack on the way. From there, we'd go to port, where we'd load the informant into a truck that would take her to a safe place.

Many years ago, I followed Tim into what men called certain death and came back certainly alive and with the Necromancer in chains. If he believed in this plan, so did I.

"Hell," I said, "let's do something crazy together one last time." I raised my glass. "For old times' sake."

"For old times' sake." We tossed our drinks and spent the rest of the night talking about the war.

Early the next morning, I was on a rickety boat with a crew of four kids who managed to look uniformed even though they wore old jeans and sweaters. I instantly understood why Tim wanted me heading the operation. These youths were hopeless, though not as hopeless as our ship, a small shrimp trawler that wouldn't pass inspection if you paid the port authority a hundred dollars.

It had some kind of a name, but it was peeled off the hull back when the demon emperor was just a demon shaman on a nameless island. The outrigging was bent and rust-eaten. I doubted it could support the weight of a shrimp, let alone a two-hundred-pound mermaid. It wasn't what I'd call seaworthy, but we'd sailed worse during the war.

Right off the bat, I discounted trawling our informant. Either the rigging would collapse, or the net would break. Instead, I decided that when we reached the designated spot, I'd get into a diving dress and haul her onto the boat myself. I'd be placing my life in the hands of a murderous mermaid, but Tim claimed she was solid, and his word was good enough for me.

So there I was, a dozen fathoms deep and straining my eyes against anything hiding in the jungle of seaweed beneath me. Pumping air and manning the cable were Milk, who was the darkest human I've ever seen, and Ralf, who was on his way to becoming the reddest human anyone has ever seen. Tim II, a smile with a person attached to it, manned the harpoon and kept an eye on the depth charges. Jackie, a giant of a woman I'd swear had some orc blood in her, either due to grandma's indiscretion or because she ate an orc, scanned the horizon through the scope of an ancient basilisk gun.

Sweat was pouring from my brow, stinging my eyes, and an itch on the tip of my nose was making it hard to focus on anything else. God, I hate those little underwater gibbets mistakenly called diving dresses.

The boys continued to lower me, the ocean growing darker with each fathom. After a few minutes, I noticed a silvery shape moving through the seaweed like a sensuous torpedo. I hoped it was our girl because if it was someone else, there wouldn't be much I'd be able to do to prevent her from sending me to the bottom. God, I really needed to pee.

A few more heartbeats that felt like hours and she came into view. She was indeed silver but otherwise didn't look at all how I imagined.

Even though I'd seen mermaids in the past, mostly their tails as they disappeared beneath the waves, my mental image was based on lurid illustrations from the yellow press, where mermaids were depicted as well-endowed ladies with gorgeous hair. The creature in front of me was a monster.

She was covered in fine scales from the top of her smooth head to the tips of her finned tail. She had no discernable ears or nose, and her mouth was a cavern brimming with sharp teeth. Her eyes were two black pits devoid of emotion. Though her figure was vaguely feminine, it was perfectly hydrodynamic—i.e. no boobs.

She held a ledger of polished bone. If what she told Tim was true, that ledger would be the downfall of many corrupt cops and politicians. It would do more damage to the mermaid mafia than a hundred submarine raids. Such a little thing, but it had more power than a ton of TNT.

I raised a hand to hail the newcomer, when I noticed something dark stalking behind her, dodging between rocks and seaweed with serpentine grace. I screamed "behind you!" only to remember that the only thing my screaming would achieve was rattle my ears.

I pointed in the direction of the stalking figure, but either Silver didn't see me, or she didn't understand the gesture. Finally, I threw a rock at her. She dodged it and tilted her head at me. At that exact moment, a trident sailed by, ripping off several scales from her flank. A cloud of dark blood rose from her injury like smoke rising from a snuffed candle.

She blocked another trident with her ledger, which cracked but didn't break, and swam to meet her attacker, who turned out to be a black-and-white striped mermaid with a finless tail and fangs like a vampire.

The two circled each other in prebattle assessment. Then, fast as a striking cobra, Zebra whipped her tail, missing Silver's face by inches. Before Zebra had time to pull back, Silver sank her teeth into her attacker's tail. Both creatures were obviously in agony, yet no sound came from them, nor did their expressions change. There was something seriously wrong with the humans who found these creatures sexy.

The striped assassin started clawing at the informant's face, tearing off scales and raising another cloud of blood. Once, twice. On the third attempt, Silver grabbed her assailant's arm and pulled her down. This time, the razor sharp teeth found her enemy's throat.

Zebra thrashed and struggled, obscuring the fight with blood and bubbles. Within seconds the fight was over. The would-be assassin floated away, and the informant swam toward me, wincing with each undulation of her body.

Thankfully, I didn't have to explain the deal to her. She grabbed me around the waist, and I tugged at the cable, indicating to Milk that he should pull me up.

As we started ascending, the mermaid pressed her forehead to my face plate. Despite myself, I recoiled. From up close, she

looked even more alien, like a fish stretched on a human skull. The
bits of flesh still clinging to her teeth didn't make it easier.

"Someone spilled the pearls!" she warbled. "That was one of
Queen Daga's girls."

"Stones and bones!" I muttered. "Did you tell anyone you were
leaving?"

"Do I look like an idiot?" She bared her teeth. "I didn't tell
anyone except your boss, and I used a secure method…"

I shrugged, which of course, she neither saw, because of my
oversized diving dress, nor would have understood due to her
people's different body language.

"Maybe the damn tadpole followed me," she went on as the
ship's hull grew larger over our heads. "She always had more ambition than brains…"

As soon as she finished theorizing, my lungs filled with brine,
and I started coughing uncontrollably. I looked up and saw a green
mermaid with a segmented tail and pincers instead of hands sawing
at our cable. My air hose was dancing about like a decapitated
snake, shooting bubbles in all directions.

"Someone really spilled the pearls!" Silver cried into my face.
"That's Hasilon, one of Daga's personal sinkers! She's bad news.
I've seen her slice through steel like it was seaweed."

I was too busy choking to comment. As I struggled for air, I
noticed two mermaids with spiky fins the color of fire swimming
toward us from below. Funny, I hadn't thought we could get any
more screwed.

"The Dariot Sisters," my companion said with a note of resig-
nation. "Their spikes are venomous. One touch and you'll experience agony that will make you wish you were in hell." She shook
her head. "I can't believe I'm going to die hugging a sweaty surface
mammal…"

Not gonna lie, that hurt my feelings a little.

Just then, a white line burst through the surface and narrowly
missed the pincered mermaid before dissipating in a cascade of
bubbles. Another line appeared, and the mermaid gave up her

attempt at slicing the cable and swam toward us, clicking her pincers menacingly. At this point, I had no air left and was struggling to stay conscious; even if I wasn't trapped in a massive diving dress, I'd be useless in a fight.

My companion bared her teeth and balled her hands into fists. However, before she had a chance to disentangle from me, the tip of a harpoon exploded from Pincers's chest in a mist of blood and viscera. An instant later, she disappeared, as if snatched by the hand of God.

With Silver clinging to me, I was dragged across the hull and dumped onto the deck. Milk jumped to unscrew my helmet before I became the first-ever victim of open-air drowning while Jackie and Ralf scanned the ocean through the scopes of their rifles.

As soon as the helmet was unscrewed from my head, I noticed Tim II approaching the twitching body of the mermaid dangling from his harpoon. She opened one orange eye to glare at him.

"Look out!" Silver and I shouted in unison, but it was too late. Despite being impaled through the chest and obviously breathing her last, Pincers managed to grab Tim with her tail and drag him into the reach of her pincers. I barely had time to blink and the kid who'd just saved my life was a headless corpse shooting blood on the deck.

"Tim!" Jackie bellowed and fired at the mermaid, leaving a hole a cat could walk through. The creature hissed, spasmed, and grew still, blue blood dripping into the sea.

"I hope you're worth it," I muttered at Silver. "That was a good kid who just died there to save your ass."

The mermaid tilted her head. "He died because he was a moron... and I don't have an ass."

She leaned against a crate and gingerly touched her wounded side while pressing the ledger to her chest like it was a talisman against all harm.

"Touché..." I mumbled. "Hey, what's your name? I think we're past code names now."

"Krisha," she said. "Look, I'm sorry about your man, but we'll probably be joining him before the sun sets." All eyes turned on the injured mermaid. "If Daga knows I betrayed her, she'll send wave after wave of sinkers until we're all crab food." She looked each of us in the eye. "I told no one. Someone spilled the pearls. Someone on *your* side."

"Let them come!" Jackie bellowed. "What can these primitive fish do against steel and lead?"

The mermaid clicked her tongue. "Do you know how many ships I've personally sunk over the years?" She winced as the boat rocked. "You think we're ignorant savages, but we have our methods... Don't you worry."

"That's exactly what I'm worried about..." I muttered. "Ralf! Call Tim on the radio. We need backup, and we need it ten minutes ago."

"Tim's dead, boss." Ralf said.

"The other Tim, you idiot!" I roared. "And stay away from the railing!" I shouted at Jackie and Milk. "They have projectiles, and the devil alone knows how high they can jump!"

"High enough..." Krisha grimaced as she pulled herself to a semi-upright position. "But they're not gonna to do that. They're gonna focus on drilling holes in your ship until it sinks. We didn't come to rule the sea by playing by your rules."

"Watch it, you talking tuna!" Jackie growled. "We already have the ledger; we don't need you alive."

The mermaid made a sound like a cat about to throw up. "Yeah? How's your Siranit? Do you think we write in English under the sea? By the Great Fertilizer, you're dumb!"

"Girls!" I shouted, "We don't have time for—" I was interrupted as the whole vessel shook and groaned as if punched in the guts. "This..." I finished lamely.

"How are they doing that?" I asked the mermaid.

"Nothing fancy. Just battering rams with spiked heads."

"We have depth charges!" Ralf shouted from the command post. "Also, Tim says to hold on. He'll be here in half an hour."

My heart sank. Half an hour was enough to destroy this ship

thirty times. Hell, I wasn't sure it would survive that much time even without a school of murderous mermaids pounding at the hull.

"Jackie! Milk!" I shouted. "Grab a depth charge each. Don't attack until I or Krisha tell you to. I'm deputizing her." I winked at the mermaid, who tilted her head at me. "I'll keep watch from the mast. If anyone gets close to the surface, I'll plug her full of lead."

Metal groaned and protested as I climbed the mast. Just as I stepped onto the platform, I heard a metallic twang and felt the mast shudder. I swirled around and saw a projectile shaped like a sea urchin sticking from a pipe less than a foot away from my face.

I scanned the water and noticed a dark figure slithering below the surface. Shouldering my gun, I aimed carefully and fired. The figure instantly dove beneath the waves, leaving a red trail in its wake. Another punch shook the ship, and I had to cling to the rigging to keep my footing.

As I did so, I lightly brushed the urchin weapon, and it sliced through my forearm as if I was made of butter. I snarled in fury and smashed it with the butt of my rifle. The urchin didn't budge, and I now had a buttless rifle. Damn mermaids!

I noticed another figure approaching the ship and fired my last shot, aiming from the hip. I missed by several yards, but at least I forced the attacker to dive, buying a spell of safety for the fearless bombers on the deck below.

"Wait!" Krisha shouted in a voice as if she swallowed a harmonica. Jackie and Milk froze, holding what looked like beer kegs over the water.

"Now!" she cried.

Jackie and Milk dropped the charges just as the ship shook again. An instant later, the ship all but jumped as the charges detonated, spraying the deck with water and dead fish.

"Did we hit them?" Milk shouted as he grabbed his rifle from the deck.

"How should I know?" Krisha shouted back. "If we're still above water in the next few minutes, then we did."

"You know," Jackie turned to stare at the mermaid sprawled on the deck. "You should really— Look out!"

I followed Jackie's gaze and saw one of the red mermaids slithering on the deck.

I aimed at her and pushed the trigger, but nothing happened. Roaring in frustration, I threw my rifle at her. She dodged it and slithered on.

Jackie charged, throwing bullet after bullet as she ran to meet the spiked monster. With unearthly speed, the creature dodged each shot as she approached the injured Krisha, who twisted around to face her assailant.

Jackie swung her weapon like a club at the red monster, who evaded it with the grace of a swirling dervish, dragging her fin rays across the woman's torso, leaving behind a dozen superficial cuts. Jackie's eyes widened, and her face twisted. She pressed a hand to her chest and started trembling.

Red turned toward Krisha, who hissed at her with her back pressed against the rigging.

"Daga sends her regards, you treasonous clam." She spread her hands and fin rays as if about to embrace the smaller mermaid. "My sister died because of you! I'm going to make your death the stuff of sea shanties!"

Red pounced but was intercepted by Jackie, her teeth bared in a feral snarl, who tackled the mermaid like a football player.

"How can this be?" Red cried. "My poison—"

"Orc blood, bitch!" Jackie roared as she smashed Red's head into the deck time after time until the monster went limp.

"Tim says he'll arrive in ten minutes!" Ralf shouted.

"Good!" I cried. "Throw me a rifle, will you!"

Tim's ship was already on the horizon, a small patrol boat bristling with guns, just like in the old days. I tore my eyes off the approaching vessel and recommenced scanning the horizon for more enemies. After a few minutes, I saw a giant clam rising from the ocean.

"Five o'clock!" I cried. "A... something."

"What the devil is that?" Milk muttered as he aimed his rifle at the thing.

"Get cover!" Krisha cried and started crawling toward an over-turned crate. "It's an urchin bomb!"

Jackie grabbed the mermaid like a knight grabbing a damsel in distress and ran for the cabin. I considered climbing down but realized I'd never make it in time. Worse, too many hasty move-ments and the rigging could collapse. Then the sharpened urchins would be the least of my troubles. Instead, I flattened myself on the platform and hoped for the best.

There was a sound like the fart to end all farts, and the bombardment commenced. The ship rattled and shook as thou-sands of spiky balls rained from above. Windows shattered, railings collapsed, metal bent, and someone cried. Something stung my shin, but my excitement all but drowned out the pain.

After a few seconds, the bombardment ceased. I carefully opened one eye and looked around. The ship looked like it was nibbled by termites but was still floating.

Fearing to move my leg, I craned my neck to see the damage. An urchin had hit the deck a few inches from my foot, and one of its spikes scratched my shin. I gave out a long sigh of relief and sat back. Just a scratch.

By now, the patrol boat was close enough to discern people. "Ralf," I shouted toward the bridge, wincing as I became aware of several glass shards sticking from my neck. "Radio Tim. Warn him that there may be more of these bombs under the water."

"Radio's dead, boss!" came the reply from the bridge.

"Then signal him manually!" I yelled back. "Use smoke signals if you have to!"

I heard Ralf rummaging through the bridge, hopefully in search of signal flags, and decided to use the lull for an attendance check. "Everyone okay?"

"Got an urchin stuck in my ass," Jackie cried, "but it wasn't much to look at to begin with."

I chortled. "Milk, what do you think of Jackie's ass?"

There was no reply.

"Milk? You alive, buddy?"

"Milk!" Jackie cried, her voice shaking. "Get your black ass over here!"

There was no reply.

I climbed down, and we hastily searched the deck. There was no trace of the man. Jackie and I stood in silence, staring at the urchin-littered floor, not daring to speak the obvious. Meanwhile, Ralf waved his flags like a high schooler doing an interpretive dance. I had no idea what he was trying to signal, but I gave him an A for effort.

There was a sound like a distant clap, and he doubled over, his flags falling by his sides.

"What the hell!" I cried as I dropped to the deck and started crawling for the injured boy.

"That was a human weapon!" Krisha cried from the bridge. "We don't use such loud ones."

"Duck!" I shouted at Jackie, who started running in my direction. "Someone on the patrol boat is shooting at us."

I checked Ralf for a pulse. There was none.

"I don't understand!" Jackie cried as she crawled to my side. "Why would they fire at us! Were they aiming at—"

A voice distorted by a megaphone provided the answer before she finished the question. "Daga and I had a deal. I'd send the people I couldn't trust to pick up her traitor, and she'd send the people she couldn't trust to take the traitor out. Isn't it just swell when the trash takes itself out?" I could hear the smile in his voice, and it cut me deeper than any urchin.

Then his tone softened. "Really sorry about this old boy, but you share too many wartime stories after a few drinks. Wouldn't be good for my political career if any of that reached the press."

I picked up a shard of glass from the deck and used it as a mirror to look at the other ship without sticking my head over the railing. There was Tim, his uniform crisp as if he'd just returned from a parade, and a dozen grinning gorillas with guns ready by his side.

Stilling my raging heart, I grabbed Jackie's rifle, rose over the railing, and took a quick shot at my brother, my killer.

Tim flew back as if punched by an invisible fist. His gorillas scattered like cockroaches, like only assholes who only care about themselves can. Satisfied, I crouched below the railing to reload the weapon. As I slid the last bullet into place, I heard Tim laughing.

"Armored suits!" he shouted. "What are they gonna think of next?"

I sighed. Now all Tim had to do was wait. If we showed our faces over the railing, he'd blow us away. If we stayed down, his mermaid allies would poke enough holes in the trawler to send us all to sleep with the fishes.

I swallowed. "Well, ladies, it was a good show. Pity no one will know about it..."

Krisha pointed at the sky. "They will..."

I looked up and saw a flock of birds circling above us. No wait! Birds don't have long hair... or machine guns! Those weren't birds at all; those were harpies!

I considered running to the bridge to get some cover, but what was the point? I was covered in lacerations, and every movement hurt. Might as well die in comfort.

"What are we gonna do, boss?" Jackie whispered, her eyes wide and bright.

I shrugged. "Enjoy the show, I guess."

The chattering of auto-fire started, but the only thing that rained on our heads was spent shells. It was the other ship that was the target of the shooting.

"Hey! They got a couple!" Jackie shouted excitedly. "Like fish in a barrel!"

"Fish are smarter than that!" Krisha protested, chin raised high.

Now, you don't sink a boat with a machine gun, but you sure make her crew consider the wisdom of sticking it out. Metal whined as a harpy with brown feathers and talons that could peel a man's face like he was an orange landed on the outrigging.

"You guys need a lift?" she croaked at us. Unlike the mermaid, her human parts looked pretty human. Pity she was ugly as a traffic accident.

"Depends on the fare," I replied, stroking my rifle.

"This one's on the eyrie matriarch," the bird woman replied. "Duck!" she cried and fired a burst in the direction of the other ship.

"And stay down, wingless losers!" She shrieked toward the other ship.

She turned back to the mermaid, orc-blood, and aging P.I. huddled below. "Let's just say she has a strong civic consciousness and wants to see half the bad cops in jail."

"Hey," I shrugged. "Half is better than none, right?"

"Smart boy!" the harpy croaked. Half a dozen harpies landed on the boat. "Where should we take you?" She narrowed her eyes at us. "And keep in mind: we don't fly over cities!"

"Somewhere with water," Krisha said.

"Somewhere with whisky," Jackie said.

I said nothing. Wherever they took us, I'd be grateful. After all, you gotta give the harpy mafia their due, or the only place you'll be flying to is some very sharp rocks.

Uri Kurliancik was born in the Soviet Union and for his sins was sent to Israel. He's an avid hiker and has gone on hundreds of small adventures all over Israel. His day job is playing D&D with kids in schools and community centers. Yeah, he can't believe it either.

His writing is deeply inspired by all of the above—the immigration experience, the exciting and secret places he found on his adventures, and the cool stories woven with his players. Also, he makes stuff up.

Uri's RPG writing has been published by Wizards of the Coast,

Paizo, Mongoose, and other less savory venues, which, if you value your sanity, you're strongly discouraged from pursuing. His latest novel is *Noblesse Oblige*.

When not writing or working, he's looking for strange new places or climbing trees for no reason. When not doing even that, he sleeps. Fitfully, like a dog chasing a rabbit in a dream.

our sky

GAMA RAY MARTINEZ

LANCE INPUT A COMMAND into *Mimir's* console. The whiteness of hyperspace peeled away as the ship burned into the physical world. His eyes roved over the status displays. The engines were running a little hot but still within acceptable levels. Fuel levels were in the green. Their destination planet was the only large body in the vicinity.

"Lance," Trace said from the seat beside him.

Lance quickly scanned the planet and sighed before looking up to meet his copilot's gaze. "What is it?"

Trace's eyes stared forward. "It's Gaia."

Lance tapped the scanners giving information on the colony world. "I can see that."

"No, *look*."

Lance rolled his eyes and looked up. Almost involuntarily, he took in a sharp breath. Gaia, the first planet discovered that was even remotely habitable, floated in space on the other side of the front window, its pink oceans surrounding a single green landmass that covered a third of the planet. In the southern hemisphere, he could just make out the huge crater that had been formed a bare handful of centuries ago, when a meteor had wiped out nearly all life. After a few seconds, he pulled his eyes away from the planet and back to the scanners, hoping the readings had changed, but of course, they hadn't.

"They're all dead," Lance said.

It was several seconds before Trace turned away from the window. "All of them?"

Lance nodded, and Trace sighed as he toggled the subspace communicator, opening a channel to Earth. "HQ, this is *Mimir*. No human life detected on Gaia."

"Roger that, *Mimir*," the voice crackled through the static. "Proceed with the investigation. Permission to land a hyperspace vessel granted. Be careful."

Trace acknowledged, and they started their descent. The ship rocked as it entered the atmosphere. Pressure spiked far more than it should have for an atmosphere this dense. The alarm blared, indicating a micro fracture. Self-repair took care of the problem a second later, and the pressure returned to normal levels. The two men exchanged glances.

"What was that?"

Lance shrugged. "A pocket of super-dense gasses?"

"Wouldn't that sink?"

"Probably. We'll put it in our report."

Trace gazed out the window in an uneasy silence before he finally spoke. "Are you really quitting the service after this?"

"Keep your eyes on the scanners," Lance said without looking up, but after a few seconds, he sighed. "Jake turns eleven next month. I've been to exactly two of his birthdays. I don't want to miss another."

It was several seconds before Trace responded. "Alli wants me to do the same."

Lance looked up from his monitor. "The two of you are that serious?"

Trace reddened. "Maybe. I don't know."

"Think about it," Lance said. "It's worth it."

Trace stared out the window, and Lance went back to the controls. They set down gently, and the next thing Lance knew,

Trace was slapping the button to open the exterior hatch. He blinked, apparently having lost track of several seconds. Before he could stop Trace, the door slid open, and a rancid smell flooded the ship.

"What is that?" Trace asked.

Lance rolled his eyes. "You know, there's a reason we have procedures before exposing ourselves to unknown environments."

Trace rubbed his forehead for a second before shrugging. "It's not exactly unknown. We had a colony here."

"Had," Lance shivered. "Before it disappeared, and I don't want whatever happened to them to happen to us." He tapped a control on the panel. "That smell is just some local vegetation. The colonists say it's harmless, and they eventually got used to it."

"Hopefully, we're not here that long." Trace shuddered. "You know if whatever happened to the colony is still here, we might have to leave in a hurry. I think we should start recharging the hyperdrive."

Lance started to argue that it was against regulations but paused. It made sense, and he nodded.

"*Mimir*, disable hyperdrive safety protocols."

The ship beeped in acknowledgement. The hyperdrive was an extraordinarily powerful piece of technology, so much so that it wasn't allowed on inhabited planets for fear of the damage a malfunction could cause. Crew had to be shuttled back and forth on sublight ships. The drive took hours to recharge after a burn, and safety protocols prevented the recharge process from engaging within the gravity well of a planet, though those could be bypassed.

"Begin hyperdrive recharge."

He was about to reengage the safety protocols when Trace laughed. "I guess we'll be able to run from any monsters, right?" Lance chuckled as Trace looked at his console. "Crap."

"What is it?"

Trace pressed several buttons. "I can't connect to the colony's main computer. It's not even sending out a signal."

Lance nodded. "We expected that."

"I know. I just hoped we'd be able to get a signal once we landed. We'll have to do this the hard way."

Lance nodded, and they stepped onto a world seventeen light-years from Earth. The grass was green. Somehow, Lance had expected it to be a different color. Blue or something. Intellectually, he knew the reason. A world hospitable to human life had to have certain similarities to Earth, and those similarities would almost have to result in green plants. Still, he was almost disappointed.

They were a quarter mile from the settlement. The land was flat and, aside from the foul-smelling wind, the walk was relatively easy. Before long, they found themselves among the squat gray structures that made up the colony. The colony ship, *Flying Dutchman,* had been built to come apart to form the colonists' first buildings. As such, they were as plain as could be.

The settlement was eerie in its stillness. Rust had started creeping onto the buildings, and wind howled as it ran through the streets, causing waves in the grass, though there was no dust. Neither were there any bodies, and that thought made Lance shiver.

In the distance, the pink waters, colored by a strange alien algae, splashed against the sand. The water purification plant stood a few yards from the shore where it would be safe from high tide but far enough to not make gathering the water inconvenient. The largest building, which had been the *Dutchman's* bridge, sat in the center of the settlement, and they headed toward it.

They stopped in front of the door, waiting for the sensors to recognize them, but the door remained still. After a few seconds, Lance tapped the side panel, but nothing happened. He grunted.

"Completely without power."

Trace lifted an eyebrow. No doubt he was thinking the same thing Lance was. The colony ship had carried enough power cells to last six months, more than enough time for the colonists to set up their own power plants. Even abandoned, the buildings should still be powered. Lance shrugged, and Trace pulled out a screw-driver. After prying the side panel open, he connected a portable power cell, and the door slid open.

A burst of clean air washed over them only to be swallowed by the rotten smell of Gaia's vegetation. Lance half expected the interior of the one-room building to be covered in a layer of dust, but though he could only see part of it without the ceiling lights, it seemed completely clean. They walked to the command console and found it dead. Trace knelt down and ran his hand along the underside before grunting in surprise.

"It's been disconnected."

"By who?"

"Your guess is as good as mine." There was a click. "That should do it."

The light sprang to life, revealing a sterile room. Aside from the control console, there were only a half dozen chairs. All had been knocked over, and one had two legs broken off. On the wall opposite the door, a bronze plaque had been mounted. A ship, only vaguely resembling the *Dutchman*, had been engraved on it, along with a couple of Latin words, *Nostrum Caleum. Our sky*. That had been humanity's rallying cry ever since they discovered how to burn their way into hyperspace.

Quickly, Lance scanned the colony's logs. He'd already seen most of the early entries. The governor had transmitted them to Earth, though after two months, the transmissions had stopped. Communications were still down, in spite of the restored power, and most of the entries after the cutoff point were garbled. He opened one of the few intact files, but it was only an entry about a child reporting a mermaid in the water. Interesting but not particularly relevant. The first line in the second file made his blood run cold.

The plague is getting worse.

"We need to get back to *Mimir*, now!"

Trace looked up from one of the other screens. "What?"

Trace's eyes went wide at the explanation. He tapped a few

buttons before following Lance. They started off at a fast walk, but the worry kept gnawing at Lance, and by the time they reached the ship, he was in a dead run. They sealed the ship, and jogged back to the medical bay.

"*Mimir,*" Lance said between heavy breaths. "Perform a full bio scan."

The ship beeped in acknowledgement.

"What kind of disease was it?" Trace asked as the green beam ran over Lance.

"No idea." Lance's words tumbled over each other. "I don't know why they didn't contact Earth."

"And you think we're infected?"

"I hope not." Lance couldn't keep the fear from his voice. If this was what had happened to the colonists...

"No anomalies found," the ship's metallic voice said.

"Unless it's something you can't detect," Lance said under his breath.

"Repeat command," the ship said.

"Examine Trace."

"I guess we can contact Earth and tell them we know what happened to the colonists."

The ship beeped again and declared Trace healthy. The copilot let out a breath of relief. Lance shook his head. "No, I don't think so."

"But you said there was a plague. No one is here. What else do you think happened?"

"Exactly," Lance said. "No one is here. If they were all killed by a disease, where are the bodies?"

"Maybe they decomposed."

Lance snorted. "A body isn't going to completely decompose without a trace in a matter of weeks, and there were two thousand people here. There should be at least *some* remains."

Trace nodded and walked to his console on the bridge.

"I opened communications with the *Dutchman*'s computer before I left. We should be able to access the logs from here."

Lance nodded. "Good idea."

He sat down next to Trace as they parsed through the logs, but they found nothing. Trace set the computer to recover some of the lost data while Lance walked to the storage area and pulled out a pair of hazmat suits. By the time they were dressed, the computer had done all it could, recovering part of some of the files. Lance scanned them and shook his head.

"There's nothing we can use. Something about the water-purification plant being under strain. Solar cells being less efficient than anticipated. Kids claiming to see mermaids, but the governor thought they were making that up. Something about toys on the beach."

"Toys?"

Lance shrugged. "I only got pieces of a bunch of files. I don't even know if they're related. Have you found any indication of a source for the disease?"

Trace shook his head.

Lance sighed. "I guess we're going back out."

Wearing the hazmat suits, they searched the settlement, confirming it was empty. In a couple of places, they found wrecked furniture, but in most, everything was in perfect condition, as if the colonists had just gotten up and left. When they found no sign of humans, they walked to the water-purification plant. It was still operational, and the cistern was full, though they couldn't say how long it had been that way.

"How can there be no sign?"

Lance thought he'd spoken quietly, but apparently, it wasn't quiet enough because Trace pointed. "Maybe not no sign."

There, about a dozen yards away, sat a teddy bear half buried in the sand. The water was at high tide and flowed around the toy. Lance walked to it and tried to pick it up by one ear, but it was too well entrenched in the sand.

Trace snorted as he pushed past Lance. "It's a teddy bear. It's not going to hurt you."

He picked up the toy in both hands and smirked before holding it out. "See?"

Lance started to respond when Trace jerked his hand back, tossing the bear ten feet away. Trace shook his hand for a few seconds.

"What happened?" Lance asked.

"I'm not sure. Something poked me."

"Are you okay?"

Trace held his hand up to the plate protecting his face. He nodded. "It tore my glove, but I'm not bleeding. It was more surprising than anything else."

Lance grunted. "We should still return to the ship to get it checked out."

Trace rolled his eyes. "Do you think the colony went to the infirmary for every scrape and bruise?"

Lance glared at him. "They did if they followed regulations. This is an alien planet, and we still haven't documented all the bacteria." Lance looked around at the landscape. Under other circumstances, it might have been almost peaceful, but now it seemed empty. "It's not like we're in a big hurry."

Trace sighed. "Fine, if you want to waste time."

Once back in *Mimir*, the ship scanned Trace. This time, it let out a series of beeps.

"Foreign organism detected."

"What?" Color drained from Trace's face. "What kind of foreign organism?"

"Unknown. Its biology resists scanning."

"How far has the infection spread?" Lance asked.

"No infection detected."

"But you said there's an organism."

"Worm-like organism currently burrowing up right shoulder. Probable destination is brain."

"What?" Trace cried. "Get it out."

"*Mimir*, program a nanobot infusion to rid Trace of the organism."

A drawer in one of the walls popped open, revealing a dozen silvery capsules, no larger than the nail of Lance's pinky. One of them pulsed green. Trace didn't hesitate. He plucked it out of the drawer and swallowed it. The nanobots inside, which could be programed to handle nearly any disease, would be breaking out of the capsule and spreading through Trace's body. For a few seconds, nothing happened. Then, Trace doubled over, gripping his neck. His skin writhed, and his eyes bulged. He tried to inhale, but it was like he lacked the strength to breathe. He fell onto the ground and curled into a fetal position and screamed.

"*Mimir*, what's happening to him?" Lance asked.

"Organism split apart. It attacked and destroyed the nanobots."

"How can it do that?"

"Unknown."

A thin layer of ooze covered Trace, and his skin gradually shifted from sun-tanned brown to dull pink, the exact same shade as the ocean outside. He stopped moving and met Lance's gaze. All color had drained from his eyes, and his face seemed rubbery. His hair and eyebrows had fallen off, and a layer of skin had grown over his nose. More than anything, he reminded Lance of a squid. The thing that had been Trace stood up, though he seemed to have trouble keeping his balance.

"Trace?" Lance asked

"Yes," Trace said in an emotionless voice. "I am Trace."

"What happened to you?"

Trace took a wobbly step toward Lance, who backed up. "I was in pain," he said. "The pain stopped. I am better now." He licked his lips. "We should return to Earth."

"*Mimir*, what happened to him?"

"Final readings from nanobots indicate genetic resequencing."

"His DNA has been rewritten? Into what?"

"I am Trace," Trace said as he took another step toward Lance.

"I am better now. We have a hyperdrive. We should return to Earth."

"Scanners unable to penetrate skin. Species type indeterminate."

Lance took another step back and spoke slowly. "Trace, why don't you stay in the infirmary? I'll contact Earth and let them know the situation."

"Sensors indicate presence of EM field," *Mimir* said. "Communications nonfunctional."

"What? How did that happen?"

"EM field appeared a few seconds ago. Origin unknown."

Lance cursed. "I guess we know why the colony stopped communication with Earth." He stepped out of the infirmary. "Seal the door."

The ship beeped in acknowledgement, and the door slid shut. Trace kept his eyes locked on Lance but didn't try to get out.

"*Mimir*, what can you tell me about what happened to him? Did your nanobots detect anything?"

"What appeared to be a single organism invaded Commander Dremond. When engaged by nanobots, it split apart, becoming thousands of single-celled organisms. They attacked the nanobots from all sides."

"How did it do that?"

"Unknown. Organisms generate EM field preventing sensors from locking on to them."

"You detected it in Trace."

"Scanners detected a parting of flesh as it burrowed through his body. Scanners did not detect the organism itself."

"We need to contact Earth. Can you reroute power from other systems into communications?"

"Diversion of power from the antimatter chamber overloaded the system. Only short-range communications are available."

That brought Lance up short. "When did that happen?"

"Operation completed fifty-three seconds ago."

"Operation? Are you saying you were instructed to do this?"

"Commander Dremond ordered it done."

"And you listened?"

"Commander Dremond is second in command. He has primary access to all systems."

Lance sighed. He should have thought of that. "Rescind all access for Commander Dermond." The ship beeped in acknowledgement. "Does he have any weapons?"

"No weapons detected."

"Good," Lance said as he pulled out his blaster and aimed. He struggled to keep it steady. "Open the door."

The door slid open. Trace stood in the doorway, staring at Lance. If he noticed the weapon, he gave no sign. His eyes were glossed over, and his skin had grown rubbery. There were suckers on the inside of his hands, and his nose had vanished completely.

"We should return to Earth."

He slurred his words, the shape of his mouth having elongated. Lance pointed the weapon at his face.

"Why did you disable long-range communications?"

"Because if I had not, you would have told Earth what happened."

"Which would've been a good thing. Maybe they could figure out how to solve this problem."

"We must return to Earth."

"Why do you want to go back so badly?"

Lance's hand opened of its own accord and the weapon fell to the ground. He looked at his fingers and saw that they had taken on a faint pink tint. For a second, Lance could only stare at the blaster. Then, he turned to look at his hand. He couldn't be sure, but his fingers seemed longer. Each had a small lump near the tip. A glance at Trace's hand revealed that the lumps were in the same spot as the suction cups.

"*Mimir*, am I infected?"

The ship beeped. "No foreign organisms detected."

"You said they generate an EM field that prevents you from seeing them."

"That is correct."

"But you could detect the field."

"Yes."

"Am I giving one off now?"

The ship scanned him and beeped after a second. "EM field surrounding you is higher than the human norm, but still within safety limit."

His blood went cold. "So that means probably."

"You should allow it to take you," Trace said.

"What?"

"Everything would be so much easier if you did not resist."

"What are you talking about?"

Trace's eyes focused behind Lance. He said something in a language Lance didn't know, but the words popped into his head of their own accord. *Sea Mother*.

The image of a mermaid formed in his mind. It was beautiful, and its voice was the loveliest thing he had ever heard. He wanted to go into the ocean to find it.

No, that wasn't right. That was how it had fooled the colonists. With that thought, the true image filled his thoughts. A thing like a massive squid formed in Lance's mind, though it had far more tentacles than any squid ever born on Earth. Too many to count. They writhed, each seeming independent of all others. Through some telepathic link, Lance knew it swam through the vast sea of this world, practically invisible in the pink water which was the same color as its rubbery skin. Though it was miles away, it was aware of him. Its lone eye focused on Lance. It let out a screech, and Lance grabbed his head. The next thing he knew, he was on the metal deck of *Mimir*. Cold washed over him, and he shivered. His arms and legs tried to move without him telling them what to do, but in a panic, he thrashed, seizing control of his limbs. Trace stood over him, wearing an empty expression.

"The Sea Mother learned what she could in taking those who lived here, but it was still not enough. She must spread."

"That was why you destroyed communications."

"Yes," Trace said. "I could not allow you to warn Earth. We will fly the ship through hyperspace. Once we reach Earth, the spawn of the Sea Mother will be dropped into the ocean."

Lance didn't need Trace to tell him. The image of what would happen filled his head. The single-celled organisms would spread through the ocean, slowly converting any life they encountered into a mindless slave, a puppet just like Trace had become. Eventually, it would spread to the surface as spores, filling the atmosphere. It would be a long time before everyone had been infected, but the Sea Mother had ways to accelerate that.

Images from the past flooded Lance's mind. He saw the Sea Mother waking as the colonists moved on the surface of the world, a new host for it to infect. It had started with the children, implanting the idea of mermaids in the water, and drawing them close so it could saturate them with its presence. Once that had been done, they walked into the ocean without anyone knowing where they were. Some had left their toys on the beach. That was what the message in the logs had meant. The creature, the Sea Mother, was intelligent. It knew that if people were looking for children and they saw discarded toys in the sand, their first instinct would be to pick them up. They had been seeded with controllers, the organism that *Mimir* had detected in Trace, which were a more concentrated version of the spores. That was what had happened to him. The toys were bait, and it hadn't been long before the creature had spread its influence to everyone, eventually consuming them to get the energy it needed to stay awake. If the same thing happened on Earth, there would be nothing left of the human race.

"We'll stop you."

Speaking those words took nearly all the strength Lance had, but even as he said them, he knew they were false. The Sea Mother laughed, and knowledge flooded into Lance's mind. Since the meteor had hit, wiping out the strange fish that had lived near the surface of the water, there had been nothing to prey on the controllers that the Sea Mother sent out. In the centuries since its only predator had been wiped out, it had spread and now inhabited every part of this world. It was in the very air. In his mind, he saw *Mimir* descending. She had been aware of them from the moment they had entered the atmosphere. The pocket of dense atmosphere that had caused the rupture had been her spores, which she appeared to have complete control over. They had been infected before they had even touched down. That had taken most of the spores in the immediate area, and it had taken a while for others to concentrate around the ship in great enough numbers to generate the EM field, but that had only been needed to prevent communication. By that point, their fate had already been sealed. The controller that had stung Trace had only accelerated the process.

"She will not use controllers again," Trace said, seemingly reading his thoughts. "She knows that if she's detected too soon, the people of Earth might find a way to resist, but your way, the slow way, allows her to spread. By the time the first symptoms are detected, it will be too late." Trace made an expression that looked almost like a smile, though it used only half his mouth and looked decidedly unnatural on his face.

"Fight her," Lance managed.

If he'd been able to cry, he would've been in tears. Trace couldn't do anything though. Trace, the real Trace, was gone, killed the moment the controller had entered his brain.

Lance was shaking as he got to his knees. Trace cocked his head, but made no move to stop him. Lance's arms were so heavy, and they kept trying to move without him telling them to. He tried to stand, but it was no use. His arms gave out, and he collapsed.

"Don't struggle," Trace said. "Look at it this way. We'll be back on Earth soon. You get to go home, with Jake."

The sound of his son's name filled him with anger. "No, I won't. I'll be dead, and she'll control my body like a puppet. She'll control Jake too. And Alli."

The names had no effect on Trace whatsoever. "She already

knows your thoughts. All your memories. Don't you understand? You will live forever as a part of her."

Strength and desperation welled up inside of him. He didn't allow himself to think. If he had, the Sea Mother would've detected it and stopped him. Instead, he just lunged for the blaster he had dropped. He pointed it at Trace and fired. His old copilot didn't even scream as his molecules were torn apart.

Lance's sense of triumph lasted only a second. Trace's body had been destroyed, but he had hurt the Sea Mother as much as cutting his hair would hurt him. Trace had only been a puppet. Even now, he felt the creature's control over him increase as it made him into the same. He rose and input a command into *Mimir*. The ship's engines hummed to life as it rose. It wouldn't even have to wait for the engine to recharge. They had left it charging in case they needed to escape quickly. Looking back, he realized they had been under her influence even then. It hadn't been enough to make them leave, but just enough to make sure she would be able to reach Earth as soon as possible. They had even joked about it. It didn't seem right that the end of the human race should be ushered in with laughter.

Trace distracted me.

The thought bubbled onto the surface of his mind. The Sea Mother examined it and dismissed it, but Lance hung on with every shred of self that he had left. Trace had distracted him, and he had never reengaged the hyperdrive safety measures. That meant they were still inactive.

They were in the upper atmosphere now. His fingers had already entered the command to return to Earth. There was only one chance. It would mean his life, but he forced the fear away. There was more at stake than just him. He threw his will against the thing controlling him. He didn't need his entire body. He just needed his mouth. His assault caught the Sea Mother by surprise, and the words slipped out of his lips, uttering a command that would've done nothing had the safety protocols still been enabled.

"*Mimir*, detonate hyperdrive."

"Hyperdrive is fully powered, but we remain in the gravity well of the planet. Detonating will release a wave of heat sufficient to ignite atmosphere and boil away the sea. Land will be scorched. Procedure not recommended. Do you wish to proceed?"

The mind of the Sea Mother welled up inside of him. It was as unstoppable as a mountain, as a storm, and Lance could no more stand against her than he could stand against either of those. He felt his mouth start to move in order to tell *Mimir* not to follow through. An image popped into his mind, one that had nothing to do with the Sea Mother. The plaque in the *Flying Dutchman*, showing an explorer ship. Beneath it were two words. *Nostrum Caleum.* The thought burned in his mind, as bright and as strong as anything the Sea Mother had ever sent.

This is our sky.

In all her long existence, the Sea Mother had never experienced a singular purpose driven by such strength. This was more that self-preservation. This was the salvation of an entire species, of a world. Now that the Sea Mother knew of Earth, she would never rest until she controlled it. Earth or Gaia. One of them would be destroyed. He remembered Jake. Lance had missed too many of his son's birthdays. He would never see another, but at least Jake would have them. All his will went to forming that one single word that would destroy an entire planet.

"Proceed."

The ship beeped in response. A high-pitched whir came from the engine room. The Sea Mother took control of Lance and tried to override his command. For a second, Lance thought he had failed, but the creature couldn't seem to form the words. She was afraid, and just like a human might have trouble holding their hands steady when overcome by fear, the Sea Mother's control over her host was tenuous. No doubt she would be able to reestablish it in a matter of seconds, but she didn't have that long. Strangely, Lance was completely calm.

The engine screamed as fire filled the cockpit. The last thought that flitted through Lance's mind was that he had saved the world. Then, everything went red.

Gama Ray Martinez lives near Salt Lake City, Utah, with his wife and kids. He moved there solely because he likes mountains. He collects weapons in case he ever needs to supply a medieval battalion, and he greatly resents when work or other real-life things get in the way of writing. He secretly hopes to one day slay a dragon in single combat and doesn't believe in letting pesky little things like reality stand in the way of dreams. His novel *Gods of Neverland* was released in 2022 by HarperVoyager.

the woman who held the sea in her hair

EM MCDERMOTT

THE MAN, like all the others, was not interesting. He had the same earnest face, the same black hair. The fur he wore was stark white. People whispered that he was a hunter to rival even the god Nanook. Yet I sat bored before my father's fire, smiling politely and dreaming of the sea.

"What is it you seek in a husband?" he asked quietly, after he'd told me all he offered—a comfortable tent, and plenty of food, and a life of peace—and I'd treated his offerings as nothing. The question was surprising. No one else had asked it before.

"Perhaps I don't seek a husband."

My father frowned at that, though it was the truth. My parents sought one for me. My father muttered of my age, and proper things, and mouths to feed. My mother, each bright day as we scraped and chewed and stomped sealskin, spoke of the value of companionship. I would enjoy it, she said, once I got used to it.

They paraded men before me, each of them with his chest puffed out like a cormorant in mating season. Fiddling with the furs they wore like gaudy feathers. Every man commented on my hair—how lush it was, how long, and deep black as the moonless night.

All but this man, who said nothing of it.

"What is it about marriage that doesn't interest you?" he asked instead.

"Perhaps it's more that there is nothing in it that does interest me."

His eyes lit up, though I could not fathom why. "Ah, then, what does?"

"Excuse me?" I asked, confused by the unexpectedness of his question.

"What interests you?" the suitor asked quietly.

I studied him anew. But there was nothing in his appearance to suggest he was unlike all the others.

"I like to sit at the water's edge," I said simply. It was not what any other woman would say. Perhaps it made me sound simple. But it was true.

"I understand," the hunter said, and left.

My mother sighed as soon as he was gone. "Sedna. You will grow old and die in this tent. He was a good match! A great hunter. Now, he will never come back."

I peered at the door flap that had closed behind him, and wondered if I cared.

As soon as I could, I escaped to the sea. The pulsing tide was the heartbeat of the Mother. It was impossible to worry over small things when I dipped my fingers into the icy water that lapped at the base of glaciers. I felt myself to be a part of everything.

Tiny ripples licked my hand. A gray fin cut like a knife through the water. I raised my hand from the sea, my heart beating fast, though I knew the predator had not come for me. The fin sank, and the surface of the water was very still. Oh, how I wished to see into its depths, to where the hunt churned.

But the hunt came to me.

The shark, its jaws a cavern, ascended from the water. Before it, the lithe black body of a seal tumbled through the air, only narrowly escaping the tiny pointed knives that lined the shark's maw.

I should not care which of them won, for to hunt was nature's way. But perhaps it was my lingering offense at the hunter's proud bearing and white fur that drove me this day to wish for the life of the seal. I stood on the edge of the ice as the seal disappeared back into the water, followed by the shark. I readied a harpoon.

I waited until I saw the tip of the shark's fin cut once more through the water. The sea was not red; the seal was not yet caught. I aimed into the sea below the fin, and let my harpoon fly.

I found my target. The line on the shaft unfurled, whizzing behind it. My fingers held on, my muscles strong beneath my gloves. The shark swam and fought, and I waited.

After, when the gray shark lay on its back on the ice, its eyes dull, the seal surfaced again. He watched me.

His eyes were a deep black to match my locks. They contained in them the soul of the Mother, as if the animal were not separate from her at all. It was for this purity that I loved animals over men.

"You're welcome," I said to him. He seemed to nod, and then he sank back below the waves.

I returned home to bring my catch to my family. Gray shark was a delicacy.

The next time I came to the water's edge, I found a seal waiting for me. Was it the same one? I could not know, but he nodded in the same almost-human way as before. He sat beside me for hours on the ice.

This continued. Sometimes he brought me fish and sometimes he brought only himself.

The seasons changed. The dark season came and went. A bright white world returned. More suitors sought my hand, and I rejected them like all before. My father's muttering grew louder. And still the seal came to sit with me, until I considered him my closest friend. By now, he knew all my secrets, for I spoke to him sometimes in the hours we sat alone.

Then one day, a day like any other, I went to sleep in my tent beside my mother and my father, and I woke in darkness, somewhere else. I was on the sea in a kayak. I could tell this from the rocking, though I could not see. My hands were tied behind my back, so I could not remove the covering that had been put on my head to block my sight.

I thrashed and kicked until I heard my father say, "Still, Sedna. Be still."

Perhaps it was surprise that made me obey, or perhaps it was stubbornness. My own father did this to me. I did not wish for him to see me afraid and desperate.

We landed on an isle. My father lifted me off his kayak and deposited me on the shore. He untied my hands and pushed off before I could rip the bag from my head and follow after him.

I would not have tried, anyway. My pride held my spine straight. I shot fire at him from my eyes, and he held his own eyes downcast, so he would not see.

"Do not worry, Sedna," he said. "I will be back for you. I am just giving you time to think."

He'd left a bag full of dried caribou and fish, and fresh water. It was not enough to last me for long. There was little on the isle to provide comfort. He might mean to teach me a lesson about gratitude, but if he didn't come back soon, I would not be alive on his return to tell him what I'd learned.

I ate little that day. It seemed smarter to save it. Snow offered fresh water, if I could only melt it. My father had left me a bow drill to make a fire. I collected driftwood and made one. I filled my pack with snow and placed it close. I curled up next to the fire for comfort, though the sun stayed high in the sky.

As I lay there, I wished for stars, though not for the cold that came with them. In winter, every star was the eye of a fish, watching me from an upside-down sea. They glinted on the water's surface. They reflected off the ice of the glaciers. I could not be alone with all those stars.

But I was not alone now. Two lights glinted in the sea. I thought at first they were only the reflection of the sun, but they swam toward me.

It was my seal. He came ashore, and crawled awkwardly across rock and snow until he reached me. He lay down beside me, and I put my arms around his blubbery form and drew from his warmth, even as I wondered that he'd come so far from the water's edge to lie beside my flames.

In the morning when I woke, the seal was gone. In his place, a man lay, naked but for the sealskin that covered him.

I started back, and reached for the bow drill to use as a weapon.

The man rolled over, revealing the hunter who'd long ago courted my hand. He opened his eyes and I recognized my seal's deep black soulful gaze.

"It's been you all this time," I said.

He smiled, pleased with himself as only men who wake up naked next to a woman can be.

"But, why wouldn't you tell me? Why not reveal yourself before now? I would've married you and avoided this exile."

The man shrugged.

"Are you a god?"

He laughed. It was easy and warm. "No. I am only a man, and a seal."

"But how are you both?"

I had heard, of course, of monsters who could change their shape. But the hunter did not look like a red-eyed ijiraq.

"I will show you," he said.

He took my hand. His felt warm while mine was cold and clammy. He was naked, but I was the one who shivered. He did not leave his sealskin behind, but took it with him, draped over one arm. He placed the sealskin gently down before he eased into the sea. "Come on," he said.

The touch of the sea on bare skin could kill in minutes. I worried that my fire would go out while we swam, and I would die of the cold. Yet I found my hands reaching to strip off my skins and furs. My feet dipping into the sea. My body following the hunter until we floated together.

My hair fanned out around my shoulders in a black cloud.

"Do you feel the sea's heartbeat?" the hunter asked me.

"Of course." I did not need to be in the sea to feel that. "Its heartbeat is the tide."

"Do you feel the power below its heartbeat?"

At this, I had to think. The water was like tiny knives against my skin. Life-giving, life-taking. It cleansed me, banishing impurities with its salt. I took a deep breath and sank below the surface. I held there, my chest aching with cold, my hair tickling my cheeks. And in my own blood, I felt the thrum of the power of the sea.

I surfaced. "Yes," I said.

"That is all there is to it," the hunter said, treading water. He did not shiver, though his skin was pale. My body was beginning to convulse, my muscles twitching as they rejected the cold.

"I don't understand."

"The Mother lives in her cave at the bottom of the sea. Once, she was alone. Life can't form out of nothing, and so she used her own life to form others. From her fingernails she made fish, and from her thumbs, man, and from her forearms, whales. From a few shapes, she made all life. The sea was flooded with her blood, which is filled with salt and magic. So long as you can taste the salt, you know her magic still lingers. It is a small matter to use it to change from one shape to another."

I'd heard the story of creation many times. Every child knew it. But never had I heard that the Mother's salt blood could change a man into a seal.

"Try it," he urged.

"To-to-to be-become a seal?" It was hard to speak now, for my teeth chattered too much.

"Something easier," he suggested. "Try to be warm."

I considered climbing out. I could stumble back to my fire, and mayhap live. But I trusted my seal. He had no reason to harm me. So I took as deep a breath as my clenched chest would allow and I sank down again below the surface.

The sea pulsed gently around me, the ever-present tide allowing me to feel the Mother's heartbeat. I opened my mouth and licked my lips, tasting the salt that came from her blood. I imagined that I was not cold. I wished for it. I believed in it.

Slowly, my shivering slowed. My consciousness began to drift away from my body until I wondered if I were dying. I felt as one with the sea, and intensely alive.

I surfaced. I was no longer shivering. The water did not feel cold. I looked down at my body and saw it had changed. I was plumper than before, as if blubber had grown up from nothing beneath my skin.

"Now you know my secrets too," my hunter said.

When my father came to retrieve me from the island, he found me with the hunter. We declared our intent to marry and my father, overjoyed, took us home in his kayak and threw us a lavish wedding. But when I became pregnant, I worried. I wished to birth in private, for I did not know what shape our children would take. But this was not the way of our people. I birthed, in a roomful of women, two children. One, a human boy. The other, a seal.

There was an uproar. I was still bleeding when they dragged me and my mewling daughter to the water's edge. Into my father's kayak I went again, my daughter clutched to my chest. She had her father's huge eyes. Light gray fur puffed as it dried. She flapped her flippers weakly.

"My husband!" I cried, but the kayak went farther and farther into the sea, and he did not come.

My own father made to throw my daughter into the waves. A newborn seal pup cannot swim any better than a newborn of any other kind, and I clutched her in my arms and screamed and fought. I was still weak from the birth, and my father's face was a mask of glacial ice.

"You have shamed our family," he said, over and over, as he tried to throw my daughter into the sea.

Cold air rushed against my skin as he tore her from my breast. She plunked into the water, same as any rock, and I wailed, and dove after her.

The water was dark and gloomy. Particles floated before my eyes. My daughter was a dark mass, turning over as she sank. I swam after her. The blood of my afterbirth trailed behind me. The ice water tingled, numbing me.

I felt for the Mother's pulse. I drew on her power as I kicked, swimming down. My body plumped and my muscles strengthened. I swam powerfully through water that felt no longer cold. But it was not enough. My human body was not fast enough to catch my sinking child.

And so I drew on her power again. My feet, so small, so useless, grew large and webbed. Scales sprouted down my legs as I held the image of a fish in my mind. The seam between my legs closed, and I kicked with a new, strong tail.

Soon, I reached my girl. I held her to my breast, which I had not changed. I would need my breasts to feed her. I swam for the surface.

We surfaced, and I held my daughter above my head. She mewled, and I breathed a sigh of relief.

"My husband!" I cried again. But my father heard me instead.

He came after me in his kayak. With cold fingers and ice in his heart, he readied his harpoons.

Rage flowed like ice through my blood. I no longer felt the chill of the ocean, yet my heart might freeze into a glacier at any moment.

Behind us was the isle where I'd been exiled. If I could get my daughter to its shore, she would be safe. But no, no. He would only come for her.

I needed an army to stand between my father and my child. I did not have that. But I had one thing that my father did not. The power of the Mother.

Giving myself up to it, I drew more power into my body. *What is form but an illusion?* I whispered to her like a lover.

And she answered, a resounding agreement.

I grew. Bigger and bigger my body became, until my daughter was like a moth on the tip of my finger. Until my hair filled the ocean like a bed of tangled seaweed. Until my father's kayak was overturned by the waves of my movements. His harpoons sank like fallen stars. His nets grew tangled in my tresses. With one long arm, I placed my daughter gently on the shore of the nearby isle and I dipped below the surface alone, to follow my father's descent.

He sank with his furs and his rage about him. He swore and cursed and fought the tangle of my hair even as its dark strands wrapped around his throat and strangled him. I stared into his eyes as they bulged. He saw a monster, in his last moments. But I saw myself as something else.

A mother.

A new kayak launched from the shore near my village. I could feel the prow set out upon the water, for there was no longer any separation between the sea and I. It rowed for the isle that cushioned my daughter.

And so I called an army.

The creatures of the sea flocked to me. They danced in my hair, silver-scaled fishes and seals that might sometimes be men. Sharks and narwhals and walruses, they came. We surrounded the isle, the waters thick and teeming.

But it was only my husband in the kayak. He'd brought our son. I allowed him passage to the isle's shore.

Years passed. My husband made a home and raised our children. He came to swim with me in the sea, weaving joyfully between the dark strands of my hair. But when he shed his skin to walk again on land, I could not follow. My legs and feet had become a tail. My skin had turned to scales. I sank into the sea and asked the Mother to change me back, but she did not.

Maybe because I did not truly wish her to.

Maybe because, once changed, you can never go back.

And so I watched from the sea as my husband raised our children on the shore. The village I came from learned to tell stories of a strange isle that could not be reached. They grew superstitious and would not pass their kayaks through the black waters that surrounded the place, for whoever tried to reach the isle did not ever come back.

My family was safe.

But this was not enough. Oh, not nearly enough.

The gift of the Mother is a curse too, I learned. The coldness of the sea cannot enter your heart without turning you cold, too. And though my children thrived in the care of their father, though they grew healthy and strong before my eyes, I could not quell the hatred that pulsed in my heart for the humans who'd banished us.

I clutched the creatures of the sea to me like adopted children. I told them never to go near the humans and their kayaks, never to give themselves up in selfless sacrifice to the harpoons and the nets. I sent fish to feed my own children while the village children starved.

The bounty of the sea had turned on them, the people of the village wailed. They could catch nothing.

Every emaciated body they put to rest in the sea gave me a surge of satisfaction. A sacrifice to the goddess Sedna, they'd call, throwing what little meat they had into the sea as an offering. I let it sink to the bottom, untouched. It was not enough. There was no enough.

At length, my children grew up. My daughter joined a pod of seals who played in the black tangles of my hair, but my son left us. He took a boat and rowed away, seeking his own kind.

Then one day, he returned.

I knew it was him right away. He had his father's soulful black eyes, and thick black hair. In his arms he held a baby, bundled in caribou fur. He stood at the edge of the water and spoke quietly of the hardship suffered by his family. There was not enough to eat.

He sang a sad song of scarcity. He called me Mother. He begged me to release the bounty of the sea so that hunters like him might feed their families.

But I was too full of vengeance to listen. I turned from his song, my heart glacial cold, and so I did not see that my husband heard too. I did not see him leave the isle and swim to the shore where my son waited. I did not see him haul out onto the ice and offer himself to sate my son's hunger. ·

My son killed him. Not knowing, of course.

When I discovered this, I shed salty tears. Tears of resentment, at first, but then of lost love, and the magic in them melted a crack in the lining of my heart.

And so the next time my son came to the shore and sang his song, I allowed a creature to go to him and feed my son's sons. Thus I became the mother of both man and beast. And the first mermaid. Sedna, goddess of the sea.

This story takes its inspiration from tales of the Inuit sea goddess, Sedna.

Em McDermott lives in a fairy-tale cottage in the secluded woods of upstate New York, but the only magic she knows is how to bake a gluten-free pie that tastes good. Growing up, Em was mentored by fierce heroines from the fantasy novels she read during math class. Her own books are dark, epic, romantic fantasies set in lush, magical worlds that are about to end. Em shares her home with two loving partners, a small flock of dragons (cough, cough, pet chickens), and more zucchini plants than is entirely reasonable. Her hobbies include planning trips to the ocean and convincing her partners to build her more bookcases.

Explore the worlds of her stories at emmcdermott.com, and receive a free story when you sign up to her newsletter.

the mermaid's song

J. LORIAN YOUNG

Doldrums hold them in its grip, no wind to fill the sail;
though prayers are rising from the ship, they come to no avail.
Aeolus does not seem to hear the pleas the men have cried,
while Neptune's quick to reappear and bind them to the tide.
As day turns into star-lit night, and night turns into day
they drift upon their seaborne plight, helpless to break away.
The limits of their minds are stretched too far beyond their power,
and sanity's tenuous grasp is wrenched long hour after hour.
The captain keeps a steady hand, the lookout keeps his guard
for any sign of distant land not written on the chart.
Horizon seems a steady line between the sea and sky;
no sandy beach's glitter and shine attracts his searching eye.
Yet somewhere to the east, it seems, or maybe to the west,
drifts an echoed sound of dreams, a lover's lost request.
It resonates and inspires their trust as it settles on their ear
and draws them by their deepest lust while calming all their fear:

Come, come, come unto me
all ye men who sail on the sea
come and lie in my shade to rest
your head upon my silken breast.

Come to valleys dark below
and I'll tell you everything that I know,
come and find a sweet release
and I will grant you peace.

"A vast!" at last, the Captain cries, "Put every man to oar!
Row hard toward the western skies and distant, hidden shore!
Go put your backs into it boys, today we'll make ye men;
we'll row her home and know the joy of solid earth again!
Hurry each man to his post! There's much work to be done
if we're to see that distant coast before the setting sun!"

Still there, somewhere, beyond the mists which creep along the brine
the haunting lullaby insists in melodies sublime:

Come, come, come unto me
all ye men who sail on the sea;
you're getting warm and drawing near
don't stop now, you're almost here.
Come to where the heavens meet earth
you will at last be safe at berth,
come and find your sweet release
and I will grant you peace.

The ship continues on its course toward the haunting voice;
their only wish, to find its source; they have no other choice.
The song has gotten to their minds, the music fills their heads;
they dream of passion most sublime in sweetest flower beds.
They know they're drawing near her, they cannot stop to rest,
the distant cape grows clearer in sunset's gleaming west.
But the craggy rocks await them as they heed the mermaid's beck;
and her soothing voice placates them as their ship is cast to wreck.
Each feels her hands upon his flesh as they dance beneath the waves

and give release to final breaths in underwater graves.
He is alone yet with his love of beauty well renowned;
she draws him deep within her cove and pulls him farther down.
He knows no fear, he's happy there, for nothing can define
the soothing sweetness that he hears carried within the brine:

Come, come, come unto me
we'll make sweet love beneath the sea.
I'll shelter you with my moist caress
and keep you here in my ancient nest.
Once beyond the veil I'll show
you everything there is to know.
Come, I am your sweet release
and I will grant you peace.

JANICE LORIANN YOUNG lives and writes in a place called Thistle Dew, nestled in the mountains of New Hampshire where she is surrounded by family, animals, and incredible nature. A love of ghost stories and the macabre led quite naturally to writing narrative poetry and short stories, often with dark and haunting themes that are sometimes based on true events.

A retired secretary and late literary bloomer, Janice is devoting her golden years to sunsets and crocheting; porch swings and family dinners; homemade breads, evenings around the bonfire and all the stories told there. She has previously been published by Silver Birch Press and is a fan of Grandma Moses, who showed by example that it's never too late for artists, writers, and dreamers of all manner and sorts to follow their bliss.

the lure of the sea

MICHELLE TANG

ALL EYES TO THE EAST!" Wai Yu screamed, voice cracking, from atop the mast. The old man, all tanned sinew and scars, struggled into a harness.

Kai followed the gazes of the crew, backs turned steadfastly against the setting sun. There was nothing to see. The cerulean waters were quiet, the sky clear. The men and women who'd laughed throughout last night's storm, who'd leapt back to the ship after every deck-scouring wave, the sharp recoil of the ropes tied around their waists making them seem capable of flight, stood silent now.

He turned his head to peek over his shoulder behind him, but the foreman's large chest blocked his view.

"Fool." Shaun smacked a palm, broad as an oar, against the back of Kai's head. "When a Drowned One is sighted, you must never look."

"What is a Drowned One?" Kai asked, but his words were lost in sudden noise. The crew, gravel-voiced and discordant, bellowed out prayers to the Sea God, their hands clapped over their ears. Kai cringed at the noise, cringed at the amount of white showing in his crewmates' eyes, cringed as something dove towards them from the sky.

It was Wai Yu, flailing in his harness like he was drowning in mid-air. He swung from one side of the ship to the other, a flesh pendulum, shrieking words snatched away by the wind, by the others' prayers.

When the old man lost momentum, when he hung like a strung deer from a tree bough, Kai found himself creeping closer. The old sailor was weeping now, moisture running from the corner of his eyes to dip into the deep crevices of his face, as if the tears were ships flowing over a rough sea. "It's a little boy," Wai Yu wept. "Please. It's a little boy that needs saving. He looks so small."

Kai was the oldest of his siblings, and at the thought of his little brother drowning in an uncaring sea while two dozen sailors turned their backs—

He sprinted to the railing, ducked under grasping hands and tripping feet. Shaun almost caught him, and Kai dove under the deck master's long reach to hit the railing hard. Hard enough that his ribs ached at the impact. Hard enough he almost went overboard himself.

It *was* a child, its features blurred beneath the water and the weakening light. The body floated just under the surface, mere inches from reaching air.

Kai panted, as if he were breathing for the both of them. He needed to tell Wai Yu that it was too late for the boy. The crew's superstition had cost an innocent life.

The child spasmed. His little face slipped above the water for a brief moment, mouth gaping, eyes wide. "Help me," the child mouthed, before water rushed into the gap where his front teeth should be.

An iron grip clamped onto Kai's shoulders, pulled him backwards so he fell roughly against the wooden deck. His breath exploded out of him like a whale geyser, and only when he saw the sailors looking down at him like brown, rugged redwoods looming over a clearing did he realize that they'd had to pull him down from the ship railing. He didn't even remember climbing up. A small deckhand sat atop his aching ribs.

"Quiet down, rookie," she hissed. "That's the Drowned One's magic. If you lay eyes on it, if you hear it...that's how it gets its hooks into you."

"It's not a... whatever you think. It's a little boy. Look for yourself!"

Now the boy's life depended on Kai's ability to convince these shipmates he'd only known a month, and from the looks on their faces it was clear he'd fail.

The child's voice was barely audible over the splashing water, even though the crew had gone quiet. "Help ... help me!" A muttering passed from one adult to the other. A few shuffled their feet.

"Mama! Help! Mommy!" The boy begged, his voice high as an angel, his words garbled with brine.

It was Shaun who first bellowed to drown out the cries. Other voices joined his, and soon the sharp thumps of fists hitting flesh joined the noise, as shipmates fought shipmates to keep them from diving into the sea.

Kai tried to breathe without pain and stared up at the darkening sky. Streaks of orange shot through the blue. They looked like the giant goldfish in the river by his house. He'd go with his siblings to throw leftover rice and chicken into the waters and watched with both fascination and repulsion as the fish slid their heavy, scaled bodies over each other in their frenzy to eat. It felt like he could reach down and scoop up a fish by hand, but his father had told him the goldfish were not for eating.

"They don't taste good." Kai's father gestured toward the beach. "You want a real meal, you get a good, strong pole and a bright lure, and you catch something from the ocean. But if you're not careful, you might become the meal."

Kai grunted at the homesickness he thought he'd conquered. "You can get off me now," he told the deckhand, shoving her to the side. The water, and the ship, had fallen silent. Kai expected anger on everyone's faces, especially those who'd been bloodied, but there was only relief.

Shaun knocked on the captain's door and slid inside at her call. She emerged, wet-eyed, a moment later, clothing rumpled, wrists rubbed raw.

"Where was she while her crew were fighting?" Kai muttered under his breath. Wai Yu, carefully wrapping up his harness, shot him a look.

"You don't know what you're talking about, so keep your mouth shut." The old man shook his head and wiped the sweat and tear-streaks from his grizzled cheeks. "She's been through enough."

"You saw him too. The boy." Kai wanted to shake Wai Yu. "You dove down from the nest to save him."

"That's what a Drowned One does," Wai Yu said. "It plays with your head, tricks you, 'til you dive within reach."

"What is it?" The sea was getting choppy as the moon rose, white caps visible against the dark. There was no sign of the boy. Another crewmate had climbed up to the nest for next watch.

"Lots of theories, but the only people who've seen it never come back." Wai Yu shrugged. "My yeye—grandfather—knew about it. He called them water ghosts. Nowadays most seamen think they're mermaids."

"Mermaids," Kai repeated.

"You know, part-fish, part-human?"

"I know what a mermaid is. That didn't look like any mermaid I've seen in books. That looked like a human child."

Wai Yu walked away. "Maybe the books are wrong. Next time we call warning, yell over the voice and look away. You could have killed someone today."

Shaun must have told the Captain about his disobedience, for she summoned him into her cabin after dinner. The room was the nicest he'd seen on the ship, with gleaming furniture and a bear rug before her large mahogany desk. Small port windows showed only darkness outside.

"I know it was the first time you've encountered a Drowned One. But your insubordination was unacceptable. You could have been killed. Members of my crew were hurt because of your distraction." Captain Vella's voice was calm, with no hint of anger.

Kai nodded, palms sweating. He couldn't tear his eyes away from the set of thin metal shackles riveted to the wall. Would he end up chained in this nice office? Or was she one to use a flog? "I'm sorry, Captain. It won't happen again." They could have warned him. If he'd known they wouldn't save a drowning child, that the captain would hide in her cabin until it was too late, maybe he would have chosen another ship to sign with.

She rubbed at her eyes, and the bands of scabbed flesh around her wrists seemed darker in the lantern light. "A warning, then. And if anyone asks, I've given you a punishment so foul you don't dare repeat it."

Kai dared to return her smile then, relief sliding over his anger for a moment. He backed away from her, slightly bowing, as he'd been taught, when a familiar face drew his eye. A family portrait hung on the cabin wall near the door. Captain Vella, a handsome man, and the young boy Kai had just watched drown.

A week passed, with no further sightings of a Drowned One. Kai trusted no one on the ship—not one of them had moved to save the Captain's son. Not even Vella herself, though she must have heard him calling for his mother in his sweet, high voice. The little voice haunted Kai's dreams, waking him with a start before he realized it was the creaking of the ship, or the whistling snores of the other sailors.

In the daylight, between tasks, he asked some more questions about the monster, but the others refused to speak of it. "It's ill luck. Naming calls," Shaun said, before deciding Kai's questions meant he had too little to do.

Surely the ship had passed the monster's territory, Kai reasoned. If the old sea hands were right, then they should be safe until they returned to the same waters. And yet a scout sat atop the mast day in and day out, looking as much around their ship as they did the horizon.

And then: "All eyes to the North!" The sailor above screamed, struggling into the nest's harness. As one, the crew turned their backs on the south and began to pray. Shaun hurried from Captain Vella's cabin, slamming the door behind his vast bulk.

Kai didn't shout prayers or sing hymns. He faced north, moving southward, until his back hit the railing, until he could hear the Drowned One's voice. If it was the same boy, then Kai would know it was a monster. And if it was *really* a monster, then Kai wouldn't be, because then he hadn't let a child drown.

The voice sounded different. Raspier. Kai whispered a prayer to the Sea God, that it was the same boy, the one he'd seen in the Captain's cabin, painted curled on his mother's lap. Kai wouldn't just watch another person die, not for any old wives' tale.

He threw a glance over his shoulder, at the water below the ship.

It was a girl this time, her sodden dress dragging her deeper, hair like sea kelp fanning around her. "Help me, please," she pleaded.

Kai dove from the railing. The warm waters seared against the fresh scratches on his arms and back, nail marks from other deckhands trying to keep him from jumping. He swam towards the girl as fast as he could.

He almost saved her. She kept dipping beyond his reach as if the very waters were keeping them apart. He took a deep breath and dove down lower, trying to get underneath her descent. Closer to the child, he hesitated. His eyes burned with sea water, and the gathering darkness made his vision blurry, but up close it seemed the girl's face wasn't quite right. Her eyes were asymmetrical, mouth crooked, nose a shapeless blob without any nostrils. And she was...connected to something. A thick muscle of flesh ran from her back, unseen from the surface, to a vast shadow in the depths. A shadow that grew larger with each second.

Kai abandoned the girl. He kicked upwards, frantically, toward the dying light. His thoughts flitted though his mind, as tumultuous as the waters around him.

Wai Yu saying the Drowned One was a ghost, or a mermaid. A creature part-fish and part-human—though no one was ever sure which parts. Kai's father teaching him about shiny lures to catch the best fish. The time an ocean storm had washed up deep sea creatures and he'd seen the grotesque fish with a light at the end of an appendage, used to lure unsuspecting prey.

Kai broke the surface and inhaled sweet air. He swam toward the ship, toward the captain who must have lost her son at sea, who had to chain herself to keep from diving in when a Drowned One came hunting.

"Help me!" Kai screamed when he got closer. "Shaun, Captain Vella! Please!" He saw their turned backs, heard their shouted prayers, and knew he would not be saved. The only thing coming for him was in the water.

The Drowned One clamped on his hips and yanked him down. He stared toward the surface as long as he could, at the sky and the ship and the waters he'd grown up fishing. He stared until there was only darkness, knowing that the next time this Drowned One was hungry, a lure approximating Kai's face would be staring up at the orange-streaked sky.

Michelle Tang writes speculative fiction from Canada, where she lives with her husband and children. Her short stories have been published by *Cemetery Gates, Escape Pod,* and Flame Tree Publishing, among others. Michelle likes to explore themes of grief and guilt in her work, and often tries to include elements of her own culture. When she's not writing, Michelle enjoys reading movie spoilers, playing video games, and lurking on social media (@a_girl_Michelle on Twitter).

cecaelia's tears

BENJAMIN TYLER SMITH

I STILL CAN'T BELIEVE the kings all agreed to this," Knight-Commander Garrett muttered, his gruff voice almost lost in the splashing of water against the longboat's hull.

He sat near the bow of the night-shrouded boat, five loyal knights at his back. Lowborn pirates filled the remaining benches. It had been a long ride from the war galleon *Fleet Empress* to this remote part of the Tritonic Strait. They looked north at the bright flashes illuminating the moonless horizon. Low rumbles and soft booms rolled across the water.

Three coffin-sized chests, filled with the finest treasure the Three Kings Alliance could offer—gold, oil, spices—paid for tonight's events, from the diversionary action to the north to this longboat full of rowdy brigands. Enough wealth to rebuild all the towns and ships the merfolk had burned since the war began, and it had been given to *pirates*.

"I can't believe they agreed to it either," said a petite redhead from the bench in front of Garrett, her suntanned features bathed in the soft blue glow from the locket she held. Her teeth glinted in the unnatural light. "Since this is bloody merfolk we're talkin' about, me and my lads would've done this for free."

Garrett glowered at her. "Don't speak to me as if we're equals, woman."

A collective gasp ran through the pirates. Boatswain Pruitt stomped toward the bow, and Knight-Lieutenant Cadel stood to block his way. Pruitt jabbed a finger over Cadel's shoulder. "You'll show Empress Molly her due respect, lander!"

"Prew, it's fine." Molly's grin widened. "Mr. Knight hasn't gotten his sea legs yet. Give him time, and he'll know his place in these waters."

Anger burned within Garrett, but Molly stood before he could respond, the glowing locket held high. A beam of light shined from the blue stone embedded in its center and pierced the dark water off the portside. "Cecaelia's Tears is directly below us. We finish this job, and we've got the merfolk by their fishy bottoms."

A hush settled over the men. Even Garrett felt awed by the declaration. Months of unrelenting massacre and enslavement could be resolved in a single night. Was it too good to be true? That thought had plagued Garrett's mind for days now.

This was why the three kings had agreed to hire Mad Molly. To hear her tell it, she alone knew the location of Cecaelia's Tears, a magical relic made by the cecaelians, a race of octopus people the merfolk had enslaved and apparently driven to extinction. The assembly of royal magicians believed it granted the merfolk unparalleled combat prowess on land and sea alike.

None in the assembly could deny the sorcerous properties of the "compass" Molly claimed would lead them directly to the relic. "This stone is a piece of the Tears," she had told them. "It yearns to be reunited with the main body."

The night assault to retake Ardburn by the combined navies of the alliance and Molly's pirate fleet had been launched to divert merfolk warriors away from this location, and it appeared to have worked. They'd encountered no resistance on the way here, something that should've been impossible for a lone boat with only two dozen souls aboard.

Or was it only twenty-two? Garrett counted heads again and frowned. Had he imagined the other two?

A hand gripped the boat's gunwale, and *something* landed at Garrett's feet. He jumped, then cursed when he realized what it was: the severed head of a merman, its green scales and black hair slick with salt water and bright red blood.

Molly chuckled. "Never seen a knight scared of a bit of gore. Are ye really up to this task?"

"I was surprised, that's all." Garrett's cheeks flushed hot, and he was glad for the dim light.

Another merman's head sailed into the boat, and the missing pair of pirates climbed aboard. Molly tossed them blankets to ward against the cool breeze. "Excellent work, lads. Were they the only sentries?"

"The only ones in the water," one of them replied. "We heard voices inside the entrance cave but couldn't find them."

"Likely echoing from deeper inside the lair," the other added.

Molly patted both on the shoulder. "We'll take it from here. Ye rest and help guard the boat." To everyone else, she said, "Check yer belongings and take yer drafts! We dive in moments."

The "drafts" Molly referred to were the underwater breathing potions each member of the dive team carried. The apothecaries in Yhul had worked tirelessly to fill this order in time for tonight. It would be weeks before all three Sister Moons again slept the night away, weeks the island kingdoms couldn't afford. These potions were as much a key to their victory as Molly's compass or the mail armor Garrett and his knights had packed away in oilskin rucksacks. By all accounts, the merfolk breathed air the same as humans, but getting down to their cities and fortresses required a bit more than a single lungful.

Garrett opened a belt pouch filled with wax-sealed vials, from antiseptics to antivenin. He removed a black one, popped the seal, and put it to his lips.

A gust of wind buffeted the boat, and someone bumped into

his back. The vial fell to the deck, its contents splattering the bench.

Cadel murmured an apology. Garrett clenched his jaw to keep from cursing. What was he going to do? They hadn't packed extras.

Molly grasped Garrett's wrist. "Ye're not the only one who hasn't gotten his sea legs yet, Mr. Knight." She pushed something into his palm. "Try not to drop it this time."

Another breathing potion. *Her* potion. "Don't you need this?"

"I spent some time with the pearl divers of Vlesia." She planted a bare foot on the gunwale. "I know how to hold my breath."

She looked past Garrett. "Ready, lads?"

A chorus of "Ayes" answered her.

"And ye, Mr. Knight?" She patted her cutlass. "Eager to slaughter some merfolk?"

Garrett drained the vial of its fruity liquid, then picked up his oilskin rucksack. "Cecaelia's Tears is our goal, Molly. We destroy it and get out. Preferably without raising the alarm."

He had another goal, one the kings had given him personally, one she didn't need to know about.

"Oh, ye've nothin' to worry about there." She stepped fully onto the gunwale. "Sneak-thievery is my third favorite pastime."

"What are the other two?"

She spun on her heel and looked down at him, eyes flashing in the light of her compass. "Mischief and mayhem."

Molly stepped backward and dropped into the water without a splash.

"At them, lads!"

Molly's voice cracked like a whip through the watery corridor. She charged, boots squelching against wet stones, cutlass gleaming in the green light of hanging aether lamps. Her pirates roared and followed her, swords and daggers held high.

Garrett chased after them, a short sword and buckler in either hand, his damp mail coif clinking against his ears. His knights were similarly armed, with Cadel and one other carrying short bows. "After them!" Garrett yelled. *So much for sneak-thievery!*

The corridor they ran through was split into two levels. The right side was filled with water several feet deep, similar to the aqueducts of Troia. The left side was a walkway fit for humans, with only an inch or so of water covering the floor. If all merfolk lairs were designed this way, it was little wonder why they could maneuver on dry land so well.

Armored merfolk warriors slithered down the corridor, their fishtails gliding over the slick stones as fast as a man could run. They clashed with Molly and the front rank of the pirates, swords, and tridents flashing. Man and merman screamed, and blood turned the churning waters red. Garrett tried to push his way through the undisciplined mass but had to settle for striking over Molly's head.

The pirate empress fought with wild abandon, her cutlass and dagger slashing and stabbing with unrelenting energy. No armor weighed her down aside from thick leather worked into parts of her captain's coat. She laughed as if she hadn't a care in the world. "Gut these fishtails and hang 'em high!"

A naked merman broke the surface of the deeper water, a javelin in his hands. Before he could throw, a crossbow quarrel pierced his skull, followed by two arrows in the torso. A mermaid popped up next to her dying comrade, javelin ready. A quarrel skittered past her.

She hurled her javelin. It struck one of Molly's crossbowmen in the heart. He toppled, his weapon clattering to the floor.

The mermaid readied another javelin, then a thrown dagger blossomed from her chest. She sank into the water, screaming.

"That's for Keegan, ye bloody bitch!" Molly shouted.

The deep peal of a conch horn reverberated through the corridor from the direction of the entry cave. "Enemy reinforcements!" Cadel yelled.

Pruitt plunged a dagger into a merman's neck, then kicked the writhing warrior into another. "We need to go, Empress!"

"Smoke 'em if ye got 'em, lads!" Molly pulled a vial of gray liquid from her belt pouch and flung it into the face of her opponent. It shattered and released a torrent of thick smoke.

The rest of the pirates threw their potions, and the corridor filled with a haze smelling of jasmine and wisteria. The strong odor tickled Garrett's nose, but it was far less irritating than he thought it would be.

The merfolk recoiled from the smoke, with several diving into the water to escape it. The ones who held their ground fell into coughing fits that ended in screams and gurgles. "This way!" Molly shouted. "Through the smoke!"

Cadel picked up the spare quiver and crossbow from the fallen pirate. "We'll all be killed if we follow this madwoman."

Garrett had to agree. "Keep your wits about you. Once we've destroyed the relic..." He trailed off, unwilling to voice the final part:

Once we've destroyed the relic, Molly and her pirates will have outlived their usefulness.

Garrett and Cadel crouched on an outcropping that overlooked a main avenue through the merfolk lair. His knights and most of the pirates waited nearby, resting or binding wounds. In addition to Keegan, Molly had lost one of her men in the melee, with another suffering a crippling blow to a shoulder.

Molly had taken Pruitt and a few of her able-bodied men to "practice a bit of stealth" and scout the area. Garrett ground his teeth. *If only she'd done that to start with.* It wasn't her fault they'd stumbled across the merfolk warriors, but couldn't she have been quieter about it?

Down below, a mermaid draped in shiny scale mail slithered along the avenue, a dozen warriors trailing after her.

"Vita have mercy," Cadel muttered. "That's General Dhesara! I saw her when Ardburn fell."

Dread and excitement warred within Garrett. Her being here made their mission more difficult, but it meant they were on the right path. *Something* had to be here if the Crimson Trident had returned when her forces were locked in a major battle elsewhere.

"Maybe we should ask her where our little relic is," Molly murmured.

Garrett jumped. When had she returned? "Did you find anything?"

Molly glared at Dhesara, the malevolence rolling off her thick enough to stab. "Hells' Foundation, I'd love to slit her open."

Garrett could respect the sentiment. He'd lost his brother and parents during Dhesara's purging of the Tritonic coastline. He wanted Dhesara dead as much as anyone who'd suffered at her hands. He placed a hand on Molly's shoulder. "Cecaelia's Tears, remember?"

"It's more efficient to catch two fish in the same net." She turned her glare on him. "Wouldn't ye agree, Mr. Knight?"

Garrett's stomach tightened. Was Molly aware of his secondary mission? Did she have plans of her own?

Molly stared a moment longer, then smiled. "Prew found a way to the lower levels. Follow me!"

She pranced back the way she had come. Cadel looked at Garrett. "She's going to be the death of us, sir."

Again, Garrett could only agree.

Molly stood next to Pruitt when they caught up with her. The boatswain shined his aether lamp down a narrow, spiral-shaped shaft cut into the stone floor. "Their version of stairs, I suppose."

"Better than a waterlogged tunnel to swim through." Molly descended into the darkness. "Come along."

The ramp led to another set of corridors. In Molly's direction, they moved through the shadows, pausing only so she could check her compass.

When they stopped at the next intersection, Garrett crouched next to Molly. "Where's the enemy?"

"Guarding their treasury, I'd wager," Molly said, her eyes never leaving her compass.

"Wouldn't the Tears be there? I'd think the source of their strength would be in the most heavily guarded part of this godforsaken fortress."

"There's a fault in yer logic, Mr. Knight." She closed the compass and looked at him, the stone's blue glow lingering in her eyes. "Cecaelia's Tears is the merfolk's weakness, not their strength."

"What do you mean?"

"Cecaelian sorcerers created it to overthrow their merfolk masters. They failed and were annihilated, yet the relic remains because they can't destroy it." Molly started down one of the corridors. "This fortress exists to keep the Tears locked away, but the merfolk don't want it anywhere near them. Makes 'em sick. Makes humans sick, too, but it's worse for the fishtails."

No historian or mage had mentioned any of that to Garrett. "Why can't they destroy it?"

"Any fishtail who touches it dies instantly, and whatever magic that protects the Tears renders it impervious to damage." She held up a hand and counted off her fingers. "Strike it, and it melts weapon *and* hand alike. Shoot it, and the arrow returns to the archer. Bury it, and the chamber it's in rebuilds within minutes." She wiggled her ring and pinky fingers. "Shall I go on?"

"How do you know this?"

"Loot isn't all I'm after. I plunder information, too." Molly tapped the compass. "I learned a lot from the crone who sold me this, the sole survivor of a small village that traded with the cecaelians before they were butchered." She scowled. "Both the cecaelians *and* the villagers. That's what this war's really about, ye know. They're huntin' people with cecaelian blood."

All this to kill a paltry number of people with mixed blood, assuming any even existed. *Will their evils never cease?* Garrett frowned. "Cecaelian merchants? Weren't they slaves?"

"All the merfolk know is war. They leave things like commerce and diplomacy to their slave class." She waved a hand. "That bit about the Tears bein' the source of their prowess is a baseless rumor. They're good fighters 'cuz they're good fighters. Yer sailors are pretty tough, but yer soldiers are soft from too many good years."

Garrett's anger flared. "You didn't tell the assembly this."

"Sometimes the right words aren't truthful ones. Besides, how can I question the assembly's wisdom?" She placed a hand on her chest. "I'm but a simple pirate, Mr. Knight."

Despite himself, Garrett chuckled. "There's *nothing* simple about you."

"You're too kind." She stopped in front of a closed door, made of oak and banded in rusty iron, likely taken from a sunken ship. Two more lay further down the corridor. "Once we get the Tears, we'll see an end to this war."

"And how truthful are your words now?"

"They're the right ones." She held up her compass, the blue beam pointing at the closest door. "We're here." She pulled a set of picks from a pocket and got to work.

Farther up the corridor, approaching lights bounced and bobbed. "Hurry," Garrett whispered.

"Ye can't rush something like this."

"Movement behind us!" Pruitt warned.

"Would ye both shut up?"

Pruitt glanced at Garrett and shrugged. Garrett ground his teeth.

"And stop that, too."

After what seemed like an age, the last tumbler clicked into place. Molly pushed the door open, and soft blue light greeted them.

A cry of alarm sounded from the approaching patrols. Garrett cursed. "Let's go!"

He and Molly ran through the doorway, the rest of the men close behind. Once inside, Garrett locked the door and ordered a handful of men to guard it. Only then did he turn to survey the room.

The chamber was as natural-looking as the entry cave, though smaller in size. Water filled much of it, except for a central island and a dry path to it from the doorway. A stone plinth stood on that island, with a glowing blue stone resting on its roughhewn surface.

Molly stared at the stone. "It's here. It's actually here." She scrubbed at her eyes. "Old nan was right."

Something struck the door. Mermen yelled on the other side, their voices muffled by the thick wood. Garrett strode forward. "Let's be quick about this."

Molly grabbed his arm. "Quick about what? We're taking the Tears with us."

"Our orders are to destroy it."

"Didn't ye listen to anything I've said?" Molly's grip tightened. "Even if we could, destroyin' it plays into their hands. We need to take it, Mr. Knight."

Garrett yanked his arm free and pointed. "That thing looks valuable. I'd wager you want to sell it."

"Ye'd be wagerin' wrong!" Molly grasped her compass. "Sellin' it is the last thing I want to do!"

"Really? And how truthful are *those* words?"

A writhing purple mass landed between them. Several more struck the cave floor nearby.

"Urchin bombs!" Pruitt yelled. "Look out!"

Molly dropped into a crouch, arms covering her body and face. Garrett raised his buckler as the bombs exploded. Ichor-covered spines buffeted the shield and struck his mail, but none of the poisonous barbs pierced his gambeson.

Not everyone had been so lucky. Several pirates screamed and moaned as the sea creatures' venom worked its way through them. "Antivenin!" Garrett barked. "Take your antivenin!"

Cadel clutched at a spine stuck in his neck and collapsed.

Pruitt was at his side in a blink, a green vial in his hand. "Hold him down! Before his throat closes!"

Garrett dropped to his knees and grabbed hold of Cadel's shoulders. Another knight pressed on his legs. Cadel writhed and squirmed, gasping for air. Pruitt shushed Cadel like a father would a child and poured the potion into his mouth. "There's a good lad. There's a good—Sir Garrett, behind you!"

A mermaid leaped from the shadows, a needle-like dagger aimed at Garrett's throat.

Molly jumped between them, and the mermaid's blade pierced her left hand. She hissed in pain and swung her fist once, twice, and again. The stunned mermaid let go of the dagger. Molly ripped the weapon free of her hand and plunged it into her opponent's naked chest. "I hope it was worth it, fishtail."

She turned toward Garrett. Urchin needles covered her outfit, and dark blood trickled down the side of her face, the color odd in the chamber's fae light. "Are ye still breathin', Mr. Knight?"

"I should ask you that." Garrett pointed. "Were you hit by the bomb? Did you take an antivenin?"

"That scent!" a feminine voice yelled, the words booming through the chamber.

Merfolk slithered from the shadows and rose up from the water. General Dhesara appeared, flanked by two of her guards. She pointed her trident at Molly. "That scent," she said in the region's trade language. "We've spent months looking for it, and it shows up *here?*"

"Well, isn't this a surprise?" Molly drew her cutlass and rested it on her shoulder. "It's not every day the Crimson Trident graces us with her presence. Tell me, Dhesara, when was the last time my lads gave ye a good wallopin'?"

"Molly," Dhesara growled. "To think in all our clashes I never once made you bleed." She put a hand to her nasal slits. "You reek of cecaelia."

"And *you* reek of desperation." Molly spread her arms. "Not so happy to finally have what ye been seekin'?"

"You never told me you were part cecaelian," Garrett whispered.

"One-eighth if my math is correct. On my nan's side. Didn't I mention that?" She touched her compass. "Where d'ye think I got this from?"

"You said you *bought* it from a crone."

"How rude! Don't talk about my nan that way."

The door to the hallway burst open, and merfolk warriors poured in. Two knights and six pirates intercepted them, but they were hard-pressed.

Dhesara raised her trident. "Kill the half-breed and her humans!"

Molly charged. "Have at ye!"

Dhesara sprang forward, her powerful tail propelling her several feet each time. Her last jump took her high into the air before she dropped toward Molly.

Molly rolled to the side, Dhesara's trident striking the floor in a spray of stone chips. Molly tried to run around her, but Dhesara recovered and lunged. The two locked blades, their faces inches apart.

"Get me the Tears, Mr. Knight!" Molly shouted. She swung at Dhesara's midsection, but the mermaid general parried with her trident. Dhesara stabbed at Molly's gut, but the pirate empress sidestepped and lashed out again. Back and forth they went, neither gaining the advantage.

Merfolk warriors slithered or swam toward the dueling females. Javelins sailed past their heads to strike at the knot of pirates behind Garrett. Arrows and quarrels flew in response.

A mermaid javelin thrower on the central island was struck in the stomach with a quarrel. She staggered and bumped into Cecaelia's Tears. Her arm burnt to ash, and fire lanced up her shoulder and into her hair. She shrieked and flung herself into the water.

Garrett swallowed. *Molly expects me to pick that up?* She said it was better for humans than merfolk, but how much better?

"Garrett!" Molly called again. She risked a glance his way, her eyes aglow with the same light as the stone. "Get me the Tears, and this all ends!"

The words and her wild expression brought him back to the assembly chamber, where she'd declared a permanent end to the merfolk threat. If he didn't do as she ordered, all this would be for naught. She truly believed that.

And so did he, he realized. *Damn that woman!*

Garrett ran for the stone. "Protect Molly!" he shouted to the men.

"Foolish human!" Dhesara tried to intercept Garrett, but Molly was on her in a flash.

Garrett skirted around their duel. Two mermaids attempted to throw javelins from the water, but crossbow quarrels forced them under. He cut down one warrior and slashed open another when he reached the central island. A third thrust a trident, but Boatswain Pruitt parried the weapon with his cutlass. "For the Fleet Empress!"

Cecaelia's Tears lay before Garrett. The glowing blue stone was larger than his fist, its surface jagged and lumpy. He hesitated a moment, thinking back on the mermaid. Then he dropped his shield and reached for the stone. *In for a copper, in for a crown!*

A burning sensation ran up his arm. Garrett clenched his teeth. Nothing caught fire, but by the gods, it *hurt!* He turned and ran toward Molly. The sooner he could get it to her, the better!

Pruitt guarded Garrett's back, but four merfolk rose from the water to block his path. The stone's light caught in their wide eyes, and he held it out as a ward. Two warriors backed away, and a third fell to a crossbow bolt. The fourth lunged, forcing Garrett to halt.

The other two regained their courage and circled Garrett.

Beyond them, Molly and Dhesara still battled. "Molly!" Garrett yelled. "Catch!"

He threw Cecaelia's Tears as hard as he could. It shot over the heads of his opponents and arced through the air. Dhesara threw herself to the side to avoid being struck, and Molly reached out to catch it with her wounded hand. The stone bounced free of her grasp and hurtled toward the water.

Molly dropped her sword and leaped for it, good hand outstretched. Dhesara pierced her exposed side with her trident, then Molly and the stone disappeared in the water.

Dhesara jumped after Molly, but bright blue energy shot from the depths and wrapped around her. She struck the ground, her body draped in glowing manacles. Those chains snaked out and coiled around the warriors closest to her, including the three Garrett faced.

Molly rose from the water, left hand to her bleeding side, Cecaelia's Tears clutched in her right. Her teeth glinted in the unnatural light. "I'd say that's enough of that. Wouldn't ye agree, *General* Dhesara?"

"Kill the half-breed!" Dhesara cried.

A javelin soared toward Molly. She held the stone high, and its energy caught the weapon, spun it about, and hurled it back. A merman screamed.

More javelins flew, with the same results. A brave mermaid leaped from the water, trident aimed at Molly's back. Cecaelia's Tears burned her to cinders.

The stone flared with bright light, and blue chains shot from it in all directions. In seconds, all the merfolk in the chamber were bound the same as their general.

Molly stomped onto dry ground and crouched next to Dhesara. "How ironic. To think the Tears would've stayed in yer possession had it not been for yer little war with the lander kingdoms. Bad enough ye had to wipe out my people, but ye had to go after their 'half-breed' descendants, too?" She shook her head. "Where's the honor in that, warrior?"

Garrett stared open-mouthed. "If Cecaelia's Tears is this powerful, how in the Eighteen Hells did the cecaelians lose?"

"Remember what I said about yer soldiers bein' soft, Garrett? The cecaelians were softer. Centuries of slavery didn't harden their pacifist souls. They thought they could make the merfolk see the error of their ways by giving 'em a taste of the bondage they subjected others to, and then there'd be peace. It didn't work."

Molly leaned over until her face almost touched Dhesara's. "Pity for you I'm not that soft."

Dhesara returned the glare, but there was fear behind the anger.

"Well, except I've a soft spot for old nan. She may have only been a quarter cecaelian, but she shared their pacifism." She held up the stone. "Dhesara, I'll promise ye this: leave these waters, and I'll not unleash the full power of Cecaelia's Tears. Ye'll be free to go.

"Cause trouble for me and mine, and yer people will suffer more horror than ye ever could inflict in a thousand lifetimes." The light in the stone flared, and every merfolk in the chamber screamed. "Ye have my word on that."

"This isn't over, half-breed." Dhesara's armor sparkled in the dawn light as she pointed up at Molly and Garrett. "We won't forget this."

"Eighth-breed, ye mean." Molly planted a foot on the long-boat's gunwale and held out Cecaelia's Tears. "See that ye don't forget."

Dhesara disappeared beneath the waves, her warriors following after her. At Molly's "request", they had helped get the dead and wounded to the surface, along with equipment too heavy to carry. Garrett stood bare-chested, his mail and gambeson once more in his oilskin rucksack. The others stood or sat in similar states of undress. At the stern, Pruitt tended to Cadel. The young knight would live. All told, they'd lost five pirates and two knights. Costly, but they'd gained so much from their sacrifices. He'd see to it all their names were remembered, noble and scoundrel alike.

"One less enemy to worry about for the moment." Molly

looked sidelong at Garrett. "D'ye still plan to carry out yer 'other' orders?"

She knew this whole time? The vixen had to have spies everywhere. "I've no idea what you're talking about, but the answer is no."

"Good to hear." Molly flopped onto one of the benches, heedless of the pirate she slammed into. She heaved a sigh. "It's been a night, lads. It's been a night."

"Doesn't that bother you?" Garrett indicated the stone. "It made my arm feel like it was on fire."

"I feel energy coursing through it, but nothing unpleasant." She shrugged. "It must be like my nan said. Only those of cecaelian blood can wield it."

And the kings had wanted her dead. "It's a good thing those orders—that don't exist, by the way—weren't carried out, then."

Molly threw back her head and laughed. "Just so, Garrett!"

Garrett sat on the bench across from her, and the weariness he'd been storing up hit him all at once. He couldn't wait to be back aboard the *Fleet Empress*. At this point, a bunk in the officers' quarters would suit him better than the plushest bed back in Yhul. "Why didn't you tell the assembly about the stone's true nature?"

"They'd have killed me on the spot." She turned Cecaelia's Tears around, watching as it caught the sunlight in different ways. "Either because they feared I'd take the stone and turn the merfolk into my thralls, or because I'd refuse to do so under *their* orders."

"Aren't you tempted by the stone's power?"

"I am many things, Garrett, but a slaver isn't one of them." Molly tucked Cecaelia's Tears into a leather pouch and rested it on her lap. She touched her bandaged side and winced. "I saw how much my nan suffered from memories she'd never directly experienced. I won't force that on another, not unless I'm left with no choice."

"What happens next?" Garrett asked. "You hold the stone now, but eventually you'll die, either of old age or in battle. What, then?"

"What, indeed?" Molly's familiar grin returned. "I guess I'll have to live forever."

"I'll be sure to impress upon my kings the need for that."

"Oh? Are those truthful words?"

Garrett returned her grin. "They're the right words."

Benjamin Tyler Smith spends his days creating maps for cemeteries and his evenings herding the undead and battling aliens. He's a writer of fantasy and science fiction, with two novels published in Blood Moon Press's Fallen World universe and numerous short stories in anthologies and magazines. Many of these tales are set in his Necrolopolis universe, a dark-fantasy world where a necromancer keeps the peace in an undead city. He is currently working on the first Necrolopolis novel.

He lives in an area of rural Pennsylvania with more cows than humans as neighbors, ruled over by a benevolent Calico Countess and her feline knight, the Earl of Grey. Helping him maintain this vast estate is a saint of a wife and a beautiful baby girl who keeps up morale, inspires story ideas, and keeps him on his toes. Follow him online at <u>BenjaminTylerSmith.com</u> and join his mailing list for free stories and regular updates! He can also be found on the Three Ravens Publishing Discord server at <u>discord.gg/ GPrRJBBmat</u>

o, my loves

KAREN DEBLIECK

In the dark
the depths
Shadows
s l i d e
across my
skin

Caress
        my shoulders

Kiss
        the nape of my neck

I y a w n
pink tongue
tasting
the salt of the sea

I
s t r e t c h my forked tail
Flicking it
in the water
Revelling
in my
strength

My
        freedom.

What has awakened me?

Around me
fish glide in schools
Jellyfish pulsate
electric
        pink and
                green

Seaweed
dances

in the heartbeat
of my home

A gentle pull
in my chest.
The same sensation
that roused me from
my slumber

Ahhhh
        Yesssss

The call of my lovers
beckoning
me:
  Please
  Come

I bare
my sharp teeth
in a smile

O, my dear ones
  I come
    I come

I slice through the water
writhing
  c o i l i n g
    against the current

My followers
swim
in my wake

My blood y e a r n s
    For them.
My heart beats
  Only
    For them

Up
  Up
    I climb

Toward the surface
toward
        my lovers.

I tear through the waves
like a babe
birthed into
the world

Each cell
        t h r u m m I n g
with anticipation

soon
        soon

The scene before me is
s c r a p e d
across the darkness
of midnight.

Tongues of light
lick
the angry clouds.

The gales moan and shriek
among tattered
sails.

The water crashes
careens
matching
the want
        Need
inside of me

I come
      I come.

Like a maiden
the ship bows
          curtsies
With the tempest

I can hear them

My loves
      my loves

Some g r o a n
their need.
Others
implore me
To come
      to come

I purr
a wordless
         song
meant to
call all
to me.

I know
they won't
      can't
resist

My followers ride the foam
joining their voices to mine
a ruinous chorale.

The heathens
p e e r
over the side.
Ghost skin
shining like the spiny eel.

Faces
        Slack
Eyes
        Vacant

Forgetting home
and wives and lovers and harlots
for me.
        For
                me

With wild abandon
they throw themselves
overboard

Hitting the water
with
a
s i g h

For a chance
to gaze
into my eyes.

A moment
in my
embrace.

My followers
greet them with
the rending of their flesh
Sweet
agony.

The other creatures from the deep join in
turning the tide red with their frenzy

But my loves
     My loves

It is you I want
          Need

You are shy
Hiding
shackled
     cheek to cheek
     breast to breast
     thigh to thigh
in the belly
of the wooden whale

O, my loves
do not play
coy
with me

Come to me
     Come
          to me.

I w r a p
my
length
around
the boat

My blood
boiling
burning
with
Desire

I come
       I come

The wood bends
and g r o a n s
in anticipation

I can sense you
waiting
       breathless

I come
       My loves

       My loves
I come

I can wait
no longer

Every fiber of my body
aches
       for you

I stretch and
      strain and
           s q u e e z e

Until the boat
          cracks
and you
spill
into
my
arms

Your inky skin against
mine.
F i n a l l y

my loves.
      My
          loves

You weep for joy.
Joy!
at our reunion.

Screaming
in ecstasy.

I can no longer contain myself.

No one else can have you
You are mine.
Mine
alone

I cradle you in my arms
gently
      rocking
you
      beneath
the swells

My mouth
tastes
your blood.

Teeth
shredding
your skin.

My hands
c r a c k i n g
your bones.

I want you
I need
     you.

My loves
     My loves
          My loves

O
My loves
Down
     Down
          Down

we
sink
e n t w I n e d
in an embrace.

Soon
your skin will crumble
and become the sand
on which
I rest
my head

I'll adorn
my raven hair
with your porcelain
bones

Drape
your shackles
and chains
around
my neck

And
     O

My loves
     My
          Loves

You will be
     safe.

You will
sleep
pressed
against my bosom

Never to part
My loves
    O

        My loves

KAREN DEBLIECK'S writing reflects the tension of identity and the sense of belonging she struggled with as an African/Korean American born in Japan and adopted by white Canadian missionaries. From a very young age she found solace in putting her thoughts and feelings down on the page. She writes about difficult truths and loves to explore history that's not taught in the classroom. Despite the divisive nature of this world, she still believes people's hearts will open to change when they hear the words "Once Upon a Time".

She dreams of travelling through space and time, being sorted into a magical house, and enjoying a lavish meal in a hobbit hole. When she's not writing, crocheting, or cooking for her hubby and four young adults, she enjoys teaching teens about life and words. Check out more about Karen, the current novel she is working on, and her blog at karendeblieck.com.

dreams of the river

D.J. BUTLER

THE MERMAID DREAMS OF THE RIVER," the grubby man holding the cloth-wrapped bundle said.

"Do you mean the sea?" Luman Walters had never heard of river mermaids. Since "mer" meant "sea," perhaps such a creature wouldn't even be a mermaid, properly speaking. "If the mermaid dreams of the river, isn't it a 'fleuvemaid,' or something to that effect?"

Assuming that "mer" came from French.

Free Imperial Youngstown, on the edge of the Eldritch kingdoms of the Ohio, was not the center of the world. And Luman still carried around a head full of questions.

The mermaid-hawker, a man with heavy calluses and dirty nails named Thornby, grimaced at Luman, then spat on the ground. "Call it what you like, the price is the same."

Luman eyed the bundle. "Can I see it first?"

Thornby sucked his teeth and peeled back the edge of the cloth. The bundle wasn't large enough to hold an adult-sized human, but it might hold a small child. With the greasy cloth peeled back, Luman saw the wrinkled, leathery skin of a small face. The face looked reasonably human, though its teeth, revealed by a curling flap of lip, were long and sharp, and its visible ear was pointed. The skin was the dull brown color of old leather, with the slightest hint of green.

Stone cold dead, of course. Thoroughly desiccated. Mummified by the passage of time.

"Satisfied?" Thornby asked.

Luman, an inveterate seeker after magical mysteries and thief of arcane traditions that were not properly his own, had encountered many frauds in his dogged quest. "Show me the tail."

To his credit, Thornby wasn't coy or theatrical. Rather than demurely hitching up another corner of the cloth to show just the tip of a tail, he pulled the cloth away entirely, tugging at it until the mermaid was fully revealed. Luman gazed upon what appeared to be a perfect little mermaid, tangled in twine, its hips segueing seamlessly into a long, fishlike tail. Or rather, it might be a flawless little merman, since its little torso was flat.

But "meer" was "sea" in German. Luman's German was reasonably good. After a youth in Haudenosaunee territory, he'd done his share of wandering in Pennsland. If that hadn't sharpened his German skills, then his sub rosa apprenticeship as a braucher had. Perhaps "mer" came from Old English. Luman didn't know Old English, but King Alfred's people had spoken something akin to German. So, what was "river" in German?

"It looks real," Luman acknowledged.

"It is real." Thornby snorted.

"Where did you get it?"

Thornby spat again. "What do you care? You ran your newspaper ad, ten shillings for a mermaid specimen, here it is."

"I have to ask you another question, Mr. Thornby," Luman said. "I shall be consulting my amulets afterward, and you'll understand that if your answer isn't precisely correct, I shall have to take action. I shall have to employ the sieve and shears on you." This was a bluff. The sieve and shears was a divination technique, not a curse. Luman didn't really know any curses. "I don't care how long you have had the mermaid, and I don't care how you obtained it.

But I need to know where the prior owner lived. When dealing with mermaids, appropriate countermagic must always be employed."

Thornby squinted, rolled his jaw about as if considering spitting a third time, and nodded. "Village outside of Youngstown. Called Marbletown."

Luman handed over the ten shillings, which were counted with a glance and a single experienced toss of the palm, and then shoveled into a purse concealed behind Thornby's belt.

Thornby turned away.

"How do you know it dreams of anything?" Luman asked.

Thornby laughed, a grating sound. "You'll see."

The laborer disappeared quickly into the thick woods, heading back to the Imperial pike that ran south of the thicket in which they stood. Luman considered. He had no countermagic to work against the former owner of the mermaid, from whom it had almost certainly been stolen. He just wanted to avoid passing close to the owner's house, if he could.

He knew Marbletown. It was south and east of Youngstown, a hamlet of no consequence. It lay to Luman's west along the pike, and would be easy enough to avoid, since Luman's route lay farther south and east still, to Pittsburgh.

To a man he knew was in the market to purchase a mermaid.

Wasn't "fluss" a "river" in German? So "flussman"?

That sounded terrible. But the word in English must be "flood," mustn't it? A "floodmaid" or a "floodman," if Luman was right to think that this creature was male? The word sounded fine enough on its own, but didn't sparkle in the mind the way "mermaid" did. No lore, no associations.

Luman grunted. He bundled the little male mermaid that apparently dreamed of a river into its swaddling clothes, sank it into the largest pocket of his long black magician's coat, beneath the shoulder and against the left breast, and walked toward the pike.

He called it his "magician's coat" because the coat had many

pockets, into which Luman stuffed a wide variety of arcane accou-
terments: a peep-stone, a ritual knife, a mouse in a box, wax, a
precious bundle of wafers of the consecrated host, and so on.
Luman's magic was miscellaneous, stolen one bit at a time from
various real magicians he had encountered since his father had cast
him out from the family farm for learning to dowse, and the tools
of his trade must be similarly miscellaneous.

Sixty miles to Pittsburgh. That was two days' long walk, and
Luman wasted no time. At the pike, Luman spun left and length-
ened his stride, stretching out his hard black leather shoes in long
paces designed to eat up the miles.

Pittsburgh was also not the center. But perhaps it was a place
where Luman could bring the center to himself and learn the
answers to some of his questions.

He had no intention of selling the little mermaid for money.
Luman could come by money easily enough on his own, inter-
preting dreams, locating stolen objects, dowsing for wells, and so
on. Not every village in the Empire had its own hedge-wizard or
cunning woman, so Luman could generally come into a town,
ascertain whether he had competition, determine whether there
were any hostile Mattheans, followers of the witchfinder St.
Matthew Hopkins, to worry about, and earn his keep. An influx of
cash for the mermaid, even above what he'd paid for it, would only
take the edge off his need to work for a few weeks. Luman wasn't
afraid of work, and that wasn't why he'd found and acquired the
mermaid.

He wanted knowledge.

The man advertising in Pittsburgh that he needed a mermaid
specimen was a famed scholar. John Bilious had once taught at
Philadelphia's Imperial College of Magic. Luman knew, because
he'd asked Bilious for help in getting admitted to the college and
had been turned away.

Not cruelly, perhaps, but coldly.

But perhaps not definitively. Now that Bilious wanted a

mermaid—for his researches? for an act of gramarye? as a teaching aid?—and Luman had one to offer, perhaps a trade could be made. Luman might be a little old to get into the Imperial College, but maybe Bilious could take him on as a private student.

Luman found himself eyeing the hills as he marched. His stomach growled, but he was good at ignoring that, for days at a time. He'd learned from his Memphite mentor how to fast. Something seemed wrong with the hills. As Luman marched between each green wooded knob and the next, he seemed to be seeing the hills for the first time.

Which he definitely wasn't. He'd spent years knocking about Pennsland and eastern Ohio. He shook his head to drive away the feeling of disorientation and nodded at two Firstborn who passed him going the other direction. In the summer heat, their long but light tunics would definitely be more comfortable than Luman's heavy coat, their light boots better than his heavy shoes.

Water flowed through the hills. It flowed south, as all the water did in these parts, gurgling together into ever-larger streams and then rivers and then wandering away across the Eldritch Kingdoms to pour into the Ohio River, then eventually into the Mississippi, and somewhere away southward, the Gulf.

Luman stopped at a trickle that flowed beside the pike. He splashed cold water on his face. A platoon of infantrymen in Imperial blue marched past, chanting off their paces and ignoring him. Their words seemed to echo up against the hills and worm away in unexpected directions, reinforcing the impression of wrongness Luman had.

The hills were wrong for the rivers.

He needed to eat something, but his last shillings had gone to Thornby. Spying a crabapple tree, he pocketed several of the sour green apples and continued on his way. He tried not to dwell on the mermaid in his pocket, or the rumbling in his stomach, or the possibility that the Marbletown constable might already be looking for him. He breathed the warm summer air deeply, took long steps, munched through a crabapple every hour or so, and imagined the arcane lore he'd learn.

No more hedge wizardry; he knew enough of that. He knew Memphite formulae and braucher prayers, dowsing, divinations, all the standard arts of the cunning man. He wanted real power. He wanted to be able to strike a man dead from a distance, or leap from New Amsterdam to New Orleans in a single step. Not that he even cared to be able to do those things, per se.

He wanted to know how to do them.

Luman had grown up poor and ignorant, doomed to a life behind a plow in a town that was nowhere. He wanted knowledge, he wanted to stand in the center.

When the sun sank beneath the western hills, he kept walking for another hour. Passing through a village with no name he could discern, he harvested a pocketful of peas from the corner of a garden, and after one last mile he secreted himself in a tangle of hawthorns in a low hollow. Against the thick bole of a tree, he wrapped himself in his coat and ate crisp sugary peas until he fell asleep.

"The river is coming back," a voice said, and he awoke.

The trees loomed huge around him. Luman's back was wet and cold, and he sprang to his feet. His hard leather shoes splashed in water up to his ankles, water filling the hollow.

"The river is coming back," the voice said again.

It came out of Luman's own armpit.

Luman dug into his coat, got his hand into the long pocket hanging beneath his shoulder, and pulled out the white bundle he found there. It squirmed to the touch, and he almost dropped it into the water.

Which now flowed around Luman's knees.

He yanked back the edge of the cloth and a long-toothed face smiled at him. The merman's skin looked faintly greenish and his hair was the flat brown color of mud. Skin and hair and eyes all gleamed with an oily sheen under the light of a moon that Luman now saw was three times too large.

"What do you want?" Luman's hands trembled. He feared to drop the merman. If he dropped the merman, Luman would never get what he wanted, what he'd acquired the merman to trade for.

"I don't want anything," the merman said. "I was at peace."

"Then why are you doing this?" The water flowed at the height of Luman's waist now, and he sloshed against the current, trying to find higher ground. Somehow, the hollow went down in every direction.

"I'm not doing this," the merman said.

"I'm not doing it, either!" Luman's voice was a shrill squeak.

"This will happen," the merman said. "This was always going to happen. This cannot be avoided. Heaven and earth shall pass away, and there shall be an old heaven, and an old earth."

"New!" Luman sputtered. "A new heaven and a new earth!"

"Old," the merman insisted. "The river is coming back."

"Which river?"

"The first river," the merman said. "The oldest one. The true river."

Luman stepped forward, and the ground beneath him fell away. He slid down only six inches, and managed to stand upright when both his feet came down on a bed of packed pebbles. Water flowed over his feet . . .

But the water flowing around Luman's ankles flowed violently to his right, while the water flowing around his legs, waist, and chest flowed away to the left. He looked up to see the dark masses of the hills beyond the hawthorn trees. They seemed to fade back and bob forward, circling him in a stony dance.

Which river did the hills align with? Which river had carved its way through these hills in the first place?

"Stop it," Luman backed up and managed to scramble out of the concealed streambed into the larger flow. Somehow, the water ran just as high on his chest. He held the merman above the flood.

"I can't," the merman said. "You can't. It happens inevitably and it will always happen. This is the covenant of the world."

Luman saw a light, away between the trees, and he moved toward it. His progress was infuriatingly slow as he pushed against the water, and mud sucked at his shoes, threatening to strip them away at every step.

"I don't want this," Luman said. The light drew closer. Was it a window? Or was it a lantern, held by a man in a long coat who sat in a canoe with a young woman, wrapped in a Firstborn-style cloak?

"You don't want understanding?" The merman flashed its long teeth at him.

"Yes," Luman said, "but that's all! Take the flood away!"

"We none of us want to be remade." The corners of the merman's mouth drooped in sorrow. "And yet the world is a machine for remaking us."

Luman's feet slipped into another unseen ditch. This time he plunged forward, slipping beneath the waters.

Luman sat up, gasping for air.

The merman dreamed of the river.

His coat was wet with fat drops and he lurched his feet, shaking them off.

There was no flood, and the hills stood still in their places.

Luman felt the fibrous grit of peas and pea-pods in his mouth and he spat until the unpleasant sensation was gone.

He patted at the large pocket and found the merman in its place. He grabbed the bundle, then hesitated. Should he pull the creature out and look? Should he leave it? Raising his head, he examined the moon and found it the normal size. Away in the hawthorns, crickets chirped. All was as it should be.

He extracted the merman and peeled back the cloth. The creature was intact, its leathery face still frozen in a smile.

Only . . . a corner of the cloth was moist. From the dew, of course. But it meant that one of the merman's arms was damp.

And was that arm lighter in color than the other? Luman poked both the merman's arms. The dry one was dark and leathery, and resisted his touch like stiff paper. The damp limb was paler and oily in appearance, and dimpled like flesh at his touch.

Luman shuddered. He wrapped the merman and stuffed it back into his coat.

Knowledge, he reminded himself. He would do this thing for knowledge.

And where he wished to know more about magic, could he now balk at the appearance of something that seemed magical?

But surely it was not. Surely, the dew had dampened part of the merman, and softened it. That would likely lead to corruption—rot and mold. He should hasten, and hand the merman over to John Bilious before any more harm came to it.

Several hours remained before dawn yet, judging by the moon, but sleep had fled him entirely. Luman clutched the merman to his own chest—to keep it safe? to be certain that it wasn't moving? to mute it?—and marched back to the Imperial pike.

John Bilious's address was included in his newspaper advertisement. Luman's, much more furtively, but also very magically, had only indicated an intersection and time at which to meet. With his early start somewhat negated by his fatigue from lack of sleep, Luman covered the miles to Pittsburgh and arrived, stomach growling, as the sun touched the western horizon.

The address identified a three-story brick house in northern Pittsburgh, surrounded by similarly large buildings. These lacked signboards out front, which made Luman think they were the homes of publishers and other people of wealth and importance. Luman double-checked the brass numbers screwed into the brick and then ascended six white-painted steps to knock on a broad door.

He waited several minutes and knocked a second time before the door opened. The man on the other side looked at Luman blankly, but Luman knew him instantly; his height, his pinched shoulders, his stoop, his bushy black eyebrows and short white hair, his nose like the beak of a toucan Luman had seen in a cage in Free Imperial Trenton, his long, thin fingers and oversized knuckles all marked the man as John Bilious. He wore a frayed yellow frock coat with overlarge cuffs over a ruffled shirt that might have looked at home in the previous century.

"Mr. Bilious," Luman said.

"Dr. Bilious," Bilious growled. "Do we have business?"

"I'm responding to your advertisement." Luman smiled. "Unless someone else has managed to bring you an authentic merman."

"Man, hmm." Bilious frowned. "I believe my ad did specify maid."

"It said 'maid,'" Luman conceded, "but if you are hoping to breed the specimen, you'll be disappointed. It's mummified."

Bilious nodded slowly. "I've been presented this week with three dead monkeys, sawn in half and stitched to trout, as well as a sadly dead infant Child of Adam with webbed toes. I've also been offered live specimens of a bird that swims and of a fish that flies, none of which satisfies my need. I have no wish to waste my time. What makes you think you're bringing me the genuine article?"

Luman smiled, but his knees shook. "I've examined it."

"Good evening, sir." Bilious moved to shut the door.

"The mermaid dreams of the river," Luman said.

Bilious hesitated. "Merman," he said.

"Merman," Luman agreed.

"Which river?" Bilious asked.

"I'm not sure," Luman said. "But it's a river in flood, and it's terrifying. The merman says it's a very old river."

Bilious harrumphed and opened the door. "Come in. The drawing room is to your left."

The drawing room was lit by two oil lanterns. Outside, through a large glass window and gauzy white curtains, Luman could see the street turning gray. A fortune in books lined the walls on heavy wooden shelves, and the center of the room held a low, polished table crowded by three stuffed armchairs.

"Tea and wine, Mrs. Hubert!" Bilious shouted.

Luman sat on the edge of a chair, leaning forward. "I was thinking, since the merman dreams of the river, maybe 'mer' isn't appropriate. Maybe he should be a 'floodman,' taxonomically speaking."

Bilious chuckled. "Bit of a scholar, are we?"

"I study arcane things," Luman said. "On my own, as I can. It's a hard road."

"Arcane studies are always a hard road," Bilious agreed, sitting on one of the other chairs. "Half the challenge is just finding the damned path. Let's see the merman. I take it you've got it in your coat there."

"Do you not remember me, Dr. Bilious?" Luman asked.

"No." Bilious frowned. "Is this some kind of ruse? Are you here to serve process? Have we a quarrel?"

"I once asked if I could study with you," Luman said. "Or if you would recommend me to the Imperial College."

"I don't write recommendations," Bilious grunted. "You say 'yes' to one poor aspirant and another hundred pop up to beg. Best to stick to a hard line, say 'no' to everyone. And study with me? Good heavens, sir, wizards' apprentices went out with Isaac Newton."

"And yet I have profitably served two apprenticeships," Luman said. "One with an old German braucher and a second with a Memphite initiand."

"Good, you see?" Bilious chuckled. "You had no need of my assistance after all."

"You know things I don't," Luman said. "I could still profit from your assistance."

Bilious's lips sank to a flat line. "I begin to apprehend that you didn't bring me a merman for the twenty promised shillings."

Luman nodded. "I will forego the shillings, if you will teach me for a year."

"A year?" Bilious leaped to his feet. "A year's servitude for twenty shillings?"

"The servitude would be mine, sir." Luman forced himself to keep his seat. "I would mind your experiments. I would clean your laboratory. I would deploy my lesser crafts to support your greater art. I would chop wood, go to the market. I would make your life easier."

"You would not make my life easier," Bilious grumbled. "No apprentice ever does."

A slouch-faced woman in a gray housedress and white apron and bonnet entered carrying a tray. On the tray stood a tea kettle and cups and a wine bottle and glasses. She deposited her burden directly on the table and retreated.

"I would pay," Luman said. "I'll work at night and pay you to teach me by day."

"I don't need money." Bilious sneered. "I am on a pension from the Imperial College."

"You don't need money," Luman agreed. "You need the merman."

Bilious froze and sucked air through his teeth.

"Show me the merman," he said.

Luman didn't hesitate. He knew what he wanted, and he was willing to negotiate hard for it, but he didn't want to seem shifty. He drew the bundle from his coat and laid it on the table.

Bilious stared at the white oblong swaddled object. He rubbed his knuckles, then cracked them, then sat down. Like Luman, he sat on the edge of his seat and leaned forward, staring.

Luman forced himself not to frown. Was the magician afraid to touch the merman? Was he staring at it with second sight, analyzing it before touching it? Or, like a disciplined child on Christmas morning, was he simply delaying his own gratification by compelling himself to wait?

Luman's stomach growled. Inspection revealed that there were no previously unnoticed biscuits or salted fish on the tray. There was wine, which Luman's Memphite oath prevented him from drinking, and there was the tea. Or rather, there were two teacups, each holding a cut plug of tea, and there was a kettle, piping out a thin jet of steam, dying by the second.

Luman picked up the kettle.

Bilious grabbed the edge of the wrapping and pulled it aside. The merman lay suddenly revealed, lying under lanternlight on the low table. Seeing it illuminated, Luman found the contrast between the one greenish arm and the brown, leathery appearance of the rest of the creature shocking.

"You've wet it," Bilious said.

"Not deliberately," Luman said. "The dew touched it. And your advertisement didn't warn the respondent not to wet the mermaid."

"If I order a quire of paper, and the tradesman arrives with a soggy mass of pulp, I do not pay him."

"That's not a quire of paper," Luman pointed out. "It's a mermaid."

"Merman."

"Also, if you don't pay the tradesman, he takes back the paper." Luman shrugged.

The merman's green arm twitched. Luman nearly dropped the kettle.

Bilious seemed not to have noticed.

"But you won't accept the twenty shillings," the elder magician said.

"I would prefer that you keep them," Luman suggested, "as payment for my first six months of tuition."

Bilious snarled. "Three months."

"Five," Luman suggested. "I shall have to work at night to earn the remaining . . ." He did quick calculation in his head. "Twenty-eight shillings. But there must be plenty of work for a hedge magician in Pittsburgh."

"You shall not use any art that I teach you to earn money while you are my apprentice," Bilious said. "You will swear an oath on it."

"I'm comfortable with oaths."

"Four months," Bilious said, "with the remaining forty shillings for the year's tuition due at the end of the four months. No room or board provided, you sleep elsewhere, and you feed yourself."

"Zero months," said a gravelly new voice. "And I take my merman back with me now."

Bilious spun in his seat to face the drawing room door. Luman turned too, and realized he was still holding the kettle. He wanted to set it down, but his hands were gripping it so tightly, he was afraid that releasing his hold would be physically painful.

A man in a red tunic stood in the door. He had the pale skin and slender frame of one of the Firstborn; his black hair hung long behind his shoulders. His arms were crossed over his chest, and he glared at Bilious with one eyebrow raised.

"Tolares," Bilious said. "I did not take you for a trespasser."

"Bilious," the Firstborn replied in a slow, flat voice. "I did not take you for a thief."

"I have stolen nothing," Bilious said.

"I saw your advertisement," Tolares told him. "Do you think the Post-Gazette does not vomit its despicable eructations into the sweet air of Marbletown?"

"And I have stolen nothing." Bilious thumped his chest with one fist.

"Because you knew others would carry out the theft for you," Tolares said. "And if it was not my mermaid to be stolen, it would have been someone else's."

"How do you know this is yours?" Bilious challenged him.

"Because my gardener Hornby has already admitted to breaking into my cabinet of wonders," Tolares said. "Whence my merman has disappeared."

"Did your merman have one green arm?" Bilious asked.

Tolares stepped forward, grinding his fists into his hips and staring at the table. "Wisdom's bees, you have wetted it. You fool, what are you planning?"

"My plans are none of your affair, elf." Bilious turned to Luman. "We have a deal."

"No," Luman said slowly. "You have made a counteroffer, which I must consider. Perhaps we should expand the conversation." To Tolares, he said, "I didn't know that Hornby was your gardener, or that he would steal from you."

"Shut up, Child of Eve." Tolares sneered. "Bilious, you've wet the merman. You must act now. What were you going to pay the thief here?"

"Not a thief," Luman said.

"Twenty shillings," Bilious grunted. "Per my advertisement."

Luman didn't think he could defeat either of these magicians, if it came to a duel. He also lacked any conventional weapon. Was it still possible that he might persuade one of the wizards to take him on and teach him?

"We were negotiating," Luman said. "I answered his advertisement because I wish an apprenticeship. But perhaps I could apprentice to you instead. I would forego any claim to reimbursement of the ten shillings Mr. Hornby took from me—"

"Chop my firewood and make my bed for a year, eh?" Tolares laughed. "I heard your pleading with Bilious here. Listen, thief. Hornby is dead, at a mere word from me. I am seriously considering killing you for your impudence. Shut up, or your chatter will make my mind up for me."

Luman threw the water. The kettle was warm, but the jet of steam had become a mere token of dying heat. He heaved the entire contents of the pot onto the merman, and as he did so he corkscrewed up and onto his feet, looking for the nearest exit, the teakettle still in his hand.

Water splashed across the table. It soaked Bilious's knees.

"No!" Bilious shouted.

Water poured from the table onto the floor. The boards were soaked, and a wave sloshed back against Luman's feet. The water was cold and dirty.

Luman stared at the kettle. He was dreaming the water that crashed against his knees, and the gleeful grin on the merman's face.

He had to be dreaming.

The merman changed color instantly. Its skin swelled, gaining an oily sheen and shading quickly from parched brown to vivid green. Suddenly, the creature's arms spun about, flopping as if to gain purchase on the table, and it shrieked without words.

Water washed across the table. Bilious grabbed for the merman and missed as the creature flopped out of his grasp.

Luman turned to the doorway, and found the Firstborn wizard blocking his path, lips curled into a sneer.

Tolares raised a finger and opened his mouth.

Luman clubbed Tolares in the nose with the kettle.

The Firstborn staggered backward, red blood exploding down his chin. "Thief!" he croaked.

The merman dove into the water. Tears stung Luman's eyes and he blinked, the salt of his own body blurring the room around him.

He turned and hurled the kettle into the glass of the window. It was a large target; even half-blind, he couldn't miss. His hand and back felt as if they were cracking from the effort, but the window shattered entirely. Fragments of glass blew out into the night air and a curtain of shards dropped from the height of the window frame.

Luman lurched away from the magicians, through water nearly up to his waist. He shrugged deeper into his coat, turning the wide collar up as he sloshed toward the window. "Don't die!" he heard Bilious screaming behind him. "The river! The river is coming!"

Luman stepped into the empty window frame, water streaming down his legs and from the lowest pockets of his coat. Then he jumped out into the cool night air. He dropped eight feet and landed on packed earth, feeling the full, jarring force of the ground up through his hard leather shoes.

Turning, he looked one last time into the drawing room of Dr. Bilious. Bilious held the flailing merman by the waist and yelled at it as at an unruly child. Tolares was covered in his own gore, and charged Bilious with his hands balled into fists.

Water was just beginning to pour over the lower lip of the window.

Then Luman was past the window, past the end of the house, down the street, and away into the falling darkness of Pittsburgh.

Questions.

Questions, always questions, and more questions.

What was the river that would return? Was the return indeed inevitable? Had it indeed returned this very night? What was the relationship between the merman and the river, and were there other mermen, and maids, in that same relationship?

No matter how many steps he took, Luman Walters always felt farther from the center than when he had begun. Where were the answers? What sacrifice would he have to make to get them?

Always more questions.

D.J. (Dave) Butler has been a lawyer, a consultant, an editor, a corporate trainer, and a registered investment banking representative, and he is now a Consulting Editor for Baen Books. His novels published by Baen Books include the Witchy War series (*Witchy Eye*, *Witchy Winter*, *Witchy Kingdom*, and *Serpent Daughter*), *In the Palace of Shadow and Joy*, and *Abbott in Darkness*, as well as *The Cunning Man* and *The Jupiter Knife*, co-written with Aaron Michael Ritchey, and *Time Trials*, co-written with M.A. Rothman. He also writes for children: the steampunk fantasy adventure tales *The Kidnap Plot*, *The Giant's Seat*, and *The Library Machine* are published by Knopf. Other novels include *City of the Saints* from WordFire Press and *The Wilding Probate* from Immortal Works. His novels have won the Whitney Award, the Association for Mormon Letters Award for Novel, and the Dragon Award.

Dave also organizes writing retreats and anarcho-libertarian writers' events, and travels the country to sell books. He tells many stories as a gamemaster with a gaming group, some of whom he's been playing with since sixth grade. He plays guitar and banjo whenever he can, and likes to hang out in Utah with his wife, their children, and the family dog.

muddy the waters

JONATHAN DUCKWORTH

POSEY GOT out through her bedroom window, the one whose lock Momma didn't know was broken. It was late, but she didn't need to see her way to find the path to the bayou. She'd had enough of Momma's rules and Momma's meanness. She was going to Water Auntie, who lived in the bayou like the fish she half resembled, and this time it would be for good.

The catspaw vines pawed at her nightclothes and the mosquitoes whined in her ears, but it was so nice to feel the pine needles and deermoss—soft from the afternoon rain—under her toes. Soon, there'd be no more groundings. No more church services, no more following Momma to the drugstore so she could talk grownup things with that Mr. Owen who poured the phosphates and mixed the malts. She'd live like a fish with Water Auntie, always safe under the care of her magic.

But halfway through the path that wound through the flatwoods, Posey heard another set of feet crunching the litter. Both Momma and Auntie had warned her the woods weren't safe at night, and so she found a biggish pine and hid herself behind its trunk. Posey snuck a glance just as the moonlight broke through the clouds. Silver light shined her Momma's dress.

Momma walked right past where Posey was hiding, and Posey

got a good look at her Momma's slumped posture, her head held low, and the dark stains streaking her clothes. Dark like molasses against the shimmering cotton folds of her bustled dress. Her gloves, the velvet gloves that reached up to her elbows, that she never took off even when she was giving Posey a bath when Posey didn't wash right—they were dripping with something like mud.

Posey held her breath, until Momma was out of sight, until her footsteps weren't as loud as the bayou frogs and the whistle of mole crickets in the dirt. What had Momma been up to? Why would she, a "good Christian woman," as she called herself, go to the bayou, a "place of devils" to hear her talk?

Posey walked like the pine needles were broken glass, following the old path to the bayou. The closer she got to the water, the quieter it got. That was all wrong—usually by night the bayou's shores were exploding with the music of frogs and insects and the splash of mullets drunk on moonlight.

But tonight—dead quiet. She came to the water's edge, where dark water and the silver-dollar moon leaned into each other. The bayou, that long tract of strangeness tonguing out to the Gulf beyond, was blacker than usual tonight. Almost like pitch.

It was still, a pane of smoked glass. No ripples. No froth. No waves. Standing on the sandy shoal, Posey found her Momma's footprints. Found something else too—the cut half of an onion.

She was holding it in her hand, some of its juices still dripping, the strong smell stinging her eyes and making her tear up, when a shimmer caught her eye, and she saw the lone moving thing in the water.

"Auntie..." she heard herself mewl, before she turned away, unable to see the floating, belly-up carcass glowing like golden foil under the moon. Auntie looked shriveled, like she'd been squeezed dry, her blood staining the bayou dark like an evil tea.

The day before had been church day at the First Methodist. Momma and Posey had sat up in the front row where Posey couldn't even fidget without the preacher seeing it. She hated church services. Hated the stale heat, hated having to sit still, hated how Billy Helm who sat in the row behind her would try to put his snotty finger into her curls. When the preacher was done with his long, dry talk about Abraham and what it meant to give up a child to God, Momma pulled Posey along to the corner where she and the other "society ladies" had their usual chat about the sermon and goings-on in town. It was when Momma was distracted talking with the mayor's wife that Posey saw her chance and snuck out.

As hot as the day was, and as stuffy as her "Sunday best" clothes were, Posey felt herself cool down just from the sight of the bayou water. It was a caramel brown today. She was so excited to get there, she let herself get snagged on a catspaw vine, and the thorn tore a nasty hole in her dress. Things got worse when she pulled herself loose and then stumbled and got turf and mud stains on the frills and tiers of her dress.

Momma wouldn't like that at all—and she'd already be in trouble for sneaking.

But she shook off her worries easily as she wriggled out of the smothering layers of her clothes. The breeze tickled her bare skin, she let out a sigh.

"Getting old for skinny-dipping."

Posey turned around, already smiling. She hadn't heard Water Auntie breach the water. Glimmering under the sun like so much brass, with big round eyes the color of bank-new pennies, Water Auntie sat halfway submerged in the shallows, watching Posey in her unblinking way.

Posey never quite knew what Water Auntie was, or if she really was her aunt. Momma called her Sister, once with fondness, but more recently with a vileness like the kindly fishwoman had done her a wrong turn or two. She was a fishy woman, scaled and finned like a fish, but with arms and legs and a head like a woman, and wide hips and a mouth almost like a woman's, except her teeth were tiny and sharp. All her life, since her first memories, Posey had known her. When Posey was littler, before Momma got so wrapped up in church and being a "good Christian mother," they'd visited Water Auntie together. But Momma hadn't been to the bayou in a long while.

"Your Momma know you're here?" Water Auntie asked, putting her webbed hands on her hips.

"Yes, ma'am."

"Don't you lie to me."

Posey walked to the water and dipped her feet in. Not too warm, not too cold. She waded in, pleased to feel the little fish nibbling at the dead skin of her ankles. "She don't want me seeing you. Won't tell me why. She's in an evil way."

Water Auntie swam over and put her arms around Posey, bringing her into a hug. Her skin wasn't slimy like it looked—it was smooth and cold, like rubber but more alive. "Wanna swim with me?"

Of course she did. Like a pair of otters they swam around, making loops and drawing crazy eights in the water. In the water, with Auntie, she always felt free. Folks talked about being free as a bird, but birds weren't really free—they had to work to keep themselves in the air. All a fish has to do is float half the time. Floating's easy.

The sun got a little lower before either of them spoke.

Auntie broke the silence. "Your Momma still down on you?"

"Worser'n ever. Don't know what's in her that's so mean."

"Sister Lorna's had a hard life. That awful man—your Pa, you know—he, well, he wasn't all that nice to my Lorna."

"She ain't talked much on him."

"The less you know the better. I still remember the night your Momma come down here, face full of crying, and she asked me, no begged me to do something—"

Water Auntie trailed off. Posey could tell there was something she remembered not to say. Posey knew from her Momma how Water Auntie used to grant wishes. Used to work her magic when Momma needed it. Usually Momma would cry into the bayou, and her tears would bring Auntie to the shore, where she'd ask what Momma needed done. Some of the stories were funny, like how Auntie witched a boy who was being mean to Momma to make him pee his pants whenever he had evil thoughts, and some were sweet, like the time Auntie witched the frogs to croak Momma a happy birthday song when her folks forgot what day it was. But she had always guessed some wishes weren't so happy.

"Asked you to do what?"

Water Auntie had stopped swimming and merely stood where she was, while Posey paddled beside her. They were in deep water, where Posey's feet couldn't touch dirt.

"Nothing I ought to tell a little girl about."

"I ain't so little."

"You're ten natural years old; a fry."

Auntie started to tickle her under the water with her slippery fingers, and Posey couldn't help but nearly giggle out of her skin.

"She forgot," Auntie said, her voice turning serious. "Maybe she forgot who and what she is. I can understand her, wanting to be different. I wanted to be different too—but the bayou always needs a Lady. Needs a witch to keep its magic going."

Posey was going to ask what she meant by all that, but from the shore came a warning harsh as a crow's caw, "Posey Elissa Carmichael!"

There was Momma, standing at the shoreline by the trees, one hand balled around a towel and the other holding up the stained and piled folds of Posey's discarded dress. She was far off, and the sun was drooling into Posey's eyes, but she knew what face Momma wore. That pinched, mean, bulldog glower, the I'll-scrub-the-foolery-off-you-and-you-won't-get-any-dinner-neither look that meant trouble wasn't coming but had in fact already come.

The lightness swimming brought boiled off, and a heavy weight sank into her gut. Auntie patted her on the small of her back, but even in this gesture there was a little push, a gentle nudge toward the shore, toward Momma.

They swam together. When Posey made it to the shore, Auntie stayed in the shallows while Momma cocooned Posey with the towel.

"Sneaking off, making a fool of me, burs in your hair, mud in your dress..."

She tried to apologize, but Momma wouldn't hear it. She told Posey to dress herself and then march back home. Posey was picking up her dress when Auntie said something quiet. It sounded like a question, one of those nothings grownups ask each other to pass the time or to be polite.

Momma answered in a different key, "I don't want my good daughter swimming in these leech-infested waters. You mark that."

Posey was fussing with the pins in her dress, her excuse to stay a little longer.

Water Auntie didn't say anything at first. Then, after a few breaths of time, "You talk like you ain't of these waters same as me."

"I am a child of Christ," Momma said, in that high, nose-up way of hers. "Jesus washes clean all stains."

"And you think your Jesus wasn't a witch too?"

"Oh, a blasphemer, too. Posey, pay attention. This is the last time I'll say this—we don't go to the bayou anymore. It's an unwholesome and ungodly place."

"But Auntie's only—"

"She's not your aunt! She's—oh, it doesn't matter. You go on home, you obstreperous child. Now!"

Posey, dressed now, wanted to say something, wanted to stick up for Auntie, for herself. But something in Momma's small, dark eyes, the hard set of her jaw, the dangerous pink in her sweaty brow told Posey this wasn't a time to be hardheaded. She started to walk. Slowly.

Their voices continued, and the salty wind from the Gulf carried them to her ears.

"Same water's in your veins, Sister."

"We are not sisters."

"You forget too much. You forget all I gave you. How much of what you have is from me, from what I done for you?"

Posey didn't hear Momma's reply. She'd walked too far. A moment later, Momma came up the path, her red lips sewn into a hard line, but her eyes soft, like any second they might start crying. For all of how angry she was with Momma, Posey couldn't help but worry for her.

Couldn't help but wonder why Momma never talked about the hard life Auntie said she'd lived.

Momma caught up to her, and even though Posey had no intention of disobeying her, one of those gloved hands clamped hard around Posey's wrist, and didn't let go until they were safe on the right side of a closed door.

Momma didn't slap or spank her. Didn't scold her anymore either. She preferred to scrub and wash. A bath like torture. Cold water, nasty suds that stung the eyes, and a boar-bristle brush that she used like she was trying to scrub Posey's skin off.

"Dirty, dirty, dirty..." Momma muttered as she washed Posey again and again. A few times, in the middle of it all, she felt Momma's hands—still protected under her gloves—feeling along the slope of Posey's neck, like she expected to find something there other than smooth little girl's skin.

The body, shriveled and spent, drifted like an eye floater across the lens of the bayou. Moonlight caught on something shiny sticking out of Auntie's neck, stuck into her gill—a knife. Posey was too shocked to even cry. In that strange space between terror and sadness and under the crushing weight of a world that refused to make sense, Posey thought about it and pieced together what'd happened.

A knife in Auntie's throat. A cut onion at Posey's feet.

The knife to cut the onion. The onion to bring tears. Tears to bring Auntie to the shore. The knife to stick in Auntie's throat.

That made sense, even if all the rest of it didn't. Even if nothing in the world felt like it should. There was a greasy, queasy feel in the air now, like Posey was breathing in something close to poison, like the earth and sky and the water between them were all crooked, a painting not set right on the nail it hung from.

Finally, her tears came. They dripped down her cheeks, like scalding drops of angel's fire. Some dribbled into her lips. They tasted like the bayou water. What was there to do?

Nothing. The water and the joy it once contained, dead. The flatwood silent. The night dark and empty.

All there was now, was Posey, and the house. And Momma.

When Posey started walking toward the house, she wasn't sure what she wanted, what she hoped would happen. What could she say, what could she ask or do that would matter now? She was a little girl, a little nothing, powerless as a grub wriggled out of its hole in a tree, or a tadpole in the shallows. Somehow, there was a whole life left, a life lived in the same house as the woman who'd killed her Auntie.

By and by, as the house appeared—one lit window, the wash-room—Posey got it in her she needed to ask Momma why she'd done it. Or better, tell Momma she was just like the awful people God drowned with the flood, or turned to salt when he smote those cities of the plain. It came to Posey that nothing would make her feel good except to hurt her, in any small way she could.

The back door creaked as Posey pushed it open. The house was dark. All except the sliver of light coming at the end of the hall, sneaking in through the crack in the washroom door.

Humming with as much righteous anger and sadness as any ten-year-old body could hold, Posey trembled with each step. But she stopped halfway down the hall, her ears pricking up as she listened to the sounds coming from the washroom. The slosh of water. Furious scrubbing. And painful, muffled sobs.

For all she felt now against her Momma, the sound of it still hurt Posey, still made her want to run in and throw her arms around her Momma, to squeeze dead whatever strange sadness had crawled into her chest. Instead, Posey kept creeping forward, but slower, more cautiously than before.

She stuck her face in the door and looked in. Under the sickly glow of a kerosene lamp, there was Momma, divested of all cloth, even her gloves gone. She was inside the tub, hunched over, desperately scrubbing her own arms with the awful boar-bristle brush.

It wasn't skin she was scrubbing. The skin had already flaked off, revealing smooth, fine scales that eagerly drank the lamplight. With the gloves off, Posey saw the fins tapering out from the insides of Momma's upper arms, terminating near the pit of the elbows. Silky fins just like Auntie's.

Posey must have done something. Moved, gasped, breathed in or out too hard. Because Momma stopped sobbing and looked to the doorway. For one blink in time, one breath, Posey stared into two fishy eyes bright as new pennies, rimmed in the soft, pink flesh of a woman's face. Then clawed hands covered the face, and the sobbing returned, then became a retch as Momma's throat split open, red slits of raw, startled flesh—gills—fissuring from what had been smooth skin.

Now Momma started to thrash, and Posey, for all she might have said and done, for all the messy soup of feelings sloshing inside her, couldn't do anything except rush over to the tub.

The bayou always needs its Lady, Auntie had said. Whatever Momma thought she'd done in killing her, be it to settle some score, prove a point, or keep her daughter to herself, those words now looked more true than wrong.

Posey jumped into the lukewarm tub water and put her arms around her Momma, and then, when Momma had stopped thrashing so much, Posey used her delicate little girl hands to find the seams of Momma's skin, and gently, carefully, began peeling it off so the scales could breathe.

Jonathan Louis Duckworth is a completely normal, entirely human person with the right number of heads and everything. He received his MFA from Florida International University. His speculative fiction work appears in *Fantasy & Science Fiction, Pseudopod, Beneath Ceaseless Skies, Southwest Review, Flash Fiction Online*, and elsewhere. He is a PhD student at University of North Texas where he serves as the interviews editor at *American Literary Review*, and he is also an active HWA member.

a flight of mermaids

BG HILTON

MERMAIDS CAN ONLY FLY in the rain. Heavy rain too, it's the only way they can keep wet enough to breathe. Most pilots hate the rain. Visibility is limited and the fragile wood and canvas fuselages of their planes become sodden and unresponsive. Even the boldest pilot would rather not take to the air in anything more than a light drizzle. Mermaids, though... mermaids will fly even in a downpour.

In the early days of the Greatest War, they tried to build mermaid planes that would fly in all weather, equipped with some sort of tank that sprayed water onto the pilots. But this slowed the planes, made them difficult to maneuvre. They cut their losses and went back to sending the mermaids up in wet weather only. Mermaids are so deadly in a steady shower that it makes up for their absence on sunnier days.

We ground soldiers all knew how much we owed to the mermaids. When tanker trucks drove the mermaids from their riverside base to the aerodrome, common soldiers—elf and orc alike—would cheer their passage.

"Get at 'em, girls!" the orcs would bellow, "Give 'em what for!"

I once saw two orc medics lay down their stretcher, just so that they could salute the mermaids as they passed. The wounded orc-lord they carried didn't protest at being laid by the stony roadside. He just called out, 'Go on, my dears! Go knock John Zombie on the head.'

The elf soldiers said nothing, of course. But when the mermaids passed behind their trenches, they must have forgotten the burning forests of their past and the ankle-deep water of their present, and their wordless songs took on a high, triumphant tone.

The mermaids—their caps pinned neatly to their flowing hair; their olive flight jackets hanging wet about their shoulders— tended not to answer. In the early days of the war they had waved back at the trenches, but once it became clear that it was unlucky to do so, they stopped. The soldiers did not mind, so long as the mermaids did their duty.

It was a mermaid squadron that claimed the unlife of Baron Sanguino in the last days of the War. This was after the Dwarfish collapse, but before the Sasquatch Brigades joined the fight, and everything hung in the balance. I was lucky enough to see the whole thing from the ground, where I was spotter for an AA gun. We goblins were much sought after for this kind of work. Our eyesight is second to none among the Peoples and works just as well in twilight or moonlight as it does in daytime.

The mermaids of the 23rd Squadron—Neptune's Thunderbolts —were flying dawn patrol over the zombie trenches. It did my heart good to watch those girls wheel and turn in the sky, their biplanes like swallows flitting over the bushes. There was not a zombie plane to be seen. The forecast said that the rain would worsen, so most of our fighters were grounded. The mermaids were the only things in the sky, made all the more beautiful by the ugliness of No One's Land beneath them; a desolate plain of mud, craters and thorny-iron vine.

It had been beautiful, once, this land. I'd visited a few times, on business. The scenery was not dramatic, like the mountains, or the coast. It was just plains and low, flat hills. But green! So green and fertile. It was filled with small farms growing wheat, dairy, hops. It was border country, and if you stopped at a market, you might see all sorts of people rubbing shoulders—orcs, elves, gnomes ... even the occasional leprechaun or dryad.

And humans of course. There were still humans in those days.

I saw the Baron before the mermaids did—a great vague blur high in the sky, descending rapidly. Looking back, I wonder how it was I recognized it so quickly. I'd seen airships on our stretch of the Elfland Front, of course, but none the size of the Baron's vast dirigible, the *Hades*. Refugees from the Dwarf Hills spoke of it with horrified awe. Now that the dwarves had surrendered, the Baron was coming for us.

By sailing high over the clouds and dropping like an overripe apple to the lower air, the *Hades* had almost taken us by surprise. I blew my bane-horn and fired a flare. Other bane-horns blared at our airfield as orcs and elves and a handful of free-dwarf pilots scrambled to their planes. Even in this weather, the Baron had to be stopped.

The mermaids of the 23rd didn't wait for reinforcements. They scattered before the great airship like a school of sardines before a predator. But unlike sardines, they turned against the shark and bit back.

How they flew! Streams of fire spewed out from the great shape of the airship, while the mermaids danced like sparks in the chimney, too light and nimble for the zombies to reach and drag to earth. That is the trick to mermaid pilots, you see. They think in three dimensions in a way that we, the land-bound, do not.

A wave of enemy planes rose unsteadily from behind the lines. Perhaps they had meant to coordinate with the arrival of the airship. If so, they had failed. Without a screen of fighters, the *Hades* was vulnerable. The mermaids had a chance—and no mermaid ever willingly gave up a chance for victory.

From my little plywood spotter's post above our bunker, I barked orders to my crew through a rubber speaking tube. The crew brought our guns to bear but couldn't fire on the great leviathan of the sky. Not with our girls engaged. My heart thundered like a freight train. *Go on, ladies! Let them have it!*

The school of biplanes dove like sea hawks, regrouped beneath the *Hades*, and rose like a fist at the airship's control cabin. I almost fainted at the sight. Hitting the *Hades* at its best defended point? Madness! Suicide!

The airship's guns roared into life, and mermaid planes began dropping from the sky like flies before a swatter. I do not like to remember that moment. Instead, I prefer to imagine the Baron, adjusting his fur-trimmed cape and chuckling at the costly gambit —laughing as plane after plane crumpled and fell before his guns— then seeing the second wave of the squadron come screaming upwards as his gunners reloaded. Then I imagine the Baron's laughter dying as his control room exploded and the airship burst into flames, a mighty bonfire in the air.

A massive cheer rang out from the trenches as fire peeled the skin off the *Hades*, leaving nothing but a charred skeletal airframe, slowly—leisurely—crumpling over the foremost zombie trenches. The remaining mermaids scattered every which way to escape the debris and hydrogen flames. One plane did not pull away in time, and the flames caught its fuselage. It would have been consumed in a minute, if not for the rain. It wheeled and thundered straight for the nearest point of our line. Straight towards me.

There was a zombie fighter on her tail. It was close enough that I could see the network of bleached bones and tanned skin that formed its airframe. Bright lines of tracers poured from his gun, but even injured, the mermaid's graceful dance continued. Her decaying pursuer did not score a hit.

I called down to my crew to fire, barely able to hear my own voice over the roar of prop-wash and the hammering of guns. But my crew heard and fired. The zombie plane shattered. Rags, bones and splinters spilled across our position. The burning mermaid plane hit the ground, its wheels shattering like glass. It skipped twice in the mud, turned over, and came to a shuddering stop.

I leapt from my post, running as fast as I possibly could across the muddy ground. There was not a thought in my head. My body ran entirely on instinct. My eyes told my legs where the obstacles in my path were, without the least consultation with my brain. I reached the plane before any other. It was on its side, one wing crushed beneath it, its mermaid pilot lying head-out and tail-in. She smelled of smoke and sea-salt. Seeing me, she reached out with both arms. Mermaids have webbed fingers. I hadn't known.

I let her take hold of me by my narrow shoulders, and I pulled. I will never know where my strength came from, but it must have come from somewhere. She was twice my height—length?—and perhaps four times my weight. My little legs ached and burned as I dragged her sinuous, scaly form away from the flaming wreckage. She had saved me, saved everyone one on this part of the front, perhaps even saved the war effort. Could I do any less for her than save her back?

When the fire hit the plane's fuel-tank, the explosion bowled us over. As the prayer-gongs in my ears subsided, I heard the crack of rifle fire. Some orcish soldiers were firing above our heads, something on our side of the trenches. The zombie pilot had survived the crash—or part of him had. Its legless torso slid like an eel through the filthy mud, as it dragged itself hand over claw-like hand.

Panicking, I tried to pull the mermaid to safety. It was then that the pain struck—agony from thigh to ankle—and I realised I was injured.

The orcs fired again and again, missing each time. The rain was worsening, and so was their aim. More soldiers were approaching —an elf with a repeating crossbow and a couple of gnolls—but I could see that they would not arrive in time. The mermaid drew her silver sidearm but, clogged and fouled with mud, it misfired.

I'd no gun, only a knife. A goblin dagger—sharp as a dragon tooth, but not much bigger. I slashed at the zombie to no avail. Rotting yellow teeth bit into my injured leg. In my agony, my knife slipped from my hand.

My mermaid picked it up between webbed fingers. With grace-ful, flowing movements, she stabbed again and again into the zombie's head and neck, until the poor, pathetic creature stopped moving.

They amputated my leg, naturally. The surgeon said that even without the zombie bite, they couldn't have saved it.

So that is my war story. Before it all started, I was a commercial traveller for a potion company. When the fighting ended, I became a junior manager at the same concern. During the conflict, I stormed no fortresses and won no medals. I slew no heroes and destroyed no idols. I never once killed anyone, nor even fired a shot, directly. Yet my mermaid pilot called me a hero, and that is a very fine thing.

I never saw that mermaid again, but I have never forgotten her.

I try not to think about her there in the stricken plane, like a landed fish. In my dreams, she's always at the controls of that craft. I see her and her sisters like whizzing spots of brightness over the blasted earth, swooping like skylarks in the downpour.

It is lucky that it was raining on that day.

Mermaids only fly in the rain.

BG Hilton is an Australian author who lives in Sydney and consequently spends a lot of time in traffic. He works in education, a fact which would probably amaze most of his teachers. He is the author of the Steampunk adventure *Champagne Charlie and the Amazing Gladys* and the South Hertling Chronicles series: *Mysterious Aisles* and the upcoming *Clocks and Boxes*. His short fiction has been published in *Andromeda Spaceways Magazine*, *Antipodean SF*, *James Gunn's Ad Astra* and elsewhere. His website is bghilton.com.

keeper of drowned souls

ELIZABETH ROSE

Hades has Charon in his ferry; the Inferno, Virgil; Valhalla,
Valkyries—
But what of a nearer Hell?

Divided, like heaven and earth, by little more than a veil of light?

Deep and dark as myth but more untouched,
cold as a coin clutched in a dead man's fingers, or the iron
fetters anchoring shiploads of slaves to the seabed.

Here among the cosmic living lantern lights of angler fish and
vipers is a man who didn't need a siren's call to leap.

A woman castaway as bad luck.

Children packed shoulder to shoulder in rusting metal coffins.

Here is a bone orchard of shipwrecks; grave of the graveless;
figments of the forgotten.

Skulls with white fire in their eyes; aequoria twitching from dark sockets; the sunken ruin of a megalodon; messages in bottles; submarines still casting sonar ghosts out into this underwater underworld; bones scaled in bioluminescence as if they, too, might stir and awaken.

Lost forever to shifting tides?

Or gated, guarded, in the only Eden unspoiled by Adam's seed, where the unnamed still drift primordial?

What fallen, darkling angel dove from grace like a mutinied sea captain off the plank? What daimon of the deep?

Nameless merrow. Less distant than the gods but shyer.

Blind as the cavefish, svelte and slippery as the ribbon eel; lightless, tongueless, without song.

Pale, luminous monstress. Careful gardener of corpses bloated and flowering larva, zooplankton, and worms; radiant maggots of this infernal abyss; this inner galaxy of carnivorous dark.

She isn't a siren.

Not a succubus with her cadaverous flesh, skin and fishbones, translucent, fang-toothed.

A scavenger. A collector and curator. Patient as the coelacanth dragging itself back from extinction.

With enough time everything returns to the sea.

ELIZABETH ROSE IS A POET, writer, and artist with a bachelor's degree in English literature. She grew up in Florida, a stone's throw from the Atlantic Ocean, and her first taste of poetry was her grandmother's old copy of *Where the Sidewalk Ends* by Shel Silverstein. These days she reads more Keats than Silverstein, living with her family and two cats in a place without sidewalks but with a lot of trees. When not writing, she can be found hiking in the woods, cooking up delicious culinary creations, or looking for cursed objects at her local antique stores.

where the nereids play

J. A. JOHNSON

THE WORLD WAS A GRAY, drizzly mess and it was perfect. Sam Baldwin swam at a sure and steady pace. Breathing twice every three strokes, he focused on maintaining his Critical Swim Speed. He could feel the plump raindrops as they struck his head and arms.

Somewhere ahead of him, hidden by the surface-level, frying-pan spatter of rain meeting lake, was Fox Isle. Little more than a pine-covered rock, Fox Isle was isolated by miles of open water in every direction. The islet, easy enough to miss on a clear day, was an almost guaranteed no-show in the rain, which of course, for Sam's purposes, was the whole point.

Although still pushing himself, Sam was confident in his endurance and pacing. His primary focus today was sighting. He had hoped for weeks for the opportunity to swim in such low-visibility conditions. Should the actual competition be held in similar weather and he couldn't find his way, then all of his months of practice would have been for naught.

Without slowing, Sam glanced back. Emily, in their two-person kayak, was rowing leisurely along in his wake as his spotter. At some point she had donned her red rain poncho. She waved. He waved back and then turned his attention forward where it belonged.

Sam never felt more in tune with himself, more alive, than when in the presence of the ocean. In his experience, most people could stand on the coastline, stare out at the endless blue vista, and see only water. Lots, and lots, and lots of water. Sam, however, saw the world, the *real* world, and it both humbled him and inspired him.

Whenever people asked him why he was an endurance swimmer, why not just run a marathon? Sam replied in the only way possible when answering someone who could never really understand the answer. He would smile.

Several minutes later, the rain began to slacken.

Emily paddled up alongside him. "Time to eat, Sport. How are you feeling?"

With an easy kick, Sam reached out and caught hold of the side of the kayak. "The water is cold, but I feel great."

They kept the chatter to a minimum. With only two minutes to eat and drink every forty-five minutes, there were no seconds to spare. Emily handed him a slice of rye bread with one of her homemade protein spreads and some water.

"At least the rain is letting up," Sam commented as he ate.

"Yeah, but there's a fog rolling in." Emily hitched a thumb behind them. "Warm, wet air over cold water. Works every time. If it overtakes us, you can forget sighting practice today, maybe even longer."

Sam knew that sea fog could last for days, but he doubted that would be the case this time. He shrugged as he swallowed the last of the bread. "Ah, worst-case scenario, we'll get turned around out here. But, you've got your GPS so we'll be fine."

Emily gave him a quizzical look. "Well, aren't we surprisingly chill, for someone on the verge of having their practice goal scuttled."

Sam eased away from the kayak and settled his goggles over his eyes. "In case you haven't noticed, I'm in the ocean with the love of my life. What's not to like?"

Emily smiled. "In case you haven't noticed, I'm not actually in the ocean. Unless, of course, you're talking about someone else."

Sam splashed her with water, then turned away from the kayak to get his bearings. He frowned when he discovered that the fog was already forming on the sea ahead of him, clinging to the face of the waves like a gauzy, cobweb blanket.

"Break's over," Emily prodded him as she slipped out of her red poncho.

Sam began to swim and was soon on pace again.

The fog continued to thicken, obscuring his view. He had never before seen fog roll in so quickly. He was just about to ask Emily to use her GPS when something brushed softly against his left leg. His heartbeat surged briefly as a parade of marine life flashed through his mind. Shark. Jellyfish. Barracuda. The list went on and on.

Face down, Sam peered into the gray-black fathoms. Nothing. The ocean was suddenly far less enchanting. Even a shark, could he have seen it, would have been preferable to the nothing. The imagination.

"What's wrong? Why'd you stop?" Emily asked as she caught up to him. She grinned. "Getting tired already?"

"No. Nothing. I just, I thought I felt something."

Emily turned, instantly serious. She snatched up her binoculars and scanned the surrounding gray water. Sam knew she was looking for a fin. "It's too foggy," she said. "I can't see clearly for more than twenty meters and half that far is already getting hazy."

Sam chewed his lip. He already regretted letting himself get spooked, stopping. He had swum with sharks before and had never been attacked. But still, something about the way the thing had touched his leg had been different, almost a caress. The more he thought about it, the less certain he was that a shark had been responsible.

"Well?" Emily asked.

Sam looked below the surface again. The view below was dim and darkening, but there was no sign of anything in the water with him. But what did that mean when a shark could appear out of the gloom in the blink of an eye. He looked up at Emily, saw the tinge of concern in her green eyes. "How far to Fox Isle?"

She consulted her GPS. "Almost exactly two miles."

He weighed his options. "Two miles," he echoed. "An hour, give or take." He looked her in her eyes. "Whatever it was is likely long gone by now, right?"

Emily shrugged. "Probably."

The idea seemed to set them both at ease for the simple reason that, in all of their time spent in oceans around the world, that was exactly how such encounters normally played out. Why should this one be any different?

Satisfied, Sam snugged his goggles into place and glanced around. The world had all but vanished, reduced to an undulating expanse, roughly the size of a baseball diamond. Damnable fog. There was no more chance to practice sighting today.

"All right, beautiful, just point me in the right direction."

Emily pointed straight ahead and Sam began to swim. After several minutes, he quickened his strokes to a fast but sustainable pace and plowed ahead.

The swells began to increase in size. It would slow him down, but more than that, it would gradually push him off course. As much as he hated it, he would have to rely totally on Emily and her GPS. He looked back and found that he could only make out the bow of the kayak, and the slow, rhythmic dip and pull of the oar.

Again, something brushed his legs. His heart leapt as something touched his side. That was enough! He was getting into the kayak and they were getting the hell off the sea.

As he turned back, Emily screamed, unseen, from somewhere deep inside the fog.

"Em!" Sam began to swim but, after just two strokes, there came a huge splash followed by a brief staccato of smaller splashes. And then silence. "Emily!"

A dozen strokes later, he came upon her red poncho, an unsettling blot of color in an otherwise colorless world. Then he saw the few bits of flotsam; a couple of energy gel packs, a flashlight, a slice of bread in a plastic baggie.

Something tapped his shoulder and he nearly screamed. It was the oar. Broken in half and ... and the blade looked to have been bitten by something; something too small to be a shark of any consequence. Whatever it was it had a bite radius only slightly larger than a human.

There was no sign of Emily or the kayak and, without the oar, it made little sense that the kayak would be very far away. "Emily!"

He dove. The lack of light from above inhibited his view but, to the extent that he could see, there was no trace of her.

Surfacing, he called to her again. "Emily!" He quieted himself to listen for her reply.

Somewhere to his right, a ripple of movement.

"Em!" He swam toward the sound. Then to his left, another ripple, like something breaking the surface and then submerging again.

"Emily, where are you? Stay put. I'll come to you."

He was beginning to feel the cold, in spite of his pounding heart and racing blood. Emily wasn't wearing a wetsuit. She would be far colder than he was.

Another ripple. No, two. One in front of him, one behind.

The panic that had been massing at the edges of his rational mind began to stir in earnest.

He tried to call Emily's name again, but his voice was suddenly choked.

"Ssssam."

"Emily," he whispered.

"Helllp meeee, Ssssam. Helllp meee, pleeeease..."

He swam toward the sound of her voice. Where was she? "Emily, say something."

She giggled coquettishly. Whoever it was, it no longer sounded like his wife.

Something below grabbed his ankle. He jerked his leg up, but whatever had him, had a grip of steel. It pulled him down. He submerged amid a flurry of bubbles. Before the fizzing cloud could dissipate enough for him to see his attacker, his ankle was released.

Sam broke the surface. His only thought now; get to Fox Isle. But which way? Which way? He was totally disoriented. *The sky!* The fog appeared brighter to his left. Follow the sun. The mainland was at least three miles away, much farther than Fox Isle, but at least he couldn't miss it.

Sam swam as fast as he could.

Something wrapped around his legs, something that he knew to be arms, slender, powerful and...

He cried out as something bit into his outer thigh. Not a mere pinch, but a bite! He felt the gaping wound where neoprene and flesh had been torn away. The arms that held him let go.

He swam again. His body electric, as adrenaline surged through his veins.

To his right, a pale shape broke the surface only to slip from his sight as it curled back into the water. It was a fleeting glimpse; a graceful, elegant shape not unlike a woman's back. But as the thing disappeared beneath the waves, the skin darkened, taking on the appearance of gray-green, iridescent scales.

I'm losing my mind, Sam thought.

His leg didn't just hurt, it burned. He knew that he was bleeding badly. The last thing he wanted to do in the open ocean was to bleed. Desperately, he pushed himself harder, in spite of the pain. What else could he do? He had to get to shore, get out of the water.

He heard his name again, "Ssssam." It was a sibilant whisper that echoed within the fog and slithered across the waves like writhing tentacles. "Ssssam, Ssssam, Ssssam."

Swim! He submerged his face as he reached out in a front crawl, once more on the move. It was after his third breath that he saw something beneath him! A vague shape, just visible where the blackness below devoured the light from above.

Sam changed course in an effort to elude the thing, but it easily matched his every move, kept pace, kept itself directly below him.

I'm being toyed with, he thought. *I'm not going to make it.*

In a rush, the thing pacing him rushed up to meet him. In a gut-wrenching instant, he recognized it.

Emily!

But how could she...

He abandoned the question and dove for her. He had to save her.

He kicked furiously. Hands outstretched, he reached down to her.

A searing ache spread from his leg to his hip, impeding his effort. *Come on, Em! Swim! Reach for me!* And then he realized that his wife was just floating there, that she wasn't even swimming, that she hadn't been the entire time.

She was dead. Something below her had been animating her like a puppet.

All at once, dark, lithe forms, half woman, half ... fish! set upon Emily's limp body from every direction, jerking her remains this way and that as they darted around her in a feeding frenzy, reducing her to bone one bite at a time.

Sam vomited, expelling bile and bread, contributing to the growing cloud of blood and particulate flesh that quickly enveloped the grisly scene.

A face rose up through the billowing gore, a face so beautiful he nearly forgot to breathe. Nearly.

Air! Sam clawed for the surface. He was aware of the woman and her companions rising up through the water all around him.

He gasped as his head broke the surface and he breathed deeply.

"Ssssam."

He turned and found the woman just feet away from him. "Ssssam," she repeated.

One after another, three other voices echoed his name.

Treading water, he spun in a circle. He was surrounded.

"What do you want?" he yelled.

"Ssssam," they replied.

They were toying with him.

"Why did you kill, Emily?" he sobbed. "Why?"

Mocking laughter encircled him. Then one of the fiends tossed something at him. He dodged, and it splashed into the black water next to him, so close that a tangle of fine threads stuck to his face and neck.

His first thought was, *jellyfish*, but he had not been stung. Thankful, he brushed the threads away only to find himself staring at the remains of Emily's decapitated head.

With the sudden courage born of hopelessness, Sam glared at the woman that had thrown it. He kicked, lashed out, but the woman slipped smoothly beneath the waves. Before Sam could check his momentum, he felt a searing pain trace itself across his stomach.

He understood sharks and other marine predators, understood their role in the life of the sea; but these, these demons of the abyss, how could the ocean that he loved so much have spawned such evil?

The four, half-human creatures began to circle him with a slow, terrifying grace. They rose and dove like dolphins, closing the circle like a noose with each circuit. He could see them more clearly, there was no denying his own eyes.

Mermaids.

Sensing the end, Sam grabbed the floating tangle of hair and drew Emily's gnawed and ravaged head to himself. He clutched it protectively to his chest, a macabre comfort, as the mermaids began to paw at him.

"Ssssam. Sssssam. Ssssam," they chanted. Their slender hands swept over his arms, his legs, his neck as they toyed with him.

Sam hated the ocean, hated it more than he had ever loved it. How naive he had been. What a fool. The true ocean was no place for humans. He had a revelation as he clutched what remained of Emily. Hell was not an inferno. Hell was a watery grave.

The mermaids dove, slapping the surface with their tail fins as they slipped from sight.

His eyes went wide as they latched onto him with fang and claw.

"Emily," he whimpered just before they pulled him beneath the waves and began to devour him.

Originally from Michigan, **J.A. Johnson** resides in South Carolina with his wife and son and their golden retriever. He is an author, illustrator, and occasional puppeteer. His books include *Treasure of the Jaguar King*, the YA fantasy *Legends of the Coast* (which he also illustrated), as well as the ongoing Wild West fantasy series, *Dragons West*. He is the co-author of the ongoing, deep-sea thriller/monster series, *The Nereus Project*. He is the author/illustrator of the sci-fi comic book, *Skyfish*, and the children's picture book, *Squeaky, Squealy, and Oink*, and many other books. He is also the creator/puppeteer of the online drawing tutorial series, *Drawing with Cheesecake the Cat*. You can learn more about J.A. Johnson and his books at, *www.evanationstudios.com*

the marks of vailulu'u

L. MICHELLE TAGO-TU'ITUPOU

THE RHYTHM of the tapping was supposed to calm me. The teardrop that fell from my eye told a different story. One of pain and uncertainty. I had been preparing for this for so long. Then the teardrop after the first strike slipped through. I didn't mean for that to happen.

Heavy, calloused hands grabbed my fists, massaging my knuckles. I felt my body relaxing and my breathing became steady. I let the teardrop fall. I focused on those hands that I knew so well. The ones I used to watch as they weaved the thin strips of pandanus leaves into beautiful fine mats.

Then I heard her voice. Sese, my aunt, began telling me a story. The tapping faded away. I could faintly hear the *tufuga* and the *koso* singing in perfect harmony. My breathing became deep.

"You know the story of how the Samoans got the tattoo. Conjoined twins, Taemā and Tilafaigā, swam to Fiji to learn the art of tattooing. When they swam back to Samoa, they chanted, '*Tatā 'o fafine, 'a e lē tatā 'o tāne.*' Tattoo the women, not the men. At some point on the journey home the conjoined area on their back was cut apart by a clam shell. They reached Samoa exhausted and bewitched from the shell's dark magic. That's when the chant changed to '*Tatā 'o tāne, 'a e lē tatā 'o fafine.* Tattoo the men, not the women. The men were given the right to give and receive the tattoo, the *pe'a*. Even though that part of the chant was lost, certain women could still receive the *malu*.

"There's another story that is not told. At least by those who embraced Christianity. It was kept in secret circles, passed down to a very small group of families. There was another set of twins. We don't speak their names. They swam with Taemā and Tilafaigā. They learned the art of tattooing. On the return home, they followed different currents. It led them to the islands of Manu'a. And Vailulu'u. They were drawn to the power of the underwater volcano. Their song never changed.

"They continued the art of tattooing, but only the *malu*. The more they tattooed, the more they changed. Vailulu'u did something to them. Something powerful. Something cursed. People began to fear their skills. Daughters with their *malu* began disappearing. They blamed the twins who were soon chased into the water. They swam and never returned. Or so we thought.

"For a few years, everything was quiet. No one got the *malu*. On one of the darkest nights ever witnessed, when there was no moon in the heavens, people heard tapping. It was the *sausau* hitting the *'au*. The sound and rhythm were unmistakable. They chose our village, Nu'uuli, in which to return. Firelight could be seen far up the mountain, but it sounded as if the tapping was right here in the middle of the *malae*.

"Village elders and *'aumaga* jumped up and began running toward the light. The tapping continued. Shouts in the dark, men running around calling to each other. The tapping kept going. For three hours, chaos ruled the jungles. Then it stopped.

"The singing began. Softly at first. It started as it always does. *'O le mafua'aga lenei na iloa, o le taaga o le tatau i Samoa.* Something was wrong. The key. The pitch. They were mocking the story. Villagers began holding their ears and falling to their knees in pain.

"The firelight from the mountain moved slowly down a hidden path. It snaked through the village. Three women total. A young woman from the village with a new *malu* and two others walking beside her. Their eyes were black as night and skin glowed red, *malu* freshly oiled on their legs. The patterns gleamed as they danced their way toward the ocean. They spun *nifo'oti* in the air, catching it before the shark's teeth on the ends could slice their skin. They sneered at the villagers bowing before them.

"The final family that was passed were crying, tears streaming down their faces. One of the ladies dared to take her hand off her ear to reach out to the one with the fresh *malu*. Through the pain, she whispered her name. The girl looked at this woman on the ground.

"'It is the only way I can save you,' the girl said. The ground shook. She walked into the ocean, never to be seen again. The wailing of the villagers lasted throughout the night into the next. That's when they knew the twins of Vailulu'u had returned. The shaking stopped. Vailulu'u was appeased."

I was so mesmerized by the story, I was surprised when Aunty Sese kissed my forehead and whispered, "*Ua uma.*"

It was done. I had my *malu*. I stared at my legs in awe. My eyes began to focus on the patterns. They seemed to reach into my soul. I saw flashes of red. Maybe it was the trick of the light and the loss of blood. I thought I felt the earth move.

When I was ready, the *koso* helped me to my feet. That's when one of my younger cousins ran into the *fale* out of breath.

"Aunty, I saw them!" He cried. "By the river, with the big banyan tree."

"No..." Aunty Sese moaned. "*Vave! Fai le samaga!*"

I heard the *koso* scrambling to get the egg and oil for the blessing ceremony. If they could bless my *malu*, I would be safe.

"I saw them," my cousin continued, ignoring the chaos around him. His eyes were wide, and his face was pale. "They used the roots of the tree to crawl out of the water. They had fish tails that were black with patterns. When their whole bodies were on land, their tails changed into legs. With the *malu*. I ran here as fast as I could."

Throwing on my yellow *'ie*, I jumped on the *fala* sitting cross legged. I closed my eyes, waiting for the blessing that would protect me. I heard the egg crack. Feeling the air go quiet around us, I knew we were too late.

I felt their presence before I heard the singing. They had come for me. Standing at the edge of the *fale*, right outside the light, were two women.

"No," Aunty Sese whispered.

"Sese," one of the women nodded at my aunt. Her voice was a low alto. Her eyes were completely black, like a shark ready to feed.

"Aunty, how do they know you?" I asked quietly, my voice shaking.

"Sese, you little devil," the other woman laughed menacingly. She carried a *nifo'oti* on her shoulder. The shark's teeth glistened in the light as if newly polished.

"I had to tell her the story." Aunty Sese stood facing the two strangers. "She has to pass it on. There's no one else left."

The two women, with their unblinking eyes, just stared at my aunt. With their attention on her, I gestured to the *tufuga* to start the blessing. He shook his head, frozen in place. That's when I lost my temper.

"What do you want?" I barked. "Get out. *Alu 'ese!* This is my family house. You don't belong here, and you cannot step onto these sacred grounds."

Their laugh was low and harmonized, grinding on my ears.

"She's a strong one," they said together, as if they had one voice.

"That's why I knew she could survive," Aunty Sese said.

"Vailulu'u is drawn to her," one of the women said flatly. "And so are we. It is her time to protect and shelter. That's what the *malu* represents, *a ea?*"

We heard rumbling coming from *moana*. I looked up into the rafters of the *fale* to seek out my spear, the one my father gave me when I was a little girl. The village murmured because he was teaching his daughter how to fight. The boys stopped playing with me once I mastered the weapon and began beating them any chance I got. They called me reckless and wild. My mother sat proudly watching her only daughter flow with the wind. She said it looked like a graceful *siva*.

"Vailulu'u calls to you, does it not?" One of the twins cocked her head to the side. "We have seen you in our dreams."

"Do you sleep underwater?" I asked bluntly.

No one moved. The twin with the *nifo'oti* lowered it to point at the ground. I watched closely, figuring out the seconds it would take for her to get to me across the *fale*, and for me to grab my spear. My eyes narrowed, focusing on any twitch of their muscles, my body ready to spring into action.

"How long has it been since you've taken a *malu* to Vailulu'u?" I asked suddenly.

"*E te fia fa'ali'i?*" They replied together.

"But how long? Ten years? Twenty? A hundred?" I watched their unblinking eyes trying to gauge their thoughts.

"More than one hundred years," came the answer.

"And what happens if you don't take back a *malu* for Vailulu'u?" I was getting angrier by the minute.

"Vailulu'u seeks payment," one of the women answered. "Would you sacrifice one, or many?"

"Since it waited this long, could it wait a little longer?" My brain began forming a plan.

"Valasi, what are you doing?" Aunty Sese whispered, looking between the evil twins and myself.

Ignoring her, I looked at the *tufuga* and *koso*, before asking, "How about we make this a contest?"

"What do you propose, insolent child?" the twins hissed.

That's when I looked more closely at their features. Their teeth were sharp, like needles. Instead of fingers, they had claws, sharp and long. They were tall and thin, muscles rippling down their arms and legs. This wouldn't be easy.

"I say we hold a contest. Three tasks. Best out of three. I get to choose one. You get to choose one. And the final task," I paused tapping my fingers on the ground. "The final task is chosen by the *tufuga*. If I win, one of you is sacrificed to Vailulu'u. If you win, I will go willingly. What do you say?"

"Or, we could just take you," they said in unison.

"You could," I said thoughtfully. "But you can't, can you? You would have crossed the threshold by now, but something is holding you back."

The thunderous looks on their faces said it all. Something was stopping them from entering our *fale*. A light breeze blew in the smell of gardenia and freshly carved wood. Mom and Dad. They were protecting me.

"You can't stay in the *fale* forever. Even with the *samaga*, we have already seen your *malu*. As soon as you step out of the *fale*, you belong to us," they snarled, teeth clicking like the tapping of the *'au*.

"I know I can't stay here forever, but come on," I put my hands out convincingly. "What do you do underwater all day, every day, for one hundred years? You must be bored. You'll probably win. At least let's have some fun before you take me to Vailulu'u."

The twin holding the *nifo'oti* began spinning it in the air effortlessly.

"What do you say, sister?" she snarled. "Let's put this arrogant child to the test."

They both nodded and stood outside the *fale* as the blessing ceremony was performed. My *siva* at the end was somber, not the usual boisterous song and dance that follows such a joyous occasion. My angry tears turned to sorrow. I wished for my parents. They would have been so proud. I looked at my Aunty Sese, seeing a reflection of my father. "They are here," I could see her whisper across the room.

I was given one week to heal and prepare. On the day of the first task, the whole village and some brave souls from neighboring villages came to watch. Word had spread quickly. Most people were terrified, yet fascinated, by the twins. We heard them singing before we saw the *nifo'oti* spinning in the air. The villagers gave them a wide path. A gasp went up through the crowd when they saw the black eyes, the *malu* on display, the sharp teeth.

I stood with Aunty Sese at the end of the *malae* with my spear in hand. Our first task was the one I chose. A spear-throwing contest hitting moving targets. The one with the most hits would win the game. Two of my cousins, Afa and Miliona, lined up items to be thrown in the air from a catapult they made a few years back. They practiced with me when no one else would.

"Are you ready?" Aunty Sese asked. Everyone had become silent.

"How do we know you aren't cheating," one of the twins asked, glaring around her.

"I drew around the catapult so you'll know if it moves," my cousin Afa explained. "We also weighed and measured each of the items. You are welcome to come and check."

"No matter," the other twin said with a haughty voice. "We will win in the end."

The *tufuga* was chosen to announce each task. He stepped up, looking more confident than the week before, and stated the rules.

Each of us stepped up as items were thrown into the air. Things that would go slower were used first like coconuts and breadfruit. Then the items became smaller; nonu, mango, kapok, whizzed through the air.

The final item was a small guava. It was picked too early, about the size of a baby's fist. My heart pounded. I had always struggled with the smaller items. The twins went first. As adept as they were with the *nifo'oti*, they were not as good with a spear. They both missed, hissing at the spear then at the villagers. Everyone took a few steps back, afraid of what might happen if they looked these evil beings in the eye.

It was my turn. I tested the air flow. I breathed in and closed my eyes. When I opened them, I nodded. Afa pulled the lever.

I made sure to keep my eye on the catapult and watched as the item flew out of the basket. My eyes connected with the tiny guava and followed it through the air. Instinctively, my arm relaxed as I drew it back. I let out my breath and let the spear fly. Breathing hard, as if I had just run ten miles, I watched. Everything seemed as if it were in slow motion.

I saw the villagers jumping up and down before I heard the cheering and *fa'aumu*. I saw my spear in the distance, stuck in the ground, with the small guava sliced in half beside the blade. Aunty Sese's hand was on my shoulder. Her eyes were bright with tears. All she could do was nod. Afa and Miliona were giving each other high fives. They knew they played a big role in my success.

The twins seethed.

"The next task," the *tufuga* announced quickly, hoping to move things along, "was chosen by the twins."

We all moved to the ocean side across from my great-grandfather's old house. The twins pointed at the reef. Things began to shift in the water. I saw little fish and small octopi darting from the rocks as their living spaces moved. The ocean bubbled. When everything stopped moving, a maze was visible. The village gasped as one. The evil twins smirked. My heart, that had just settled down, sped up again. A swimming contest? Against two mermaids?

"At the blow of the conch shell, you will start," the *tufuga* called out. He looked pale as he saw the reef and pathway we would be taking. The uppermost part was very close to the deep blue of the ocean.

I stretched my arms and legs, cracking out the kinks in my neck. I had already resigned myself to losing this round. Regardless, I would swim as hard as I could.

The sound of the conch shell made me jump, then run into the water. I glanced to my side as the twins sauntered in. As they reached the water up to their waists, I saw the tails grow where their legs had been. They swished around, sand swirling beneath them.

I started swimming to the first obstacle. It was a tunnel within the reef. Purple sea urchins waved just underneath the water line.

These weren't the small ones my aunt used to find and eat. These were the larger flower urchins with sharp, venomous spines.

Taking a deep breath, I dove and swam. I tried to keep in the middle of the tunnel. The current was a little rough in this area. As much as I tried to keep going straight ahead, I kept drifting toward the spines that surrounded me. Soon, I felt a sting. Then another, then another. There was no use trying to avoid them so I just swam as hard as I could.

I surfaced on the other end. My head felt dizzy. Shaking it, I tried to focus and find the twins. Maybe they had blown the conch shell for the win, and I didn't hear it? Looking toward the shore, the villagers were still there, watching me. I could hear them cheering me on. My skin was still tingling. Looking down, I saw the spines. Pulling them out made my head clear a bit.

I started swimming again. Rounding the curve near the deep blue water, the hairs on the back of my neck stood up. There was a thin strip of reef between me and dorsal fins circling nearby.

I looked back when I heard water splashing behind me. The twins had just surfaced from the first obstacle. I heard them swearing as they pulled the flower urchin spines from their bodies. I made my way to the next obstacle. I couldn't believe I was beating them!

Diving under the next tunnel, I began to see blue bubbles creeping out of the holes. My heart lurched as I swam. The stinging began just a moment later. By the time I got out of the tunnel, I saw blue tentacles clinging to my exposed skin. Grabbing a smooth rock, I gently scraped the pieces off my body.

I heard more splashing and saw the mermaid twins shoot out of the second tunnel and leap into the air. They actually looked graceful and almost beautiful. Their tails were black, but you could still see the *malu* design. The patterns were glistening in the sunlight.

Hearing the villagers screaming, I stopped to tread water. A feeling of dread came over me as I saw something jump over the reef's barrier. A dark shadow moved toward me. The dorsal fin made an appearance above the water's surface. Turning around, I started swimming as fast as I could.

I could feel its presence behind me. I felt something bump into my leg and almost froze. There was no way I could outrun it. Treading water again, I tried to think. That's when my dad's voice floated into my head, and I remembered what to do.

I let myself go underwater. Black beady eyes stared at me. A tiger shark. Probably a young one, but a shark, nonetheless. It looked hungry.

As the shark neared, I reached out my hand, touching its nose. Pushing as hard as I could, I turned it away from me. The shark was now facing my path to the shore. Instinctively, I grabbed onto its gills and rode it toward the finish line.

The shark swerved as we reached shallower waters. I let go, half swimming and half running as my feet touched the sand. I heard the villagers yelling clearly. I was close to the finish line. If I won this race, I would win the wager. The finish line got closer and closer. Just when I was reaching the end, two tails darted past me. The conch shell blew. The villagers fell silent. The twins had won.

I stumbled out of the water then dropped to the sand. Aunty Sese came up with a towel and wrapped it around me. She looked at the wounds on the exposed parts of my body. Her look was thunderous. I grabbed her hand and held on tight.

"I'm okay," I breathed out. "I almost won."

"Almost is not going to save your life," she whispered, holding me tightly.

The twins stayed in the ocean, tails stirring the water around them.

"We will rest tonight," the *tufuga* called out to the village. "Tomorrow will be the final task."

Silently, everyone left. They would go to the comfort of their homes. The twins followed a pathway toward the deepest blue of the ocean. The maze closed as soon as they reached the outer edge of the reef. The dropping sun highlighted the black tails flipping in the air.

"*Sau*," Aunty Sese put her arm around my shoulder. "Let's get some rest."

The next morning, everyone gathered on the *malae* again. The *tufuga* waited for the twins to arrive then made his announcement.

"The final task is a hunt for a sacred item," he said to murmurs from the crowd. "Each of you is allowed one weapon. They are not to be used on each other. Only on things you may encounter.

"The clue is in Logomē." The *tufuga* looked pointedly at me.

I breathed in sharply. Logomē was a place where people went and were lost, not physically, but mentally. Well, I thought, if I lose, at least I won't be thinking clearly when the mermaids take me to Vailulu'u.

"Look for the place where the ancestors rest," the *tufuga* announced, then signaled for the conch shell to blow.

Surprised at how quickly we were starting, I only had time to give Aunty Sese, Afa, and Miliona a quick hug before taking off running with my spear. The twins jogged beside me. They looked relaxed, *nifo'oti* sitting lightly on their shoulders. Sighing, I turned to focus on the clue.

Pushing my way through vines and underbrush, I aimed for the old graves of the Manu'a chiefs. They were large rock structures almost in the middle of the small jungle space. I hoped the mermaids wouldn't follow me. I knew approximately where the graves were located from stories my parents told me when I was young.

I finally saw the mounds ahead of me after a few minutes. As I approached, I could feel something watching me. My skin prickled.

Whispering quietly, I bowed my head saying, "*Tulou lava.*"

The feeling that spirits were surrounding me disappeared. I felt comforted. I had heard stories of villagers coming onto the sacred land only to exit with a fever that lasted many moon risings. They would toss and turn during this sickness talking about things they saw. Those stories made my skin crawl.

I walked around the large mounds. Rocks bigger than my head

were stacked four layers high with a flat area at the top. The entire structure was covered in moss and vines. The area smelled of earth, some places rotting. I looked into crevices and on the ground to see if anything had been disturbed. Nothing was there. Continuing my pacing, I kept repeating the *tufuga's* words. The place where the ancestors rest. The place where the ancestors rest. The place where the...

I was in the wrong area. Yes, these were the old chiefs of Manu'a, but not the ancestors. Not the Nu'uuli ancestors. We weren't looking for a burial ground. Going back into the jungle, I reached a clearing not far from the burial mounds. The place where the ancestors rest. It wasn't a riddle. It was a literal place where the Nu'uuli ancestors would rest when they would visit Logomē. There were several smaller rock structures in the area. Some were used to hold items; others were used to lean against. I walked quickly, looking for the clue.

A breeze blew through the area shifting leaves overhead. With a streak of sunlight, I saw a rock glistening to my right. It was stuck into one of the mounds. Grabbing it, I read the next clue. 'In shallow waters, near a lonely rise, leaves of green grab hold. A rock of life, small piece to take, with a story to be told. From the waters, feet will make, legs on sand unfold."

I heard the twins crashing through the brush. Taking off with the rock, I ran toward the Pala Lagoon. The waters were shallow and there was a lot of seaweed. That had to be the first part. Catching my breath on the shore, I saw a small islet several yards from the shoreline. That had to be the rise.

I jumped as I heard yelling then squeals. Those were not human. Crashing sounds echoed around me. I turned with my spear, trying to see through the tangled leaves. To my left, the twins came flying from the jungle. Their *nifo'oti* lifted in the air. One of their weapons had some specks of blood. Whatever they'd hit hadn't died. It sounded really angry.

A flash of brown and white barreled through the trees. Before the tusks of the beast could hit me, I jumped into the water. It was shallow and only came up to my knees. Out of the corner of my eye, I saw the twins as they turned into their mermaid form. I silently cursed them and their carelessness before diving toward the islet. The boar, thank the gods, stayed put on land.

Seaweed and undergrowth from mangrove trees slowed the twins' progress. I was able to half swim; half pull myself through the water. Climbing onto the small piece of land, I looked around for rocks that brought life. I saw basalt and regular types of earth. Leaning over the side, a flash came as the current flowed. I put my head underwater and reached, grasping something that came off in a small, fist sized piece. It was lava rock. Rock of life!

I jumped back into the water and headed for shore. The twins were right behind me. We swam away from where we entered, just in case the boar was hiding and waiting. The twins' tails took a few seconds to turn into legs. That gave me a head start.

I could hear their breath behind me as we ran back to the village. Branches and vines whipped my face, legs, and arms. I heard grunting from the side, which made me run faster. The tusks came into view before the rest of the body did. In a split second, I jabbed my spear into the body of the hulking beast then hurdled over it. My spear came out easily as I continued to run.

We all reached the *malae* at the same time. I bent over trying to catch my breath. The twins stood there, black eyes almost lifeless. Neither one was out of breath. We all held out the lava rock at the same time.

The conch shell didn't blow. I looked at the *tufuga*, confused. The mermaids continued with their blank stare.

Think, I told myself. Then I remembered.

"Tagaloa created everything," I began. "He made the water. Then he pulled the land from it."

"Humans thought once the land was raised," one of the twins continued, "all would be well."

"Tagaloa never stopped creating," the other twin chimed in. "Humans cannot see it, but creation continues."

They were referring to Vailulu'u. The lava rocks brought new life. We could feel its presence when the earth moved, when the water boiled, but we always forgot. Until the next earthquake. Or the next *malu*.

The conch shell blew.

The color of moana *changed as I went deeper into her depths. From a light, translucent blue to a darker, midnight color like the night sky at its most quiet time. Only there are no stars to light the way. Fish with built-in lights flashed, distracting me with their antics. Claw-like fingers wrapped tightly around my wrist. I saw the smiles filled with sharp teeth. Somehow, I could hear their voices. They were singing a song in a minor key. I realized what song it was. The patterns on my legs began to ache, almost as if I were receiving the marks for a second time.*

The twins dragged me through the water. I could see the glow forming in the deepest part of moana. *Vailulu'u was beautiful. Bubbles of bright red rose from a mound of volcanic rock and basalt. Just when I thought they would reach us, the bubbles would implode. It was beautiful. And terrifying.*

It had been a tie. We had all finished the final task. Now it was up to Vailulu'u to decide. Which one of us would be sacrificed to end her cravings for another hundred years? I had said my final goodbyes. I shed no tears. I knew my fate and if it would keep my people safe, so be it.

The twins let go of my arm. The three of us floated together, looking at the glory of Vailulu'u. The swirl of steam and silt became mesmerizing. The swirl surrounded us. I closed my eyes. The screams in the deep blue ocean were like nothing I've ever heard before, or since. They tore at my eardrums. My insides felt as if they were on fire. I reached out to Vailulu'u.

I awoke on the sand, Aunty Sese's face looming over me. I sat up and looked out beyond the reef. My *malu* was still intact. The screams were gone. Afa and Miliona came running over and helped me stand up.

"Valasi, you're alive!" they both cried, hugging me tightly.

We started walking toward home. In the light of the setting sun, my *malu* began to glow.

L. Michelle Tago-Tu'itupou was born and raised in American Samoa in the proud village of Nu'uuli to a Samoan dad and a Palagi (Caucasian) mom. As the middle child of five siblings, she loved to lose herself in books. While eating lots of chocolate. She passed on her love for reading and storytelling (and chocolate!) to her four daughters. She plans to continue writing so that Pasifika communities around the world can see themselves in stories written for and about them by someone who is "them." Michelle currently lives in Salt Lake City, Utah with her husband, four daughters, and two dogs, dreaming of returning to the ocean to feel the sand between her toes.

apex predators

ZACH SHEPHARD

THEY CALL ME "BLOODSUCKER" and corner me under the jungle moon. With pathetic spears they impale me, and I dismember three for the insult. Alas, I'm eventually overwhelmed.

Not knowing about wooden stakes, they cannot end me. Instead they bind me to a raft, at the ocean's mercy. Come sunrise, I'll expire.

I spot my salvation: a woman with a shimmering tail for legs, far out to sea. Her lifeblood could grant me the strength to break my bonds. My gaze beckons her over, mesmerizing.

She approaches. When she smiles, I realize my mistake.

Her fangs are larger than mine.

Zach Shephard lives in Enumclaw, Washington, where he occasionally writes fantasy, science fiction, and horror stories. Most of his work is either humorous or dark, with very little middle ground. (If you're reading something of Zach's and haven't at least chuckled by the end of the first page, you can safely assume the protagonist is in for a rough time.) He's had stories appear in places like *Fantasy & Science Fiction*, the Unidentified

Funny Objects anthology series, and a number of Flame Tree Publishing's gorgeous Gothic Fantasy books.

Zach's interests include board games, exercise, a medically concerning level of sugar intake, and chronic back pain. His life is filled with regret and *Home Alone* quotes.

For more of Zach's work, check out zachshephard.com

the daughters of atargatis

PAUL STANSBURY

A Pantoum

DEEP UNDER THE SEA, the mermaids do dance,
  When Atargatis's daughters are stirred.
  And sailors look about with furtive glance,
  When the sweet calls of the sirens are heard.

When Atargatis's daughters are stirred,
  Up from the cold, murky depths they arise.
  When the sweet calls of the sirens are heard,
  Many a sailor has met his demise.

Up from the cold, murky depths they arise,
  The mermaids' desires are most devious.
  Many a sailor has met his demise,
  Falling prey to their spells mischievous.

. . .

The mermaids' desires are most devious,
    The warm flesh of mortals is their desire.
    Falling prey to their spells mischievous,
    The fate of those so enchanted is dire.

The warm flesh of mortals is their desire,
    A mermaid's kiss bodes a watery grave.
    The fate of those so enchanted is dire,
    Your final resting place marked by a wave.

A mermaid's kiss bodes a watery grave.
    Once caught, men can never escape their trance.
    Your final resting place marked by a wave,
    Deep in the sea, where the mermaids do dance.

Paul Stansbury is a Kentucky native, author of *Inversion—Not Your Ordinary Stories; Inversion II—Creatures, Fairies, and Haints, Oh My!; Inversion III—The Lighter Shades of Greys; Inversion IV—Another Infusion of Speculative Fiction;* and *Down By the Creek—Ripples and Reflections.* Over one hundred of his works have been published. His speculative fiction stories have appeared in a number of print anthologies as well as a variety of online publications. His poetry has appeared in *The Rising Phoenix Review, Young Ravens Literary Review, Strange Poetry*, and *Kentucky Monthly* and read as part of a concert, *A Woman's Life,* by the choral group, Sounding Joy. He is Scheduling Coordinator for The Jeanne Penn Lane Celebration of Kentucky Writers. He is the owner of Sheppard Press. Now retired, he lives in Danville, Kentucky.

the lost ones of earth and sea

JULIA VEE

WHEN THE WITCH of Monterey agreed to meet me, I sent a prayer to the moon that she would find my son. I would pay anything, do anything, for his safe return. No cost was too high—even banishment.

The witch waited for me on the shore at dawn. My great white escorts couldn't continue through the kelp forest, so I swam alone through the shallow waters of the cove and the tall tangle of brown algae towers. I rose in mist and sand, a swirl of seawater obscuring my transformation.

My gills lay flat and my nostrils flared as I adjusted to the air. My scales faded down to a faint girdle above my hips. Where I had strong fins and a tail before, I now had two pale green legs. Weak legs.

I hated wearing them here.

My feelings were not shared by the younger jiaoren. They longed to abandon the deep reaches of the Pacific Ocean that were our home. They wanted to run on the land with humans.

But humans were dangerous. They exploited us. They coveted our silk. When they wounded us, we cried pearls. That only made them torture us more.

We had fled the warm seas to come here to this wild place. But after millennia, their ships were everywhere, their numbers, prolific.

Stay hidden. Do not show them what we are.

That was our one guiding tenet and those who broke it were banished.

I would break it a thousand times if it meant I could bring Luk home.

The witch stood like stone on the shore, her hands deep in the pockets of a gray trench coat, her legs anchored in black rubber boots. Her black hair whipped about her as the ocean winds roared with my slow approach.

I unwound the seasilk I'd braided into my hair and pulled it flat. Light and strong, the shimmering fabric dried in an instant. The seasilk we wove radiated illusion. If I wrapped it around me, humans would not see a tall, muscular woman with pale green skin —they'd see what their mind told them to see and have only the vaguest memories of it.

Seasilk wouldn't fool the witch. She saw deeply. She saw me truly as I was, the Queen of Sharks. I was not in the least bit human, for all my humanoid form. I stood before her, armored in a chitin chest plate and a serpentine blade at my hip.

But I didn't wrap it around me. It was not mine—it belonged to my son.

We said nothing for long moments. I needed her, and she would demand a boon. That was how she worked. If I was lucky, she would not call on me for a few turns of the moon. But I would take what I could get because I came to her not as a queen but as a mother.

It would have to be enough.

I handed her Luk's seasilk. She ran it through her fingers, and the expression on her face shifted from aloofness to curiosity. She was Wu, an oneiromancer of old, and her curse was to travel the dreams of others. For me and others desperate like me, it meant she could tell us whether our missing loved ones still lived because the dead didn't dream.

"Can you tell me if Luk is still alive?"

She held out her palm.

I pressed a silken pouch laden with pearls into it. She hefted it before putting it in her coat pocket.

"I haven't walked with your kind before, but I will try."

Wu's eyes reminded me of the ocean at night, gray at the surface, black in its depths. She raised the seasilk to her pale cheek, her eyes going half-mast. Seconds passed. Then minutes. Her eyelashes fluttered as I waited, and it felt endless.

An eternity later, her eyes snapped open and that far-seeing gaze drilled into me. "He lives."

My heartbeat raced and hope made me dizzy. He was alive! The only thing that mattered was getting him back.

"Where is he?"

"That's a different price altogether."

"More gems?"

"A boon."

I would have given the witch a prince's body weight in pearls and other treasure. But that was not her price. She demanded something rarer.

I nodded and removed the serpentine blade I wore. The green stone of the knife was cool and sharp. I wedged the tip of the blade into a large scale above my right hip bone and pried loose the scale. Blood welled up, hot and red against my cool skin.

I gestured to her left arm. "Give me your hand."

She obeyed and I turned it palm out. I pierced the tender flesh with the tip of the blade. Her blood welled up, coppery hot. My nostrils flared and the sweet scent hit me hard. Witch blood was more potent than most. I pressed my scale there, melding it to blood and skin. Despite the dim gray of morning light and drizzle, it gleamed, pearly and iridescent like the inside of an abalone shell. It pulsed over her blood. As if it were still on my body. It lived on her skin as it had lived on mine. This was our jiaoren magic, one of transmutation.

My thumb was covered in the witch's blood. I brought it up to my face and tasted the salt of her lifebood and dreams. I bared my razor-sharp teeth at her. She didn't flinch.

"When you find him, you can summon me thus."

Our dreams were not like human dreams. We were creatures of the deep and our lives had a stillness and timeless quality, unlike humans with their life squandered in minutes and seconds of frenetic activity. We saw things where no human machines could ever venture. I wondered how Wu could handle so many visions, but the purple shadows under her eyes told me that maybe she didn't handle it well. Maybe the flip side of walking while others slept was to not ever truly rest.

I left the witch and returned to the sea with hope in my heart. I dove into the kelp forest and willed forth my change, summoning my tail and fins. If I swam a little slower, it was to savor these precious moments in my home—before my inevitable banishment once they discovered what I had done. I had broken our sacred rule, and it felt like a betrayal to question why we still had this rule when all it did was cause us to lose our kin to the land.

I greeted my shark escort and sent them thoughts of their prince. We were aligned in this. Nothing was more important than bringing him home to the sea. Their immense white bodies cut through the water with menace, their flat eyes promising retribution to those who would interfere.

We swam south along the coastline and I emerged in the royal grotto. The air scoured my skin and raked my lungs after the cocoon of the sea. This was where we were safe from humans. Here, I didn't resent my legs. Here, they were my choice. The smooth limestone walls rose high above me, graceful arches and crags. The grotto was a maze of clearings where we could meet, create, rest, or study. Though we avoided humans, we never ceased to study them. We kept the things they valued—the gold, the weapons, and trinkets.

Two bottlenose dolphins popped up in the grotto pool, their clicks and squeaks greeting me. I had swum with them since they were calves. Luk had named them Smiles and Pip, one for his perpetual grin and the other for the little sound he made when he was playing.

I preferred my dolphin companions, but as a royal I had an image to uphold. We flexed our power and dominion with the fearsome visage of the great whites. Only the royals were able to communicate and influence these sharks. I appreciated their strength, but our interactions lacked the warmth of my dolphin companions. The dolphins were smarter, and I felt more connected with them as our young grew up together.

Smiles butted my hand with his snout and I gave him a fond pat. "Soon, Luk will be home to swim and hunt with you."

He clicked in reply and I sent them off to return to their pod before I went to my chambers. Once, I'd had everything—a consort and our son. Now these rooms were empty of life, holding only my seasilk robes, chitin armor, and swords.

I shook off the memories and donned my robes. I wasn't cold but they would hide the wound of my missing scale from prying eyes. When Luk had gone missing, I'd dismissed my attendants and guards. Now I was glad for it because it meant I could hide my transgression a little longer.

As always, the feel of the seasilk was a comfort, and I braided a long swathe of it into my hair.

I walked to the weaving area, searching for distraction from the waiting. The witch had said Luk was alive, and the rest demanded my patience. The looms were still, and the sea silk hung in shimmering swathes. It was our art and our shroud. Even in my banishment, my people would leave me with my silk.

Because I knew that's what this would come to. Everyone knew the prince was missing. When I garnered his return, there would be no way to squelch what had happened. The punishment was banishment, mine and Luk's. But I would fight to the death for him to stay.

I passed the looms and wandered through the archway to the research area. The chamber was piled high with the detritus we had taken from shipwrecks and drowned sailors. Here we learned their languages, studied their maps, and played with their toys.

Luk loved their art and their musical instruments and had a vast array of them across a long plinth. His favorite had been the jade horse.

"Have you ever seen a horse, mother?"

"Years ago, when we roamed freely on land."

"Have you ridden one?"

"No, Luk."

His young face had been wistful, and he'd run around the room with that polished jade horse in hand.

I thought of the way I swam with the orcas and how free I felt on the ocean. Maybe humans felt that way when they rode horses.

I'd been more partial to the swords. The metals had rusted away long ago but the gems on the ceremonial hilts still glittered. I picked up the nephrite daggers that were as sharp as when they had been carved millennia ago. My serpentine blade was the milky green of a lagoon, held a wicked edge, and never rusted. It had been my father's before me, and his father's before him, the official symbol of our authority.

Weapons were one thing we had quickly adopted from the humans. But maybe Luk had been onto something, and we should have spent more time on appreciating their art and their music.

"Mei Mei, you should rest."

I whirled around to face the speaker. It was our great general, one who wielded the might of the sea—my cousin Rōng.

While his words said one thing, his tone and informal address said, "You're weak and unfit."

We were the same height and broad build, but physical attributes aside, we could not be more different. Where my training had been spent on history and diplomacy, his time had been spent on military strategy.

Rōng's seasilk robes were dyed by squid ink, their folds dark as a starless night. His black hair was streaked with white and braided into a waterfall of small plaits that were knotted in a single larger twist. He looked dignified and strong, like a good general should.

We jiaoren were many, but our pods spread out far. It was not so much a kingdom as vast collection of tribes under one silk banner. Rōng wielded the coral spear of his rank, but he would not be satisfied until he held the serpentine blade I carried as well.

I wasn't his little sister. But when others weren't present, he didn't accede to my status as his ruler and referred to me as Mei Mei. He was older, and we had the same grandsire. But for the accident of birth, he would be King now instead of me.

"Thank you for your concern." I knew better than to get into an argument with him.

"Any news of our Luk?"

"I am confident he will return soon."

Rōng's voice took on a soothing note. "I hope for all our sakes, that is true..."

He paused. "...We should be making alternate arrangements should the worst come to pass," he concluded.

Our kind often had curiosity of humans. Luk especially so. Visiting land was not forbidden, but mingling was. If we lived among humans as humans a full turn of the moon, we were jiaoren no longer. Our skin would fade, our teeth would dull, and our fins could no longer be summoned. Time was running out for Luk, which is why I had gone to the witch.

Rōng's concern rang hollow. With Luk missing, I had no heirs of my body. Should anything happen to me, Rōng would take the throne. Some of the advisors would no doubt welcome it. We were long-lived, but the ocean was a vast and dangerous place. Our gifts let us commune with the creatures of the deep, but we had no such luck with humans and ships. We were constantly evading them, retreating lower into the deep.

Rōng wanted to go on the offense, to use our ocean allies to create a boundary and enforce our territory. To no longer be hidden.

I also didn't want to stay hidden, but I didn't want to go to war with the humans. We needed to negotiate. We needed intermediaries. I believed in diplomacy, lest we continue to lose our more free-spirited kin. Like my consort. And now my son.

"Your intelligence assets will be reporting in soon?"

Rōng gave me a noncommittal shrug. "They have much territory to cover."

And they were loyal to their general.

This is why I was counting on the witch. Because I knew Rōng had nothing to gain by finding Luk.

Pain smashed into my hip, radiating outward in dull throbs. It was from the wound of my missing scale—the witch was summoning me. My pulse skyrocketed and I struggled to stay upright. I prayed to the moon that my face didn't reveal anything to Rōng. Maybe he would think any pain he saw was attributable to Luk. I had to get rid of Rōng and answer the witch's call.

"Thank you for your report, General." I injected at much authority as I could into my voice.

His lips twisted at my dismissal and he gave me a perfunctory bow before turning away.

I waited three heartbeats, then three more. After I was sure my cousin had left the area, I walked quickly to the grotto pool. No one could see me or interfere. Then I slipped into the water, my fins flaring with a satisfying rush. I pumped hard, and this time did not summon my shark escorts. They couldn't cross the kelp forest anyway.

In the end, I wasn't alone. Smiles and Pip followed me, their sleek bodies cutting through the water to give me a smoother path to the witch's cove. It was as if they had sensed that Luk was close. Their pod spread out around us, near but not pressing. Their sounds and thoughts soothed me during our swim. It was a comfort that I hadn't known I needed.

We navigated the waving stalks of the towering kelp, and at last, I rose from the waves. I tied my silk around me and walked through the fog. Three figures stood on the shore and my heart leapt in my throat.

Though the witch and another man were there, I had eyes only for Luk.

He looked thinner. His skin no longer held the green of the sea. But his eyes were my eyes, and his blood was my blood. When his arms wrapped around me in a hug, hot tears fell down my cheeks, pearls scattering to the sand.

The young man next to Luk cleared his throat, and I now gave him a thorough once-over. His skin was smooth and brown, and he wore his dark hair closely cropped. One of his eyes had a milky tint and that's when I noticed his fingertips lightly resting on Luk's shoulder. "Luk, you should introduce us."

Luk smiled and his eyes crinkled like upside down half-moons. "Mother, this is Gabriel. Gabriel, this is Nǚwáng."

Gabriel extended his other hand. "So nice to meet you, Nǚwáng."

My son had given my title rather than my name.

I didn't want to shake this man's hand. I didn't like the way Luk looked at him. It was the way I had looked at my consort—with stars in my eyes.

The witch said nothing, her fathomless eyes taking in our tableau.

The moment stretched out and finally I took Gabriel's hand. His skin radiated heat like he was lit by the sun. I saw the pulse of his lifeblood and how his vitality shone from him. It burned me.

I dropped his hand and turned to my son. "Luk, we don't have much time."

He shook his head. "I'm not going back."

"Please. The moon turns soon."

He shook his head again and despair swamped me. If he'd come back with me, at least we'd have more time, talk it over further.

I tried again. "It doesn't have to be all or nothing, Luk."

"For me, it is. This is everything."

Again, that look that said he'd found what he was looking for.

My shoulders sagged in defeat.

I pressed my hands against Gabriel's cheeks and drank in his dear, dear face. I kissed his forehead and closed my eyes. His hair smelled like linen and sunshine. Like a human. I gave him my blessing.

"Open seas, my son."

"Open seas, mother."

My heart split cleanly in two, leaving me hollowed out inside.

I turned to the witch. "You knew."

She hesitated. "When I saw his dreamline, he was happy. It was filled with love."

Her sentimental characterization hurt so I rushed to conclude our business. "You brought him to me, so our bargain is fulfilled."

She held out her palm. Though I hadn't asked, she added, "It was love from his childhood memories too."

Tears burned my eyes, but I held them back. With a flick of my serpentine blade, I cut my finger and pressed it against her palm. My scale pulsed as I fed it my blood.

The witch tilted her head, curiosity in her gaze but all she said was, "I will take my boon shortly."

"You know how to call me."

Luk pressed his palms together and bowed low, his last tribute to me not as his mother but as his sovereign.

When I dove back to the sea, there were no more tears. I was going home empty handed, but I had seen Luk one last time.

Pip nudged me gently as we swam through the kelp and I leaned against his small body, drawing comfort from him and Smiles.

But did it have to be the last time I saw Luk? Now that he wasn't returning, no one else knew what I had done. I could hide my involvement with the witch and work towards a compromise— a way to see Luk again. A way for all our people to see all our lost ones again.

Emerging into the open sea, I was nearly blinded as a massive wall of smooth gray-white flesh slammed into my head and neck. Stunned, I flipped to the side and glided back through the wake of bubbles left behind by the great white. I sent a command to halt but was met with a wall of resistance as if it were shielded.

Only another of the royal line could do that. The shark's attack had been only a gentle nudge rather than a killing blow. My cousin wanted to talk. I pushed hard, my tail undulating with a powerful beat. Smiles lifted me, the force of his fins and mine propelling us rapidly toward the surface.

Rōng awaited me there, his face twisted in disgust. He had scouts everywhere and he knew what I had done. I hadn't been careful enough.

"Your line is weak, you are weak," he spat.

"You overstep yourself, General."

My punishment would be banishment, but it wasn't up to him to enforce. He could go to the council and I would abdicate.

The shark swam around us both in wide circles. It was well and truly bonded to my cousin. I hadn't been able to pry its mind from Rōng's control. I wanted to summon my own escort, but they were far away and wouldn't get to me in time.

"Your reign is over. Maybe you can find your consort on land," Rōng sneered.

My head and heart were already sore. Rōng's words sent anger coursing through my veins. I had given everything for my people, lost everything while following their tenets. And it was for nothing. So that this warmonger could usurp my place. It was wrong. He was wrong.

"Poor little general. How can you show your worth when there is no war to fight?" I taunted.

He lunged at me and I darted away.

"More valuable than you and your worthless son!"

I bared my teeth at him. "I'm still your sovereign."

"No one will miss you," he snarled. Madness glinted in his eyes, sparking a hint of fear in me.

The shark circled tighter and now I realized that he didn't have to tell anyone what had happened. I had dismissed my normal bevy of attendants and guards. I had come to the witch without my own shark escort. I was alone and if my cousin wanted to do away with me now, it was the perfect time. I would be declared missing and Rōng would take the throne. Just as he'd always wanted.

The shark's fin dipped with menace and I drew my blade. Waves slammed over us and I sank low to see the shark's approach.

A mass of small bodies surrounded us, appearing from all directions. Relief flooded me as I saw Pip and Smiles lead the charge to attack the great white. Their beaks were relentless, but my relief was short-lived as Rōng's hands closed around my neck.

His fingers were brutal around my gills, the pain muted only by my struggle to breathe. Instinctively I reached to pull his hands away.

And then I remembered my knife. I stabbed wildy upward, my arm feeling sluggish.

The blade glanced off his ribcage and he tightened his chokehold. My vision narrowed and I didn't want to die like this, with his face as the last one I saw. My thoughts scattered but I tried to reach Pip and any other member of his pod.

My tail beat upward, tilting us back in a macabre dance that forced Rōng's fingers to slide and free up the barest edge of my gills. Sweet relief flooded me and I aimed the knife higher, under his exposed armpit.

I looked into his eyes and smiled as my blade slid home. From behind him, Pip's beak rammed down. Rōng's eyes and mouth opened wide, and a ghastly outpouring of bubbles and dark blood streamed out. We were locked together and I felt his death throes as he bled out.

Goodbye, cousin.

I wrenched my blade free and relinquished the body. It lingered there, his face a mask of eternal disbelief. I couldn't bear to look at it. Pip nudged me and I held onto him, his compact frame pulling us up to the surface. I gasped the harsh air and sobbed. Once I started, I couldn't stop, great wracking shudders ripping through me. The pod of dolphins surrounded me, keeping me afloat, comforting me with gentle clicks of sound.

At last, I could draw breath without crying. Pearls fell from my body. The sky loomed above me, gray and muted. Seagulls squawked in the distance and waves lapped against my skin.

I was still here. I drew in another deep shuddering breath, feeling my ribcage expand.

Luk was still alive. I still had a chance to work for reconciliation of land and sea. As long as I drew breath, I could work towards that. I would work towards that.

For me. For all of us.

Open seas.

Julia Vee is a writer with a passion for magic, monsters, and the rich flavors of East Asian cuisine. Born in Macao and raised in Northern California, Vee's academic focus on Asian Studies at U.C Berkeley deepened her appreciation for the history and lore of the region. With over two decades of experience as a trial lawyer in Silicon Valley, Vee has always made room for her creative pursuits, as well as teaching courses on business and property law as an adjunct faculty member in colleges and law schools.

Outside the courtroom, Vee's heart beats strongest for the fantastical. A graduate of the Viable Paradise residential workshop, Vee collaborates with co-author Ken Bebelle to craft thrilling fantasy stories that blend action and East Asian elements. Their forthcoming trilogy, beginning with *Ebony Gate* (July 2023) and followed by *Blood Jade* in July 2024, from Tor Books, promises to transport readers to a world of wonder.

beneath the deepening sea

E.H. GASKINS

Sailors dread the depths of the Deepening Sea. There are things there that no man was ever meant to see.

I FOUND MYSELF, young and wide-eyed, on the bow of a brigantine, headed to whatever desolate tract of land we could find. I was intoxicated with the thought of discovering new places and plants and creatures to cull my appetite for learning. A fledgling naturalist, philosophic and free to roam, fed the chance of a lifetime to look for new life to study, with the *RMS Descartes* as my vessel, a gift granted by the crown itself.

Then the storm came, and with it, the horror.

As the waves rocked and the clouds crackled with fearsome thunder, the tentacles tangled about the deck, taking their hold around the hull. Forty sailors fell victim to the dreaded deep, and the tendrils took me.

Panicking, I was pulled to the depths of the Deepening Sea. Descending slowly, I suffered the sickening weight of the water. The air was squeezed from my screaming lungs by the cold. But no matter how deep I went—how desperately I begged to die—I could not. The horror below left me living, unimpressed by my mortal plight.

It dragged me down, down, until light became void, and the weight of the water threatened to crush my bones into gems. And then, I descended no deeper.

Finally facing the being, I found it not a faceless freak, but an angelic humanoid set upon a sprout of tentacles blacker than the steep noir of the Deepening Sea.

"Speak," said he, in a voice not unkind.

"Can I?" asked I, finding my voice not audible, but transmitted betwixt our minds. I gazed in wonder at the beast in the deep and asked, "Why do you leave me alive? Here, where no mortal man should be?"

"I've told you once, I want to hear you speak," said he, "here in the depths of the Deepening Sea."

I knew not what to say—what could he want to hear from me? What knowledge could I hope to give he who dwelled in the bosom of the deep?

"What say you," asked he when I did not speak, "of the knowledge of the world? Do you find the finding of facts pleasing or flighting?"

"Pleasing," said I. "There is no higher honor than to stretch one's intellect to its border."

The mermyd slid a pitch tentacle across his porcelain chin and peered at me with pensive eyes of sparkling sapphire.

"And you," asked he, "who values his intellect above all other, do you see this call to honor as a prided privilege or caustic curse?"

"A privilege, surely," said I without a hesitant thought. "It is a gift for thinking minds to think. For to not have a thinking mind, that is the curse. It is the thing that allows us to know we truly *are*, and not simply *could be*."

The monster lingered in tidewater static silence.

"And what of you, great beast of the Deepening Sea?" asked I, growing brazenly bolder, the heat of my curiosity warming my chill-brittled bones.

"I once thought as you, that the pursuit of knowledge was noblest, though now I think to be a fool would be freer."

I was shocked, a sketch of surprise. "You think it freeing to be a fool? To have the simple mind of a moron?"

"You think to be simpler is to be an imbecile? That one cannot navigate the wonders of life without a wealth of knowledge?"

I quickly considered. "I think many make do justly. They meander about their meager lives, unconcerned with the knowledge that could be. I suppose that you could call them lucky, unaware that they languish in a haze of ignorance. And I suppose, then, that the intellectual is cursed with the gnawing desire for knowledge."

"And yet you still seek it?"

"Unwaveringly."

The creature considered once more, glancing upward to the farthest hint of the surface light. "I've dragged you far down into the depths of the Deepening Sea—too far for any mortal to have a hope of surviving."

I felt Death's chill grip wrap around my heart, ready to wrench the life from my already frigid chest. The porcelain monster's eyes returned to mine.

"You, who are so engulfed in his own philosophies, do you want to linger in this life?"

"I very much do wish to linger," said I, "for there is so much left to learn. But I fear, as you said, should you release me here, I shall be crushed by the depths of the Deepening Sea."

"It is true, you would not return to your world above unscathed," said he. "When you tread the depths, there is always a mark remaining. But let me posit a proposition for you, fragile mortal. Two paths, but you may only stride one. I can let you return to the surface, but your mind will be tainted by the tides. You will live as a normal man, capable of maintaining a normal profession, but your craving for knowledge of the world will be lost. Or, you can stay here, in the depths, and I will give you all there is to know."

It was my turn to peer toward the world above, contemplating the choice set in front of my feet. "To secure all the knowledge of the world is what I've set out to do. It is what excites me most, but to be confined below the seas, that is not appealing."

"So you choose to return as a simple man?"

"No," I said slowly. "For it is also the greatest fear of the scholar to be stricken with simpleness."

"So you choose the depths?"

There was a precious pause, a minute or a millennium, I could not know. I carefully searched the corners of my mind for the answer, but perhaps I should have searched my soul.

"I value my life, and I do wish to continue to do so above. But, to take away the intricate workings of my mind is to give up myself. So, I will do it, oh, Beast of the Deep. I will stay here in the bosom of the sea, with all the knowledge of the world to share with the currents."

The creature nodded, its face shimmering in the black water. "So be it."

I felt the sea tug against me, a swirling waterspout in the deep. I lurched toward the beast, guided not by my limbs or his tendrils, but by the water itself. The world flipped on its head, and I began to lurch and contort, a victim to some vicious morph.

And then, just as quickly as it had started, it was done.

I was no longer a blood-and-bone man, but a cosmic deity of the deep. I'd become omniscient, an all-knowing being confined to the tidewaters. In front of me floated a boy, not unlike my former self, who wore a face like porcelain. He smiled at me as he ascended to the surface, an expression I knew was reaped from the feeling of freedom.

I know now that the boy was the monster I met in the deeps of the sea. And now I, as he, crave simplicity. I float across the ocean floor, searching for ships above to bring down into my ichor dark. I hope to find a fool who thinks himself a master of the mind who might give me what the beast offered so very long ago.

Until then, I wait, in the crushing cold black, praying to a God I now know is not there, that I may one day escape the depths of the Deepening Sea.

Raised on *Lord of the Rings, Star Wars*, and *Dungeons & Dragons*, **Ethan (E.H.) Gaskins** (not surprisingly) adores everything science fiction and fantasy. He holds his MFA in Creative Writing from Western Colorado University and his B.A. in Philosophy from East Carolina University. Originally from the Carolinas, Ethan currently lives in Denver with his fiancée and four rambunctious pets. He's a jack of many trades, desperately trying to master at least one. That's why, although he hass worked in marketing, a retail pharmacy, and even spent several years as a tanker in the Marine Corps Reserve, his heart lies with creating the most wondrous fictional worlds and characters he can.

fading song at midnight

CHRISTOPHER BAXTER

THE DRAGON CRASHED against the rusty gate, snarling and hissing. It belched flames, but the old runes along the bars flared white-hot, containing the fire.

"Hey, girl," Niketa whispered. She'd hoped that the old drake would calm down once she arrived; her elfin blood tended to endear her to beasts. But no luck. It'd gotten a taste of human flesh—virgin, what was worse—and had gone feral.

She aimed her revolver between its eyes. The runic bullet pierced scales and skull with ease.

The dragon collapsed. Niketa rested a hand on its snout until it was completely still. Then, sighing, she left. The ranch hands would butcher it—the drake's scales, bones, spit, blood, and meat would be worth a fair haul.

She headed down the slope to her farmhouse. Her muscles were sore and she'd gotten burned along one arm that morning. It'd been a damn long day.

Her son Dweym waited on the porch, head low. His bandaged arm rested in a sling.

"Sorry, ma," he muttered. "I know she were one a' your favorites."

Niketa entered the kitchen. "Ain't your fault, boy." At the basin, she washed the splattered, steaming blood from her hands.

"I shoulda been more careful."

"That's true. But sometimes it don't matter—dragons'll get the better of you."

"She coulda laid two or three more clutches at her age."

"No use frettin'. Had to be done, and that's that. Ain't the first blood-mad dragon we put down, won't be the last."

She patted her son's cheek—boy was almost taller than her already, though that was no great feat. Took after his father, with tiny tusks that jutted up just past his lip, but with her dark coloring.

"Get your brothers and help with the butcherin'. And send your sister in to help me."

Dweym frowned. "Ain't seen Veli since you took her to the upper eyries this mornin'."

"I sent her home with Russet n' Mynalynn—she's probably at their cabin. Fetch her for me?"

Dweym nodded and hurried away. Niketa started chopping vegetables, shaking her head. Russet and Mynalynn stole Veli away at least twice a week. Ladies needed to get about having one of their own.

But when Dweym returned, he was alone. "Ain't nobody home. And ain't no mud on the step—don't think anyone's been in since it rained this afternoon."

Niketa stared at the fire, worrying over the mountain paths and their dangers. They'd checked every trail Russet and Mynalynn could have taken and had found nothing. Now they had search parties ranging the mountains in the darkness. She needed to get back out there. The flames danced, sparks drifting.

"Hey." Creyne shook her gently. "Y'still here?"

Niketa started. She hadn't heard her husband approach. "Sorry," she muttered. "Done got lost in the fire."

"Got a signal from left-hand fork," he said. "You wanna wait here?"

"No chance." She led the way to their tethered wyvern. Creyne took the reins and she clung to the back of his duster as the wyvern leapt into the sky.

Creyne sat straight and broad-shouldered, unbowed by a day of wrangling dragons and a night of searching. She stretched her sore shoulders, a little envious—troll-blooded folk like Creyne tended to stay energetic and healthy longer than others. All that her elfin ancestry seemed to have left her of late was a tendency to get distracted by fire when she was tired. Weren't fair.

They flew into the mountain valleys and circled down to a wooded vale. Niketa almost slid out of the saddle to squint at the clearing below. Most of the ranch hands were clustered around a flickering signal fire, which threatened to consume her attention; but she managed to spot two bodies lying beneath the trees.

"Gods," she gasped. "Russet and Mynalynn?"

"Might be so." Creyne's words were muffled by the icy wind and the heavy flap of the wyvern's wings, but Niketa caught the tight worry in his voice.

She wrapped her arms around his chest, hoping she'd been wrong. But as the autumn-brown clearing drew nearer, she was able to get a better look at the bodies—one woman with skin almost as dark as her own, and one short and pale with honey-colored hair. It was them.

As the wyvern settled to the ground, Niketa leapt from the saddle and ducked under the flapping wings to check the bodies. She couldn't see any injury, and they were still warm. She felt for a pulse.

"They's alive." MacDugan, one of their oldest workers, approached. His face was as weathered and gnarled as any of the gray pines. "But we can't wake 'em."

"What happened?" Creyne called as he dismounted, at the

same time as Niketa burst out, "Where's Veli?"

"Ah... don't rightly know," MacDugan replied. "On neither count. But we found 'em o'er here." He gestured with a lamp into the trees. "There's, ah... somethin' odd goin' on."

They followed MacDugan into the woods, the warmth of the bonfire fading to autumn mountain cold. As she ducked beneath a low branch, Niketa caught an unexpected scent in the air. She paused, bewildered. It was a scent of salt and brine—of the ocean. But it was also oddly sweet, like a flower right at your nose.

Old memories burst through her. It was the smell of the Aethereal Lands.

She caught Creyne's arm. "You smell that?"

He sniffed the air and frowned. "Is that...?"

Niketa realized suddenly that she was clutching Creyne's arm too hard, her fingers digging into his skin. She let him go and picked her way lightly over the rocky ground. Creyne stumbled along just behind her, cursing the uneven footing.

MacDugan stopped beside a towering dead pine, its bare branches like white bones in the night. The trees ahead looked no different from those behind, but she could feel a boundary before her, a line where the world began to change into something else.

"A fading," she whispered.

Creyne looked around. "What?"

"An opening into the Aethereal Lands." Niketa eyed the forest ahead, wary. Elfin could open these passages, but it was a long and difficult process—most of the flighty fair folk had no patience for it. Usually, fadings appeared and vanished on their own, at the whim of the Aethereal Lands themselves. How had this found her?

When Creyne placed a calming hand on her shoulder, she realized that her breathing had grown ragged.

"The woods, uh... *change* up ahead," MacDugan said. "We found Russet n' Myna out there. Then some've the other workers started passin' out."

"The air over there is poison," Creyne said. "Veli's probably asleep somewhere close."

"Maybe." Niketa could feel the effects of that air drifting through the fading—it soothed her, calming her more painful emotions. It felt... wonderful. She hated it. She ground her teeth, trying to clear her mind. "Veli's elfin enough; she might could be awake. Lost."

Creyne turned to MacDugan. "You got everyone else out of there?"

The old man nodded. "Most woke up right quick. We're just lucky the song stopped."

Niketa felt like someone had dropped her into a frozen pond. "What song?"

"A woman—prettiest voice I ever heard." MacDugan eyes went wistful. "Drew us right in. Was downright painful, when she stopped..." He shook himself. "But I don't think any of us woulda come back, if she hadn't."

The calmness of the Aethereal air was gone. "Get everyone back to the ranch." Niketa spun and ran back to the wyvern.

"Niketa?" Creyne called, following. "What is it?"

"A siren." Niketa dug through the saddlebags. "Lures folks to their deaths. Get everyone outta Dodge before she sings again."

Creyne and MacDugan shouted orders. The ranch hands were soon carrying Russet and Mynalynn down the trail, with MacDugan bringing up the rear. Creyne stepped to Niketa's side.

"So it lures people to their deaths," he whispered, "...you thinkin' that's what happened to Veli?"

"No. I think she took Veli to get me to follow."

"You...?" Creyne frowned, comprehension dawning on his face. "Wait, so this is *personal*? That thing came here for you?" His voice grew louder. "For our daughter?"

"Seems that way." Niketa removed a small box of matches and a flask of flammable dragon spit from the saddlebags and slipped them into her pocket.

Creyne took a slow, calming breath and patted the wyvern, which had gotten skittish. "How do we deal with this?"

"You go in there, and come five minutes you'll be snorin'." She took a deep breath. "I'll get Veli."

Creyne grimaced but didn't argue. The man was stubborn, but knew reason when he heard it. Usually.

In a large sack behind the saddle, Niketa found a length of narrow iron chain that they sometimes used to tether the wyvern. It wasn't pure-forged, but it might could weaken a full-blooded elfin. She hung the coil on the back of her belt, hidden under her duster.

"You get gone, hear? 'Fore she starts singing again."

"I can't follow you, but I ain't leavin', neither."

"Idjit." She went up on tip-toes to kiss him. Then she headed back into the trees.

Creyne followed. "What's to stop this thing from bewitching you?"

"I'll... I'll manage."

They stopped beside the dead pine. Creyne frowned, chewing his lip in obvious frustration. Then he slipped his heavy revolver from its holster and held it out. "Just in case."

Niketa stared at the pistol's black wooden grip. She'd left hers on the saddle. "This ain't gonna be that kind of problem."

Creyne held out the revolver for a few more seconds before letting his arm fall. Niketa cupped his cheek in her hand. Then the first few words of a song reached her ears. She knew the voice, high and perfect. The sound pulled at Niketa's mind and heart, drawing forth a painful longing. She stepped forward without thinking.

Creyne caught her arm. "You okay?"

She looked up at him, standing firm, his eyes worried. He didn't seem inclined in the slightest to follow the song. Stubborn as a mule. She forced a smile and kissed him.

"Don't follow me, hear? Not one step. Ain't gonna do us any good if you pass out over there."

Creyne nodded. "I'll be right here."

Niketa squeezed his hand and turned to face the fading. The music pulled her, and the air of the Aethereal Lands clouded her thoughts. She'd never wanted to go back here again, and she'd never wanted to deal with Lideia again. Her mind fought instinctively against the siren song, urging her to turn and run. She was afraid, but not for her life.

If she returned to the Aethereal Lands... could she come back?

Niketa took a slow breath. Her daughter needed her. She crossed the boundary. After a few steps, she began to catch glimpses of greener growth at the edge of her vision. The grass poking through the rocks grew lush, until finally it obscured the rocks from view. The trees grew thick and tall, their trunks a deep green that was almost black. After a hundred paces, she'd entered a completely different wood, an ancient forest the likes of which couldn't be found within weeks of her dry, dusty ranch.

But most noticeable was the air—warm, humid, and thick, almost smothering, but in a way that felt like a comfortable blanket wrapping around you on a cold evening. Mercy, she hated admitting it... but she had missed that air.

The siren song was clearer here, beautiful and melancholy. It told her the path to take, reassured her that she was going where she ought. Even though she followed it, she fought against its hold on her mind. She was going where *she* wanted.

Finally, the trees parted, revealing a tall bluff overlooking the black waves of an ocean. Teal clouds drifted across the slate-gray sky, and golden stars left blazing fire-trails as they burned slowly through the heavens.

A gravel path switched back and forth down the bluff toward a beach of night-blue sand. Sitting on a gray rock out in the water was Veli, happily kicking her feet in the surf while the wind tousled her dark hair. And beside her sat Lideia.

Part of Niketa had still been hoping that somehow, by pure happenstance, some strange siren had lured Veli here all unknowing. But even from this distance, Lideia was unmistakable. Her skin was pale as marble and her long, feathery hair was the deep teal of the clouds reflected in the dark ocean waters, the same shade as her long tail.

Niketa started down the trail toward the beach. Lideia stopped singing. Niketa could feel the siren's eyes following her. When she reached the sand, Lideia slipped from the rock and floated gently with the surf to the shore. Veli remained on the rock and waved with a dreamy smile.

Niketa forced a smile and waved back, relieved to find her daughter alive and well. She noted, though, that Lideia had left Veli where Niketa couldn't reach her—but where the ocean could.

The surf surged around Lideia. When it withdrew, her tail had vanished; she walked on a pair of long, pale legs. A sheer white dress, like sea foam that had decided not to return with the tide, only accentuated her curves. Niketa forced her gaze to stay on Lideia's sky-gray eyes.

"Oh, Niketa. I have spent so long looking for you." Her voice was melodious, even when speaking. She pursed her lips in a sympathetic wince. "Look at you. What has become of you?"

"Lideia," Niketa replied. "Why're you here?"

"You've gotten so *old*, and you look so tired." Lideia circled her. "If only you'd stayed in the Aethereal Lands, love."

Niketa flushed, but she kept her chin high and her eyes on the siren. Lideia studied her with a mix of pity and smugness. Niketa was acutely aware that Lideia looked the same as she had twenty years past—as perfect as ever.

"You're dirty, too." Lideia gestured toward the sea, and the waves rushed forward in response. "You should take a bath."

"You ain't gonna make me feel bad about myself, Lideia," Niketa snapped. "Get to the point. What're you doing here?"

"Oh stars, *listen* to you—why are you talking like that?" Lideia's eyes were wide and perplexed. "You sound like a *troll*."

Niketa clenched her jaw. She remembered the tone in Lideia's voice—once, she would have called it teasing. But after so many years away from the elfin folk, she could hear it for the cruelty it was.

"Bring me my daughter."

"She's fine, don't worry. Don't be so tense." Lideia smirked, walking down the beach. "Come on—I was serious about that bath."

"Lideia!" Niketa shouted, the words echoing off the rocks. "You have *kidnapped* my daughter. Give her *back*."

Lideia's looked shocked. "No. No, I didn't."

"You did." Niketa sighed. Elfin folk—*her* folk—could be self-centered to the point of blindness. She'd once been that way herself. Gods, she didn't want to be here. "Bring her to me."

"That's *not* what..." Lideia shouted, clenching her fists at her side. The winds picked up and the black seawater surged forward up the shore—and crashed over the rock where Veli sat, nearly washing the girl away. Niketa jumped, alarmed, but Veli simply giggled.

Lideia let out her breath. "Look, I'm... *sorry,* okay?" The mocking cruelty was gone from her voice. "I just wanted you to come here."

"Okay." Niketa tried to keep her tone neutral. She didn't dare upset Lideia as long as Veli was on that rock. "What for?"

Lideia smiled slightly, a real smile, and shrugged. "To save you, I guess."

Niketa stared. "To save me."

"Yes."

"From what?"

Lideia rolled her eyes. "From this!" She waved her hands at Niketa. "From your *life!* I came to bring you home, where you can be happy again."

Niketa shook her head slowly. "Lideia, I am happy where I'm at."

"Oh, please," Lideia scoffed. "I can see that you're not. Not like we used to be."

Niketa glanced past the siren. Veli had pulled her feet up onto the rock, safe for now—but the surf was growing agitated again, reflecting Lideia's mood.

"Look, Lideia... why don't you come stay with us a few days? See my life, my family, for yourself."

Lideia stepped back, a look of disgust on her face. "I'm not staying with a *troll*." She stalked across the beach to a black rock that jutted up, waist high, from the blue sand. "And I've seen your life."

Niketa glanced again at Veli and then followed the siren. The top of the rock was hollow, forming a shallow bowl filled with clear water.

"A watchin' pool," Niketa breathed. As with fadings, most elfin knew how to make them, but rarely took the time.

Lideia plunged her hand into the water without even a single ripple. The pool began to glow with images: Niketa's farmhouse, her sons sitting up worried on the porch, her dragons in their dens.

"You work yourself to exhaustion taking care of that troll's dragons," Lideia said. The pool showed Niketa, earlier that day, wrestling a feisty grey serpent. "Then you stagger home in the evening to give up your sleep over fussing children. You're perpetually tired, dirty, and sore. And for what?" The image in the pool shifted, showing Creyne. Niketa frowned—he stood on this side of the fading, in the Aethereal Lands, holding his breath.

"For a troll. A *troll*, Niketa." Lideia's expression was a mix of fury and heartbreak. "You *know* they're monsters. How they've hunted our people. My song doesn't even affect him—he doesn't have the heart, the *soul*, to hear it properly. Look at him!" She hit the water with her free hand, sending a single ripple across the surface. "He doesn't respect you. He promised to wait on the other side of the fading, and yet here he is. All trolls care for is themselves, and you've *always* known that."

Niketa bit back a sharp reply—the waves and wind were growing rough again, splashing up onto the rock where Veli sat.

"Auntie Lidi," Veli called. Her voice sounded drowsy. "I'm gettin' cold."

"You'll be fine," Lideia replied, absently waving a hand. She let the image in the watching pool fade away.

Niketa took a deep breath. "Lideia, please—"

"Come back home with me," Lideia interrupted, catching

Niketa's hands. "This is where you belong—with your people. I know you feel it."

Niketa winced and looked away. She *could* feel the air of the Aethereal Lands working into her, calming her. Calling her back to her old life. Lideia's proximity, her voice, her smell—all of it brought back memories, and most of them weren't bad.

Lideia pulled Niketa down the shore. "You were so happy here, in the wilds by the ocean. Remember? You can be happy again."

It was tempting. Niketa had known it would be, but even so, she hadn't been prepared to face it. The taste of the Aethereal air, the call of the wilds, of a life free of work or responsibilities. Days running through the trees, nights dancing round clearings to satyr music. With Lideia.

She looked up and met the siren's eyes—so eager and hopeful. Desperate. Niketa winced and pulled Lideia to a stop. The wind and waves picked up again, worse than before.

"Lideia, I'm married now. And my children—"

"No, I know!" Lideia blurted. "I understand. You always wanted children, wanted to try living like the mortals. I never listened. But that's why I called to her first." She waved toward Veli. "We can take her with us. She can be ours, together. You can have it all. Your daughter, your people... me."

"I have more than one child, Lideia."

Lideia blinked, confused. Niketa sighed. To elfin folk, children were inconsequential; young elfin were turned loose into the wild to survive—or not—on their own. Lideia probably couldn't grasp why Niketa would be concerned with having all four of hers.

But Lideia nodded anyway, without any understanding in her eyes. "All right. Fine. We'll get the others, then. Bring them all."

"Auntie Lidi!" Veli shouted. The girl was standing with her arms wrapped around herself. "It's cold. Please get me off the rock."

"Not right now!" Lideia snapped. A wave surged over the rock, sweeping Veli's feet out from under her. Niketa's heart jumped into her throat as Veli fell, barely catching herself on her perch.

Niketa pulled her hands free. "Lideia, I made my choice a long time ago. I'm makin' it again. *Please*—accept that. Let me take my daughter home."

The wind began to howl, and the waves rolled higher and higher. And then it all went still. Lideia stared at Niketa, her face cold.

"Fine," Lideia said. "Veli!" she called in a sing-song tone. "Come here, dear."

A large wave swept Veli from her perch. Niketa cried out, but her daughter was fine—the wave cradled her to shore.

"Come here," Lideia said, still sing-song, holding out her hand. Veli ran up the shore and took it, smiling. "Veli, your mother wants to take you home."

Veli's face fell. She turned distant, sleepy eyes to Niketa.

"Time to go home, dear," Niketa said, holding out her arms.

"I wanna stay here."

"We need to go home."

Veli stepped back to hide behind Lideia's pale legs. "No. Auntie Lidi told me I could live here, and I won't have to do no chores or go to bed when I don't wanna."

Niketa stared at her daughter, startled by how detached she sounded. How elfin.

"Well, Niketa?" Lideia arched an eyebrow. "The girl has made her choice. Weren't you just saying something about respecting choices?"

Niketa clenched her teeth. Then she swept Veli onto her shoulder, carrying her like a stubborn hog. "When you're grown, girl, you can decide to go wherever you like. But right now you're comin' home." Veli kicked and screamed, but Niketa was used to wrangling upset dragons.

Lideia caught her by the arm. "She wants to stay, Niketa." The siren's voice was ice. "Leave her here."

Niketa slipped her free hand into her pocket for the flask of dragon spit. "We're leavin', Lideia." Behind her back, she poured the spit out onto the sand.

Anger flashed through the siren's eyes, the cold, petty fury of the elfin. Then Lideia's face smoothed into a smile. "I want her to stay here," she said in the sing-song tone she'd used to call Veli before.

Niketa felt an urge to set her daughter down, a subtle prompting similar to the siren's full song. "You've gotten good at that." She slipped her hand into her pocket again and pulled out a match.

Lideia opened her mouth, still smiling, and then frowned— she'd spotted the match. The wind howled, and the waves crashed. Niketa struck the match with her fingernail and dropped it into the dragon spit.

The fire flared, and Lideia's eyes went vacant. She stared at the flames with her mouth agape. Niketa pulled free of the siren's grasp and stumbled away, running for the trail to the forest.

Then a massive wave crashed into her back, throwing her into the rocky bluffs. She twisted to protect Veli from the blow. She hit the cliffside, and the air left her lungs. The water washed away, dragging her along.

"You want to come with me, Niketa," Lideia said. The words became a song, surging through Niketa's mind, obliterating thought. She *did* want to go; so badly that it hurt. Lideia pulled her to her feet, smiling and singing. Stars, not a day had gone by that Niketa hadn't missed this woman. They had been perfect together. They were—

A wet hand closed about Niketa's ankle. She looked down to find Veli laying in the blue sand, shivering and coughing up water. Her eyes were terrified and confused.

Niketa stared at her daughter, concern warring with the song in her ears. The song that told her to leave the girl. Her daughter. Niketa took a deep breath, reached under her coat for the iron chain, and wrapped it around her fist.

She punched Lideia in the face. The siren dropped to the sand like a poleaxed steer, unmoving.

Niketa scooped up her daughter and ran up the trail that climbed the bluffs. She needed to be out of hearing range before

Lideia awoke. The trees enveloped them, muffling the dull roar of the ocean. Niketa slipped and tripped in the damp undergrowth as she worked her way back toward the fading.

The song tore through the quiet forest like a bullet through flesh. It assaulted Niketa's mind and heart. Niketa clenched her teeth and pressed forward. She couldn't cover her ears without setting down Veli, and the girl had begun struggling again, fighting to go back. Each step was harder to take than the one before it. Niketa soon realized that she had begun to turn, twisting gradually back toward the ocean.

She groaned and righted herself, her head pulsing with the effort. Her next step didn't find ground where she'd expected, and she tumbled down a slippery slope, clutching Veli to her chest.

When they reached the bottom, Veli began to claw her way back up the hill, screaming. Niketa clung to her, but couldn't summon the stamina to move forward again. The song was growing louder, drowning out her thoughts.

A shadow fell over them. Creyne scooped them into his arms. Niketa held tight to Veli and pressed her head to her husband's chest, listening to his heart beat.

Creyne ran to the fading, his face red from holding his breath. The vibrant greenery around them grew dull and pale, and the grass grew brittle and yellow. The trees slowly became shorter and thinner until they were once again beside the dead pine. Creyne collapsed, gasping. Niketa held her husband and her daughter tight, panting, praying that the song would end. It didn't.

Veli tried to escape. Niketa pushed her into Creyne's arms. "Get her away from here."

Creyne nodded, panting. "What about you?"

Trembling, Niketa pulled the pistol from his hip. "I'll be back soon."

She took a deep breath of the crisp, dry mountain air and returned through the fading. The song pulled her forward—she ran through the darkness, letting it guide her steps.

Lideia stood on the sand beside the watching pool, her hair

disheveled and speckled with sand. A dark bruise was swelling up across her cheekbone. Her eyes were stormy, but she smiled grimly when she spotted Niketa climbing down the bluff.

Niketa stopped at the edge of the sand, raised the revolver in both hands, and fired—high enough that she knew it wouldn't hit the siren, but low enough that Lideia probably felt the bullet pass. Lideia's song ended with a startled yelp. She stared at Niketa, incredulous.

"That's your only warnin' shot."

"You... I..." Lideia's face firmed into appalled anger. "I'm trying to *help* you!"

Niketa sighed. "Factually, Lideia... I know it. I know you are. But now my daughter's safe, I need to make a few matters clear." Niketa took a few slow steps forward. "First off, I didn't leave home because I wanted a family."

Lideia frowned. "What?"

"I left 'cause I realized that I didn't like who I was back then. So I left to see who else I could be. And I found a place for myself."

"With a dirty troll?" Lideia snarled.

"I know our kind's had trouble with 'em in the past, but he ain't what you say and I can damn well be with anyone I please, understand?"

"You're not happy!" Lideia shouted over the rising wind. Behind her, the waves crashed up the shore, roaring. "How can you not see it?"

"I'm tired," Niketa admitted. "I'm sore. The kids and the dragons've all done a number on me. My life is hard. But I love it. I'm happier than I've ever been. Don't care how it looks to you—no one gets to tell me otherwise."

Lideia shook her head. "This isn't who you are!"

"That *ain't* your call to make." Niketa stepped close enough to be sure Lideia heard her over the ocean and the wind. The rich air of the Aethereal Lands calmed her, beckoned her back. But she had a better home. And she would do what was needed to keep it safe.

"Lideia, I... I know you don't understand. I wish you could. What I want just ain't what you are. Don't mean I don't still... care for you. I don't want you to leave here angry with me." She raised the revolver. "But understand—you're gonna leave, without another verse. And you ain't gonna come back."

Lideia's face twisted in cold fury. "Someday you'll return. The Aethereal Lands are calling to you—I can see that you want them. You want *me*."

"Probably always will." Niketa swallowed and shook her head. "But I've wanted a lot of things in my life, and I can't have 'em all. No one can. I've chosen what I want most, and it ain't you. You can deal with that however you like, as long as it's away from me and mine."

Slowly, the wind and the waves quieted. Lideia glared at Niketa. Then she shrugged and looked away. "Fine."

Niketa's stomach dropped. She knew Lideia—she could hear the lie in the siren's voice, see it in her refusal to meet Niketa's eyes.

"Just go, Lideia," she whispered. "Please."

Lideia pursed her lips, petulant, furious—greedy. She inhaled, a breath too deep for just speaking. She opened her mouth.

Niketa pulled the trigger.

Christopher Baxter got in trouble for reading books in class from kindergarten through high school. To stop his teachers from getting upset, he began writing stories instead (it looked like he was taking notes). This tactic proved to be effective through college and all sorts of jobs, too, so he never stopped. You can find more of his projects, from the 2022 Baen Fantasy Adventure Award to *A More Civilized Podcast* at Writerinthehat.com.

my ex comes in with the tide

M. LOPES DA SILVA

my ex comes in with the tide
　　　she crashes
against the shore beats
my window with fingers
drums knives in the water that trickles down
my hairline to call me coward, gently

　　　coward
　　　　　coward

her tremble fingering the lobe of my ear she
whispers about the old dreams I wish
we'd never had, the ones she won't let die
pledged drunk fizzy in cherry soda anticipation by young fools

　　　us
　　　　　us

and on long REM shores eternal rolls the rocks she delights
over cutting off my feet
and becoming foam together

M. LOPES DA SILVA (HE/THEY/SHE) is a white Latinx, non-binary trans masc and bisexual author from Los Angeles. They write pulp and poetry, and sometimes the two get mixed up together. Their poetry has been published in *is this up*, *The Dead Inside*, and Electric Literature. Dread Stone Press just published his first novelette *What Ate the Angels*—a queer vore sludgefest that travels beneath the streets of Los Angeles—as part of their new Split series.

the last ounce of flesh

KEN BEBELLE

I ELUDED *my captors and won my freedom three hundred years ago,
and yet I still revisit my imprisonment in my dreams.*

*A moment of youthful foolishness led to my bondage. I swam too close to
examine a boat, bobbing in the waves off the coast of Nihon. Darkness
sweeps up from beneath and then a tangle of ropes and wriggling fish drags
me out of the water, dangling over the prow of the boat. The Walkers on the
boat shout and point at me. Pinned by the weight of the ropes, I can't even
raise my arms to defend myself as one of them clubs me across the face.*

*I awake in water that tastes wrong and stings my gills. I thrash and
slam my face into something hard and clear, as if the water simply stops
before my face. This will be my prison for years.*

*The enclosure is a pale mockery of my home, barely enough water for
me to turn around, the glass painted with broad strokes of blue and green. I
think they are meant to evoke the kelp forests, but they just seem like bars on
the windows. The water is tepid and stale with the stink of my waste and
my fear. My prison sits inside a tent of stained canvas with a dirt floor. A
rusting brazier stands at the other end, filling the air with oily smoke and
fitful light. When I raise my head from the rank water I choke on the
ash-laden air.*

The Walkers hold me here as a curiosity. They come to see me, to make faces of disgust and horror, to thump the glass with their fists and hammer my ears. It is an unending parade of shame and humiliation.

And yet it is not the worst.

I have come to recognize those who are not satisfied with the simple terror of my appearance. They come dressed in rich clothing and painted faces, followed by a train of simpering attendants. The man who enters my tent tonight wears a jikitotsu of embroidered green and silver silk over jet-black hakama. The sword at his side is housed in a scabbard of dark wood inlaid with mother of pearl. His servants bow and scrape as he examines me.

He looks at me and nods approvingly. "Ningyo. A rare find, indeed."

Behind him, my jailer bows low. "We have kept her in good health, daimyo."

The daimyo snaps his fingers.

I know what comes next.

What comes next is grasping hands, roiling water, and chaos. Thick, smoke-filled air scrapes my throat as they drag me out of my prison. I fight and writhe, but strong hands throw me to the dirt and hold me down. I tell myself I will be silent, I will not give them the satisfaction.

Cold steel bites my flesh and I cry out in agony. The daimyo smiles at my pain and passes a heavy bag to my jailers.

The Walkers bind my wound and pour me back into my prison, my body violated, my mind shattered. It is my turn to watch in horror as the man nibbles delicately at a bloody chunk of my flesh. I turn away as he greedily swallows.

I float in my prison, in water that stinks of my blood. In time, my body heals and I wait, dread filling my days, for another Walker who fancies a taste of forbidden flesh.

My crutches scrape against the polished hardwood of the table as I adjust my seat, trying to find a comfortable position. It is nearly impossible since my feet dangle above the floor. If only the shaman had made the flesh mask with longer legs. I lean back and stretch my hip, willing the ache in my knee to quiet down enough for me to read the menu.

Not that it matters. What I am looking for won't be on the menu. At least, not any menu that would be put down on paper.

Enough time passes that the waiter is starting to look uncomfortable. Long silences tend to do that, and in a moment I know he will clear his throat, or offer a suggestion. Something to fill the quiet. It is a rather irritating trait of their entire species. A byproduct of lives spent in constant, noisy communion with each other. How I long for the quiet darkness of home, where the softest sound carries the most weight.

I look up at my beleaguered waiter and make eye contact before he can make any of his inane throat noises.

"I'd like to see another menu." Talking like this always irritates my throat. I pick up the water glass and swallow some of the cool, tasteless liquid.

The waiter seems to understand me after a moment. "I'm sorry, miss, is there something specific you're looking for?"

I set the glass down on the table, the linen cloth rough across my arm. The remaining water in the glass trembles. I squash my anxiety before it can show, and the water stills. "I'd like to see the *other* menu."

When the waiter hesitates I wave him off. "Ask your superior to attend to me, if you are unable to fulfill my wishes."

Visibly flustered, the waiter moves off, leaving the private room through a door blocked with discreet silk privacy screens. Graceful impressions of koi are painted on the silk in stark strokes of black ink with sparse red accents. The restaurant's decor is aligned with the privacy screens—elegant and understated. Furniture made from real wood, a rarity in these times of scarcity, hand crafted and finished to exacting standards that have not been seen in over three hundred years. Very few appreciate the quality on display here, but the details leap out at me like a blazing neon sign.

Edomae has been open since last week, a simple, brash name for a new restaurant in the middle of Kagurazaka Street. Nestled amidst buildings that reflect more modern architecture and materials, Edomae is a paragon of elegantly simple black wood and polished stonework.

Sato Ren, Edomae's owner, is known to be a ruthless businessman, with intellect as sharp as the creases in his slacks, and a taste for running his competition to their graves. He learned his trade at his father's side and assumed ownership of their conglomerate only a few years ago. His venture into small, chic restaurants is something of a hobby.

I shift again in my seat as I wait, trying to keep my irritation off my face. The face is already itchy enough without making it worse by doing anything other than smiling through it. I paid a fortune for this face, it would be a shame to ruin it early.

The waiter's superior enters the room, an older woman with a competent look. She gives me a placating smile.

"Is there something special you wished to order?"

My limbs feel heavy and slow, and my eyes burn. Beneath the flesh mask that smiles at the woman, my face is hot in the confined space. I pray this is worth it. I just want this to be over. "I have heard you serve ningyo."

The woman's eyes flick briefly to my crutches and back. Her smile does not falter. "I'm sorry, I don't know—"

"Ningyo. Fish-man. Or fish-woman, whatever you have in the tank. I don't care. "

The woman hesitates, and I know I am in the right place. She only needs something to help her make the decision. I beckon her closer so I can give that to her. She leans in and I whisper a name into her ear.

It is an old name, not used in many years, but popular during the Edo period. Her eyes widen a fraction and sweat breaks out on her neck. Even in the stale air of this room I can taste her anxiety on my lips. She backs away, her eyes darting around the room.

"Excuse me, I will go ask."

I dismiss her.

The *kyokubadan* is hardly even that, a ragtag collection of what the Walkers consider oddities, held on display in dirty canvas tents. Those like me. Sometimes I am the only one in my tent. Other times I may share the tent with a bear, or a kirin. At least, I think it is a kirin. It is hard to tell because the creature is filthy and covered in oozing sores.

I make a morose game of trying to guess which of us will perish first.

I hope it is me.

The *daimyo* in the green and silver silks returns, this time with a younger man behind him, also dressed in green and silver. The elder man gestures to my tank and barks an order.

I fight. I always fight, hoping that I can make it too hard for them, to make it cost too much to take my flesh.

It never works.

They pin me down, gasping like a mindless fish. The *daimyo's* eyes blaze with greed. The younger man looks uncertain, perhaps he is about to be sick.

The steel bites through my scales and I scream. I can't help it, can't hold back, even though I hate myself for showing weakness. The younger man flinches back at the raw sound of my voice. His elbow jerks and strikes the smoking brazier. The shadows tip and dance as the brazier falls over.

The tent ignites and then everything is shouting voices, flickering orange light, blistering heat, and choking smoke. I wriggle and this time, my captors lose their grip. I drag myself to the edge of the tent, a layer of cheap, burning canvas separating me from freedom. The flames lick at my body as I plunge through and into the cool darkness of night.

The briny smell of home calls to me, so close. It is dark, too dark for the Walkers to see, but it is not nearly as dark as the bottom of the sea. I can see well enough to evade my captors and drag myself to the edge of the small village. From there I find my way down a small hill to a narrow beach, and frothing, salty waves. I plunge into the cold, welcoming waters.

The next figure to enter the private room is Sato himself. Like his unassuming name, he too, is easily forgettable. An average haircut, atop an average frame, dressed in clothing that is clean and functional, but not stylish or noteworthy. It is the disguise of a man who has learned to hide in plain sight. He may not be a daimyo's son anymore, but he still carries himself with the arrogance of wealth and privilege.

He holds an ornate covered tray in one hand and he sits across from me. Like the waitress, his eyes also notice my crutches.

"Are you sure you have enough money to order this, miss?"

If there is one thing we have beneath the waves, it is the silly things the Walkers attribute wealth to. I pull out a stack of crisp bills and lay it on the table. I also bring out the shaman's bauble, a sphere of sea water as large as my fist, sparkling with its own inner light. Sato's eyes slide off the money and land on the bauble. He puts the tray down and pushes it to me. I pull the bauble back before he can touch it.

"How do I know this is real ningyo?"

He laughs. "Just one bite and you won't need those crutches."

"What about the curse?"

Sato leans back in his chair and gives me a calculating look. "A myth."

"The benefits of ningyo flesh are a myth," I counter.

He eyes the water bauble. "Somehow I don't think you believe that."

Sato lifts the cover off the tray with a flourish. A purple-red slab of meat quivers like jelly in the center of a crystal plate. The smell is powerful, but all wrong. I touch my finger to the meat and then to my tongue. Sato watches carefully as I do this.

Relief washes over me. This fool has not captured another of my people. It's shark meat. I tell him so and he sighs.

"How do you know?"

It's my turn to spear him with a look. "Why don't you ask me the real question you've been holding back?"

Sato covers the chunk of dead fish and leans forward on his

elbows. His eyes are bright and I can smell the thrill of fear coming off him like salt spray from a wave.

"How do you know my real name?"

Years pass after my escape. My crippled body barely serves my needs and is as much of a prison as the box of water ever was. Still, returning to my home waters is a balm that heals my mind, if not my body. Floating in the water, my body feels at least a little less broken.

Some of our kind still venture onto dry land and mingle with the Walkers, despite my warnings. If they will not heed my warnings, they can at least bring me information. They bring me stories, and I wait. Sometimes they bring me a story that I recognize, and I return to dry land to investigate. This happens rarely, but the results are satisfying. With each trip, my body heals and I grow stronger.

The stories become less frequent. I am almost fully healed. When the stories stop, I search through my memories. There must be one more, one that I overlooked. I have waited this long, I can afford to be patient.

Finally, the day comes when one of the young ones brings me the story I have been waiting for. Hundreds of years have passed since I returned home, and the world of the Walkers has changed. It does not matter. I pay a fortune in scales and shells to the shaman to buy a flesh mask and bauble. I return to dry land and search for the last ounce of my flesh.

I say, "I've been looking for you for a while now."

"Oh? Why is that?"

I roll the bauble of water over my fingers. Sato's eyes follow it like kelp caught in the tides. "You have something of mine. Something I lost a long time ago."

"Maybe I can help you find it."

"Oh, you can help, I just didn't know until recently. In fact, for a long time, I assumed you didn't have it, but that was my mistake.

I should have realized that even in the midst of a fire, something as precious as an ounce of ningyo flesh would not have been lost. The daimyo even knew to save it before it could burn, to ensure it granted you your longevity."

It takes a moment for my words to register. The minds of Walkers are small, petty things, not made for living this long. But after a moment he manages to dredge up the appropriate memory and when the look of comprehension dawns on his face, I squeeze the bauble of seawater and the shaman's magic blooms around us.

Magic fills the room with the smell of brine and salt. The bauble leaps from my hand and flies to Sato's open mouth and nose. It plunges down his throat before he can even blink.

Sato spasms as the water blocks his airway. He jerks and falls out of his chair, hands clutching at his throat. While he struggles, I grab my crutches and hobble over to the door. I close and lock it.

I'll need some privacy for what's coming next.

With a twitch of my finger the bauble shifts and allows Sato a quick breath. He heaves in a great gasp of air before I shut it down again.

I kneel so I can meet him eye to eye. "Unfortunately, I do not have time to subject you to the years of agony I endured, breathing stale water and smoke in that disgusting tent."

His lips are turning blue. Years of my pent-up rage boil just beneath the surface, straining to get out. "This is just a taste."

I grab his jaw, fingers digging in, and force him to look at me. His eyes tear up, water streams past his ears. "Just a taste, like you had of me."

My fingers tuck under my neck and I pull aside the flesh mask, so I can enjoy this with my own eyes. I endure the sting of air on my face and stare down the last human to have eaten my flesh. I grin and show him my sharp teeth. His eyes track across my wide mouth, my eyes, too large and liquid to ever be confused as human.

He falls from my hand, body convulsing from lack of air, like a fish out of water. I open the hollow shaft of my crutch and pull out a sword, sheathed in dark lacquered wood, inlaid with mother of pearl.

When Sato sees the sword, he has an obvious moment of chilling clarity. I will savor this moment for the rest of my life.

Steel bites into flesh.

I leave the crutches, but keep the sword.

The briny smell of the sea calls to me. I walk across the city, following the scent. My steps are awkward, but stable. After today, I vow I will never walk on dry land again. I make my way to the beach in the middle of the night and joyfully discard the flesh mask. Luminous scales cover my body like supple armor. Walking legs merge into my powerful tail. For the first time in hundreds of years my body is whole again. I plunge into the waves and go home.

Ken Bebelle has been an avid reader of fantasy, science fiction, and comic books his entire life. His first foray into writing was in the eighth grade with a sword-and-sorcery fantasy story stored on a 5.25" floppy disk.

Ken and his co-author Julia Vee recently finished *Ebony Gate*, an Asian-inspired contemporary fantasy set in the Pacific Rim. *Ebony Gate* will be published by Tor Books in summer 2023 as the first in a trilogy. Ken and Julia have also self-published another series, *Seattle Slayers*, an urban fantasy set in a post-apocalyptic Seattle. In his spare time, Ken is married, has two grown children, ponders the cyberpunk novel that he has yet to write, and tries to grow tomatoes in his meager backyard.

we are ocean

T. THORN COYLE

WE SWIM.

One being. Many bodies. One mind. Many facets.

The inky depths surround us, cradling our fatty flesh in indigo. Our scales shimmer in the filtered light from above. Iridescent shards of blue, green, turquoise, and umber.

We turn as one. We dive as one. We rise as one. We breathe with separate lungs, as one.

We are unstoppable.

Beautiful.

Peaceful.

And deadly.

Captain Tracy Hawkins' day was not going well. She scrubbed at her scalp, fingers reaching past dense curls to massage away the headache that had been building all day.

The *Doria*'s crew, a crack team of sailors and technicians, grew more demoralized by the second.

"I don't understand what's happening, Captain," said Jace.

Jace was a short, chubby, androgynous person with glowing

golden skin and the most arresting blue eyes the captain had ever seen. Jace and Tracy were occasional bedmates, though they tried to keep it under wraps. Be discreet. Nothing was ever truly secret on a ship, with every crew member firmly in each other's pockets, but the captain needed to not rub anyone's noses in it.

Life in any small community was that way. People knew things, but if you didn't shove it in their faces, they could choose to politely ignore it. And there was no need to upset the balance of power.

Her crew came from all over the world. From cities in Nigeria to small holdings in Bulgaria, together, they formed a little floating village.

Out here, it was band together or die.

The few who failed to adapt to that one rule didn't last on Tracy's ship. Not for long, anyway.

Tracy sighed, looking at the confusing sonar readings.

"Is it jammed?"

Jace ran a hand through their short, straight dark hair. The untidy mop needed a cut, but then, so did the hair of most everyone on the crew. Tracy insisted people bathe and not wear perfume—tight quarters and all—but other than that? You looked how you wanted.

"I can't tell. If I didn't know where we were, I'd think we were bouncing off the ocean floor, but we should be over deep waters."

"Sand bar?" Tracy asked.

Jace shrugged, flipped some switches, and rotated some dials.

"Your guess is as good as mine."

"Well, whatever it is, we need to keep going. We have a whaler to intercept."

A whaler called the *Pequod*, to be exact.

We are aware of the ship above us. A small ship with a steady gait, it tracks the whaler that is the very reason we are massing here, now, during our main feeding season.

We follow whales of many kinds, our ocean siblings, eating what they do not, and avoiding the creatures that would dine on us as well.

The gray bulk of the whale bodies protect us from predators. Not that we cannot protect ourselves, with the shell knives strapped to our broad chests and around our fleshy hips. And with our rows of teeth, should it come to that.

But, as I said, we are peaceful. Who wishes to fight, when one can swim and dive?

Oh, all things must eat, including orca, walrus, and the largest octopus. We do not fault them for their needs.

But that does not mean we wish to become dinner, as the krill, bluefish, and kelp are ours.

Blood in the water is no good thing.

But if the light ship above us does not move more rapidly, blood in the water there will be.

The captain looked out over the bow, wind whipping at her face. Tracy tugged her red knit watch cap more snugly over her ears. The air was frigid out here, the water choppy and gray.

There was no sign of the whaler or the tiny pod of minke whales they were supposedly following. With the busted sonar, Tracy had to rely on other means to track their prey. Ordinary sight. Sound. A shift in water coloration. All the things that sailors had relied upon before technology grew so fancy, when crew and captains both became dependent on screens instead of eyes, ears, and noses. Even tongues.

Tracy tasted the salty air. Just open ocean, nothing more.

But there, just up ahead, the water shifted.

"Pod ahead!" Tracy spoke into her comms.

Static. Then Jace's voice came from the control room. "Dolphins? Whales? What?"

Tracy raised her binoculars, sweeping the churning waves.

"Can't tell yet. But it's big."

Too big for a typical pod of four or five smallish minke whales, that was for sure.

On we swim, feeling the excitement of the humans on the small ship.

Good. They need to know we are here. What exactly they think we are, we do not know. I do not know. My small mind casts the question to the larger whole.

We share a vast wealth of knowledge in our collective mind. But without individual minds contributing, the large mind would falter, founder. Sink to the Stygian depths beneath our corpulent, muscular forms.

They do not know what we are. The answer echoed from mind, to mind, to mind. *But they will not harm us. They suppose we must be friends.*

That was good, I supposed. And if friends mean people with a common enemy? Then friends we are.

I kick my green spangled tail, forcing my graceful bulk forward. Onward, chasing toward the larger ship come to menace our segment of the seas.

Tracy paced the deck, worry hounding her heels. Not only was the sonar still jammed, making it hard to track the whaler, something felt off about that pod. Very off. Whatever the mass was moved in a similar way to dolphins, but not quite. And her binoculars caught the occasional bright color, flashing beneath the surface.

Nothing that large should be so bright, especially not in cold water like this. And a pod should not be that varied.

The ocean was filled with technicolor bright schools of fish. But no school moved this way.

She studied the writhing mass as it dove deeper, then rose again toward the surface.

"It's so beautiful," Tracy whispered. Out here on the open ocean, beautiful could mean deadly. Especially when she couldn't tell what the fuck it was.

"Boss?" Jace's voice cracked over Tracy's comms.

"Yeah?"

"I caught a blip. Just a few seconds in between the static."

Tracy lowered her binoculars.

"And?"

"The whaler is just where we thought she'd be. A few degrees off, is all."

"Adjust course," Tracy snapped.

"Already done."

The crew raced around, preparing for what was to come. Her second in command barked orders and would be along to confer soon.

Tracy needed to be at her second's side. To give direction. Make decisions.

But her duck boots were planted firmly, glued to the rolling deck. She was unable to move. Unable to do anything but raise her binoculars again.

The strange pod was still there, just ahead. Between the *Doria* and a Norwegian whaler named *Pequod* that she couldn't yet see.

Whatever the large group was, they moved more like seals than anything else, but no seal was spangled with green, umber, or yellow.

A creature surfaced.

Tracy gasped.

The human holds a device up to their eyes, lenses reflecting the sun.

A dark-skinned human, slight of build beneath a yellow covering and some sort of red cap, lowers the device.

I drink in the vibrancy of her warm dark eyes, wide open with shock, just like her mouth. With a blink, I transfer the image to the rest of us. A murmur rises inside my head. Conversation. Discussion.

It washes through me as the woman—I assume it is a woman, though I have scant direct experience with humankind—still stares at me, agape. I stare right back.

We are with you. I send our thought her way.

She blinks and closes her mouth, hiding those small white, ineffective teeth away.

She nods.

How humans kill anything with teeth like that, I have no idea. Our rows upon rows of pointed teeth are far more effective. But perhaps human beings do not feast on bluefin or the occasional seal. Or if they do, they must use the deadly weapons of the larger ship we stalk in common.

There is so much for us to learn. Of all the things we know, the knowledge of how humans live is patchy. Slim.

They barely swim, after all.

Tracy couldn't believe her eyes.

The creature was impossibly gorgeous, like some shimmering, sparkling green manatee. With a fleshy, humanoid face, dark seal-like eyes, a bulbous nose, and lips that skinned back into a brief, but terrifying smile.

Were those shark teeth? And a knife strapped across its chest? Holy hell.

It raised a muscular, vaguely human-shaped arm and waved.

Tracy was too shocked to wave back.

Her second, Manuel, stepped up beside her. "Crew's ready for the next order. What's the hold up?"

Tracy pointed mutely, but all that was left of the creature was a circle of bubbles and the shimmering of green.

And then, through her binoculars, the whaler appeared. Twice larger than the *Doria*, the *Pequod* was white and red.

Tracy hated it on sight.

There is nothing to do to assuage the human's fear. We must hope that she is smart enough to see that we can be of help. If her ship attacks us, that will only waste our time.

Besides, none of us are swimming to kill the small ally ship.

We writhe here at a distance from the dwarf piked whales—friends we should be feeding with—to take down the hulking whaler intent on destroying our lives.

We merfolk have no quarrel with those hunters who pilot cunning small boats on the frigid waters, taking one whale during season to feed their people for a year. As I said, all things must eat.

But the hideous white ship with a long, blood red stripe down its side, painted like blood? That sort of ship we cannot abide.

Cowards, every one of them. They have no need of whales for their survival.

Not like we do.

Shall we swim? The voices echo in my head.

We shall swim, we answer.

That is always, ever, the answer.

Tracy's comms crackled.

"Whale pod sighted!" Jace's excited voice came through, loud and clear. "Five adults, and some calves."

"Shit," Tracy spat. Of course, the pod would appear with the whaler nearby. The *Pequod's* sonar likely wasn't jammed. Tracy bet everything on that damn ship was in top condition.

Whalers had more money than the *Doria's* ragtag operation, and always would.

But did they have cunning?

Manuel's head whipped around. His blue watch cap rode low over bushy eyebrows and his dark eyes were wide with urgency.

"We have to act. Now!" he said, as if Tracy didn't know that.

"Get ready to maneuver between the *Pequod* and the whales," Tracy snapped into her comms.

"And you," she turned to Manuel, "get everyone in position. We're going in quiet if we can, but if we can't?"

She skinned her lips back from her teeth, feeling as fierce as a cold-water shark.

"We blast them all to hell."

The water churns with tension and activity. Our pod races toward our gray friends. Not the largest whales in the ocean, but still three times our size, the small pod protects three calves. We cannot let the larger ship near them, and the smaller ship?

Well. It is on the wrong side of the whaler.

It is coming, a susurrus of voices clamor in my head. And I feel it then, that sensation of disturbance the rest of the pod has been signaling for minutes now. The smaller craft moves above us in the water, shifting course. Aiming toward the hulking steel carapace set between us and the whales.

And I feel *her.* The small dark woman in her yellow coat and red cap. Perhaps, despite her ineffective teeth, she is ready to fight with us after all.

Beneath the larger ship! I cry out as several other voices say the same. We speak in unison. We move as one mighty, fluid shape. Diving beneath the massive white beast, heading for the whales.

The *Doria* picked up speed, whipping icy wind against Tracy's exposed skin, riming her lips and cheeks with salt.

Surely the *Pequod* knew the smaller ship was there. The larger ship floated, unconcerned, as if the *Doria* had no weapons. As if the *Doria* was not about to skirt the *Pequod's* nose, placing its proud body between the whaler and the whales.

The waters churned below as the flashing, shimmering jewel shapes dove.

"They're going under the ship," Tracy whispered.

That was good. At least, she hoped that was good. If the pod of whatever-they-were could get to the other side without being ripped to bloody bits by whirling rotors, they could shove the minke pod further away.

If they couldn't?

Well. The *Doria* had fighters on board, didn't she?

We swim.

Our whale friends are a mass of confusion, anger, and fear. Some are ready to fight, others wish to run. All have placed their graceful gray bodies to surround the vulnerable calves.

They move in concert, though they are not one.

Not like we are. We are deadly grace in motion. We are beautiful.

All things native to these waters are beautiful.

Not steel and grease. Not clanging and clanking and pulses that scramble whale brains into confusion.

We were confused once, too. But we learned. We adapted.

The strange rumbling and pulsing noises no longer shatter our concentration, impeding our ability to communicate.

All they do is serve our anger.

I smile.

Around me, we smile.

Ready. Ready. Ready. Ready. Our voices are sweet music beneath the icy waves.

We turn as one, a gorgeous, shimmering mass, moving like a school of bright fish through the cold refreshing waters. The waters that slide around me. Around us.

The waters that give us life.

We prepare to offer death.

"We're not going to make it in time!" Manuel shouted, racing across the deck in a foolhardy scramble. He was a graceful one, Tracy's second, but even he knew better than to clamber like a monkey when on the verge of battle on a water-slicked deck.

Looking out over the white-capped gray ocean, Tracy cursed.

Manuel was right. There was no way to reach the whales in time.

"Turn and halt!" Tracy shout into her comms, knowing that Jace would do all within their power to make it so. She heard the grinding of the *Doria*, shifting gears.

The *Doria* was close to the *Pequod* now. Too close for comfort.

But close enough to fire.

"Ready the harpoons!" Tracy shouted at Manuel over the groaning of the *Doria's* engines and the roaring sound of choppy, open ocean.

"Ready!" Manuel shouted back.

"Aim!"

"Fire!" his voice bellowed back in answer.

Half of our body shoves at the whale pod, shifting them further from the dangerous bulk of the ship. The other half of our body faces the enemy.

We are ready. We are one.

The whales click and whisper.

Then we hear it, echoing through the waters.

Shrieeeek. Thunk.

Shriiieeeek. Thunk.

Shriiieek. Thunk.

Above us, we hear human voices, shouting.

I smell oil in the water. See men falling, small limbs whirling, air compressed into bubbles, exiting their lungs.

It seems the small ship has bought us time.

Push harder! I scream into our mind.

I feel us moving the whales. I feel us readying to strike.

I feel us, split in twain, working together.

We are glorious.

The harpoons shot true. Several whalers screamed, shaken from their perches. They fell into the water and would be dead in minutes. Water that cold kills a human being more quickly than a gun.

"They're about to fire back!" Manuel yelled. Around Tracy, the deck was a frenzy of coordinated movement. Everyone raced, sure footed or slipping, grabbing ropes and weapons.

The *Doria's* engines screamed as Jace fought to control the pull of the larger ship on the smaller vessel. The metal hull creaked and groaned.

Maybe attaching to its sides was a mistake. If the *Pequod* decided to give up on this pod, they could focus their efforts on Tracy's ship, rending it to bits.

And perhaps they would.

The whole crew knew it, going in.

But it would save this pod, at least.

Then Tracy saw a way through.

At least, she hoped she did.

The smaller vessel could not take much more. It had bought us time, it was true, but we were not so churlish as to let the small craft go without a fight.

I felt the whale pod move to safety. One half of our body was still with them, with one quarter of that number preparing to join us back in the fight.

No! I shouted. *Stay!*

Stay! Stay! Stay! our voices echoed through the waters.

The pod was more important than our single lives. We would survive. We are ocean.

We are endless.

Even if my single drop should die.

The *Doria* lurched beneath Tracy's boots. She grasped teakwood and metal, steadying herself on the slick deck.

"Captain?" Jace's voice was edged with panic in her ear.

Tracy ignored her friend and sometime lover.

"Cut the ropes!" Her voice rang above the noise.

"Cut the ropes!" Manuel bellowed.

"Cut the ropes!" The call went down the line.

With a buzzing of saws and the slashing of knives, her crew attacked the lines tethering them to the *Pequod*.

Sailors on the other ship opened fire.

With a scream, one of her mates fell to the deck, and another windmilled toward the sea.

Mouth set in a grim line, Tracy shouted into her comms.

"Now! Turn!"

The *Doria's* engines reversed, freeing their craft from the *Pequod's* deadly embrace.

Tracy turned toward Manuel, who stood, stock still, mouth agape in horror, staring at the whaler.

Then Tracy heard the screams.

We do not move as well on land as in the water. Our grace comes from our fat, buoying us in salt and brine. But we are muscular as walruses, larger than the largest humans.

My own singular body bunches and slides across the deck, rushing the smaller creatures as they scream and slash. Fire shoots through my shoulder, exiting to hit a screaming man behind.

Three of our singular bodies roll across the teak as one, crushing, smothering, slapping with strong hands.

A man comes at me with a knife, flashing in the sun.

I slap the sharpened metal with one hand, and with the other, pull him toward me.

He screams. Cries out. Shouts. I see the panic in his eyes. I taste the warmth of his spit.

I open my mouth and bite his neck in two. Not seal or bluefin, but tasty in its own, peculiar way.

No time to feed.

I heave toward the next sailor as the others roll and crush around me.

We are deadly.

We are one.

There is blood staining the gray water.

But it is not the blood of whales.

Tracy stood on the deck, chest heaving.

"Oh, my Goddesses," she whispered to the wind.

The creatures, large as walruses or manatees, scaled bodies shining blue and green, gold and umber, writhed across the deck of the *Pequod*. Their human arms fought. Their inhuman mouths gnashed, and rent bodies in two.

Blood slicked the deck. A deck that had been washed with whale blood too many times.

Half a kilometer distant, a whale spouted. A tail slapped. The pod moved on.

"Captain?" Jace's voice sounded in Tracy's ears.

"Set a course for land."

"But Captain!" Manuel's voice was hoarse from shouting. "We can't just leave them!"

Her eyes scanned the deck of the whaler, taking in the carnage, then swept back to her second.

The screaming had made way to gasps and moans.

"They're all dead or dying, Manuel. There is no saving them."

She raised her binoculars and trained them on the pod.

"The whales are safe for now. Our work here is done."

She spoke into her comms again.

"Set a course for home."

The Coast Guard or the military could deal with the whaler. They would find it eventually.

The *Doria* needed to get out of there before any human authorities showed up to blame them for the floating abattoir.

Once all are dead, we eat our fill. Human flesh is not a favored meat, but better than letting it rot and waste. We shall leave plenty for any scavengers who come this way.

The rest of us will hunt for fish, with the pod, as our people are meant to do. It is the way of things, to swim and eat.

But sometimes, it is the way of things to kill that which places us in danger.

Soon enough, we slip from the blood-slicked vessel, back into the frigid, cleansing waters of the sea.

We join the rest of our body, carrying those of us too injured to swim well on our own.

There is no rejoicing, other than the joy of being one again. One body. One ocean. One mind.

The waters give life.

The waters take life away.

We are water. We are ocean.

We are one.

T. Thorn Coyle worked in many strange and diverse occupations before settling in to write novels. Buy them a cup of tea and perhaps they'll tell you about it.

Author of *The Steel Clan Saga*, *The Witches of Portland*, the *Seashell Cove Paranormal Mystery* series, the *Pride Street Paranormal Cozy Mysteries*, and *The Panther Chronicles*, Thorn's multiple non-fiction books include *Sigil Magic for Writers, Artists & Other Creatives*, *Crafting a Daily Practice*, and *Evolutionary Witchcraft*. Thorn's work also appears in many anthologies, magazines, and collections. An interloper to the Pacific Northwest U.S., Thorn pays proper tribute to the neighborhood cats, and talks to crows, squirrels, and trees. You can find them at thorncoyle.com.

europa's children

MARELLA SANDS

"IT LOOKS SO DREARY," said the woman next to me.

We were sharing a view of Europa through a tiny porthole. From here, the brilliant whiteness of Europa's icy surface was sliding into a deep ocean blue as *Reefs of Sirenia* crossed the terminator into the night side. The ice was not what drew me to the porthole, however. I was here to listen to the song of the underlying ocean, which had recently sprung to life in my veins. It was almost like the pulse of the ocean of home. *Earth!* The ocean of my heart, of my ancestresses, of my goddess. It was dead and gone and millions of miles behind.

The misery of that knowledge was too big to truly grasp. The pain of it was often too much to bear.

"It's not dreary," I said to distract myself from my wretchedness. "Think about the waters under the ice. The waters are so vast, they haven't even been mapped yet." In my blood, the pulse grew stronger. *Home home home*. A new beat, a new pulse, a new ocean. For the first time in years, I could relax. I had fulfilled my purpose.

The woman shuddered. "That's what scares me. There're miles of water beneath your feet." She made a concerted effort to appear more cheerful, though the expression she put on was more pained than happy. I had noticed the same look on many passengers' faces. Few really wanted to leave Earth, even as the ecosystem collapsed around them.

The weak overhead lights washed out the woman's skin so that she appeared almost ghost-like. Her eyes and the edges of her lips were dyed slightly green due to the hatchlings in her body. She had no idea they were there. They swam through the arteries and along the nerves of every human on this ship. My kind. My offspring. I had ensured this place would be safe for them.

The woman leaned on the cold metal wall and continued, "Why are we homesteading *here* when humans have settled on Titan? And the Mars colony is well-established. Why do we have to go to *this* world?"

I didn't answer; the question wasn't a serious one. Mars was closed to new colonists now, and the Titan settlement was on the verge of complete collapse after the failure of their first crops. Europa was the only option if you won the lottery and your opportunity to leave Earth became real.

The woman blinked a few times and wiped her eyes with the back of a hand. "They must keep this air so dry for a reason," she said unhappily.

I managed to do nothing more than smile despite my joy at her discomfort. "I've heard that's common. It will pass." That was certainly true. There was no need to elaborate that it would pass because she, and every other human on this ship, would be dead. The hatchlings growing inside her eyes needed water more than this woman did.

A small boy ran up to the woman. "Can you see it?" he asked excitedly. A tall man with white lines of pain bordering his eyes and lips approached slowly. The lighting made his sunken eyes seem to disappear back into his skull. He was desperately thin, as were many of the humans at this point. The offspring of my kind were enjoying the meal they needed to grow into the next stage of their life cycle.

"Joey's been talking about nothing except Europa and the landing," said the man.

I looked down at the child, who bore the faint green in his skin. He, too, was feeding the hatchlings. "We were just talking about Europa's ocean," I said to the boy. "But you can't see it because of the ice that covers the entire moon."

"Do you think anyone lives down there?" the boy, Joey, asked. "I'd love to see a fish!"

I did my best to keep a sneer from crossing my face. This small human hadn't killed Earth's oceans, but his kind had, and now he wanted to see a fish? I wanted to be back home in my own ocean, listening to the goddess my mother singing to our next generation. To know that the ocean held us, comforted us, taught us, and, in the end, folded us into itself once our long lives were over.

My lost home, my heart wanted to keen. *My goddess. All my sisters and mothers!*

All gone now. All dead. Humans' fault.

"Maybe there are fish here, though I doubt they'd look like the fish of Earth," I said.

"The last fish died in 2267," said Joey as if he were parroting something from a school lesson. "That's... one hundred and... six years ago?" The boy's expression showed he was trying to do the math in his head.

"Almost," I said. "One hundred and sixteen years ago."

The man put an arm around the woman's shoulders. "At least we're almost there. Maybe then we can rest, get some good food in us, and get our health back. This voyage has been a nightmare."

"Colonies don't generally have much in the way of good food to begin with," I said with disdain. The whining of the human male angered me. He thought this *voyage* had been a nightmare? His kind had killed an entire planet's ecosystem and still considered themselves victims of the catastrophe, as if they weren't directly responsible. Enduring a "nightmare voyage" was not nearly adequate recompense. Even enduring being eaten alive by my offspring was not enough suffering to atone for what his kind had done.

"Do you think anything lives in the ocean?" asked Joey.

"No one knows," said the woman.

"I'm sure there's life," I said. I knew it for a fact, because the call of the ocean below was full of the songs of living organisms. "Europa has an ocean just like Earth did. I'm sure it's simply teeming with life."

"Fanciful," said the man. "Nothing lives in Earth's oceans anymore. This one's just as dead."

"But what if it's not?" The child was so excited. "Maybe we could meet them. Maybe we could be friends. We haven't met anyone on Mars or Titan yet."

"You'd want to meet alien life?" I asked. The young one snagged one tendril of curiosity out of me. "Why?"

"To be friends," he said, as if I hadn't heard what he'd said less than a minute ago. "We could learn all kinds of things."

"Your kind could have learned all sorts of things from your home ocean," I said with undisguised bitterness. "You could have learned so much from the sea and her creatures."

"You talk like there's intelligent life in Earth's oceans," said the man drily. His sunken eyes narrowed as he scrutinized me. Let him look. It was far too late for him, or any other human, to do anything to save themselves.

I ignored him and concentrated again on the child. "Have you never heard of whales? Dolphins? Octopuses? The ocean of Earth sheltered many forms of intelligence before humans destroyed it all."

The boy sucked in his breath. "A whale! Wouldn't it be grand to see a whale!"

I did my best not to scream at him with the force of my hatred and sorrow. I was old enough to remember the last of the whales, an ancient cow who had borne her children into the goddess' embrace for decades. But they were all gone now. Every single one. Because of humans.

"Well," I said once I could choke out the words without shouting them. "Once the fish were gone and the whales, too, the last of Ocean's Children knew they had to do something drastic, or even they would die. They sang to the goddess for a path of deliverance."

"Ocean's Children?" The man sounded more disdainful than curious.

His tone made me want to spit venom at him. But of course, I no longer had venom since I wore a human form. I missed my old body; it was one more thing lost to me because of humans.

Forget the man. I would concentrate on the young one. "Ocean's Children are what they called themselves. You called them mermaids. Or sirens, or sea maidens, though they had males among them, of course. For thousands of years, they sang their worship to the Ocean, their goddess and their mother, asking for clear waters and schools of fish. They lacked for nothing. The brood males bore the young and the fry wriggled themselves into the deep to eat and grow into the next generation."

The boy screwed up his face. "Bood male? What's that?"

"Brood," I corrected. "The females bore the eggs, of course, and these were fertilized by the breeding males. It was up to the brood males to take the eggs inside their bodies and shelter them until they were ready to be born."

I closed my eyes briefly, recalling the last hatching. Thousands of fry had exploded out of the husks of the brood males. Those of us who observed had encouraged the young to swim down, down, down to the very bottom of the ocean, to root themselves in the silt of the abyss. For centuries, they would devour any food that came by until they were large enough to squirm free of their old forms and swim toward the light, to join the rest of us and sing our songs to our mother, the Ocean.

But that entire brood had died before ever reaching the abyssal depths. The ocean was too toxic, even for our kind. We had to find another way to survive.

The goddess understood. Even as she died, she was powerful

enough to discover that the humans had found a way to get to an ocean world far away. *Ocean!* We could go there. We could live there and swim freely in the waters of a new ocean.

As her last act of devotion to her children, the goddess had changed me into something that looked human and breathed air. I had been given the wretched ugly countenance of a human. My tail had become two legs with feet. My fins had become arms tipped with clever monkey hands. My mouth gave forth sounds almost as melodious as that of the dolphin. Deeply blue hair cascaded down my shoulders and back, while my human eyes were bright green. My new lips were the pale pink of a conch, my skin a dewy beige like the sands of a tropical beach. I knew I must be attractive due to the looks I got from the human males and not a few of the women. But I missed my old form, even as I endured this new form for love of my goddess and my sisters and my mothers.

But before the change, there had been one last spawning. Every fertile female had laid her eggs in the dark chamber that had held our eggs since time immemorial. For one last time, I had joyously spread my eggs onto the algae-covered sands, bearing the pains that must be endured to expel the eggs from my body, grateful to the goddess for this last opportunity to be mother to my kind. Then I and my sisters had watched as the breeding males had spread their milt over the entire mass. Hours later, once it was clear the eggs were fertilized successfully, the brood males had taken the eggs into their bodies. The eggs of the last great spawning were concealed and made safe. They were the only hope of my species.

"They had to leave Earth, just as the humans were doing," I said to Joey. "The last thing their goddess did was to make one of them into a human, with human legs and feet, and eyes as green as the sea."

"Like you," said Joey.

"Indeed." I laughed somewhat sadly, but of course the boy thought I was telling a story, not reciting the facts of my life. "Let's say it was me. That makes the story more interesting, don't you think? So, I was changed. I got myself passage on a ship. I secured the brood males in the water system. As soon as the ship left Earth's orbit, the brood males' task was complete. They were the first food for the hatchlings, who then entered the water filtration system and were drunk by the humans on the ship. Within a few days, every single human became host to thousands of hatchlings."

"What's the point?" asked the man, who shook his head in disbelief. "Europa's oceans can't be the same as Earth's. Anything from Earth that entered that water thinking it could live there would die. But, I guess, it's just a story."

"Just a story," I agreed. "But Europa's ocean is the abode of its own goddess, and she has promised that the fry will be changed. They will adapt to this world."

"Then we can meet them," said the boy with confidence.

I said nothing. I did not want to gloat that he and all his kind would be dead, served up to the fry as food. Even I, ultimately, would be consumed, once my guardianship was over. I could no more live on Europa unchanged than a human. But the young, oh yes, the young would survive.

The man blinked and rubbed the arteries in his neck with a thin hand. He had clearly already been significantly consumed. "Everyone on this ship has felt tired lately," he said slowly. "The medbots can't determine why. It's always 'Unknown Pathogen,' but no one's sick, exactly. There's something else going on." He hesitated a moment, and then added, "Isn't there?"

I shrugged. "Perhaps. For the purposes of this story, we can posit that the changed mermaid could have altered the medbots' programming enough to conceal the presence of the hatchlings, make them invisible to digital devices, just as they were invisible to the bots that kept the ship's drinking water pure enough to be safely consumed by humans. Any computer can be fooled if you feed it the right code."

The ship shuddered as it began its landing procedures. Later colonists might be deposited on Europa's surface by drop ships, but this first ship needed to land so it could be cannibalized for parts. Unfortunately, that was not what would happen; the humans would be dead and my kind had no need of metal and wiring.

The woman shook her head. "That's a terrible story. People infected... infested... with baby mermaids? Where's the happy ending? Real life can be tragic, but stories should end happily."

"The ending will be very happy," I said. "Ocean's Children will adapt; they will have their own ocean, their own *world*, and they will not have to deal with humans ever again."

"Why not? We'll be there," said Joey with confusion.

"But the story hasn't finished," I said, giving Joey a conspiratorial smile, as if we were in on some joke being played on his mother. "The human part of the story is that all the humans die when the mermaid children burst from their bodies. The brood males did their job to get the eggs on board, and now humans are offering their flesh to be consumed by the young until the fry are strong enough to leave you for the ocean."

"That's not right," said Joey with rising alarm. "They're going to kill all the people? That's not fair! I hate this story!"

"It's entirely fair," I said. "Humans killed the ocean. The fish are dead. The reefs are dead. The whales are dead. Even the goddess and her children are dead. Nothing lives in Earth's ocean. *Nothing*. How can your kind ever make up for that?" Now I couldn't keep the hatred out of my voice. For so long, I had pretended to be one of them while despising them. Hating that I had to wear their form for the years it had taken for this plan to come to fruition. Knowing my goddess was dead and all my sisters and mothers had died with her. The breeding males and brood males were gone. Even the hatching ground was devoid of its cushion of algae. Only I remained.

And yet, the hatchlings of the last fertilization swam through the bodies of every human here. That pleased me. That my kind would inherit an entire world of their own filled me with joy. Still, I was resigned that I could never live in Europa's ocean myself. I would never swim with the tides again, nor spawn, nor sing to my goddess. These fry were the last of my children but I would not see their triumph. Where they were destined to go, I could not follow.

The man had continued observing me closely. The truth appeared to dawn on him, though it took minutes for him to finally decide that his fears and my story might actually be the truth.

Words seemed to be dragged out of him against his will. "I keep dreaming of the ocean. The dark, deep parts. I've seen small, tentacled creatures swimming with the tides. I've watched those tentacles grab sailors or pull ships down. My dreams always seem to end in the death. For humans, anyway."

The woman frowned. "Me, too."

Joey held his head as if it hurt. "My dreams are all dark, like I'm underwater and drowning. And then things wiggle out of my mouth."

"You've dealt out death for centuries," I said. "Now it's our turn. We will use you and discard your bodies. We will have our own world and a new goddess. Europa is ours."

The man clutched at the boy and dragged the child away from me. "I'll tell the medbots you're not human. That you're harming us. Something can be done."

The ship shuddered as the descent began. There was more shaking than I had anticipated. Could the ship survive the descent? The first ship of colonists on Mars had exploded on entry to Mars' atmosphere. Supposedly, the manufacturing defects were corrected, but there was always that chance we could all die in a fiery explosion so close to our victory. So close to securing our future.

"Nothing can stop this ship from landing," I said, keeping the fear out of my voice. "Nothing can stop the fry in your blood from being born. Once we've reached the surface, the fry will go out onto the ice and burrow through to their new home."

The woman finally turned around. "What do you mean?"

"She said we're all hosting parasites that will kill us and take Europa for their own," said the man from between gritted teeth.

He shoved the boy at the woman. "She's either crazy or about to commit mass murder. Take Joey, get to the cafeteria. I'll get some service bots to deal with her."

The woman blinked her dry eyes a few times and shoved the child behind her. The man ran off shouting for help. Well, *ran* wasn't quite accurate, considering how weak he was. More like he moved off at a stumbling fast walk.

"You're mean!" said Joey from behind the woman

"And you are the species who killed everything and everyone important to me. You don't even deserve my hate. You are nothing but a force for destruction. You will all die."

The woman sobbed in terror and dragged the boy by the hand and they disappeared down the corridor. I followed more slowly, remembering that the safety briefing had encouraged everyone to be strapped in to a seat during the descent to the surface. I didn't have that luxury at the moment. But it hardly mattered if turbulence slammed me into a wall or the ceiling before dropping me to the floor. We were here. The ship was descending, and the fry were ready. Within hours, they would burrow through the ice and become a part of Europa forever.

The cafeteria was only dimly lit as the ship sent most of its power to the systems engaged for landing. Ambient lighting was at a minimum.

"Get away from us, bitch," shouted the woman. She turned to the roughly one dozen humans in the room who had also decided to ignore the rule of being strapped in during landing. More than likely, they were too weak to get to their seats, just as the man was almost too weak to walk.

I sat down, disliking the effort it took to keep standing on my alien feet. Though I sometimes actually liked the hair and the eyes, and especially the hands, I could never accept legs and feet in place of my tail.

It hardly mattered now. I merely had to wait for the fry to consume me on their way to Europa's surface.

The man entered the room with two service bots. His face was pale and he panted heavily. He pointed at me. "She's the one poisoning us somehow! Take her to security."

The service bots approached, ready to drag me to some quarantine cell and question me. But that would not be my destiny.

Joey suddenly clutched at his abdomen and fell to his knees, retching the contents of his stomach onto the metal decking. His mother screamed his name and leaped toward him. I did, too, as I did not see any motion in the vomit. Were the hatchlings dead? But then, after a few moments, the nearly transparent fry began flopping across the floor toward me and the humans. Joey's mother drew back in alarm. I steadied myself, the momentary scare causing my human heart to beat heavily.

The man fell to his knees and began vomiting. More fry moved across the floor toward more of the humans. They were hungry. I barely remembered my fry days; all I could truly recall was the ever-present gnawing hunger. These offspring of mine would be equally famished.

The service bots continued to remove me from the room. That had been the last instruction they were given and they would see it carried out. But it didn't matter. I felt one of the fry latch onto the flesh of my lower leg.

I laughed. The screams of the humans in the room were drowned out by the sudden increase of noise from the engines labored to make the landing as soft as possible, and then, with a solid bump, we were there, on Europa.

Welcome. The voice was there in my mind. It was deep and sweet like the currents of the abyss. Tears sprang to my human eyes. I had never dared hope Europa's ocean would speak to me.

Thank you, goddess. Thank you for making our offspring your children.

It is I who thank you for bringing me children.

More bites along my limbs. Blood ran freely from my body onto the floor, where more fry drank it eagerly.

Fear not, said the goddess in farewell to me. *They are safe here. I promise you and all your dead sisters. Their children will inherit this world.*

That was enough. I closed my eyes and enjoyed the sounds of human screams, now more closely resembling animalistic howls. *Come*, I thought to the newborns. *Come and eat. And take this world that is now yours.*

Fry burrowed their way into my neck, my groin, my eyes, even my ears. The agony was much greater than the pains of bearing eggs, or even the pain of being changed to a new form, and my howls joined those of the humans. But that didn't matter. My kind would survive. Europa was ours.

When not writing, **Marella Sands** spends her time watching superhero movies and scanning Etsy for more craft materials to buy. She escapes her keyboard to bake and make jelly. She was fortunate to be able to teach in Tashkent, Uzbekistan, for the spring semester 2022. While there, she stood in the ruins of a city built by Alexander the Great, rode a Bactrian camel, and toured the bazaars of Samarkand. In her stateside classes, Marella watches students teach each other skills such as origami and improv, and referees debates on whether Steve Rogers is a utilitarian or a deon-tologist (for the record, he's a deontologist).

Marella currently has three series out: her *Tales from the Angels' Share*, about a bartender who encounters the supernatural and gets tossed into the age-old conflict head-first; *Escaping Normal*, a nonfiction series about the paranormal; and her alternate-history series, which is being reissued by Untreed Reads. She is also working on the third edition of her Twi-English Dictionary.

tovarishch

JONATHAN FICKE

THE VILLAGERS NEVER MOURNED ME, banishing me to the dark waters. They whispered their warnings: "Do not go to the beautiful rusalka, young man." They feared me. I sang to them, but they ignored me.

And then came the soldiers in their gray uniforms with fire and thunder and blood. They listened to my song, and I welcomed them into my embrace. I took them into me, tangling them in my legs and hair, pulling them down and holding forever.

Now I am not scorned. The villagers whisper "tovarishch" to me and send another Nazi to die in my arms.

Jonathan Ficke lives outside of Milwaukee, Wisconsin with his wife and children. His fiction has been published in Flame Tree Fiction's *Compelling Science Fiction, Cossmass Infinities*, and *Writers of the Future, Vol. 34,* as well as been translated into Spanish, Estonian, Bulgarian, and Galician. When not writing fiction, he turns lumber into sawdust, and when all goes according to plan, furniture. Find him at jonficke.com, and (until the edifice crumbles under the weight of hubris and neglect) at Twitter @jonficke.

something rare

JOHN MABEY

LIKE JARS OF SAND, Joe Gibson's lungs rattled with each cough. Doubled over, a hanky pressed to his mouth, he expelled more mud from his chest. The dust was everywhere. It darkened their skies, smothered their homes, and pricked their lungs. At thirty-two, Joe had been a strong, confident farmer in his small Kansas town. Then the soil betrayed him, and like so many others, he wasted away just as the crops did. Most left town, others lost their homes and turned to the local Hooverville. But not Joe, he still had ambition and determined to turn things around.

Wiping his lips, he pocketed the hanky and returned to the only work left to do.

A pencil clenched in his teeth, he rubbed an eraser frantically over his sketch. Hair always took the longest to draw. Curly, wavy, straight; wasn't enough to just draw lines, you needed volume and depth. But the real challenge came in beards. No one's beard and hair were the same. That day's subject proved no different. Brushing the eraser crumbs to the hay below, he retrieved the pencil and looked to his client.

"You do this much?"

"Do what?" Joe muttered.

"Draw us freaks."

"As often as work comes." Joe smeared beard-lines into a smooth blend with his thumb. He looked up for comparison.

His subject sat on a throne of flaking gold and red velvet. Their wardrobe mocked royalty with spotted furs and soiled purple silk. Arms draped lazily over the throne's sides, the Bearded Lady pointed her regal chin into the air. She raised a painted brow. "And how often does work come to Kansas?"

"Not often enough." He brushed more crumbles aside. "Most carnivals have their own artisans to keep things up, but every so often"—he bent down and redrew her brow with the arch it now held—"one comes through in need of someone to fix up their banners."

A smirk at her lips. "Ever draw anyone pretty?"

He shrugged and thumbed more lines smooth.

She huffed. "Would it be so bad to make a lady feel special?" Breaking her pose she leaned forward. "You know, I've been told a little tickle of beard isn't"—her eyes dropped briefly to his lap— "unpleasant."

Joe's cheeks burned bright under the muted tones of beige tent walls.

"Gibson!"

The gruff outside voice hailed with a wind that rippled the tent's sidewall. Both turned as the flap opened, blinding them with brash sunlight and dust. In the doorway stood the antithesis of Joe's subject; bald, beardless, and dressed only in overalls. The brawny man with black snake tattoos twisting up his forearms pointed at Joe. "You Gibson?"

Intimidated, Joe jumped to his feet. "Yes, sir. Joe Gibson ... sir."

"Management wants you."

Joe thumbed back. "Just finishing—"

"Now, Gibson."

The Bearded Lady pouted. "Come on Biggs, a little longer? I was gonna show him my trick." She offered a knowing smile. "You know the one."

The man, Biggs, impatiently motioned for Joe to follow. "He

can mess up your beard another time, darling. Management needs him to see the Maiden."

She slumped back in her chair. "Come back and see me, sweet pea."

Joe nodded as he gathered his things.

Outside, the afternoon sun held mercy for no one as it singed the skin and burned up all shadow. Rows of sideshow tents flapped and bobbed in the hot chapped wind. Joe took note of several banners they passed. Sun and sandpaper-wind stripped most of their colorful flare and left a few ragged. He hoped the carnies could pay to have them all touched up—if not remade for double the price.

Biggs stopped before a tent at the end of the midway. Though no different than any of the others, Joe noticed the tent flaps were secured with thick ropes snaking through eyelets and padlocked.

"Management wants you to fix her up," Biggs said. He pointed to the banner beside the closed flap.

"Maiden of the Sea," Joe read aloud. The words—painted in blocky lettering strangled by seaweed—sat above a faded image of a woman. He smirked. "You saying there's a mermaid in there?"

"Ain't just a mermaid," Biggs said in a matter-of-fact way. "She's a siren. Dangerous devil of a woman."

Joe let out a snort. "Okay, I get the bearded lady, even the alligator guy with the skin thing, but a mermaid? Come on. People can't seriously buy into this?"

Biggs thumbed back at the banner. "You want the job or not?"

Joe nodded. "Yeah, I'll take it."

"Great." Biggs turned to leave but paused to look over his shoulder. "We open tonight. Tear down's Monday. You get it to us before tomorrow night, and you get double. Get it to us before tonight and you get more. Give it to us at tear down, you get what we agreed upon."

"Hold on." Joe meant to reach for the man but thought better of it. "You gonna let me in? Can't exactly draw a siren without seeing one."

"Ain't my place to say," Biggs said. "Not for this one. Gonna need to talk with Management first."

"It's fine, Biggs," another voice said from behind. A tall slender man wearing a sharp black suit, white button-up, and black bolo tie offered a pleasant smile to Joe as he approached. Wisps of brown hair stuck out from beneath a frayed top hat, which he briefly doffed in Joe's direction. "Look around you, Biggs. The poor man's from Kansas. I hardly think we can trust a farmer's vision of an ocean-bound witch, do you?" He briefly tipped a hand toward Joe in a sort of 'no offense' kind of gesture. "Let the man see her and wonder. Isn't that what we're all about?"

Biggs grunted but nodded. He pulled out a large ring full of keys and began to slide each aside in search for the right one.

"You must forgive, Biggs," the man said, turning to Joe. "He means well. This carnival would hardly be standing if it weren't for him." He held out a hand, its long fingers reaching toward Joe. "And you must be Mister Gibson."

Joe took the man's hand and felt a boa-like grip as the slender fingers curled around his. "Joe Gibson, sir."

Again, the man tipped his head. "Management, at your service."

"Pleasure to meet you," Joe said, flexing his wrung hand open and closed.

"It was fortunate we found you. Oklahoma's dust got to our last artist. Coughed up his own red paint." A smile curled at the edge of his slender lips. "We wish him the best, of course."

"Of course," Joe muttered.

"Now, as you may have assessed, this isn't your average specta-cle. No sir, unlike most of our medical oddities, this one's the real deal; the genuine article. Found her stranded on a beach down in Florida. People pay over and over to see her. Most return 'cause their eyes didn't believe it the first time."

Joe raised a brow. "You're saying there's a real mermaid in there?"

"That's right, no carny trick here. As real as you or I."

Biggs finished unthreading the rope and opened one of the tent flaps to reveal the black beyond.

"Before we go in, Mister Gibson, there's a matter of the rule. Don't speak to her; not ever. This ain't the mermaid of your childhood. This is a siren: sinker of ships, drowner of men, and devilish granter of wishes."

"Wishes?" Joe asked. Hungry for pay, he chose to play along with whatever wonder they sold.

"Sure. A siren's voice is haunting and alluring. It'll drive you to drown in a thimble of water. To hear her is to hear death himself speak your name. But there's also another side of her. In the rarest of occasions, it's said a siren may be compelled to grant a wish to one to whom she's indebted." Management smirked. "That being the trick of course, how does one get a siren in their debt without drowning themselves first?" He leaned down and whispered a quip. "That's the biggest reason so many return. They beg her to grant them wishes but have nothing to offer but coin. And what's a siren to do with that?" He chuckled and straightened up. "Silly really, but our pockets don't complain."

And with that, he disappeared into the tent's black maw.

Joe remained behind with unease. From inside he could hear Management's steps crunch over gravel and hay, and beyond that ... something wet.

"Do come in Mister Gibson. I assure you, she's quite harmless in her current state."

Readying his notebook and pencil, Joe breathed in the sun and dove into darkness.

It took a moment to adjust in the dim bulb light. As things became apparent, he noticed another man. Older and slightly hunched, the man wore suspenders that hung loose at his sides as he clutched a bowler hat respectfully to his chest; his balding head bent low.

Management waved Joe closer. "This here's Andy. He takes care of our guests in this tent." Then, without reason or warning, he snapped his fingers beside both of Andy's ears. "The man's deaf as a corpse. Couldn't hear a pin drop, let alone a train. These are the kind of precautions we take around ... our siren." Management waved a dramatic arm toward a platform at the front of the tent.

There, in a glass tank the size of a large tub, floated the Maiden of the Sea.

"Jesus," Joe muttered.

"My dear friend," Management said as he strolled toward the tank, "there's nothing to be afraid of. This may be no girl in the fishbowl, but I assure you, you're quite safe."

Joe licked chapped lips and approached.

The woman lay the length of the tub, her upper torso above the water. She wore a gold sequined bikini top with matching shells molded over each breast. Hands bound by leather shackles; they were suspended above her head by a chain attached to tent supports above. Her upper half looked like a witch about to be burned at the stake. But that wasn't what bothered Joe the most. A leather muzzle covered her mouth and chin. The severity of its hold seen in the bulge of cheeks beneath her eyes. Her eyes—wide and afraid—watched Joe.

Management waved Joe closer. "Come, come, she'll not bite, nor sing for that matter."

Closer now, Joe followed the woman's slender naked torso into the water. Just below her navel, scales glittered. They shone all the way down in a mesmerizing oil slick of color. At the end of those scales fluttered a wide and nearly translucent tattered fin.

"Still not convinced?" Management asked. "Certainly don't blame you." He removed his coat jacket and rolled up his sleeves. "Allow me to put you at ease, sir." The siren went wild as Management reached in. Despite her physical protest, he grasped a handful of scales just below her waistline and tugged.

Though muffled, the wail that came from beneath the muzzle conveyed a pain that staggered Joe's stance.

Management shook the water from his hand. He accepted a towel from Andy. "See, no gaff here. That tail is attached my friend."

Joe watched the Maiden of the Sea hang her head down, despondent. "Good lord," he whispered.

Management laughed. "My dear sir, I don't think the Lord has anything to do with it." He rolled down his sleeves and accepted his coat from Biggs. "Sailors thought these creatures to be witches of the sea. I'm inclined to agree."

A wink of his eye, and Management made for the open tent flap. "Make her beautiful, make her enticing, and again, don't speak with her. Do that, and I'll pay you triple what we agreed upon." He pointed to Andy now seated at the back corner of the tent. "Andy here will make sure your time is a safe one. Be good to her as there are few things rarer than a mermaid."

Joe broke his gaze on the enigma. "What could possibly be rarer than a mermaid?"

Management only offered a knowing smile before he and Biggs vanished into the blinding white of the tent opening.

In the open tent space where a paying audience would later stand and gawk, they'd given Joe a chair. From there he observed the impossible—nothing being overlooked. With some revulsion, he regarded stringy pieces of tail fin, ripped off and swirling in the tank. He found the flex of her stomach and quiver of her exposed navel bewitching. He'd fixed many carnival hootchy-kootchy banners, but never beheld the softness of a real woman's bare belly. His gaze roamed over the golden shells, the horrific muzzle, and stopped at her eyes.

She'd done her fair share of watching too. But where his scrutiny tended to wander, hers remained sharp and focused. Like an ocean's high tide, the blue in her eyes overwhelmed the brown of his.

Embarrassed, he dropped his attention to the sketch.

With pencil, he took the horrific and turned it playful. A flirtatious swish in her tail. A delicious curve of scales at her hip. A shadow of depth at her navel. He rounded her breasts and put full lips where none could be seen. At first, he thought to draw a horrific monster, but she seemed so beautifully plain that even the muzzle struck pangs of sadness rather than ferocity. To sell a monster where only this pitiful creature resided; he'd let the Talker persuade the crowd.

Setting his tools down, Joe stood and stretched. Hands on his lower back, he looked to the mermaid. Hungry eyes watched him. She was starved—surely—but this didn't seem to be a craving for food as much as freedom to move.

From behind, Andy clapped his hands. Joe's time was up, and a blinding reality of dust and poverty awaited. Packing his things, Joe offered his subject another look. In the tent's gently waning bulbs, the Maiden of the Sea entreated him with a misty-eyed gaze.

Outside his decrepit farmhouse, the wind cast dirt against his windows in a mockery of rain. His home had been beautiful ... once. Just as the acres of dried-up soil had been once. Now windows and doors needed to be resealed against the daily gale of grit. The foundation required attention after a shift of stone. And there was the dilapidated roof—though he hardly worried about a threat of rain.

Sitting in a parlor chair, Joe hung his head in defeat.

Across from him, his absurd depiction of the horrific spectacle hung pinned to the wall as an icon poised for worship. He hadn't returned since that afternoon, and yet he couldn't stop thinking about her. Lifting his eyes, he met his sketch's amorous gaze. That coy smile and frisky tail couldn't soften the truth of what he'd witnessed.

She seemed to watch him back.

"I can't live like this," he said. Hands folded together, Joe found he seemed to be begging, maybe even praying, to the woman on his wall. And the Maiden of the Sea watched over him as he slid off the chair to his knees. In a whisper, "Please, I'll do anything."

The depiction remained impassive.

Joe sank lower on his knees.

Then, whether out of madness or magic, a thought whispered back.

Heart thumping with revelation, he focused on the sketch and knew what must be done.

On his feet, Joe pulled yellowed curtains back. The dusky sky had gone from light brown to a burnt orange under the setting sun. Soon carnival fireworks would paint vivid colors in a muted sky and bait the ailing denizens of his small Kansas town. He let the curtains fall and looked over his parlor. Couch, chair, dusty white walls; it'd take a moment to prepare, but a moment brimming with life-changing possibility.

He wanted out of this existence; something his siren wanted as well.

Joe drove his farm truck slowly along the back of the carnival tents. Most nights, carnies prowled tent alleys for drunks and lurking kids. But this night the crowds were big and ravenous. It'd take every carny to relieve every mark of their coin. He backed up to the Maiden's tent and waited. If spotted, he'd feign ignorance: just another look before finishing the banner, sir. When no one approached, he stepped from his truck with baseball bat and bolt cutter in hand.

Surprisingly, the tent's back entrance stood open. A crowd could be heard musing as they filed out of the main entrance. Once silent, Joe dared to peek inside. Alone with his back turned, Andy stood securing the entrance flap. Outside a boom of fireworks followed by avid cheers drowned out all other sounds. But what was that to Andy? A problem that needed immediate remedy.

Rushing the space, Joe brought the bat down on the unsuspecting deaf man's head. With a *squak,* the old man fell forward, his dented bowler tumbling over the hay.

"Shit." Joe stepped back, a smear of red on his bat. He hadn't meant to hit so hard. Regardless, blood ran stark against the man's bald head. Crouched down, he checked the body. A small plume of dust curled out from beneath Andy's nostrils.

Joe's relief was cut short when he remembered another set of eyes in the tent.

From over his shoulder, the Maiden of the Sea watched him. He tucked the bat and cutters under his arm and approached. *I'm getting you out*, he mouthed. The closer he got, the more he could see that those saucer eyes weren't wide with terror but, rather, hope.

He made quick work of the chain suspending her arms. A muffled gasp came from the muzzle. Her face convulsed with the agony of moving stiff, atrophied limbs. She motioned to the shackles binding her hands.

"Not yet," he whispered. "First, we get you out."

He set the cutters aside and investigated the tank. Coins glittered its bottom; wishes for someone else's pocket. Plunging his hands into the chilly water, he ignored the payout below and curled his arms under cold slick scales. Beneath the plated layer her muscles and bones felt jumbled, jagged.

A sharp intake of breath filled her muzzle as he hoisted her out of the tank. Wide dilated eyes gave away the pain she tried to quell, before they rolled back into her skull. Overcome with agony, the Maiden of the Sea went limp in his arms.

Though the unconscious mermaid lay hidden between layers of blankets in his truck bed, an uneasy chill overcame Joe as he drove off the carnival grounds. Passing the entrance, he caught sight of Biggs tossing out two youths. The formidable man barely glanced as he passed, but the brief hold of his gaze broke Joe into a sweat.

At home, he carried the mermaid into his parlor where a cleaned and filled large metal feeding trough waited. He gently lowered her into the steel tank, the water overflowing and pooling across the floor. Panicked blue eyes opened the moment her skin touched water.

"It's okay," Joe said, hands out before him. "This is my home. You're safe here."

A series of emotions flashed in her eyes. Relief. Gratitude. Confusion. She glanced at the water and cuffs, muttering something against the muzzle.

"I know. I know." Again, Joe held up calming hands. "I intend to take all that off—really, I do—but there's something we oughta discuss first."

She shook her head and thrust bound hands at him.

"No. You're a siren, and I need to know I can trust you."

Something else in her eyes. Shock, disbelief ... maybe hate? She tapped her bound hands against the muzzle insisting, *At least this.*

"Now see"—Joe pointed a finger at her—"I ain't an idiot. I know what you're gonna do the moment I take that off." He pulled a chair near the trough and sat. "Let me be clear. You're in the middle of a farm in Kansas. That water there is the most you're gonna find for miles outside the carnival. You've no idea the hell I went through to gather it. That being said, can't imagine a creature such as yourself is gonna get far on their own."

The siren screamed. There was no doubt, the sharpness of the sound beneath the muzzle lent a ferociousness dampened by moist leather. She rocked back and forth banging against the sidewalls. Water splashed across his wood floor.

Joe remained calm in his chair, waiting out the siren's fit.

Exhausted, she let out a final sob before resting her head against the trough.

"Are you done?" Joe asked. The siren stared at the wall. "I don't think you realize how lucky you are. I mean, you hardly seem grateful for where you are, as opposed to where you were." Joe shrugged. "I've no intentions to harm you. I just wanna help."

At this, her gaze slid over to him. She looked more haggard than before, her skin an ashen hue in the light. She tried to sit up, but winced and slumped back.

Joe leaned forward. "I'm willing to free you, but there's gotta be an understanding. You keep wailing like that ..." He shook his head. "I've no desire to drown myself in that tub tonight. So, if you want the mask off, I got terms."

Something in her eyes died then. The shimmer of hope he'd seen fizzled as she nodded her agreement.

"Good. I think we can make this work." He clapped his hands. "You wanna be free, yeah?" Another slow nod from her. "And I wanna get the hell outta here. Grant my wish, and I'll grant yours."

Despite her growing lethargy, the siren managed to raise her brows.

"Oh, don't be so surprised," Joe said. "I want my one wish, and considering what I've done for you ..." He tilted his head. "I think a creature like yourself can see the benefits of our arrangement. What I want—my wish—is a life of fame. I wanna see the world. I want riches. I want people to seek *me* out for once." He relaxed in the chair, a thoughtful finger at his lips. "Maybe in California—"

The siren's eyes fluttered; her muzzle dipped into the water.

"Hey!" Joe ran to the tub's side. He hadn't noticed before, not with the darkness of the wood flooring. The water around the tub carried in it a pink hue. The water in the tub, a bold red.

"Oh, lord!" He lifted her head out of the water. Her eyes were half open. Reaching into the tub, he hefted her out. She arched with a muted scream as he held her. Rushing into the kitchen, he laid her on the table. Blood immediately pooled beneath her.

Joe grabbed rags and put a kettle of water on the stove. Rushing back to her, he rolled her onto her side. Blood oozed and smeared from a place where the scales of her tail met the flesh off her torso. He recalled the hard painful tug Management gave earlier and thought maybe her thrashing made something worse. "I —I don't know what I'm doing," he stammered.

The siren's eyes rolled about in her head as her chest rose and fell in a pant. She lifted cuffed hands and clawed uselessly at the muzzle.

Shaking the water and blood from his hands, Joe relented. A desperate prayer, and he unstrapped the muzzle.

The siren's eyes came alive as the leather tore away with strands of skin and saliva. She opened her mouth, taking in a lungful of air and screamed. Joe Gibson covered his ears and waited for death....

But death never came.

Confused, Joe lowered his hands. Maybe she'd keep her part of the bargain after all.

With the last aching notes out of her, the siren took in another breath and dropped her head to the table. She pushed bound hands down her scales. Her voice nothing more than a rasp, she begged, "Get it off."

"I don't understand. Get what off?"

The siren's eyes rolled up again but still she managed to repeat, "Get it ... off."

Behind Joe the tea kettle shrieked. "Let me just—your wound first." He emptied the kettle into a bowl and soaked the rags in it. By the time he got back to her, the siren had already passed out. For the better, Joe thought. Turning her over he looked for the wound. The blood flowed sluggishly down her back as he pressed his fingers between scale and flesh. Then he saw it.

"No, no, no," Joe repeated. He pinched a thick black thread between his fingers and lifted. The siren's tail was no more than a prop ... sewn directly to her. The ghastly thread wove in and out— skin to scale—in a circle around her body. Suppressing his rising bile, Joe trimmed some of the thread away and lifted a portion of tail from her skin.

The cloying smell broke his resolve.

Doubled over the sink, Joe expelled dinner and tears. "What did they do to you? God, what did they do?" He nearly collapsed to the floor were it not for his hold on the counter. "Oh, Jesus!" Coughing and gagging, he lumbered over to her. It was clear now.

The way her tail felt when he lifted her. They'd broken her legs and sewn her into a shiny sack.

"I want to go home," a weak voice pleaded. Awake, her unfocused eyes moved about the room. Her mouth opened and closed as she tried to speak again. "I want ... to go home." Those last words came out as nothing more than a faint whisper.

Joe paced the floor wringing blood-stained hands. This wasn't how it should've gone. He should be rich, far away from such horrors, and somewhere else—anywhere else. "I can't deal with this." He didn't even know if she could hear him, but he didn't care. This couldn't be his problem. Not another burden to bear.

He carried the unconscious woman back to his truck. He'd drop her off on Doc Jacobson's porch. The Doc would know what to do.

Opening the driver side door, he glanced toward the carnival in the distance. Dark skies hung over the space. They probably figured out what happened and cut it short. They'd be ghosts long before the police were called.

"Good riddance," Joe said as he shut the door and turned the ignition.

Back home, Joe leaned against his truck. She'd been left on the Doc's dark front porch. Driving off, wailing on the horn, he looked back and saw the porch light turn on. She'd be in better hands now. As for himself ...

He needed to get out of town. No doubt Doc would call the police. Tomorrow they'd look for someone to pay for what'd been done, and with the carnies gone, Joe would surely be next in line.

Opening his front door, he walked into a parlor puddled with bloody, brackish water. A subtle sweet scent of rotten fruit permeated the air. Suppressing a gag, he made his way across the room to pack. From the corner of his eye, something advanced—and all went black.

Joe struggled to open his eyes. An ache at the side of his head pulsed every time he tried. Still foggy, he looked about through half-closed lids. Lying on his back on the table, he saw the kitchen light glare above him. Everything else remained in shadow. He went to move his hands but found them pinned. When he looked to his wrists, black snakes coiled around each of his arms.

"Wh-what ... is this?" The snakes tightened, and he grimaced.

A click of shoe and a man dressed in black emerged into the circle of light. "Ah, you're awake," Management said.

Terror pulled Joe's eyes open. More aware, he looked back to the black snakes. Tattoos. Their wearer, Biggs, stood over him, his hands a vice-grip over Joe's wrists. Other carnies stood in the shadows. One of them stepped forward, a bandage over the right side of his head.

"Andy," Joe breathed in.

Management circled the table. "You know, I liked you when I met you. Felt like we had ... a connection. Even thought about asking you to be one of us." He leaned in close and whispered. "But it's much better this way, I think." He patted Joe on the chest. "I'm gonna make you famous, Joe Gibson. Show you the world. People are gonna to throw money at you. How's that sound?"

"I'm sorry," was all Joe could say. Then came the sob. "Please, God! I'm sorry!"

"Now, now," Management soothed. "None of that." A nod to Andy, and the old deaf man approached with something in hand.

Joe strained to see and caught a glimpse of leather. He squirmed and screamed but fighting against Biggs was futile. A smell of old leather filled his nose. The straps tightened and the muzzle's rough inner layer warmed with his breath.

Management withdrew a long needle and spool of black thread from his jacket. "You asked what could possibly be rarer than a mermaid."

Joe wailed into the muzzle as Management fed the black thread through the needle's eye.

"It's simple really. A merman."

John Mabey's journey started with the mysterious arrival of a Bookmobile. A scrawny nine-year-old, he found himself with copies of *The Shining* and *Alfred Hitchcock's Tales of Terror* weighing down his arms. Curious, the enigmatic librarian offered him this challenge: start with Bradbury; finish with King. By ten, John finished both author's extensive catalogs and never returned to the real world again.

Now, whether taking notes from the ceiling of a Mystery Spot, listening to tales recounted by retired carnival acts, or looking for apparitions hitchhiking on Route 66, you can be sure John is creating a world beyond the everyday. Inspired by early American history, folklore, and campfire tales, John's stories are lessons steeped in archaic lore and sweeping prose.

Find more about John and his first upcoming novel on Instagram @JohnMabeyAuthor and his personal website John-Mabey.com.

mermaids, monsters, and mayhem

ELIZA CARNS

I

THE FIRST THING TO know about merpeople is that they're not quite right in the head. One too many shark attacks, maybe, or tentacled fights with the Kraken. They would as soon gut you as greet you. And don't let them catch you making a joke about a certain red-haired warbler; you'll find yourself sunk so far to the depths, you'll be spouting water on the other side of the globe.

Me, I stay away from them and any pool of water I can't see the bottom of. You never hear of a goblin scuba diving, do you? Goblins are strictly landlubbers, content to keep their feet firmly planted on dry land. If I'm seeing a merperson, something has gone seriously wrong.

And something must have gone seriously wrong, because I'm looking at two of them now as I stand on a long dock over the ocean waves crashing against Northport's rocky shores. The first one, Arran, looks like he lost a fight with a boat propeller. His heavily muscled upper body is covered in scars upon scars. But I would take him any day over his colleague, Atl, who clearly spends a lot of quality time in the dark. His body is so white that it is almost translucent, and while one eye is fixed on me, the other roves around, likely in search of a tasty snack. I just hope goblins aren't on his menu.

"The answer is no, Zeke," Arran says. "As representatives of the Mer And Finperson International Alliance, we are not joining your council of magical beings."

I shrug. "Suit yourselves." I turn to go. I hadn't wanted to ask them in the first place, but Fiona, the love of my life and a witch enthusiast, had insisted. Now I can return home, sit in my comfy chair, and drink my delicious nightcap of strained bone marrow. Fiona will be happy, I will be happy, and—

"Wait," says Arran. I turn to see him exchanging glances with Atl. "We might be willing to join your council if you do us a favor."

I sigh. On the one hand, this sounds like a time commitment, and I want to get home in time for *Jeopardy!* On the other, as a goblin, I have a deep appreciation for the art of driving a hard bargain. "What do you want? My firstborn child?" I add with a chuckle.

"Good oceans, no," Arran says, wrinkling his nose in disgust.

I glare at him. "It was a joke. I'm a goblin, get it?"

Arran and Atl stare blankly at me.

"Ever hear of Rumplestiltskin?" I hint.

Nothing.

I sigh again. I should have remembered that merpeople have no sense of humor. Another black mark against them. Still, it is disappointing when they have never heard of the most infamous goblin in history. "Just tell me what you want."

Atl reaches into a pouch he has belted around his waist and tosses something onto the dock.

I'm almost afraid to look. Is it a severed limb? Whale intestines? Some horror of the deep? I squint my eyes to peer at the object, only to widen them again. On the dock lies a tiara of sparkling gold encrusted with jewels.

Instantly, my mouth gapes and my fingers twitch. I step forward, reaching down to grasp it, running my fingertips reverently over its sparkly surface. I'm not ashamed to say I maybe even drool a little. Hey, I'm a goblin, and coveting shiny things is what we do. "Magnificent," I breathe.

"It belongs to Marina, our princess," Arran says. "She went missing two weeks ago. All that we can find is her tiara."

"And?" Frankly, one found tiara in exchange for one less fishy twit seems like a net gain.

"And we fear something terrible has beset her."

"And you want me to do what?" I ask, turning it over and over in my hands, caressing it.

"Find the princess," he says. "She is the youngest daughter of our king, the fairest of our maidens, innocent and pure. Our king is distraught at her loss. She is barely more than a child."

"What has any of this to do with me?"

Arran shrugs. "We heard that you are good at solving mysteries. And we can't walk on land."

"I'm just a pawn shop owner," I grumble. Solving mysteries is usually a lot of work and has caused me more than one close call. But I can't look away from the tiara in my hands. "Do I get to keep it if I find her?"

"No," Arran says.

"Then forget it," I snap. I force myself to toss the tiara back at them. Atl easily catches it. "I'm too busy to go chasing after runaway sea tarts."

Atl makes an angry sound like the bleat of a dolphin, and his hand goes to one of the many vicious-looking knives strapped across his chest.

Arran holds him back with a gesture. "You can't have the tiara, but we'll pay you handsomely. And we will join your council."

I cross my arms. "How handsomely?"

Arran names a figure that makes my heart do the rumba in my chest.

But I, too, know how to drive a bargain, and I don't want to seem like I'm giving in too easily. "I'm not going in the water."

"You don't have to. We have already investigated everyone and everything under the water. All we can figure is she left the ocean.

She had a disgusting habit of doing that." His mouth twists into the same expression I make when I bite into a bit of rotten fish. There's clearly more to the story of Marina's little field trips on dry land.

"Mermaids can't live for long outside of the water," I say, my voice a hard edge underscoring my words. I don't want them to renege on the payment when all I find is one dead mermaid.

He looks back at me with a sneer. "We know."

I clear my throat. "And when I find whoever is responsible...?"

"You bring him here," Arran says, his thin lips drawing back in the semblance of a smile. "We will deal with him."

No doubt about how that will end up. Shark bait. Stories abound of how the enemies of the Mer And Finperson International Alliance often disappear, hogtied to an anchor at the bottom of the ocean or fed to the Kraken.

But what do I care? That's their problem. I just have to find her. "Done."

Arran lifts up his hand to shake on it. I step forward to grasp it, and instantly wish I hadn't. He grips my hand, his skin moist and cold. When I meet his eyes, a predator stares back at me from the inky depths. I am close enough to see his nostrils flare as he sniffs the air. His fingers tighten around mine, pulling me towards the water.

I jerk my hand away and wipe it against my leg. "What's your interest in this?"

"She's my sister."

I've heard sworn blood enemies speak with more affection. I head back up the dock, shuddering as I feel the stares of both of them on my back. I make a mental note to tell Fiona to keep seafood off the dinner menu for at least a week.

II

The second thing to know about merpeople is that they stay close to the water, a lack of legs being the first impediment to venturing far afield from the waves. You won't see merpeople climbing Mount Rainier, for example, or spending much time in Kansas.

I head to the docks as the most obvious place to start. Someone must have seen something; say, a certain mermaid princess flopping and wriggling her way toward town.

I approach the shipping docks with a little trepidation dogging my steps. Not too long ago, the thought of approaching humans to ask about a mermaid would have been unthinkable. The few magical beings who lived in Northport had hidden their true selves, passing as human, and avoiding even a whisper that vampires, witches, and goblins were more than fairy tales. But a series of events—starting with the death of a devious warlock—had collapsed the magical border between the human and the magical realms, and the village was overrun by seemingly every gnome, orc, and fae in existence. The border had been reestablished, but the genie had been let out of the proverbial bottle. (His name is Frank and he plays a mean piccolo.)

Now we are all figuring out the way forward—humans and magical beings alike—but the peace seems tenuous at best. Hence the need to establish the magical council with representation from every group: stronger together, yada yada yada. Goblins are generally solitary beings, so the thought of joining such an organization is generally anathema to me, let alone leading it, but my darling Fiona has made it clear that doing good deeds is the way to her heart. So, however reluctantly, here I am.

I hail the first grizzled worker that I see on the docks. He looks about fifty, with wiry gray hair peeking out from under a knitted beanie, his arms covered in faded blue tattoos, thigh-high waders protecting his lower half from the bloody slosh. He unloads crates of fish, barely bothering to look at me as I approach. "Excuse me," I say, clearing my throat, "I know this is going to sound very odd, but I'm looking for a mermaid—"

"Marina," the man says, pausing in his work to look at me with an odd gleam in his eye.

"Oh, you know her?" I ask, excitement flaring in my belly. What are the chances the first person I run into knows the princess? Maybe I will have this wrapped up by supper time after all. I can hear the *Jeopardy!* theme music now.

"Aye," he cackles, "everyone around here does."

My eyes narrow. "What do you mean?"

"Marina's been coming out on the docks every night at dusk."

Something about his tone gives me pause. It's the same one I would use to describe a particularly enticing jewel, or a buttery lemon scone fresh from the oven at the Wicked Good Bakery. "To do what?"

He waggles his eyebrows. "To sing to the men."

I purse my lips. Not exactly the mental image I had formed of the young princess. "Well, mermaids are called sirens of the sea, after all..." I try to imagine what a mermaid princess might sing. Old whaling hymns of lost loves at sea, perhaps.

The older man cackles again. "That's one word for it. If sirens sang about Pam, the lusty clam, who liked to be tickled with a lick and a tease—"

My eyebrows shoot up. "Excuse me?"

"—or Neil, the long, thick eel, who liked a good rub and a tug in the tub. Or Sally—"

"I get the picture," I cut him off. "So you're saying Marina would sing dirty ditties on a nightly basis and then return to the sea?"

"Aye, usually with a man or two who wanted a dip, if you get my drift." He winks.

I grimace. "Why?"

"Why does any young person do it?" He shrugs and hitches his thumbs under the straps of his coveralls. "I sowed my own oats as a lad. Can't say it was ever with a mermaid, but there was a particular lass named Carla, who liked to burnish my barracuda..."

I block out his voice as he waxes on. His story about Marina doesn't make any sense. Why would a princess want to sing dirty songs on a dock to humans? Surely there are plenty of merfolk who would have loved to dally with her. "She disappeared a few days ago," I say, relieved to interrupt him as he begins to describe an improbable act involving a lobster trap and a buoy. "When did you last see her?"

He pauses, seemingly sensing that my questions have veered from the lascivious to the suspicious. "Don't know anything about that and don't know when I last saw her." He frowns. "I heard she was affiliated with the Alliance, so I wouldn't be asking around none either, if you know what's good for you." And with that, he strides off.

Left with more questions than before, I roam the docks, asking anyone I see about Marina. Each time, the same story is repeated, punctuated by winks and nods. In fact, it would have been more difficult to find someone who *hadn't* heard of Marina, the Lusty, Foul-Mouthed Mermaid. Everyone seems to know her, but the memories all become curiously dim when I ask about when they last saw her or where she might be now, muttering about the Alliance.

As time ticks forward, I despair of ever making it home in time for dinner with Fiona. I am in the midst of a fond daydream of Fiona's specialty—roasted tongue and sweetbreads with a side of black pudding—when I am distracted by the flashing red-and-blue lights of Northport's local fuzz.

The Northport Chief of Police, with whom I have the misfortune of being well acquainted, stands to the side of an ambulance. He's holding a bag with what looks like a knife in it. Paramedics roll a gurney with a body on it to the ambulance. An ominous white sheet covers most of the figure. I step closer, trying to get an idea of what lies beneath. As the paramedics lift the gurney, something flops out from under the sheet, flashing iridescent in the sunlight.

A mermaid tail.

III

The third thing to know about merpeople is that they don't take disappointment very well. For a long second after seeing the tail, I strongly consider declaring "mission accomplished" and heading home. Let the cops find the perpetrator. They probably enjoy that kind of thing and don't have a warm cup of oxblood soup waiting for them.

But the odds of me getting poked by a trident in the eye aren't good if I don't find out who is responsible for harming Marina. And Fiona is rather fond of my eyes.

Heaving a sigh, I turn into The Lucky Charm for a fortifying drink. The bar is owned by Finnegan, a leprechaun with a shock of red hair who is built like a bull on steroids and has a temper to match. He looks up as I enter.

"You," he snarls. "Get out."

Okay, so I'm perhaps not his favorite person, based on some earlier, small misunderstandings. "I'm just here for some juice," I say, raising my hands.

"You cause trouble every time you come." He points to the door. "Out."

"Look, what you call trouble, I call a series of unfortunate coincidences and bad luck," I say, but Finnegan doesn't appear to be softening. "Okay, okay, just one drink and then I'll go. I promise."

Finnegan grunts, which I take to mean consent, and I hop up on the barstool. Finnegan passes me my usual: prune juice.

"One drink," he warns. "And no trouble."

"Scout's honor." I give him my most winning smile.

A growl rumbles out of Finnegan, but he walks away, albeit muttering epithets as he goes.

I settle in to enjoy my drink. Unfortunately, Finnegan's absence is replaced by the grating sound of crying from a patron at the bar. I turn to glare at the cause of the noise, a young man with sandy hair and reddened eyes. "Do you mind?"

"I'm so sorry," he sobs, "it's just...my girlfriend..."

"Left you, did she? Smart girl."

"No! My girlfriend Marina. She—"

Hello, there. I paste a concerned expression on my face as I slide down the bar and examine him more closely. Weak chin, broad forehead, squinty eyes—I'm not sure which is uglier, him or a mermaid. "You poor thing. What happened?"

He looks at me, tears running down his face. "My girlfriend, Marina, is a real, honest-to-God mermaid."

"Go on," I encourage.

His voice drops to a whisper as he casts a glance around. "Her father is the king of the merpeople and the highest-ranking official of the Mer And Finperson International Alliance."

"You don't say." I prop my chin on my hand, hoping against hope that he quickly gets to something I haven't already heard.

He nods. "We met one night under the full moon and it was like magic—"

"Enchanting, I'm sure," I interrupt, barely stopping myself from rolling my eyes. "And the problem is..."

"Can't you see?" he cries. "I'm human! A mermaid princess can't marry a human!"

I frown. "The logistics do seem a bit challenging."

"No, I mean she told her father we were going to get married, and he tried to kill her." He drops his head in his hands and wails.

Well, this puts a new spin on things. I rub my chin. The Alliance is certainly capable of criminal acts. Ever since the magical border dropped, the Alliance has engaged in small-time extortion, drug peddling, prostitution, and other grifts, not to mention the rumors of the odd murder or two.

I take a sip of my juice as I consider. "Why would he try to kill her? Why not just kill you?"

The boyfriend stops mid-wail and stares at me. "You think they meant to get me and instead got her?"

"Well, I don't—"

"That's even worse!" he cries. "It should have been me!" He wails harder than before.

I inch away, taking my drink with me. I can appreciate the tragedy of true love lost—and I would behave the same if anything happened to my Fiona—but he is frankly getting on my nerves. Furthermore, it still doesn't add up to me. No matter how mad he may have been, would the king really risk his daughter's life? Plus, if the Alliance had something to do with her disappearance, why employ me to find her?

My thoughts are interrupted by a giant cracking sound. Dirt, wood, and bricks rain down like hail. Steel beams squeal. Screams rend the air as people take cover. I squint up as a section of the roof is ripped away and a giant, tentacled monster of nightmares appears. *Dear heavens. It's the actual Kraken.*

A terrifying dark maw of jagged teeth opens, sending half-eaten fish heads and bits of entrails dripping down. The horrific smell is enough to knock a shark dead at twenty feet. A deep voice booms, the sound reverberating through my bones. "Where. Is. The. Goblin?"

IV

I do what any hero might: I hide under the nearest table. Maybe—probably—the Kraken is searching for a different goblin who also happens, quite coincidentally, to be at the bar.

"You," Finnegan hisses. I turn to see him hiding in the corner. "I knew you would be trouble. You owe me a new roof."

"What?" I hiss back. "I didn't rip off your roof. And I certainly don't know any sea monster—"

"Where is Zeke the goblin?" the voice booms again.

Son of a gorgon. I wonder if I should try to leave Fiona some sort of last message before I am devoured.

"Give him up or I will rip this place apart!" the voice thunders.

"He's right here," Finnegan says, pointing at me with a smirk.

I glare at him. "Thanks a lot."

He gives me the finger. Great guy.

I push myself to standing, brushing the dirt off my pants as I try not to show how close I am to wetting myself. "I'm Zeke. What do you want?"

The Kraken's head lowers, the crooked, razor-sharp teeth approaching. I hunch, thinking I'm about to become an afternoon snack. Instead, I see a humanoid face balanced on top of a muscular torso appear above the Kraken, his silver hair flowing in the wind like a fishy Fabio.

"I am Marinus, King of the Merpeople and President of the Mer and Finperson International Alliance." I am relieved to realize it has been the merman and not the Kraken who has been speaking. Nothing more terrifying than a monster that can converse with you before eating you.

I clear my throat. I'm not about to show that I'm intimidated by him, whether he showed up riding the Kraken or a seahorse. "I'm Zeke, Owner of the Golden Ring Pawn Shop and, uh, Part-Time Online Purveyor of Secondhand Goods," I say, trying to make my voice sound just as Loud and Important. "Nice ride."

"All sea creatures obey me," Marinus says, lifting his arms wide and displaying a massive chest roped with muscle and covered in tattoos and battle wounds. The Kraken growls upon his command, a thunderous sound that causes more bricks to tumble down.

I puff out my chest. "Well, I'm obeyed by, uh, all ghosts and spirits." I cross my fingers behind my back. It's just one ghost, really, and only because I employ him in my shop. And he isn't even that obedient.

"Where is my daughter?" Marinus intones. "Arran reports employing you to find her on my behalf."

I have a sneaking suspicion he won't be happy to hear the answer. "Before we get to that, I think we should just clarify the terms of our agreement. I get paid whether I find her alive or, well, let's just say less than alive—"

"If my daughter has perished, I will rain down terror from the seas!" Marinus bellows. The Kraken roars in an answering echo.

"Sure, whatever floats your boat. But I still get paid either way, right?"

Marinus gestures with a hand, and the Kraken's tentacle whips out to grab me, lifting me into the air. I shriek, struggling against the wet limb grasping me, but it won't budge. It tightens like a python around my middle, constricting my air.

"Have you found my daughter?" Marinus asks me once we are eye level. Up close, he is impressive in his own right, at least seven feet from head to tail.

"I saw her, briefly," I say, wheezing.

"And is she alive or dead?"

I debate. Angering the king while the Kraken could either squeeze the life out of me or drop me to my death feels like a bad choice. "Alive." I mean, she very easily could have been. She hadn't been in a body bag. Yet.

"Where is she?" he asks, his question sounding like a threat.

Probably the city morgue. "I couldn't say exactly…"

Marinus growls at me, and the Kraken responds by tightening its grip until I can't breathe. Black spots dance in front of my eyes. I struggle to free myself, but my feet kick uselessly in the air, and the tentacle doesn't move no matter how much I claw at it with my nails. As my vision darkens, I think of Fiona and send out a mental love note, imagining what we might have been.

"Murderer!" I hear a cry below me, momentarily distracting me and ruining my last vision of my love. There's only one thing that would surely seal my fate and enrage Marinus to the point of murder. *Please don't be*—but it is. It's the boyfriend, whatever his name is, who clearly has the common sense of a scallop.

"You!" Marinus exclaims. He stabs a hand toward the boyfriend, and the Kraken's tentacle lashes out, wrapping around the boyfriend and yanking him into the air.

With their attention diverted, the tentacle wrapped around me loosens enough for me to suck in a breath before I pass out.

"You're a murderer!" the witless boyfriend is still screaming at Marinus. "You tried to kill Marina!"

"Stop talking," I wheeze. "Before he kills us both."

Marinus's head swings back and forth between us. I don't much like where this is heading. "My adopted son hired you to find my daughter," he snarls at me, "and you're in league with *him*?"

"I don't even know him!" I say.

"You're lying!" Marinus gestures, and before I can say *son of a gorgon*, the Kraken slithers off the tavern and starts lumbering toward the ocean, one still-screaming boyfriend and one terrified goblin in its slippery grasp.

V

The last thing to know about merpersons is that you don't ever —and I mean ever—want to piss them off. Especially not merpersons who can ride a Kraken like some sort of blasted sea dragon.

In my mind, I am strong, courageous, willing to take on and defeat monsters of any size. I have stared down orcs, trolls, warlocks, witches, and even the odd werewolf or two. But if there's one thing that terrifies me more than any monster, it's the frigid waves of the Salish Sea, which are rapidly approaching as the Kraken slithers forward.

"Put me down!" I yell. "I don't know him! I've never met him! He's a complete wanker!" I imagine being dragged down to the depths of the ocean by the Kraken, and tremble at the thought of the icy waves rolling over me. I turn my head to Marina's boyfriend who's being carried along beside me. "Tell him you don't know me!"

"You didn't tell me you were working for him!" the boyfriend yells back. "I'm not helping you!"

Too soon, the Kraken undulates off the dock and plunges into the waves. Marinus leaps from its back and dives under the water. Droplets spray my face and I prepare myself for death. Yet even as the Kraken submerges itself, Marina's boyfriend and I are held aloft over the waves like we are riding some sort of odd oceanic vessel.

We finally come to a stop at least a mile from shore. Nothing but waves surround us. Marinus arises from the sea like a cross between the Birth of Venus and an angry David Hasselhoff. He's accompanied by Arran and Atl.

"Is it true?" Arran asks. "Is Princess Marina dead?"

The boyfriend makes a noise, but I speak over whatever blabber he intends to say. "I don't know! And even if she is, I certainly didn't kill her! I found her because you asked me to. I didn't even want to do that. Now get me out of here!"

"Silence!" Marinus commands. "The one standing charged here is the human who dared to love a mermaid princess, and you as his accomplice."

The boyfriend tries to speak, and I again cut him off. "First off, I'm not his accomplice. Second, I don't think he killed her. He thinks you did."

"Me?" Marinus asks. "She was my daughter! I loved her!"

"So do I!" the boyfriend says, finally getting a word in, although not one that either Marinus or myself care about. "I love her with a fire that burns brighter than a thousand suns, a love deeper than a thousand oceans—"

"Then who did?" Marinus asks, cutting him off.

"As Marina is no longer with us," Arran quickly says, "I am now the King's Royal Heir, and, as such, I decree that both of these perpetrators are guilty of the princess's murder. They should be dragged to the bottom of the sea and then fed to the Kraken."

Atl smiles, running his thumb over his knife. His roving eye fixes on me with an unblinking stare.

"Now, let's not be hasty—" I start.

"I command the Kraken—" Marinus begins.

"Marina isn't dead!" the boyfriend yells.

Everyone falls silent.

"What did you say?" Arran asks sharply.

"Someone *tried* to hurt her, but they missed. They took her to the hospital and they want a statement. She'll be fine." He glares at Marinus. "But that doesn't excuse that someone tried."

"Well, if it wasn't you, then who?" Marinus asks.

While Marinus is turned toward us, Arran and Atl begin to

back away. A memory flashes through my mind of the knife that I saw the chief of police holding as evidence...which looked an awful lot like the knives strapped across Atl's chest.

"Those two," I say, taking a chance this won't land me at the bottom of the ocean.

"What?" Arran asks, barking a laugh as the others turn to look at them. "Why would I do that? I hired you!"

"With Marina out of the way, you become the royal heir. The knife that was used to harm her is from Atl, your friend. And you hired me to either be your alibi or your patsy, a role I was about to play just now." Total shot in the dark, but if it delays my demise, it's a win.

"Is this true, Arran?" Marinus asks. "You, my adopted son, would harm my daughter?"

"Of course not!" Arran protests. "He's lying!"

"Well, we'll see what Marina says," the boyfriend chimes in, which is the second useful thing I've heard him say, and vastly improves my opinion of him.

Arran pales, which, for a cold-water animal, is saying something.

Epilogue

After that, Arran and Atl soon crack. The tale emerges that Arran wanted to be king and feared any future progeny Marina might have with the boyfriend (the logistics of which still escape me). Marina turns out to be just fine, if you don't count her terrible taste in men. Marinus upholds Arran's commitment for the Alliance to join my council. And I make it home to Fiona (although sadly I missed *Jeopardy!*, blast it).

As I sit in my recliner next to my dearest love at the end of one of the most fraught days of my life, I realize what truly matters: always get payment in advance, because there's no way that sea louse, Arran, is going to pay up now. *Son of a gorgon.*

Eliza Carns lives on an inlet in the chilly Pacific Northwest with her delightfully human husband and child. She generally enjoys the fine art of snark, cozy bonfires, and reading way past her bedtime, and she has a sneaking suspicion that she just might be a witch (despite all evidence to the contrary). For more stories about Zeke, Fiona, and their rather misguided exploits, you can find them on Kindle Vella or Amazon.

the storyteller

RICK WILBER

AOIFE and I were talking amiably in the front bar of Dick
Mack's pub on Green Street in Dingle, that large town near the far
end of the Dingle Peninsula in County Kerry, Ireland. I'd been in
town for all of a couple of hours after a long five-hour drive from
Dublin, where I'd escaped my troubles and come to find enough
solitude to get back to storytelling. I'd left almost everything
behind in the Shelburne Hotel there in Dublin, including my
laptop.

I was on a book tour for *Love's Enemy*, which was number one
in the U.K. and Ireland and had been for weeks. Promoting it was
driving me toward a breakdown. I'm not a great socializer, I'm not
great in front of crowds and being interviewed. I'd reached the
point where I was lying on my bed in Dublin staring at the ceiling
instead of meeting the Irish Times writer for lunch and a pint at
Davy Byrnes pub, just around the corner. I'd hit the wall.

So I ran. I shoved some clothes into a duffel bag I bought on
Grafton Street, brought my journal and my pens, asked the
concierge to get me a decent hire car, and I took off, heading west,
on a random path to somewhere calm and quiet.

Like Dick Mack's, where Aoife was tending bar. I'd checked
into a nice hotel, Benners on Main Street, right in the heart of the

town. The hotel looked like it might once have been the manor house of some English aristocrat back in the days before Irish independence, so I wasn't surprised to find that my room was big, airy, with a high ceiling, a fireplace with turf ready to light, a nice writing desk next to a window that looked out down the hill to the town and, beyond that, Dingle Bay. The bay was dotted with a few sailboats weathering the rain that seemed to have followed me all the way across the country. There were patches of blue sky in the distance, sure, but rain at the moment. Call it Irish weather. Call it soft so.

The fireplace, and the desk, and that view had looked promising. Maybe here I'd be able to write a chapter of the novel that had me stumped. I knew my agent and editor must be going nuts, so I sent them a text saying I needed a break for a week and I was unplugging and didn't want to be contacted unless it was an emergency. I'd be back, maybe with a chapter of that second novel. I sent that and turned off my mobile. They knew how bad my stress levels had been.

So here I was. I took a deep breath. Calm. I'd taken a quick shower to wash off the tension that came with my dereliction of duties back in Dublin and gone for a walk. Not more than ten minutes up the road was Dick Mack's, a pub that looked authentic and uncrowded. There were stars in the sidewalk of famous celebrities and politicians who'd been there; and when I'd walked inside I saw why. There was a long, narrow front room with a classic bar, mirrors behind, armed with shelves holding bottles of various beers and whiskeys of all sorts and other liquors. On the bar itself was a row of taps, Guinness and Beamish and Smithwick's and Carlsberg and five or six others. Behind those taps stood Aoife, toweling off a few glasses and putting them onto the shelves. She'd looked up to see me and smile and nod hello.

The place was nearly empty, with just one older couple in the back nook sharing a drink and a chat, having come in from that cold October rain. As I folded my umbrella and hung it over a peg on the wall, Aoife had said, "Good day to get out of the rain for a while, right? What can I do for you? A pint?"

"And a whiskey," I'd said, "Writers' Tears, if you have it."

"I certainly do," she said, and got the pint of Guinness started so she could let it sit and settle for a minute or two while getting the whiskey. "Ice?" she asked, "you Yanks usually want that."

"Yes, please," I said, not denying where I was from. Then I sat down on the bar stool as she put a few ice cubes in the glass and set the Tears down in front of me. I took a sip. Nice. She tended the Guinness, I knew the ritual of a pour by now, having been in Ireland for all of a week. She'd leave room at the top of the pint glass and let the stout settle for a bit before topping it off and sending it my way.

"First time in Dingle?" she asked.

"Yep," I said, embracing that inner Yank. "A little getaway for me for a few days. Some room to breathe."

"Ah, well, this is the place for that so," she said, giving it a little stage Irish and a wink. "Welcome to your safe place, then. Nice and quiet here this time of year. In summer it gets busy, but now? Not too bad."

"Thank god for that," I said, and took another sip. It helped. I shook my head, "It was crazy in Dublin, too much happening at once."

She nodded, "That's Dublin, in a nutshell."

"So I got a hire car and started driving west."

"And now here you are so. Can't get much farther west, you know. Next parish Boston, is what they say."

I laughed. "I get it. The whole Irish Catholic diaspora thing, right?"

She tilted her head, "My, that's very thoughtful," she said, and abruptly stuck out her hand for a shake. "I'm Aoife." She pronounced it "ee' fuh."

I took her hand and we shook. "I'm Patrick," I said. "Pleased to meet you."

"Padraig," she said, pronouncing it "pod' rig." "That's what I'll call you while you're here. That's the Irish of it and we have a lot of that in the West. Gaeltacht, you know. "

I did know. The Gaeltacht was those parts of Ireland where the primary language was Irish. "Slainte," I said and raised my glass to the Gaeltacht.

"Slainte," she said back and set the Guinness, perfectly ready now, in front of me.

I liked her immediately. Blue eyes, black hair tied back in a ponytail, a bit taller than myself and I'm five-foot-ten. Much more physically fit than I'd ever been. Smart, too, you could tell that instantly, and no doubt better educated than me. I'd gone to a local college in Illinois, nabbed a journalism degree just in time for the newspaper business to start collapsing, gone back for an MFA at the big state university so I'd have the credentials to teach, and then I'd been lucky with the thesis novel that capped the program.

I told her all that and admitted more. This was my first time abroad, at age thirty-one. I was divorced, with one child who spent most of her time with my ex. I was a writer, touring around to promote that thesis, which had become the novel, which was *Love's Enemy*, and had hit the top spot in bestseller lists and nabbed starred reviews, and so I was, as they say, on my way.

Or not. "It was eating me up," I said. "Day after day of interviews and bookstore signings and readings. All that travel, all those people standing in line or sitting there hanging on my every word. It was frightening. I needed a break. I rented a car, and here I am."

"*Love's Enemy*," she said. "I've seen that in Mahoney's Books in the front window. Well done you."

"Thanks," I said, and held up my glass for another whiskey. The Guinness sat there but eventually I got to it, and then a second.

We talked for a couple of hours over Guinness and whiskey and it turned into an impromptu story slam. I told a tall tale about Paul Bunyan and Babe the blue ox, who died from the cold in a heatwave when all the popcorn popped in the fields and Babe thought it was snow. She told me about Tír na nÓg, the Otherworld, and the love story of Oisín, the great poet, and Niamh, the fairy woman that he saves from tragedy so together they can rule. And she told me about fairy trees and selkies, those seductive creatures who shed their seal skin to take human form and how hard it can be for them to find that seal skin and return to the sea. I countered with the Navajo creation story that tells of the Ni'hookaa Diyan Diné, the Holy Earth People and that's why today the Navajos call themselves "Diné" or "The People." It went on, Aoife having the better of it so, but I held my own.

Eventually more customers trickled in and then some musicians showed up with a fiddle, a bodhrán, a flute and a tin whistle, and a banjo. In minutes they had a session underway. I listened for a while, calm as I could be, really past my crisis, and then grabbed my umbrella and started out the door.

"Soon again, Padraig," Aoife yelled at me over the music as I was leaving and so I turned and waved and smiled at her and stepped outside. The rain was gone and there was a blue late evening sky and brisk breeze off the water. I enjoyed the pleasant downhill walk back to Benners' and my comfortable room. There, I unpacked a bit, put some clothes in drawers and hung up a coat and a few shirts and then sat down at the writing desk and used the journal and pen I'd brought to start writing.

In the morning I had no book signings to do, no interviews, no lunches or dinners, nothing to do but relax in Dingle, look out the window in my room to see the town down below at the bottom of the hill, and beyond that Dingle Bay and out there, visible in the bright, sunny morning, a few islands.

It was the best I'd felt in months. I described it for myself on that notepad, noted the clouds on the far side of the bay, Mount Eagle in the distance straight ahead, those distant islands. What was it like out there, I wondered? Secluded? Safe? I supposed so.

And the town below. How was that? I headed down to the hotel restaurant for breakfast, full Irish, and then decided to go for a long walk along the main road past the Dingle Oceanic Aquarium before crossing the street and coming back along the harbor, seeing the fishing boats and the statue to Fungie the dolphin who'd entertained tourists for decades before disappearing during the pandemic when there was no one out on the harbor to hold his interest.

It was a beautiful day, sunny with a light breeze off the water, light jacket weather in October. There were seals in the harbor, I could see them poking their heads up from time to time to look around. Two of them were waiting patiently at the stern of a large fishing boat. Honesty was the name on the prow. The crew was at work on the deck but I didn't see any fish being thrown the seals' way as I walked by. I took a picture with my phone. As I did that the seals came closer, and then closer still, right up to the edge of the dock where I stood, so they were five feet below me in the water but looking right at me. I smiled and said hello but they were impassive, those doglike faces and those big whiskers and those large dark eyes impassive, watching me. I didn't have any more fish to throw them than did the crew on Honesty, so eventually I waved and turned to walk away. They barked at me as I left, one bark followed by another, and I turned to look at them, but they had dived down into the water and were gone.

I did the whole town on foot, looking in the shop windows, checking out the grocery store and the pharmacy as if I was planning to stay a while, then, after an hour or so of this, I stopped in Moriarty's to buy a bottle of whiskey, Writers' Tears of course, to take back to the room. If whiskey was what had me writing, I was glad to find that out. Anything would do. It had been a long, long dry spell, blocked by my anxiety. Back in the room, I opened the whiskey, poured a glass (no ice, sadly) and got to writing, taking pleasure in the physicality of writing longhand.

My first novel, the one making all the noise right now, was set in Occupied France during World War II. I wrote it as spy novel but it crossed genres to Romance: two lovers risking their lives to find out the details on Rommel's Atlantic Wall and get the information to Eisenhower in the spring of 1944. Lots of spycraft tension involved in that, and then the action took over as the Gestapo figured them out and gave chase.

They ran, together at first, with lots of heated lovemaking in barns and on hillsides as the danger ignited their passion. Eventually, with the Gestapo knocking on the front door as they fled out the back, they were forced to split up, going their separate ways to get back to London and, they hoped, each other.

She made her way to Dinard on the French coast, a village looking out toward the Channel Islands of Jersey and Guernsey. A stolen boat, a dangerous Channel Island full of Nazis, a harrowing escape from there to Dover, and then a train to London where her lover hadn't been heard from and was presumed dead at the hands of the Gestapo.

He wasn't dead. With the Gestapo hot on his trail, he went south into Vichy, and from there over the Pyrenees to Spain and thence to Portugal and from there a fishing boat to neutral Ireland and from there, at last, across the Irish Sea to Holyhead in Wales and a train ride to Paddington Station, London.

He arrived after curfew but was happy to walk across the city to the flat where they'd promised to meet. He stopped a couple of times at pay phones but she didn't answer. He kept walking.

The Luftwaffe attacked London that night, just a nuisance raid to remind Londoners that the war was going on. He kept walking during the bombing, thinking nothing could kill him now after what he'd been through.

She was huddled in an Anderson shelter in the vegetable garden behind the flat when a bomb destroyed the pub next door and the debris fell on the shelter and, stunned but otherwise unharmed, she staggered out into the street to see her lover walking, then running, toward her as the bombs were falling all around them. One of them hit the building he was running by and it collapsed on him. He died in her arms as she was pulling him out of the rubble.

It was a weeper, in other words. Nicely told, a good historical I'd like to think; I had all the facts straight enough. But it was just a weeper. To my surprise it outsold Hilary Mantel for the number six spot in the Times top ten. It earned out in two months, and just like that I was on my way, with a mid-six-figure advance for the second novel.

Which I hadn't been able to work on since the tour started. And now, here, it was moving nicely, page after page. I was in the zone! Locked in, at last, as the young sailor and his pretty Yank were busy falling in love while Margaret Thatcher, Britain's prime minister who'd earned the nickname the Iron Lady, responded to the Argentinians takeover of the Falklands with belligerence. The Royal Navy would put together a fleet and go take back those islands. Rule Britannia!

Our young hero, in love with his pretty American girl, was called to duty by the Royal Navy. He was a petty officer, working in the computer room of HMS Sheffield, a newer, high-tech destroyer, and he needed to be in Portsmouth in three days. Sheffield was doomed. It would be sunk by a French-built Exocet missile dropped by an Argentinian jet.

It would be a lot of fun to write that scene. Would our petty officer survive? Be a hero? A coward? I'd know soon. It felt good to be at work.

I stopped for the evening. I was hungry. In this rush to write I'd forgotten about lunch, forgotten about dinner, forgotten about Aoife and Dick Mack's. Did they serve food there? They did, my phone told me when I asked Google. Turning on the phone brought a rush of texts and emails. I ignored them all and turned it back off.

In fifteen minutes I was walking in the door of Dick Mack's, and there was Aoife with a warm "Hello, Padraig," and a smile and I felt at home. The hamburger was excellent, the conversation even better as I banged on about the Falklands War and about the Scots strange relationship with the English, which was nearly as fraught as that of the Irish and yet they were all on board to win the Falklands war. She had started a Guinness and poured me some Writers' Tears without my asking and when I paused for a breath, she laughed, and said, like we were old pals, "You must be having a good day there, Padraig."

I set my hamburger down, took a sip of the whiskey, and admitted that things were much improved over yesterday. I'd been writing, and perhaps it was pretty good, I told her.

"That's the new novel you were talking about yesterday so? The one that had you stumped?"

"The very thing," I said.

Had I talked about it the day before? I suppose so. Truth was, Aoife was a classic bartender. A good listener, a few supportive comments here and there. Attractive, hell, beautiful, and so I was flattered she was willing to talk with me at all. By the second whiskey yesterday I was willing to share my life: the divorce and the one great kid I really missed seeing, the death of my journalism career and the birth of my success as a novelist. All of that, in some real detail; the crazy first agent, the brilliant second one, the editor who made my work better, the promotions people who made my life worse, the panic that had gripped me in Dublin. All of that.

"You're a natural, Padraig, you know that, right? You're a great storyteller, and I've known a lot of good ones."

"You know some other writers?" I asked. So much for my being something special in her life, which I'd sort of been hoping for.

"Sure and I have, Padraig. This is Dingle, you can't swing a hurley around here without hitting an artist of one kind or another." She smiled. "You've seen those stars on the sidewalk outside, right? This place has been chock-full of writers and actors and directors and musicians and athletes. And now you!"

She reached down below the bar and brought out a copy of *Love's Enemy* and handed it to me, then reached up to her ear where a pen was perched and handed that to me, too. "There's one less copy at Mahoney's now, Padraig. Would you sign it for me? Make it 'To Aoife and her sisters,' please and I'll make sure both of my sisters get to see it soon, all right?"

I took it from her hand, inscribed it the way she asked, and handed it back. "I hope you like it," I said.

"It's really grand, Padraig," she said, "I bought it during my break after you left yesterday, and then stayed up all the night with it. It's wonderful. I can see why it's so popular. You tell a great story so."

"Thank you. I'm really pleased," I said, and I was, to my own surprise. I'd been hearing so much praise for the past year from agents and editors and publishers and readers that I'd become pretty numb to it. But it was nice to hear it from Aoife.

She laughed, "But what a sad ending!"

"Sorry," I said, "but that's just how I saw it in my head. Sad, yes, but he died for love, so there's that."

She laughed. "Don't be sorry at all, it works perfectly." She leaned over the bar, the place pretty crowded by that time, and slipped me a piece of paper. "I'm off at nine tonight. Text me when you're ready to take a break from this new work of genius and I'll take you on a little pub crawl. How's that sound? It'll be great craic."

Great craic, I'd learned in my brief time in Ireland meant conversation and maybe some music and everyone in good spirits. "I'm in," I said. "I'll send you a shout just after nine and we'll meet, all right?"

"Perfect," she said, and it was.

The next morning, Dunquin was just twenty minutes by car from Dingle Town, up around the inner bay then cut across to the north of Mount Eagle and down to Dunquin. We walked down the switched-back steep stone steps from the parking lot to Dunquin pier, where the boat was waiting for us. Dermot O'Connor Blasket Tours said the sign on the pier, and Dermot himself stood in the boat and waved us in. Its name was the Kerry Gold, a long, narrow boat with an upthrust prow and gunwales low on the sides, for hauling in crab traps or nets, I guessed. But today it was a tourist boat, and there were four rows of three seats each, anchored firmly into the boat's decking. Aoife and I were the only passengers and we sat at the rear, where Dermot stood handling the outboard motor that would take us to Great Blasket.

Dermot was a small, bow-legged Irishman utterly at home on the Kerry Gold, steady as you go in the slight swell coming in as we stepped from the concrete pier. I got the feeling he was more at home on the water than he was on the land.

He wore an Aran sweater against the chill off the water, one of those thick white sweaters with patterns in the stitching. He wore a Man U. cap backward on his head and a smile on his face as he handed us life vests, and reached back into a bag to pull out an Aran sweater for me, too; something to ward off the chill. I was glad to have it.

Dermot was, by god, the real thing, and he was taking us out to Great Blasket, with its abandoned village and its long and strange and wonderful history of literature and storytelling. We would spend the night out there, with Aoife's sisters and their friends who were already there. A ceilidh, Aoife called it, some traditional music and food and drink in an old traditional home.

She'd talked me into this little adventure last night after we'd found our way back to my room in Benners Hotel and talked and drank some more there.

It was the islands, the Blaskets and the Aran islands up near Galway, that were the real Ireland, she'd said as we sat and had a glass or two each of my Writers' Tears. She had the day off tomorrow and was going out to Great Blasket to meet her sisters and spend the day hiking and the night with some great craic before coming back the next morning. Would I join her?

Of course I would. She'd told me then about how the village on Great Blasket, in its heyday, had been a marvel of storytelling, as scholars and writers came to the island to hear that pure Irish spoken and those great stories told by the village's seanchaís.

The scholars and artists encouraged the islanders to tell the story of their lives in books, and when they did, writing in Irish and translated into English and other languages, the books were read by many thousands and were still in print. People like Carl

Mastrander and J.M. Synge helped islanders like Tomas O'Crohan and Maurice O'Sullivan detail what life was like in a small fishing village isolated from the mainland much of the time, a village living by its own rhythms and dreams and stories.

The most famous of them all was Peig Sayers, a great story-teller, the best seanchaí on the island, said Aoife. Peig's book became standard reading for Irish schoolchildren, who could learn the language as they learned of the life the islanders had led.

The village was abandoned in 1953, Dermot told us as we made our way across from Dunquin to the pier at Great Blasket. As the young had left for easier lives, often to America, the final few dozen had moved to the mainland. Their homes, shops, and the schoolhouse all lay empty for years, save for occasional scholars studying what once had been, and tourists in the summer who chose to stay there for a while in quiet simplicity.

It was a beautiful morning but bad weather was coming, Dermot told us, but not till late in the day, when we'd be snug in Peig's old home. Dermot would see us tomorrow, about this same time. For today, the Atlantic welcomed us for the crossing with a light breeze driving low waves toward us as we headed across the Sound. I was thinking how lucky I was. The whole island was ours. We'd made love the night before. It had seemed inevitable to me from the moment I'd first seen her in Dick Mack's. We hardly knew each other but that didn't seem to matter.

Walking with her as we followed a trail that led steeply uphill from the village to the top of a ridge that ran along the length of the narrow island, I felt that I'd found my true love, crazy as that sounds. Her melodic voice when she'd talked to me in Irish as we'd made love then lay there together, sated, carried stories that I could sense, if not understand, stories of a magical culture, isolated out here, surrounded by sea and storms and sunshine by turn.

In an hour we'd reached the peak of the island's ridged back. The view was stunning. Great Blasket below us had low-lying fog moving in and we could watch its progress from our height. Beyond that low fog she pointed out the details to me, Skellig

THE STORYTELLER · 319

Michael in the distance that way, Dingle Bay over there, the Sleeping Giant island that way, Slea Head in front of us.

We walked back a different way to go by the beach, where dozens of seals were either in the water or lying on the beach in the sunshine as the fog began to move in. Aoife and I were the only people there, and maybe the only people on the whole island. I wasn't sure when the sisters would arrive. The isolation felt wonderful.

We walked right up to two of the seals lying on the beach in the sunshine. The fog was offshore and surreal, a gray wall coming our way as the seals eyed us, offered a little bark of hello, it seemed to me, then, to my amazement, rolled over on their backs so Aoife could walk up and rub them on their bellies. She spoke to them quietly, in Irish, as she rubbed.

I'd never seen such a thing. Those seals looked at me, languid in their enjoyment of Aoife's pats and rubs on their stomachs. Then one, then the other, nodded to me. Aoife spoke to them again in Irish, turned to me and said, "They'd like you to come here and do this, too."

"You're kidding."

"Not at all," she said. "They like you."

"They like me? How can you know that?"

"These are my sisters, Padraig. Niamh," who eyed me and nodded, "and Siobhan," who blinked her eyes and raised one flipper. Crazy, absolutely crazy.

I patted and rubbed until that offshore fog finally rolled in over us and all went to gray. "To the ceilidh!" said Aoife. Two barks came from Niamh, and Siobhan followed that and off we walked or waddled.

Aoife was well ahead and then came back to hold my hand and walk me along the path that led from the seal beach to the village and, at the top of the village, Peig's house. As we went steeply uphill, we left the fog behind again, deep gray to light and then gone, and ahead was Peig's house. It was mid-afternoon by my watch but here it was a moonless night on the outside of that fog.

The only lights showing were straight ahead. Aoife squeezed my hand, and said, "You'll love this Padraig. It's the way it was. It's the way it can be for us."

"Us?" I asked.

She smiled and held my hand as two people came walking up from behind, catching up with us. Niamh and Siobhan, two smiling women. "Padraig," said one, "I'm Niamh," and she took my other hand. And "I'm Siobhan," said the other and leaned in to kiss me on the cheek. The sisters. They looked it, for sure, as Aoife and her sisters smiled and hugged each other and then led me up to reach a wide flat plot of land and Peig's cottage, lights shining and music playing as we walked in.

The place was packed. Musicians were just sitting down to play. There were two fiddlers, one of them an older man, his face worn from toil at sea, his clothes roughly woven but sturdy, his sweater just like the one I was wearing. The other was a young woman, very pale and thin but smiling, happy to be there.

Over by the fireplace was John Millington Synge, the playwright, looking just like the photographs I've seen of him in Dingle, chatting with Carl Mastrander and Tomas O'Crohan, unmistakable in his cap and sweater. All three men smoked pipes. By the window was Maurice O'Sullivan, talking with Robin Flower, another scholar. And there, sitting by herself, looking right at me, was Peig Sayers, with Aoife leaning over her to whisper in her ear. Peig was smiling and nodding.

Aoife walked away, back toward her sisters near the door. I watched as she reached the sisters and spoke to them and they smiled and nodded and then all three looked at me. They were beautiful, the three of them. Aoife gave me slight smile and then left her sisters to walk toward me.

She put her arms around me and said, "Hold me, Padraig," and I did, a possessive arm around her waist as the pale, thin fiddler struck the first notes and the session was off and running with them playing some reel that made my head spin even as Aoife leaned over and kissed me on the cheek to say, "Peig would like to say hello to you, Padraig, my love."

My love! That's what she called me. I looked at her. She looked at me. We kissed, briefly, and I wanted more but she laughed and pushed me away, toward Peig.

I walked over there. Peig was smiling and had just lit her pipe. She waved at me to sit and I did that, next to her. She took a puff on the pipe and said, "She's a wonder so, that Aoife."

"I know," I said.

"Will you tell stories about her, then? About us here and what we have? You're a seanchaí, I can see that. We'll have sessions, you and I, telling the truth of things, keeping the past alive."

"Like now," I say.

"Like now," she agreed. "Now go, lad, to your Aoife and her sisters. Aoife needs you. We'll talk again soon so."

The music was wild and infectious, the fiddles leading the way, the bodhran moving things along, the tin whistle piping up. There was toe-tapping and occasional yells all around, with Tomas O'Crohan step dancing, his feet flashing on the stone floor.

I got to my Aoife. She was smiling and gave me a hug. I looked at Niamh and Siobhan and they stepped my way to hug me, as well.

Aoife pointed toward the far wall, to the left of that solitary window, to the peg where a sealskin was hanging. "Will you get that for me, Padraig?" she asked.

I kissed her again lightly and again she laughed and pushed me away, toward that sealskin. I turned and walked over to it. The music had stopped. The place had gone quiet. I reached up try to take the sealskin but it wouldn't come loose from the peg. I tried again but it wouldn't come loose. I looked back toward Aoife and her sisters. They were smiling. Aoife nodded at me, winked, said, "My love to you, Padraig." I turned back, held the sealskin in both hands, pushed it upward to get it off the peg and then brought it down and into my hands.

There was an exhalation in the room, a great moment of

tension resolved. The music started again, frenetic, Tomas's feet were flying.

Aoife took me by my right hand, my left holding the sealskin, and we turned and left the ceilidh, leaving it all behind and starting to walk back down the hill toward the beach, nobody saying anything, but Aoife squeezing my hand. The sisters followed behind us.

We reached the beach, that large boulder to our left, the rough sand in front. We stopped before we set foot on the sand. "Here," said Niamh, and "Here," echoed Siobhan and they started to walk behind the large boulder. They turned back to look at us.

Aoife put her arms around my neck and brought me to her. We kissed. We pulled apart. I knew what to do. I handed her the seal-skin and she left me, walking toward the boulder to join her sisters who'd waited for her and then all three disappeared behind it.

The fog had thickened again, and then there was a light rain washing through it as I waited and waited some more.

I heard a bark and then another and another still in the dark-ness, down by the water, where waves were coming in and reaching halfway up to sand before washing back down. I walked toward the sound of those barks and at the water's edge the fog had disap-peared and there, in the water, looking at me, were three seals. They watched me. I watched them.

I'm writing this now in Peig Sayers' cottage on the abandoned village on the abandoned island of Great Blasket. Out the window I can see the Sleeping Giant in the distance, lying on his back, bathing in the warm waters of the Atlantic Drift. The sun is shin-ing, the air is cool, there are children playing camogie in the flat open field that's at the top of the hill that Peig's cabin sits on.

I write all day, taking breaks now and again to walk down to the beach and see the seals lying on the sand, floating in the water, only their heads show. They're beautiful.

At night, I dance and sing and drink with the sisters and all the others. The sisters come up as the sun sets in the west, walking up from the beach, dressed for the dancing that is to come. Aoife sings, that wonderful voice of hers carrying across the island, while Niamh plays her fiddle and Siobhan plays the tin whistle. I play the bodhrán and I've become quite good at it. We play lilts and reels and the occasional dirge, though there is nothing here to be sad about.

And then when everyone leaves, Aoife stays behind to lie with me in our bed so I can tell her the stories I've written that day.

And then we fall asleep and in the morning she is gone. It's a good life. It's a very good life.

Dermot O'Connor walked down to the steep switch-back path that led from the parking area to the pier at Dunquin. It was a beautiful fall dawn, the newly risen sun glinting off the dew still lying on the metal railings that ran along the pier. It was eight-thirty in the morning. He had a group from Switzerland that was scheduled for nine-fifteen, several language scholars and their spouses and friends who wanted to see the famous Great Blasket, where so many scholars had gone before them.

It was a good day for it, the calm following last night's storm. Today, the water was flat here in the harbor and there were gentle rollers out in Blasket Sound. Twenty minutes was all it would take to get the Swiss there and leave them for the day. He'd pick them up at six P.M. at the pier on the island, so they could see the sunset to the west as they motored out into the sound. They'd like that. An easy day for all concerned.

He walked onto the Kerry Gold carrying a ten-liter can of petrol to top off the gas tank on the outboard. He set it down and leaned over to unscrew the gas cap and noticed something large under the dock, caught on the pilings. Not something, but someone, he knew as he looked closer. A body. Someone who'd drowned in last night's weather.

Someone wearing an Aran sweater. One of Dermot's, by god. Jesus, it was that Yank writer, it had to be. Poor fellow, so much for worrying about him out in Peig's place. He must have gone for a walk down to Seal Beach to see the waves crashing in and it had cost him his life. The tides had pushed him in from there.

Ah, well. Tragic. Dermot pulled out his mobile and called the Gardai. Best to let them take it from here. It would be a grand story to tell, though, wouldn't it, in the years to come? The Yank who'd wandered into trouble? The one who was always scribbling into that journal of his, taking notes for that next great novel, he said. That journal might be in Peig's place, come to think on it. Dermot would check for that when he dropped off the Swiss scholars. Now wouldn't that make for a grand story?

Rick Wilber has published a half-dozen novels and short-story collections for WordFire Press, Tor Books, and other publishers. He has published more than sixty short stories in major markets, most often in *Asimov's Science Fiction* magazine. For twenty-five years he and his wife Robin, a finance professor, have led college study tours to Ireland and he often has Irish settings in his stories and novels. His work has won or been shortlisted for a number of awards, including the John W. Campbell Memorial Award for Best Science Fiction Novel of the Year, the Sidewise Award for Best Alternate-History—Short Form, the *Asimov's* Readers' Choice Award (shared with co-author Kevin J. Anderson), and the Canopus Award for Excellence in Interstellar Writing (shared with co-author Kevin J. Anderson). He is visiting assistant professor and thesis coordinator in the low-residency Graduate Program in Creative Writing—Genre Fiction at Western Colorado University.

copyright information

acknowledgments

This anthology was made possible with the generous support of Draft2Digital and Western Colorado University's Graduate Program in Creative Writing.

if you enjoyed merciless mermaids, you may also like

Monsters, Movies & Mayhem

Unmasked: Tales of Risk and Revelation

Gilded Glass: Shattered Myths and Fractured Fairy Tales

www.ingramcontent.com/pod-product-compliance
Lightning Source LLC
Chambersburg PA
CBHW020557120726
47903CB00001B/287